HARPER'S FINALE

HARPER SUTTON

F. C. Clark

Matador
9 Priory Business Park,
Wistow Road, Kibworth Beauchamp,
Leicestershire. LE8 0RX
Tel: 0116 279 2299
Email: books@troubador.co.uk
Web: www.troubador.co.uk/matador
Twitter: @matadorbooks

ISBN 978 1838593 490

British Library Cataloguing in Publication Data.
A catalogue record for this book is available from the British Library.

Printed and bound in the UK by TJ International, Padstow, Cornwall
Typeset in 11pt Aldine401 BT by Troubador Publishing Ltd, Leicester, UK

Matador is an imprint of Troubador Publishing Ltd

To my Mr C

Acknowledgments

I have so many people to thank, not only for their support, but also for believing in me.

My amazing family have been by my side through the ups and downs, laughter and tears, moments of 'can I do this' and moments of doubt. I could not have done it without you. In addition, my friends – who are my lifeline, my extended family – who have held my hand along the way.

Thank you to all the readers of Harper's Fate and Harper's Fortune, your continued support in the love story of Kate and Luke has been overwhelming.

Thank you for all your shares and likes on Facebook, I am indebted to you all. Thank you also for supporting me through Instagram, where I have shared the Harper's series and also met some incredible women – you know who you are, and I am so grateful for your continued support and friendship.

This journey would not have been possible without Erica and Sophie from EKC, and Luke and Brendan from FMC – did I mention I have a new book?! Finally, Jane Hammett, my amazing editor, who has taught me so many lessons that will stay with me forever.

Chase your dreams…

Kate Harper and Luke Sutton have been on a wild journey, taking myself and my readers with them… Maybe one day they will return, watch this space.

1

A humming echoes through my head. I open my eyes and try to focus, but I'm completely disorientated.

'Boss, she's awake!' a man yells.

Slowly I begin to absorb my surroundings. Shit. I'm on a jet – a private jet similar to Luke's, the same plane we took to Venice five days ago to get married.

'Pleased you could join us, Miss Harper – I mean, Mrs Sutton.'

My skin crawls. I know who's speaking. A short, balding man stands in front of me. I close my eyes. This isn't real. It can't be. A flashback to the front door bursting open at Sandbanks almost stops me from breathing. I open my eyes to see my worst nightmare: Philip Cooper.

He leers over me, wearing an expression that scares me. This has to do with my inherited Bagrov and Cooper shares. It must be. I think back to a few hours ago, when Alexis Cooper told me that her father, Philip, planted the bomb at Luke's house in South Kensington that almost killed him six months ago.

But where is he taking me? I'm no use to him. Unless he's heard that Luke is planning to take over my shares?

I try to think. Would Luke have instructed his lawyers to start buying my Bagrov and Cooper shares? It's too soon for anyone to have found out. *Keep your mouth shut, Kate Harper*, goes around and around in my head. No problem. I am silenced by fear.

He looks at his watch. 'One hour, then your fate – and my fortune – will be revealed. Let's just say your finale will be… memorable.'

I look around the jet. 'Where are you taking me?'

'At last she speaks,' he says. 'Have you ever wondered if that pretty little mouth is what gets you into trouble?' He runs his fingers along my jawline, brushing my lower lip with his thumb. I turn my head and push his hand away.

'Don't touch me,' I whisper.

With no warning he grabs hold of my long blonde hair and yanks my head towards him.

'I'll touch you if I want.'

Fuck – this is wrong. My dread is spiralling out of control.

'Daddy,' a voice murmurs from the far corner of the plane.

Philip releases my hair and turns. I look across the plane. It's Alexis Cooper, Philip's daughter. He walks towards her.

'You promised me no one would get hurt,' she says.

'I told you to sit there and be quiet.' His harsh voice echoes through my entire body.

She bows her head, and her short dark hair curtains her face. This isn't the superbitch Alexis I know. She looks scared. Yes, she's my enemy, but earlier today she tried to save me. What am I missing? He wants my late mother's company, I get that, but why are we both here?

'You nearly killed Luke,' I say.

'I assume my daughter has been shooting her mouth off.'

He raises his hand and strikes Alexis hard across the face. Her head hits the aircraft window.

Holy shit, this is his daughter! Our love–hate relationship is far from my mind as I run to her defence. 'Leave her alone!'

Philip shoves me hard in the chest, causing me to fall.

'Sit the fuck down, unless you want some of this too.' He raises his hand threateningly.

I scurry to my seat, my body shaking and my heart beating frantically. I push up the cuff of Luke's sweatshirt and grip what lies beneath it. My birthday gift: a watch with a built-in tracking device. For the first time, I am grateful for Luke's need to control everything in his life. I close my eyes as I remember his last words: *Stay alive, Kate. I will find you.*

Please find me, Luke.

The rest of the journey feels like an eternity. At least I'm still alive. After a bumpy landing, the aircraft taxis to a halt. *My fate awaits*, Philip Cooper said. What did he mean?

Philip leaves his seat and heads down the gangway. 'Tie their hands together,' he orders.

'Yeah, boss.' The man dressed in black answers and pulls my arms. 'Don't move.' He begins to bind my wrists. I look across at Alexis. Another man is tying her wrists.

The men pull us towards the exit. I squint in the sunshine, and look around. Crap. It looks familiar. We're surrounded by barren wasteland. No passport control. It's obviously a tiny airport – if it's even an airport. Reminds me of when I met my elusive Russian father eight months ago. Where the hell are we?

Philip rallies his troops while Alexis and I stand behind him with our guards. She looks at me then bows her head. Undoubtedly Philip's violent behaviour started long before today, and I now feel a different emotion towards the woman I have despised since we met: empathy.

'You all have your location points? As you know, the exchange will not take place until tomorrow lunchtime. It needs to run smoothly. Walsh, check in with the team at the house,' Philip bellows.

A tall, dark-haired man steps forward. 'All sorted.'

'Good. Let the fun commence,' Philip says and smiles.

Fun! Furthermore, what exchange?

'Move,' the guard says, yanking on my arm and dragging me towards one of four black 4×4s waiting in a row. Alexis is taken to another car.

'Oi, eyes forward,' the guard says and pulls my arms.

In my mind, I can hear Luke's voice – not my husband's normal voice, but his military voice. Commander Sutton. *Stay calm and think on your feet, Harper.* With that thought, I see my first clue: the number plate of the 4×4. Jesus Christ. Russia may well be in my blood, but I've had enough visits here to last a lifetime. This is my second, and I pray it's my last.

The man opens the passenger door. 'Get in,' he says. Without hesitation I climb in.

'Scoot over.'

I scramble across and he slides in next to me. Another man is already sitting behind the steering wheel. I scan the area, but there is nothing for miles. Then the front passenger door opens and Philip Cooper gets in.

'Let's go,' he says to the driver.

'Where are we going?' I ask.

'Make sure Walsh leads the convoy. Follow close behind. I don't want any gaps left for a possible intervention. Got it?'

Intervention?

'Yeah,' the driver responds.

I take a deep breath. 'I know we're in Russia.'

Philip ignores me and checks his phone. 'The lodge is ready. We need to stick to the route we planned.'

'My real father lives here – in Russia. He's ruthless.' This isn't a coincidence – I'm sure of it. 'He will know I'm here.' I pray he is watching me.

Philip looks over his shoulder. 'Shut her up.' He waves his hand to the man holding my arm, who clamps both hands around my throat, squeezing my neck and compressing my windpipe. Holy shit, this is it! My legs thrash against the seat and I slap his hands away. I try to breathe but I can feel my lungs labouring. I can't breathe…

'Enough! I need her alive, which is a fucking shame.'

He lets go. I cough and splutter, gasping for air. My hands touch my neck, which feels bruised. I fight back tears, wanting to appear strong, not terrified that I was seconds away from death. *Please find me, Luke.*

'Cover her head,' Philip says, looking at me. 'I suggest you keep quiet, bitch, or you will have a repeat performance – and this time I won't be so fucking nice.'

The burly man next to me picks up a black cloth from the floor and slides it over my head. I take a deep breath, hoping to calm my trembling body. I think of Luke: what would he do? Other than kick their fucking arses? Think, Kate, think.

Despite being terrified, I begin to make mental notes on the journey. We took a left fairly soon after leaving the airport, and since then the car has travelled at a reasonable speed – maybe fifty miles per hour. The last turn was a sharp right onto what feels like an unmade road. After some time, the car begins to slow.

'Boss?' the driver says.

'Over there – park in the garage and make sure the other vehicles are covered. Just use your brain,' Philip orders.

Moments later, my door opens and someone yanks at my hands. I step out of the car, still in complete darkness. My legs feel weak, and I stumble.

'Jesus, take off her fucking hood,' Philip yells.

The cloth is pulled off. I remain silent as my eyes adjust to the light.

The car is parked in a large wooden outbuilding surrounded by trees. Another vehicle arrives. The guard drags me towards the entrance of a large, single-storey building. Philip is ahead, talking to some tough-looking men. I hear footsteps, and turn. It's Alexis.

The burly man leads me through the rear entrance into the building. My initial thoughts are that someone lives here, although it is incredibly dated and a little rundown. Nonetheless, it looks like someone's home – and I'm certain it doesn't belong to Philip.

'You know where to take them.'

I'm scared. What does he mean?

His eyes meet mine, then he turns and walks off.

The guard almost yanks my arms out of their sockets. I fall to my knees.

'Get up, bitch,' the man hisses.

Bitch? I'll give him bitch. Christ, I wish Luke was here.

We walk down a corridor and stop outside a door. As I run through potential exit strategies, two issues face me: first, this is the only door along the long corridor and, second, an opportunity to escape is unlikely. The burly man unlocks the door and pulls me inside a cold, sterile room. It's roughly thirty foot square, with a long, narrow window in the far corner, plus a black wrought iron bed and a few wooden chairs.

Within seconds Alexis joins me.

'Sit on the chair,' the guard orders. Alexis is made to do the same. My guard produces a knife, cuts the rope around my wrists, and reties them to the rear of the chair and my legs to the front. He then does the same to Alexis.

'Go and tell Cooper they're waiting. I'm going to take a piss. I'll meet you out the front.'

Waiting – for what?

He closes the door. I hear the sound of the key in the lock, then silence.

My head bows as I swallow the lump of fear in my throat.

'Please tell me you know what the hell is going on?' I look down at the front legs of the chair, hoping to see a frayed edge of rope or a sharp piece of wood. My hands begin to explore – and get nothing except friction burn. 'Shit! This is seriously fucked up.' I shake my head and blink hard to stop myself crying.

'Alexis.'

Nothing. She remains silent.

'Jesus, Alexis, bloody answer me – what the hell is going on? I think your dad is going to—' I take a deep breath. 'Alexis, look at me.'

Her eyes meet mine.

'We need to find a way out of here.'

'What's the point? We're in the middle of nowhere. He'll be one step ahead of us – he always is.'

'We are going to get out of here! Try to loosen the rope. Scrape it against your chair.' My feet work hard. 'Alexis, copy me.'

Her eyes are empty – and for good reason. How can he do this to his daughter?

'Alexis, please try.'

She nods and begins to mimic my actions.

'That's it – keep rubbing against the wood.'

We both work at my plan – if nothing else, it distracts us from the here and now. I look across at the woman I have detested for so long, and the evidence is shining like the North Star: she came to me because she loved my husband. Maybe she has never stopped loving him.

'What does he want with us?'

She shakes her head and continues to scrape the rope. This is another first. Alexis Cooper – silent.

'Why are we in Russia?'

Her eyes lock on mine. 'Russia!'

'Yeah, I recognised the number plates.'

She takes a deep breath. 'I – I don't know.'

'Jesus, Alexis, we need to get out of here.'

'Optimistic, Kate.'

'I'll go with desperate Kate and a little optimism. I heard your dad talking about an exchange. Do you know what he's exchanging?'

'No.'

'Fathers can be shit. My dad abandoned me – and, strangely enough, he tied me to a chair. Déjà vu.'

The sound of the key in the lock stops us dead. It triggers a cold rush of panic through my body, which heightens when the door handle turns.

'Ladies, are you bonding?' Philip says, strolling in and locking it behind him.

He walks slowly, circling our chairs while drinking from a crystal tumbler. He has a plan, I'm certain. He collects a chair from the far corner of the room and places it in front of me. He sits, resting one foot on his knee, and downs his drink before placing the tumbler on the floor.

He smirks. God, I hate him more than I hate any other human being on the planet. 'I suspect you have many questions racing through that pretty little head of yours.'

The scales of liberty rock back and forth. Do I answer? No. I draw my lips inwards.

'Silence.' He smirks. 'Like I said, this is something you should learn to do more often, but after tomorrow my problem, which is you, will no longer be. You mentioned your father, Ivor Varizin. He's a popular man. The problem with popularity is it can bring enemies to your doorstep – and some enemies seek revenge.' He leans back in the chair, relishing the clear rise of fear inside me. 'Strangely, you are worth more than I imagined.'

My eyes flit to Alexis's. She looks confused. This is news to her too.

'I struck a deal with Chekhol, Yura Chekhol. Does the name mean anything to you?'

I remain expressionless. I haven't got a bloody clue.

'As luck would have it, he contacted me, and for whatever reason he wants to use you to hurt your father. I need you away from Bagrov and Cooper – two birds, one stone. So you will sign your shares over to me before you meet your fate.' He sneers.

God, I hate him.

'Getting married was not a wise decision, Kate. It means Sutton will have some control over your fortune and my business. No, no, no, not very smart. You could say it was the final nail in your coffin.' He chuckles coldly.

My breathing quickens.

He stands and walks behind me, placing his hands on either side of my face. I try to turn away from his touch. His grip tightens and he brushes his rough, bristly cheek against my face.

'No, you will be still,' he whispers before he sweeps his tongue across my jaw. Bile rises to my mouth. I close my eyes to rid myself of his touch and the smell of alcohol that lingers on his breath.

'You remind me so much of your mother.'

His words rotate in my head. Mother! Which one, my dead Russian mother or my adopted mother?

My mouth is so dry I can barely muster a response. 'I don't understand.'

'Katenka Bagrov.' He releases me and returns to his chair.

'You knew my mum?' I'm confused. Did they work together? I had assumed that Philip joined the company long after Katenka had died.

'We met briefly – four, maybe five times. Let's just say they were all memorable encounters.'

I close my eyes, trying to piece together his tale.

He sniggers. 'You look surprised; nearly as surprised as I was when I found out she had a child.'

'Two,' I blurt.

'Bagrov, as it was back then, was struggling to survive. Financially, the company managed to sustain itself, but it needed modernising. I was young and ambitious. I knew I could turn the company into the success it is today. Katenka was beautiful, her skin was...' He sits back in his chair, lost in a memory, a memory that causes me to feel nauseous. 'Sadly, she was a little... frigid.' His eyes lock on mine as he waits for a reaction. I feel numb. I can only just breathe.

'You see, life was swimming along nicely. My career with Bagrov began in London. They saw my potential and transferred me to New York.' He pauses. 'The second time I met your mother, she declined my offer to buy her shares. The last time I saw her in New York was... let's just say it didn't go to plan. Why she refused to have sex with me I will never understand. You women are difficult creatures.' He leans towards me and runs his finger down my cheek. 'You have your mother's complexion.' He blinks, and leans back in his chair again. 'After our brief moment of intimacy she fled to London with you. As I said, I was unaware you existed. She was good at keeping secrets.'

Intimacy! This can't be real.

He stands in front of Alexis, then runs his hand through her dark hair. 'My dear Alexis, you are turning into your mother.'

She closes her eyes.

Something is raw between them. None of this makes any sense; this is not the power father-and-daughter couple I have witnessed in the boardroom.

'Daddy, I'll do whatever you need. Please let us go before it's too late.' Her soft voice is sharp with fear.

Once again he laughs at her before he slaps her face hard.

'No – stop – please,' I beg.

He whirls around and slaps me. My vision blurs.

His rage seems to have altered; this is now about power and control. He manoeuvres his chair closer and sits down. 'When I first saw you at Luke's parents' party, you reminded me of Katenka. Little did I know why – and just how much you were going to affect my life. Cunning bitch, leaving her shares in trust until last year – your birthday. That was a fatal blow to my plan – and to you, it would seem.' He takes a breath and smiles, basking in my distress. 'You are related to Katenka Bagrov. The whore left my shares – my fucking shares – to the stupid cunt who's shacked up with Luke Sutton! Who would have thought such a story would be true?' He peers at me. 'Your mother left you with a death sentence. Ah, you can't beat a mother's love.' His hands slide slowly up my legs. 'I think you and I could have some fun. I could compare you to your mother. I wonder, are you as frigid as her?'

Holy fuck. I never met her, but I am certain Katenka would not have had sex with this weasel – no way. Adrenalin pumps through my blood after hearing about his plan. I swallow hard and look across at Alexis. Our eyes meet before she looks away. Another revelation hits me like a lightning bolt – Alexis has been here before, at the hands of her father.

'Don't touch us,' I say, compelled to fight.

Suddenly he grips my hair, yanking it hard.

'Argh – get off me!' I yell and try to squirm away, but it's pointless. He's too strong.

From nowhere I feel something cold at my temple.

'Fucking talk to me like that again, bitch, and I'll shoot you, do I make myself clear? Open your mouth.'

What?

'Now, or I will shoot you and let you bleed to fucking death.'

Reluctantly, I part my lips. He shoves the barrel of his gun in my mouth.

'Oh, to fuck with Sutton's wife. What a pleasure that will be! I suggest you don't try to fight. That didn't work for Katenka.'

He pushes the gun further in, almost choking me. My eyes glaze over as I desperately try to fight back my emotions. What does he mean, it didn't work?

'You'd better get used to this. I'm going to fuck you very soon.'

He looks at Alexis. 'Don't worry, you will get your turn.'

I try to stop gagging, but with the gun jammed into my mouth, it's impossible.

Thankfully, he removes the weapon and sits back on his chair, leaving me to splutter and gasp for air. I inhale deeply, hoping to regulate my breathing and to stop my body from trembling. But I can't stop shaking. I'm in shock. Would he have shot me? I'm certain he would.

'You see, after I met Katenka in New York I decided to play a game. I threatened her, attacked her, sent her love letters hinting at what I'm capable of.' His eyes gleam with delight: the sick bastard is getting off on his violent behaviour. 'For a while it was fun, knowing she lived in fear, and it wasn't until I came to London the following year that I knew she wouldn't change her mind. Once again the whore refused to sign over her shares. Taking her again made me feel a little better. It would seem you have her fighting spirit. Like mother, like daughter.' His hands slide up my sweatshirt towards my neck. 'I put my hands round her throat and just kept squeezing. I wanted to scare her.' He laughs. 'Killing her was never my intention – but I can't deny it gave me pleasure.'

A cold wave of fear washes over me. I feel numb. The pounding of my heart against my ribcage makes my body vibrate. He killed her – he killed my mum.

A single tear rolls down my cheek for her, Katenka Bagrov, my mum. One thing is for certain: his confession means he's going to kill me. He can't afford to let me go.

His thumb traces my tear. 'Very touching.'

'You're an evil bastard. I hope you rot in hell.'

'Maybe, but life will be better once you sign your shares over to me.'

'Take them! I don't want the bloody shares. Just let us go,' I plead.

'No… I shall have the company shares and then you, and then I will deliver you to Chekhol. I have a feeling it won't be pleasant. I assume you understand what I'm saying.'

He stands and looks at his watch. The glow from the window is dimming; I'm guessing a couple of hours of daylight remain. *Luke, where the hell are you?*

14

'So, ladies, this evening will be fun.'

Fun! Oh God, I want to throw up.

He walks behind Alexis and drags her chair across the room, scraping it against the wooden floor towards the bed.

'I have no use for your cunt this evening. But you're welcome to watch – you may learn something. Sutton wouldn't marry a woman who couldn't fuck, I'm certain of it.'

No. I begin to shut down.

He drags my chair in front of Alexis.

We watch him undo Alexis's wrists.

'Untie her hands and don't try anything.'

She looks blankly at Philip.

'It's quite simple, Alexis, untie her fucking hands.'

She leans towards me and loosens my wrists.

'Now her ankles.'

She folds forward and her trembling hands work fairly quickly, while Philip still holds his gun at my temple.

'Get up,' he commands, but I can't. 'Move, or I'll shoot her.' He swings his gun round to Alexis's temple. My eyes meet hers as I stand.

'Good girl. Now take off your clothes.'

I shake my head.

Without hesitation he strikes Alexis.

'Now!' he yells.

I shake in fear. I slip off Luke's sweatshirt and my T-shirt, then my Converse and jeans. All that remains is my underwear and socks.

He waves his gun in the air. 'Everything.'

I close my eyes and remove the last few items.

'Hmm, Sutton has good taste. I'll reserve judgement until I've fucked your tight cunt.'

Luke – please. Where are you?

'Tie her hands together.' He passes Alexis a piece of rope and gestures with his gun to get on with it. 'Move,' he says and shoves me forward. 'Wrists together.' She ties my hands looser than they were.

He tugs at the rope.

'Ow!' I moan, although there is no pain. But I have begun to hatch a plan – I hope.

'Get on the bed. If you try to run, I'll shoot you... I have no problem ending your life and changing my plans.'

I believe him. He's unstable enough to kill me if I fight him.

Unsteadily, I perch on the edge of the bed. Suddenly he punches me on the side of my face, forcing me to the mattress. My vision blurs. He's cut my lip; I can taste iron.

'Middle of the bed,' he says.

Shaking, I comply. He tugs my ankles, causing me to slide nearer to the metal footboard. I watch his every move. He drags Alexis's chair towards my feet and throws her extra pieces of rope.

'Tie her up, make sure her legs are spread wide.'

She leans forward as far as she can and ties my legs.

I close my eyes. *Oh God, please take me away. I would rather die than allow him to touch me. Please, Katenka, take me with you.*

Tears roll down my cheeks. He hits me again. I'm still here. No amount of praying will help me.

I turn away, not wanting to look at him.

He roughly grips my face. 'You will look at me.' He waves his gun at me.

'Daddy, no,' Alexis whispers, 'please don't do this—'

'Shut the fuck up.'

He kneels between my legs. I desperately want to hit him, but my wrists are bound together, and he's still got his gun at my temple.

He rears up and begins to undo his trousers. He has to lower his gun and use both hands. This may be my only chance. I club him as hard as I can with my bound hands. He falls sideways. I sit up, but he recovers quickly.

'You fucking bitch!' he screams and uses his hand to wipe his mouth. 'You've cut my fucking lip.'

'Good, you disgusting fucking pig.'

This time he uses his gun against my ribs, followed by a hard blow to my face, knocking my senses into tiny pieces. Once isn't enough. He continues to pistol-whip me, too many times for me to count. Then he's at my throat, his hands locked tightly, squeezing.

'Is this what you want? To die like your fucking mother, you fucking whore?'

I try to fight him, but he increases the pressure and I'm almost gone. I begin to lose consciousness for the second time today.

I don't know what happens next, but suddenly I can breathe. I gasp for air, panting and crying. I manage to sit up. Alexis stands at the foot of the bed, the remains of her chair in her hand. Philip lies, squalling like a demented animal, on the floor.

'You forgot to tie my hands, you fucking arsehole.' Her eyes are on fire.

'Alexis, grab the gun!'

She grabs the weapon from the floor and holds it in trembling hands. She walks towards Philip, who is trying to crawl away, and kicks him in the head. Again. Again. He lies still.

'Quickly, untie my hands.'

She lowers the gun and fumbles with the rope. Once my hands are free, I loosen my ankles and scramble off the bed. I'm sore all over, but I can just about stand. Quickly, I dress.

Now what? I turn to see Alexis pointing the loaded gun at Philip. I walk towards her, feeling unsteady on my feet, and slide my hand over the gun.

'Give it to me.'

Her glazed eyes meet mine.

'I know how to shoot,' I say.

She hands over the weapon and I check the chamber.

I hear him coming round, and cast my eyes around the room.

'There's only one way out.' I point to the window. 'We need to buy ourselves some time.'

'How far do you think you'll get?' Philip manages to croak.

'Shut the fuck up.' I walk towards him and kick his face, knocking him sideways. 'God, that felt good... Luke said I'd get my day.' I kick him again. 'That's for my mum, you murdering bastard.' I lean towards him. 'Don't ever hurt my family again. When Luke finds you, you'll be sorry – and dead.' Quickly, I grab the rope and bind his feet. Thankfully he's too weak to fight. 'Tie his wrists.'

'The gun?' Her words are chilling.

'We can't shoot him! The noise, and—' God, I feel sick. This is her dad – a poor excuse of a human being, but he's still her dad.

She nods, her eyes murderous.

I move to the bed. 'Help me block the door.' We work in silence and quietly push the bed in front of the door. 'OK, now drag his sorry arse.' I yank his ankles while Alexis pulls him towards the bed. Somehow we tie his bound ankles to the leg of the bed. We stretch his arms above his head and tie his arms. He lies under the bed tied like the animal he is.

'They won't be able to open the door,' I say.

He begins to groan.

I look around and see my socks on the floor; I ball them up and shove them in his mouth. 'Choke on that, you sick fucker.'

'What's the plan?' Alexis asks.

I look across to our only escape route, the high window.

'It's our only option, and it's getting dark so we don't have a lot of time.'

I push the chair against the wall and try to open the window. Unsurprisingly, it's locked. Crap! Breaking the window might attract attention, but I have no choice. I use the butt of the gun to break the glass and the jagged edges. Too loud – shit! I tuck the gun in the waistband of my jeans.

'You go first.' I clasp my fingers, ready to give Alexis a leg up.

'Wait.' She strides towards her father and presses her foot against his throat. 'I hate you – you deserve to die.' She kicks him hard in the head, enough for him to fall unconscious again.

She reaches my side and stands on the chair. 'Ready?' I say and give her a leg up. 'One, two, three.'

She boosts herself up and pulls herself through the window, then lowers herself on the other side. 'Give me your hands.'

It's ironic that I'm depending on Alexis to survive. I loathed her, but now we are fighting for survival together. Jesus Christ, life tests me at every corner.

Alexis helps me hoist myself out of the room and through the window. As I slump to the grass I feel an intense pain in my side.

'Shit!' I hold myself and stagger to my feet.

'Kate, you're bleeding.'

I look down at my blood-soaked sweatshirt. A sharp piece of glass is sticking out of my side.

'Shit, I thought I cleared it all.'

'Jesus.'

'Pull it out. Bloody hell, it hurts. But quickly, we need to run.'

'OK. On three. And no screaming.'

'Really, are you shitting me?' I take a deep breath.

Tentatively, she grips the glass poking out of my sweatshirt.

'Three.' Alexis pulls it out and throws it to the ground.

'Holy fuck.' I hold my side and she helps me to remain upright. 'What happened to one and two?'

'We don't have time. Now run,' she says.

2

We run into the woods until the lodge is out of sight. It feels like an eternity, but must only be about twenty minutes or so.

I stop, mainly due to the pain shooting through my body.

'OK, we don't have long before it's dark,' I whisper, trying to regulate my breathing. 'I think we're about fifteen miles from the main road. I was making mental notes on the way here. We took a sharp right onto the dirt road.' I take a breath. 'For what it's worth, my gut says they would expect us to head towards the road. I think we should stay in the woods then head to the road in the daylight.'

'Jesus, Kate, I was thinking let's run and hope for the best!'

'Let's assume they've realised we've gone, so from this point on no talking, stay alert and look where you're walking. If you need me, pull my arm. Got it?'

After another twenty minutes, we're even deeper in the forest, surrounded by tall dark trees that take on intimidating silhouettes as night arrives. My senses are on high alert, but there are no sounds except our light footsteps. I shiver, not just because of the cool air but because of blood loss. I can feel blood seeping through Luke's hoodie. We need to find somewhere to pitch up until sunlight.

A little while later, I hear a noise and stop dead. I reach for Alexis, who stops and holds her breath. I bring my index finger to my lips, although we have barely spoken since we escaped.

'Can you hear that?' I whisper.

Her brows arch. 'What?'

'Water. It's really faint. Listen.'

We stand still, straining our ears. I'm truly hoping it's not in my head, but after several blows anything is possible.

She nods and points. 'Over there.'

'Let's go.'

Within a few minutes we arrive at a small stream. We rush to it and kneel down to lap up small handfuls of icy water. It may be cold, but we're dehydrated.

I look around. 'We can stop here. You go that way and I'll look up here.' As I walk further upstream I spot an old tree with a hollow trunk. I turn when I hear Alexis.

'Welcome to five-star shit-hole.'

'Will we fit?'

I begin to dig out the soil. 'It's loose and dry.' The dirt breaks away fairly easy. 'It'll do for tonight.'

'What do you want me to do?'

'Get some branches that we can use as camouflage in case the scumbags come to find us.'

'OK.'

She walks away while I continue to make the hole a little less crappy, but it is mud and tree roots, so there's a limit to what I can do! It's pitch-black – apart from the stars that light the night sky for us.

'I need your help,' I say, and lift up my sweatshirt to assess my wound.

Alexis leans closer and gently touches my skin. 'Jesus, Kate, that looks bad.'

'It hurts like hell.' I look down. Even though it is dark, I can just about make out the wound across my ribs. It must be three inches long.

'You need stitches.'

'Shit, it kills. I need to bandage it.' I look at Alexis. 'Take off your belt.'

I slip off my sweatshirt and T-shirt. I then fold my T-shirt in half and half again – a makeshift bandage.

'Tie your belt around me.' I hold the T-shirt over the laceration and Alexis ties the belt. 'Ow. Jesus Christ, that hurts like hell.'

'Sorry. Is that tight enough?'

I nod and blow air through pursed lips. I try to slip Luke's Abercrombie hoodie on, but as soon as I raise my arms the pain kicks in.

'Let me.' Alexis slips it over my head and then carefully manoeuvres my arms one at a time. 'OK?'

'Yeah, I'm just so cold.'

'Me too.'

We crawl into the tree hollow. It's tiny, and we have to sit with our knees drawn up. I rest the gun next to me and continue to keep a watchful eye.

I rub my grubby hands against my forehead. 'Bloody hell, this is fucked up. I've been married for five days… Five bloody days and now I'm in Russia – again, with you – superbitch – as my rescue partner.'

'Superbitch!' Alexis whips back.

'Come on, you know that's what I called you. To be fair, you deserved it.'

She smirks. 'I can be a little… forward.'

'Forward? Christ, Alexis, you targeted me from the onset. You hated me. Now I know where you learned that.'

Her face drops.

'Crap. Sorry, I didn't mean—' I reach for her hand. 'You're nothing like your – him. It was a slip of the tongue.'

'You're right,' she says and closes her eyes.

'No, he's worse than evil. You have a sharp tongue. There's a difference.'

'Kate Harper, sorry, Kate Sutton, are you trying to make me feel better?'

'Maybe.'

Alexis releases a small smile. This friendship has to be the most bizarre alliance I have ever formed.

She takes a deep breath. 'I did love Luke once. I know you think I still do, and there is a small part of me that always will, but you make him happy.'

'Oh.' What the hell do I say to that? 'Your families have been friends for years; you could have ended up together.'

'I don't think marriage has ever crossed my mind.'

'Luke knows you slept with Ollie. I sort of told him in Dubai.' Even in the darkness I can see she looks alarmed – almost as much as Luke, when he found out she took Ollie's virginity for a joke. 'Besides, you did have your mouth stuck to Luke's face.'

'Poor judgement, and I was drunk.'

'I know, water under the bridge.'

'I can imagine Luke's reaction… The Sutton brothers stick together. They always have.'

'He was furious.' That's an understatement; it was a Luke Sutton 'code red' moment, one I won't forget. Bizarrely, it led to him planning our wedding a week later.

'Do I regret it? Yes. But I was young and carefree.'

'Declan told me,' I say.

'Declan hates me, and Ollie avoids me at all costs. I don't blame either of them… I assumed Luke would have found out – well, he knows now.'

'Ollie is nothing like his brothers. Luke wants to run the world and Declan is… a shag monster.'

'Suits him,' she says.

'Did you know Ollie tried to…' My words trail off.

'Commit suicide? We all knew, but no one spoke about it.'

'Declan blames some of it on you, and that's why he—'

'He hates me. I deserve it, Kate!'

'Shit – I shouldn't have said anything. Look, it was a long time ago and Ollie's happy now.'

'Kate, I'm sorry that my father…' She swallows. 'He should never have brought you here.' She looks down. 'Taking your mother from you is unforgivable. I can't change what's happened, but I have honestly never felt so empty.'

'It's not your fault; he's sick in the head. Alexis, you saved my life! He was going to…' I can't say the words out loud, ever, but even in the darkness I can see the painful look in her eyes. She saved me, but who rescued her? 'I'm so confused. I thought my mum committed suicide.'

'But D—' She can't finish his name. Besides, he's not worthy of the title.

'I've seen her death certificate and it says suicide. You know George Williams?'

'As in Matthew's father? He's a coroner.'

I nod. 'He signed her report, and Joseph Morley kept a copy.'

'Why? I know he's a judge, but why would he keep a copy of every case?'

'It doesn't make sense – a bit like Philip didn't know I existed.'

'He didn't. Believe me, he was shocked when he found out.'

'They all grew up together, right?' I ask.

She nods. 'George, Joseph and – him.'

I take her hand. God, this is so painful for her.

'Plus Luke's dad,' she says.

'Yeah, Luke told me they all went to the same school. One thing's for certain: someone's lied.'

'After today, you can see that my dad's capable of anything. He must have something on George and Joseph – they aren't bad, not like him. There must be more to it.'

'None of this makes sense,' I say.

'What about your Russian father?' she asks.

'Ivor Varizin? Luke thinks he's watching me. He turned up at our wedding in Venice, I know he watched us get married. Well, he was hiding, I just happened to catch sight of him.'

'Do you think he knows you're here?'

'I bloody hope so. I mean, if you're stalking me, at least have the decency to stalk me when I need rescuing.'

Alexis smiles. 'I get why Luke likes you, Kate. Maybe I always have.'

How can I answer that?

'Philip said you're like your mum. Where is she?' I ask, but now I wonder about my question.

'The last time I saw her was in a psychiatric ward. I remember it so clearly. I was wearing the most beautiful yellow sundress with daises. Sh-she went mad, lashing out and harming herself. That was the last time I saw her. I guess I was six, maybe seven.'

'Oh God, I'm so sorry.'

'Don't be. I barely remember her. I was ten when she died. Dad told me when he put me to bed one evening. He was so matter-of-fact about it that I accepted the news as though he had told me to brush my teeth.'

'That's so sad.'

'It was a long time ago. Anyway, you only recently found out you were adopted. That must have been difficult.'

'It was. "Oh, by the way, you're twenty-seven, your parents are Russian and now you've been given a shitload of money, plus your mum is dead, but don't worry, she's left you her business too."' I lean my head against the tree. 'Sorry! I just can't believe my life has turned on its arse in a year.' I take a deep breath and look at her. 'How long has he been abusing you?'

She drops her chin.

'Shit – you don't have to answer. Sorry.' I draw her closer, and the stabbing pain in my ribs takes my breath away.

The moonlight seeping through the foliage is reflected in her eyes, revealing the depth of her sadness in the iridescent droplets of water trickling down her cheeks.

'Alexis, don't answer, it's too personal, I'm completely out of line putting you on the spot.'

'It's OK,' she whispers, and sighs. 'The first time he raped me, I was twelve and I'd just bought my first bra. I was so proud. All I could think about was my new bra.'

Jesus – I feel sick. It's painful, but I hug her. She tries to pull away but I hold her trembling body until she feels warmer.

'Sick fucking bastard… You poor love.'

'I don't want your pity, Kate.'

'It's not pity. I'm furious he's got away with it. It will never happen again, I promise you… Luke will find us and he'll kill him.'

She starts to cry. Her cries increase until they fill the tree hollow. They're pitiful cries, like you would expect to hear from a child, not a woman. How long has she held on to this pain?

'Shh, let it go. I'm so sorry I've dragged you into this,' I say.

'I would rather die than feel him touch me again.' Her voice is low and her tears continue to flow – driven by a sense of relief, perhaps.

'He will never touch you again, I promise you.'

I have no idea how long I have held her, but she is sound asleep.

My shoulders relax slightly but I feel weak – due mainly to blood loss and, of course, fear. What will happen if he finds us?

Exhausted, I close my eyes. At least, one shuts, but the other is swollen and was already closed. In my mind's eye, I see Katenka. My heart aches knowing what she went through. I just lived the last chapter of her life and survived. I feel totally humbled that she protected Harry and me from *him*. Philip Cooper. He murdered her.

Thoughts race through my head, and suddenly it hits me. *Holy fuck! No.* I run over the facts of Philip's story. Katenka was in New York, he raped her and she fled to London. I was a baby at this point... She then bought a house, met Malcolm Harper. The next time she visited Malcolm she had two children, so the likelihood is that she was already pregnant when she met Malcolm... Holy shit. Philip Cooper must be Harry's father.

You have to be kidding. How can *he* be part of my sister? Denial is my first reaction, but I know my gut instinct is right: the dates and timing make sense. Oh God, this will kill her...

Is knowledge power? No, it's not. Knowledge is overrated and leaves you feeling crappy.

'Please, Katenka. Mum. Help me.' Tears roll down my cheeks at the thought of her and how she died. Forgiveness for Cooper is not in my soul.

My thoughts return to Luke. I can feel in my heart he's trying to find me. I look at my wrist. *Where are you? I need help. Please find me.*

The sound of a twig breaking wakes me. I peek out of the tree hollow. It's daylight. A small deer walks past. It's quite surreal to witness nature so close – it's even more surreal that yesterday was not a dream. Reality kicks in as I look to my right and see Alexis asleep.

I brush her hair from her face. 'Alexis.'

She stirs.

'It's time to go.'

She lifts her head. 'Oh my God, Kate, you look like shit.' Her assessment is probably on point.

'Well, that's handy, because I feel like shit.' My hand rests against my blood-soaked wound.

'Your eye.' She gently touches my swollen socket. 'Can you open it?'

'No, it hurts too much. Anyway, I don't want to burst your bubble but you're not looking so hot yourself.'

We smile.

'I'm freezing,' she says.

'Me too. It's early – we'll warm up once we start moving. OK, we need a plan – other than to get the hell out of here. I think we should head for the main road, look for a house or a garage. Christ, I need a coffee and a doctor.' Plus a miracle.

We sit for a couple of minutes enjoying the peace, knowing how long today will be.

I crawl out of the hole. Alexis follows. Trying to stand is a little challenging.

'Steady – lean on me,' Alexis says and holds me close.

'I'm fine.'

She steps away and I manage to remain stable. 'Luke – please find us,' I mutter.

'Kate, no one knows where we are.'

'Trust me, he'll find us.'

She takes a breath. She might think I'm being irrational, but what she does not know is that Luke has the ability to track me 24/7, with the help of his Secret Service friends.

'Ready?' I remove the gun from my jeans and check the safety. 'Let's not forget the exchange is today. Philip's crew won't be alone. Today will be another peachy day in paradise...'

'Paradise!' she repeats.

Silently, we tread along the grassy bank, heading away from the stream. The wood is dense and the ground is littered with tree stumps and thorny bushes. I can barely see out of one eye, which is still swollen shut, and feel almost too weak to walk.

How long have we walked? The sun is directly above us; it must be midday, although it feels like we have been walking for days.

We are silent, so the sound of a male voice stops us dead in our tracks. Nervously, I hold the gun. Thankfully, we are shielded by a mass of bushes and I can't see who's speaking. Then a man comes into view. He's one of the scumbags from the house. I look at Alexis.

'Nothing. Over,' he says.

Another voice echoes through the forest.

'They have to be there. We have two hours before the handover. Find them!' Philip Cooper screams over the radio, making us jump.

The man stops and looks towards our hiding spot. Alexis looks at me, using her fingers to mime walking, then points to the gun. I shake my head and mouth 'no'. It's too late. She appears from the bush.

He strides towards her and yanks her arm. 'One down, one to go. Now where's your mate?'

'I don't know. We got separated last night. Do you have any water?'

Wow – not bad, Alexis!

Quietly, I edge round to the other side of the bush and creep behind the man. I raise my gun and swing it with all my strength. It cracks against his head, and he slumps to the ground. I almost collapse too.

I hold my side and take deep breaths. 'Shit, Alexis, he could have killed you.'

'Yes, but he didn't.'

'Grab his radio and gun, and check to see if he has a phone.'

She searches his pockets and passes me his gun and radio.

I bend down, which hurts like hell, but I need to find a pulse.

'He's alive.'

'Should we kill him?' Alexis asks.

I shake my head. 'I know he would kill us, but I can't kill him. Plus, the noise. We need to keep moving.'

The radio bellows in my hand. I shriek.

'Continue north. Peterson, where are you? Over.'

'I'm guessing he's Peterson. Sleep well, Peterson… Let's go,' I say and offer Alexis his gun.

She shakes her head. 'I don't know how to use it.'

'Take it. The safety is off. You just point and pull the trigger. Please, you may need it.'

'OK.' Reluctantly, she takes it from me.

We continue our journey in silence. I am beginning to feel light-headed. I look down at my sweatshirt. I'm certain there's more blood. I need a doctor.

After a while the trees become sparse and the ground becomes more open. The thick foliage helped us to be less conspicuous; now we need to remain alert.

I stop for a moment, resting my hands on my thighs.

Alexis comes to my side. 'Kate?'

'I need a minute.'

'You look pale – we need to get you to a doctor.'

I nod. 'I'm fine. Let's go.'

'You're not, you're too weak.'

'We don't have a choice… I can't spend another night here.' I can't.

Although the warm sun shines through the gaps between the trees, the air is cool. I wrap my arms around myself.

Another hour passes. Our surroundings look familiar. Alexis stops, holding her hand in the air.

'A car,' I whisper. 'We must be near the road.' *Thank God.* 'Let's walk along the edge… just in case it's Philip's men or the Russians!'

'Great.'

Then we hear it: the thump of heavy footsteps.

I turn to see burly men heading our way. *Oh, fuck.*

'Run, Alexis!'

We run, but we are weak and too slow for the men who are charging after us.

A bullet whines past me and hits a tree. Now the open space means we're mice in their game of cat and mouse – we don't stand a chance.

'Stop, or we will shoot!' a male voice bellows.

My legs freeze, as do Alexis's. She reaches for my hand.

'Turn around slowly,' the husky voice commands.

We turn to face four of Philip's men.

He reaches for his radio. 'We have them. Over.' His cold eyes scan us. He frisks us and removes our weapons.

From a distance I watch Philip charge towards us. His smirk is chilling.

'Thought you'd be able to get away? For two strong women, you are both fucking useless.'

'Something happen to your face?' I can't help myself. My life hangs in the balance, so I may as well go down fighting.

'I suggest you shut the fuck up or your other eye will look the same.'

'Kill me, I don't care. You're a fucked-up weasel who hurts women – you must be so proud of yourself.' I look at the burly men surrounding him. 'You call yourself men? Listen to the shit that comes out of his mouth. Grow a pair of balls, for Christ's sake.'

'Kate!' Alexis tugs at my hand.

Philip lunges towards me and slaps my face.

'Is that it, you fucking prick?' I cough, and spit out blood.

He grabs my hair. 'You need to learn some manners.'

'And you need to learn not to molest and rape children, you fucking pig.'

He releases my hair and turns to Alexis. 'What have you been saying?'

Her face is pale and filled with fear.

'I'm waiting.' He raises his hand.

'Leave her alone.' I push him. I'm furious. Then I kick the back of his knee. He buckles and falls to the ground. Just one of my husband's 007 moves... He glares at me, his face full of fury. 'I promised her you will never lay a finger on her again – ever.'

'You want to die, bitch? It will be my pleasure.' He scrambles to his feet.

'I told you I don't care... You're a sick fucker. Actually, you're a paedophile.' I look at his entourage. 'You know you work for a man who fucks children? I hope you're proud of yourselves.' I'm also hopeful some of his workers are fathers and it may spark their morals.

I look at Alexis, who has tears rolling down her cheeks. Is this the first time anyone has defended her?

My hand slips into hers. 'Let's go,' I say. After all, we have nothing to lose. I either die here or with the Russians. I'll take my chances.

Philip pulls his gun and points it at my head. 'If you walk, I will shoot you.'

'Go ahead. I don't care.' I pray he's bluffing. I inhale possibly my last breath. *I love you to the end, Luke Sutton.*

Then I hear a gunshot. Alexis screams my name and pushes me down. My head makes contact with the hard ground and I feel intense pain, but also a sense of peace. I look up at the sun beaming through the trees. My eyes feel heavy.

'Stay with me, baby,' a voice whispers in my ear as my body shuts down.

3

Slowly, I surface. I'm in a dimly lit room, not the forest. I open my eye, painfully, and there he is. Luke. Please, God, let this be real and not a dream.

My heart pounds. It's him – my Luke, dressed in black, sitting in a chair by my bed. He told me to stay alive and he would find me, and he did.

My entire body feels weighted down. With a huge effort I skim my hand across his dark hair. *Please wake up.*

'Luke.' My voice is barely a whisper.

Once more I touch his hair. This time he stirs and his dark eyes find me.

'Hi,' he whispers and gently kisses my lips. My relief is too much. Tears roll down my cheeks, and I sob.

'Shh, it's OK. I've got you.'

'Luke, I'm sorry,' I mutter.

'You're safe.'

'But—'

'You're with me.'

I nod. As long as he's with me, everything will be OK. It's been that way from the beginning.

'Where are we?' I ask.

'Kudrovo,' he says.

'Where?'

'Your favourite country – Russia!' His brow shoots up.

'Take me home, please.'

'You're too weak. This hospital bed is the only place you'll be until the doctors say otherwise.'

'I feel like crap.'

'You look hot!' His smile warms my heart.

'Argh, don't make me laugh. Everywhere hurts.'

'You were unconscious when I got to you, plus you've lost a lot of blood.'

'Luke, I was so scared… Philip.' I shut my eyes; just the mention of his name causes panic.

'He's dead.'

What? He will never touch another woman again – except I can feel him, his hands around my throat. I can't breathe.

'Calm down. Kate, look at me.' Luke inhales and exhales slowly; I mirror his motion. 'That's it, in and out.'

Within a few seconds my breathing settles.

'Thank you for…' *For killing the man who killed my mum.*

I feel a firm grip on my other hand.

'Katarina, no one will ever hurt you, I promise.'

Ivor! I look at Luke.

'What's going on?' I never thought I would see him again, let alone hear him call me by my birth name.

'We met Ivor's team en route and he insisted this was the best private hospital.' Luke's eyes flit from mine to the man he hoped would never return to my life. 'We were trying to reach you when Philip fired his gun. Kate, Ivor shot Philip.'

My eyes flick back to my Russian father. I prayed he was watching me – and he was.

'The gun…' Oh God, a memory comes flooding back. 'Philip fired – I remember. Where is Alexis?'

Luke looks across at Ivor.

'Where is she, Luke?' I attempt to pull myself up from the bed 'Ouch.'

'Careful, you're attached to IVs and you have stitches,' Luke says.

'I don't care. Where's Alexis?'

'Kate, the bullet…'

'No!' I say.

'Calm down. She was hit, but they managed to remove the bullet. She's stable.' Tenderly, Luke touches my check.

'She's been through so much. I need to see her.' I try to sit up again, but it hurts too much. 'Luke, please.'

'Katarina, excuse me – Kate, your husband is right, you are too weak.'

'You don't understand – she saved me.' Twice.

'She's in recovery – no one can see her yet,' Luke says. 'The bullet skimmed her femoral artery.'

'This can't be happening. That's major, right?' I can't think straight.

Luke nods. 'She's lost a lot of blood.'

'Give her some. Luke, you help everyone. I'm begging you to do something.'

'She's in the best hands. She has a rare blood type – AB negative – which hasn't helped.'

'Siblings.' I close my good eye, then look at Luke. 'Can siblings help?'

Luke's brows knit. 'Possibly, but she doesn't have any. Besides, they have located some blood now.'

'I think she does.' I swallow. 'Harry.'

'Kate, you're not making sense.' Our dark eyes lock. 'Talk to me.'

'Bloody hell, my stomach really hurts.'

'You have lacerations on both sides of your ribcage. Ivor, give me a hand.'

Ivor and Luke place their hands under my arms and lift me to a sitting position.

'This may hurt.'

I hold my breath.

'Is that better?'

'Yes.'

I reach for Ivor's hand, knowing I have to explain what happened to my mother, the love of his life.

'Dad, I need to tell you something.'

He nods and takes my hand. It's the first time I've called him 'Dad'. His eyes gleam – with pride?

'OK, Philip told me.' I bite my lip and look across at Luke.

'He raped Katenka in New York, and again in London, and—' My words trail off. 'He murdered her. He strangled her.' My free hand travels to my neck with the memory of what he did to us both. 'I'm so sorry. He took her from you – from us.' I sob.

'It is OK. I knew your mother would not have taken her own life.' Ivor places his lips on my forehead. 'Shh, it is OK, my child.'

'But it's not… When Alexis and I were hiding last night I kept playing back the story Philip told me, and then it hit me. The timing. I'm pretty sure Philip is Harry's dad.'

Luke bows his head.

'I can't keep this from Harry… I pray he's not her—'

'She has to be told, or at least given the choice to find out,' Luke says.

'I didn't think you would agree.'

'This is not our decision to make, Kate,' he says.

'Luke, so much doesn't add up… I can't take much more.'

'Please rest, Katarina. Your body needs to mend.' Ivor tries to smile, but how can he? His wife was raped and murdered, and now he has killed a man for me.

'Ivor's right.' Luke stands and runs his hand through his hair. 'Christ, this is a mess. I need to make a call.'

'What about my mum and dad, Luke? They need to know.'

He shakes his head. 'Not now – one step at a time. Besides, I need to contain what happened to Philip. We're all implicated in what went down, Kate.'

'But he's dead, and Harry might tell them, and what about me? How can I explain this?'

'Calm down! First things first. I need you healthy so we can go home, OK?'

I nod.

'I'll go and make a phone call. Ivor, do not leave her alone, understood?' Luke's tone is direct. As I predicted, he remains cold towards Ivor, with a chill that will not thaw any time soon.

Ivor's loss is clear to see. His dark eyes are sad. I wonder if there is a small part of him that feels relieved knowing his wife did not leave the world of her own accord.

'I'm sorry about Mum.'

'Please, this is not your fault. I have taken revenge for Katenka, and of course for you too.'

'What happens now?' I take a deep breath, which hurts like hell. 'Please don't tell me this is it, you're going to disappear out of my life.' I can't cope with another year of wondering where he is.

Tenderly he strokes my face. 'If you want me in your life, then I will stay… Your safety comes first and Luke must agree,' he says. 'Katarina, please sleep. I will still be here when you wake.'

'Can you hold my hand?' A residue of fear from the last twenty-four hours circulates through my body, but when his hand slips over mine all the security I need is right here.

I wake when I feel someone place a cuff on my arm to take my blood pressure. Luke is at my side with a doctor. They then walk to the doorway. Luke glances across at me. I know my husband, and I certainly know the look he wears when he's holding out on me.

He returns to my side and perches on the edge of the bed. 'How are you feeling?'

'Hungry. I need a cup of tea.'

'Good. I'll get you something to eat.' Luke looks at Ivor and reluctantly leaves him alone with me.

If Ivor stays in my life, which I bloody hope he does, I now face a new battle – Sutton verses Varizin. God help me!

Ivor takes my hand.

'I saw you at my wedding,' I announce.

Ivor chuckles. 'I know.'

'Your hiding skills weren't great.'

He smiles. 'I am too old to hide.' He wanted me to see him – I know that in my heart.

'Thank you for the white rose... In the picture you gave me of your wedding day, Mum was holding the same kind of rose – is that why you left it on my pillow?'

'Yes.' He nods. 'I wanted your mother to be with you.'

Tears roll down my cheeks. 'She is – well, in my head and heart. I guess that's all I'll ever have.'

'And that is all you need. Now, please rest.'

Before long Luke returns with a tray of tea and toast, which smells divine.

'OK. Let's sit you up.'

I nod. Luke flashes a half-hearted smile. *What's up with him?* He pulls the table closer and takes the chair next to me.

'Did you get hold of Harry?' Just the thought of Harry's news kills my appetite.

'Yes. Now please eat.'

'How was she?'

'I spoke to Raymond, then to Harry.'

'What did she say? I should have spoken to her.'

Luke passes me my tea. 'Kate, please.'

My trembling hands take the cup.

'I told her, and asked if she wanted to take a DNA test,' Luke says.

'God, I pray that I'm wrong.'

'Harry agreed to the test. I've arranged for an appointment.'

'And Alexis?' I ask.

'I need a sample of her saliva,' he says.

'Is she back from theatre? Did you ask her?'

'No.' Luke drags his chair closer.

'No? What, to the theatre or asking?'

'Kate, please, just eat.'

'Isn't that, like, breaking the law? I mean, you can't just test her, can you?'

'What I need is for you to eat and drink.'

I put my cup back on the tray. 'But Harry is more important. I need to speak to her.'

'Not now,' Luke commands.

'Luke, she needs me.'

'Yes, and I need you to rest. It goes against my better judgement, but I told them both about the last twenty-four hours.'

'What? That Philip was shot and…'

Luke nods. 'She knows everything. I had no choice.'

'Poor Harry. He may not be her dad, but—'

'Eat.' Ivor feels the need to join in. *Great, just what I want: another controlling man in my life.*

'I'm not hungry, I feel sick.'

'It's shock,' Luke says.

'Can you go and see how Alexis is? Please, Luke.'

'She's in ICU.'

'Crap!'

'For observation, that's all. Honestly, she's incredibly lucky,' Luke says.

'Lucky! Luck hasn't been on her side.' I close my eyes for a second. 'That's twice she's saved my life in twenty-four hours.'

'I don't want to push you, but I need to know what happened so I can come up with a cover story,' Luke says.

'What do you mean?'

Luke looks at Ivor. 'Philip Cooper was shot on a hunting trip. It was an accident.'

'Well, I guess he was hunting me, so that's not total bullshit.'

'Katarina!' Ivor bellows.

Now he wants to play Dad!

'I want you to tell me what happened, Kate. Take it slow, OK?'

'I don't think I can, Luke.' I shake my head.

'It's just us, me and you, remember?'

'It's…'

'I know it's difficult. Just start from the beginning.'

'OK. So I called you when Alexis turned up at Sandbanks.'

'Because she overheard Philip say he planted the bomb at our house,' Luke says, 'and they planned to take you.'

I nod. 'After they broke in at Sandbanks, I woke up on a plane.' I run a hand through my matted hair. 'Philip was evil, Luke, he—'

I think Luke is going to speak, but he says nothing. His mouth is a thin line.

'Luke, this is too much for you.'

'No, carry on,' he says, but the tell-tale signs of him losing control are mapped across his face – alongside the fear of nearly losing me.

'When we landed I went in a car with Philip, and Alexis followed in another. Luke, I thought I was going to – one

44

of his men squeezed my throat…' I touch my neck. 'The men were—'

Luke takes my hand away from my neck. 'You're safe – no one will ever touch you again. Carry on.'

'You saw the building we were taken to?'

'Yes,' Ivor says.

'They tied us up in a room. I tried to get free, Luke, I tried, but…' I take a breath.

'I know. Did you smash the window?' Luke asks.

'It was the only way out, and that's how I cut myself.'

'Before that, what happened?' Luke asks.

'We were on our own for a while. Alexis was in shock, we both were. He came to the room – I mean, Philip.'

I take a moment.

'Go on,' Luke says.

'He told me what he did to Katenka. Apparently he never knew I existed until I inherited the Bagrov shares.' I take Ivor's hand. 'It kills me knowing how scared Mum must have been.'

'She is at peace,' Ivor says.

'But it doesn't make sense. We've seen the official report Charles took from his dad's office. I don't know Joseph Morley or George Williams, but do you think they would lie? Alexis said maybe Philip had something on them.'

'You know who these men are?' Ivor asks.

'I don't know them, but Luke does.'

'They are my father's old school friends, and I know their sons. Charles is Joseph's son – he took a copy of Katenka's paperwork.'

'Luke, they know something, I know they do,' I say.

'I have no idea why they would lie, or even if they knew Katenka. Kate, your mum was cremated, so we have no proof. All we have is paperwork and speculation,' Luke says.

'So they get away with it?'

'Get away with what? Did Philip implicate either man?'

I shake my head. 'No. He never mentioned them, and neither did I.'

'I can dig around, but I don't want to open up a can of worms. Philip was shot, which we all played a part in.' Luke looks across to Ivor. 'These two men are the elite in their industry. Joseph Morley is a judge and George Williams is a coroner. They could search for justice – and they may not find in our favour.'

'Kate, justice has been served for Katenka. We can now be at peace,' Ivor says. 'Luke is right. I agree to let this lie.'

'But Mum, what about justice for her?' My eyes sting.

'He is dead. She has justice – we all do.'

'Kate,' Luke says, 'and then what happened?'

Although Luke changes the subject away from Katenka, I still feel justice has not been done for her.

'After Philip told us about Katenka…' I run my hands through my hair.

'Then what? Tell me.'

I bite my lip. 'I don't think I can.'

'Why? Because of me?'

I nod.

'Nothing you can say will alter how much I love you.'

'But it's bad…' I look at both men. 'He – hit me – too many times to count.'

'Fuck.' Luke stands, his fists clenched.

'I'll stop,' I cry.

Luke takes my hand and sits on the bed. 'No.'

'I don't want to hurt you,' I say.

'You won't. I need to deal with this, Kate.'

'He untied Alexis so she could help him. I had to take off my clothes and get on the bed. I couldn't do anything else. He had a gun at my head, Luke.' Defensively, I fold my arms across my chest.

Luke closes his eyes for a second. 'You did the right thing. I told you to do whatever they said to stay alive.' His words have little effect. This is torture for him as much as it is for me. My husband, an ex-SAS soldier, failed to protect me.

I nod. 'Alexis had to tie my feet to the footboard, and…'

Ivor stands. 'I cannot listen.'

'He didn't rape me,' I blurt. 'He didn't get a chance to. I managed to hit him, and then he went mad, his hands were at my throat – but he forgot to retie Alexis and she knocked him out.'

'My child.' Ivor touches my cheek. Luke remains unnervingly silent.

'I don't know how, but we tied him to the bed.' *Luke, say something. Rescue me, don't shut down.* I take his hand.

'This should never have happened, Kate. I let you down.'

'I should never have met Matthew Williams or run off to Sandbanks, but I did. Philip should not have planted a bomb at our home last year or raped his daughter from the age of twelve, but he did.'

Luke bows his head. 'Baby, I just…'

'Hold me, Luke, tell me that everything is fine, and we can go home and eat French toast and—' I cry again. I just want things to be back to normal.

He raises his head. His eyes are full of anguish, the identical look he wears when he talks about how his best friend Paul died. He's guilty. He thinks he should have saved me. He's trained to kill and protect, but he didn't protect his most precious possession – me.

'French toast, Luke.' I try to smile through the pain.

'French toast.' He takes a breath.

'Yep, you and me, and French toast, nothing more. Simple.'

'When I get you home, that's the only thing you will be doing.'

'Good. Take me back to the old days of boss and cook, please.' My words hit a nerve – and his heart. His dark eyes connect with mine, and he comes back to me.

'I'll settle for my wife at home.' He leans forward and kisses me.

'Katarina, did he mention the name Chekhol?' Ivor asks.

'I don't know. Honestly, I can't think straight. Say the name again.'

'Chekhol. Yura Chekhol?'

'It rings a bell. He did say I was going to be delivered to someone who has a grudge against you.'

Luke glares at Ivor. 'You mentioned Chekhol when we met.'

'It is an old family name.'

'No!' Luke shakes his head. 'I've heard it before. You do know Kate was drugged and tied to a chair the last time you met.' Luke will never forgive Ivor for leaving me alone in Russia.

Ivor takes a deep breath.

'Of course you do,' Luke snaps.

I watch Luke closely. He is in fighting mode. 'Are these the same people, Ivor?'

'We dealt with it back then. I have one of Chekhol's men – he told me where Kate was.'

'So you knew?' I ask.

Ivor shakes his head. 'No. One of my men heard about Chekhol's deal with Cooper. It was too late, Katarina, you had been taken.'

'I was bait,' I say.

'It looks that way,' Luke says.

'Luke, let me deal with this,' Ivor says.

'Deal with it, like you did when your daughter was left for dead?' Luke's brows snap together and his jaw tightens. I remain silent. 'I'll deal with it myself,' he barks.

'She is my daughter! I would never hurt her. Trust me, this is already being taken care of.'

'Forgive me for not trusting you, Ivor.' Luke stands.

'The Chekhol family did have a long-standing feud with the Varizin family, but for years we have been at peace. Gideon Chekhol has recently inherited the Chekhol fortune, and he has a lot to learn.' Ivor stands too. 'Believe me when I say I am dealing with it. We have much in common: if you hurt my daughter, I will kill you.' Ivor extends his hand across the bed. 'I will honour my word, Luke.'

'Ivor, a warning to you – never underestimate me.' Eventually, Luke slips his hand in Ivor's. 'I need visual evidence.'

Evidence! What? Post a body in a bag!

'OK, I've seriously had enough of this. I need to go and check on Alexis.'

'Like hell you do.' Luke diverts his temper towards me.

'I just want to go home, Luke. Can you help me get up?' But I can already feel my eyes closing.

'Maybe tomorrow.' Commander Sutton is in the house. I wondered when he would make an appearance. Secretly, I've bloody missed him.

'Katarina, I have to leave, but please listen to your husband. I will return later, my precious daughter.'

'Don't walk out on me again,' I plead.

'I promise I will return.'

We are alone. Mr and Mrs Sutton.

'I need to feel you, Luke.'

He flashes his best Sutton smile, the one that captured my heart.

'It's difficult to hold you.' He cups my face in his hands and gently presses his lips to mine.

'I'm sorry for all this.'

'Kate, this isn't your fault.'

'You're all I could think about last night. You kept me alive.'

'You're trouble, Mrs Sutton, but you're mine, and I'm never going to let you go.'

'No regrets.'

He rubs his nose against mine. 'Never – six days of bliss.'

We smile.

'You know how much I love your black 007 wannabe outfit, but it's a little dramatic just to get my attention.'

'It's the only way.'

I giggle, and a sharp pain shoots across my torso. 'Ow, this is driving me mad.' I feel my gown. It's damp. I look at my fingers. 'Shit – is that blood?'

Luke lifts my gown. 'Your dressing needs replacing. Stay there.'

'I'm not going anywhere,' I say.

He disappears and returns in a couple of minutes, pushing a triage trolley.

'Are you allowed to help yourself?'

'I've lost count of the number of times I've done this.' He slips on surgical gloves and begins to remove the soaked gauze. 'This may sting a little.'

'I'm used to pain, go for it.'

He shoots me a look, not appreciating my humour. Silently he cleans the area and applies a new dressing.

'It's weeping; there's no blood. Better?'

I nod. 'I need the bathroom.'

'OK. I can change your gown too.'

'What about these?' I look at my arms.

Luke assesses the drips. 'You have a few more hours in these, plus another round.'

'What's in them?'

'Glucose, saline, antibiotics… Your vitals were all over the place, and you were dehydrated.' Luke puts pressure on the cannula, unscrews the drip and places a cap on the end. 'Let's get you changed.'

He seems guarded. I can't work out what's bothering him – maybe shock.

'Take it slowly.' He pulls back my blankets and slides his hands under my shoulders. 'Ready?'

'Yes,' I whisper. Aided by Luke, I manage to sit up.

Luke swings my legs round. I take his hands, ready to stand for the first time.

After what feels like a ridiculous ten-mile hike, but which is only roughly six feet, I reach the en suite. After a much-needed bathroom break, Luke undoes my gown. In front of me is a mirror offering me the first glimpse of my injuries.

'Oh God, Luke!' I'm unrecognisable. Is this what he's been hiding? My horrific body? My face is shades of purple and I have a deep cut on my lip. One eye is swollen shut. A chill washes over me when I see the livid handprints on my neck. The marks are an instant reminder of what Philip did, and how much worse things could have been. The remainder of my body is as I thought: all the colours of the rainbow float across my ribcage.

'Luke,' I murmur.

'Shh, it will fade.' He rests his hand over my heart. 'This concerns me the most. You need time.'

I begin to cry. Luke folds me into his arms. 'I'm sorry that I wasn't there to help you, Kate.'

I pull away. Sadness clouds his features.

'No, never say that. I need your strength, Luke... Please, I need you to carry me through this, not beat yourself up.'

'As long as I live, no one will ever touch you again. You have my word.'

The day passes. I sleep. I wake with a start, gasping for air.

'Luke?' I pant.

'It's OK, I'm here.'

The room is dimly lit. Evening must be approaching.

'How long have I been asleep?' I try to sit up. 'Have you heard from Harry, and Alexis? Is Ivor back?'

'One question at a time. You've been asleep for a while, which is exactly what you should be doing.' He steps closer.

I try to move. 'Argh, this is really getting on my bloody nerves.'

'Take it easy.'

'I need to call Harry. She's probably hurting and…'

Luke's silence is not comforting.

'What is it?'

'I spoke to Raymond.'

'And?'

'She's not ready to talk to you.'

'What do you mean, talk to me? Harry wouldn't say that, she wouldn't push me away.' Would she?

'Understandably, she's devastated.'

'Too devastated to talk to me? I don't understand. I would never hurt her.'

Lovingly, he presses his lips to my forehead. 'Don't take it personally.'

'How can I not take it personally?'

'You need to calm down. This is not about you.' His firm response echoes around the room.

'What? And don't shout at me.' I fold my arms. 'Argh, even being cross hurts – this is really getting on my tits.'

'You're being unreasonable. Your sister has just learned that her father may be the same man who raped and murdered your mother, and nearly killed you, and potentially her half-sister… I think she is entitled to some time and distance, even from you.'

'Well, I suppose, if you put it like that, but I feel like I've let her down. Maybe I should never have said anything. Having information is shit.'

'Look, you've done the right thing. Would you like something to eat and drink?'

I look away, cross with Harry. Why would she shut me out?

He lifts my chin so I am looking at him. 'Food. I need you to get strong.'

After some food I fall back to sleep. Again my sleep is disturbed, but this time it's due to the pain in my ribs. I open my eyes to see a darkened room.

I try to sit up. 'Shit.' Pain shoots through me.

'Hey, you're awake.' I recognise the voice.

'James!'

It's James Sullivan, Luke's former SAS partner and closest friend.

'Where's Luke?'

'Max has just landed. I told him to take Luke back to the hotel for a shower and a change of clothes.' He turns on the bedside light.

'What's the time?' I ask.

'Early. So, how are you feeling?'

'Like crap. Tell me, were you part of the rescue mission?'

He's dressed identically to Luke. They have a similar muscular build, but James is blond.

'Sutton called. Why wasn't I surprised that you needed help – again? You have a habit of pulling your husband out of retirement.'

'Retirement? Really? Why don't I believe he ever left his 007 job?'

James laughs. '007!'

'Yeah. So, you mentioned retirement?'

'He is retired, Kate.'

'Whatever. Anyway, this time it wasn't my fault, and I'm sorry for dragging you here again. Have you seen Alexis? You know, the girl I was brought in with?'

'Yeah, she's been bloody lucky.'

'Can you make yourself useful? I really need a cup of tea.'

'Sure. Anything else?'

'No.'

He leaves the room. I pull the covers back and somehow manage to pull myself to a seated position. I swing my legs round and lower one foot at a time to the floor. Here goes. I muster all my energy and strength, and stand. The first few steps are OK. I use the drip tripod to support me and slowly head for the door. However, it opens before I can reach it.

'Where do you think you're going? Back to bed, Harper – now!' James quickly puts a tray on the table. 'Kate, don't move.'

'I want to see Alexis. I need to see how she's doing.'

'Not on my watch. You can wait for Luke.'

'For Christ's sake, I'm going to see her! You can either help me or I'll do it myself.' My legs feel like they're about to give way.

'Fine, then let me get you a wheelchair.' He steps into the corridor and returns with a chair. 'You're a pain in the arse, do you know that?'

'Old news, Sullivan.'

James pushes me down the brightly lit passageway towards Alexis's room. The door is ajar; I can hear machines bleeping. James pushes me closer to her. The sun is rising and bathes the room in a warm glow. Alexis lies in bed, asleep or anaesthetised – I'm not sure which.

'Is she asleep?' I look up at James.

'Her sedation is wearing off. She is probably in and out of semi-consciousness.' He reads her medical notes and whistles. 'She's doing well, considering.'

'Good.' I reach for her hand, which is warm and soft.

'Kate,' she whispers.

God, I want to cry. 'Hi, how are you feeling?'

'Tired.'

'Want me to get the doctor?'

'No.'

'Apparently your vitals are good.' I take her hand. 'I'm here for you. I want you to know that.'

Tears begin to roll down her cheeks, and I wipe them away. 'We're OK, we're safe. He's—' *Shit. Does she know her dad is dead?*

'Luke… he was in here earlier.'

'Oh. Did he – explain everything?'

Her eyes flood with tears. She knows he is gone.

I can't help crying too, out of relief and sadness. 'We can get through this together, I promise.'

She attempts to squeeze my hand.

The door burst opens and Luke appears.

'Kate.' He glares at me from the doorway. 'You're supposed to be in bed.'

'I know, but I wanted to see Alexis.' *Oh, here goes, Mr Moody Bollocks Sutton has arrived.* 'James said her vitals have improved.'

'Sullivan, a word,' Luke snaps.

I raise my brows at Alexis. 'Married life is just peachy, did I mention that to you?'

She tries to smile.

'Look, I need to get back to bed… I think I'll be leaving soon, but I'll be waiting for you in London.'

Luke returns to the room. 'Kate – bed.'

I kiss her hand. 'Be strong and remember what I said.'

She looks at me, her weary eyes already beginning to close.

Luke silently returns me to my room and helps me back into bed.

'How was your shower?'

'Fine.'

Here we go – one-word answers. What's up, Sutton?

'Can I have a shower?' It's fair to say I need one. Actually, I need a complete makeover – but swollen eye sockets, a bruised neck and deep cuts are far from makeover material!

'Later. I need to speak to the doctor.'

'OK, so the reason you're pissed off is…' I can hear a drum roll in my head.

'Is it too much to ask for you to rest?'

'I was resting, but I needed to see Alexis – and you know why, especially now she knows Philip is dead. I can't imagine how she feels.'

'Knock knock.' A familiar voice comes from the doorway. *Perfect timing, Max.* 'Jesus Christ, look at the state of you. Bloody hell, Luke, you said she was bruised, but…' Max walks to the side of the bed.

'It looks worse than it is,' I say.

'Kate, you are severely injured. Don't play it down. Accept that you need to rest.' Luke shoots me down. I look up at Max. He's seen us argue many times. His role alters daily, from father figure and driver to Luke's primary confidant.

'Don't test me, Kate.' Luke looks at his watch. 'Seven o'clock – you need some breakfast. Stay with her,' he says to Max, 'and do not get out of bed,' he adds to me.

Max perches on the bed and rubs his forehead, flashing me a rueful look.

'I'm sorry I wasn't there for you,' he says quietly.

'I'm fine, honestly.' I take his hands.

'Kate, you're not fine. Look at the bloody state of you! You've had the shit kicked out of you, so don't tell me you're OK.'

'But I'm here, and breathing… Twenty-four hours ago I thought—'

'Luke told me everything back at the hotel. He's in shock, Kate.'

'I feel so guilty.'

'You did nothing wrong… That sick fucker, I should have taken him out when I had the chance.' His voice rises with anger. 'If he wasn't dead, I'd kill him with my bare hands.'

I know he would. Max protects me like I'm his own. His only son, Paul, who was Luke's best friend was murdered when he was seventeen, and he still wants revenge.

'I feel bad sending you on a wild-goose chase so I could go to Sandbanks.'

'Pain in the arse, that's what you are.' He takes my hands.

'Is he OK? I mean…' I look down. Although Luke is strong, strength only carries you so far.

'He'll be OK now you're safe. Anyway, I'm worried about you, not Luke. He can take care of himself.'

The door opens and Luke joins us with a tray of food that smells amazing.

'I'm starving.'

He pushes the table towards me. Scrambled egg, bacon, orange juice and tea. I immediately begin to eat.

'Max, did Luke tell you Ivor's here? Actually, where is he?'

'He was here all night, but you won't see him now until he visits London.'

'Oh, but I thought… Why didn't he wake me?'

'He didn't want to disturb you.'

'But he promised not to disappear again.'

'You and I know he can't be part of your life while he has enemies that are willing to use you as bait. Kate, let him deal with things,' Luke says.

I lay my knife and fork down. Although I haven't eaten much, I'm full. 'When can we go home? I assume you have a plan?'

'Yes. Your story is that you arrived two days ago and you were in a car accident,' he says, reading my medical records. I sense he is holding back.

'Paperwork? I mean my passport.'

'Sullivan has sorted it,' he says.

'Oh, what about at home? I mean, do I tell people I was in Russia?'

'No. Sandbanks. Another car accident.'

'Christ, Luke, you must have serious issues with my driving skills.'

'Add them to the list, Mrs Sutton.'

For the remainder of the day I rest, then I convince Luke to shower me. I believe I begged him to wash me, so he lightly sponged my entire body. Lying on my bed wearing fresh clothes from home is perfect. I am aware the water has had no effect on my appearance, but at least some of yesterday has disappeared. Max drops in to see me every so often, and James said his goodbyes before returning to Zurich.

Later, I watch Luke speak to the doctor outside my room. They shake hands and grin. I think a negotiation has just taken place for our journey home. The doctor enters the room, Luke close behind.

'Mrs Sutton, you look brighter today,' the doctor says.

I nod. 'I feel better, thank you.'

'Good. I have completed your paperwork and have agreed that you may leave, but you must visit your doctor at home.'

'OK.' I can't believe I'm going home.

'Very well. I will say goodbye.'

'Thank you.'

The doctor leaves the room and Max follows him.

Luke perches on the bed and takes my hand, running his fingers over my wedding ring. 'We need to talk about your health.'

'Why? Am I ill?'

'No, but I haven't told you everything.'

I nod, feeling a little uneasy.

'When women are admitted to hospital, the doctors have to perform certain tests before starting treatment. One of those tests is a…' He hesitates. 'A pregnancy test.'

What?

'Kate, you're pregnant.'

4

'What did you say?' I snap.

'Baby, you're pregnant.'

A single word rotates in my head – pregnant! 'There must be a mistake.'

'There isn't.'

'Maybe the tests are different here – less accurate? They must have me mixed up with someone else. Ask yourself, Luke, do you trust the doctors here?'

He begins to laugh.

'Do you think this is funny?' I say.

'As usual, you make me laugh.'

'Have you seen the test? I mean, did they show you the results?'

'Kate, the facts are clear, you're pregnant.'

'OK. Why are you so calm? We've not even been married for a bloody week, and now this… Jesus, Luke, I can just about take care of myself, let alone you and now a baby.'

'Admittedly, I was shocked when the doctor told me, but I've had time to adjust.'

'When did they tell you? And shouldn't they have told me first?'

'They told me yesterday. You were taken straight to surgery. I assume they told me as I'm your next of kin, and—'

'Yesterday! Why didn't you tell me then?'

'For obvious reasons, and for the record I'm not disappointed.'

Crap. I am. Get a grip, Harper. No, I'm not ready for motherhood, but it's here now. Part of Luke is growing inside me.

'Give yourself time,' Luke says.

'What – about nine months?'

He smiles. 'If that's what you need.'

I need to not be pregnant!

'OK. Let me process this. Indulge me?'

He smiles. 'Go for it.'

'I'm pregnant and you're happy with the news… So how did this happen?'

Luke's brow knit.

'Yes, I know *how*, but when? Shit, did I miss my pill? I must have. Luke, I can't think straight. How many weeks pregnant am I?'

'First, I am happy with the news. My beautiful wife, who I adore, is carrying our child. Our birth control failed – or we were careless. Anyway, you're pregnant, but in the very early stages – possibly six weeks. Kate, your body has been through a great deal, and…' His words trail off.

My hands cradle my stomach. 'What are you saying? That I could lose the baby?'

'They can't answer that. You lost a lot of blood, and you were dehydrated. Shocked.'

'What? You've given me this amazing news and then told me it could all go wrong? That bastard murdered my mum and now he could do the same to our baby!'

'Let's not get ahead of ourselves. We have to stay positive, OK?'

'Yes, but most expectant mothers have not had twenty-four hours of hell.'

'True, but you're strong, and if our child is anything like its mother, it will be fine.'

'Oh my God, Luke, can we do this?'

He takes my hands.

'I don't think I can take much more' I say.

'That's the reason I didn't tell you. Even now I don't think you're ready to hear the news.' He leans forward and kisses my stomach. God, my heart melts; he's ready to be a parent, noticeably more than I am. My eyes fill with tears.

'We can do this, Kate.'

I nod.

'Have you told anyone?'

'Max and James know, and Ivor was there when the doctor told me.'

'Oh, so everyone knew before I did. Last on the list, there's a surprise.'

He frowns. 'The people who know are here to protect you, and our child.'

'Holy shit, Luke, you're going to be a dad... A dad! Are you sure this is what you want? I would never have an abortion.'

'Agreed – no abortion.' He gets off the bed and sits back in his chair. 'I don't lie – you of all people should know that. I am happy with the news. Would I like to have spent more time with you alone? Yes, but I also didn't want to wait too much longer to start a family.'

'Thirty-two is bloody old. I'm married to a geriatric,' I say and laugh.

'I'll take it as a good sign that your sense of humour has returned. I can't wait to get you home. After this little expedition you will be tied to our bed – for your safety and my pleasure.'

'As long as you can get it up, my eighty-year-old kinky codger.' I laugh, then wince.

'Now I have two reasons to lock you up… Maybe three. My wife, my child and my need to have you when you're well.'

His words are music to my ears.

It's early evening. After a short car journey, we arrive at a nearby private airstrip. Luke's jet is waiting. As soon as I step out of the car, the chilly wind brushes against my face. I don't remember it being this cold while we were playing hide and seek, but the last forty-eight hours are sketchy.

'Take one step at a time. I wish I could carry you, but…'

'I'm OK.' Within a few minutes, using Luke for support, I reach the steps to the jet.

'That's it, nice and slow,' Max says at the entrance of the plane. 'Take my hand.'

Two more steps and I'm there.

'Let's get you home.'

Home. I want to cry. Max takes my coat and helps me take my usual seat. When I'm safely seated, Luke fastens my belt and tucks a blanket around me.

'OK.' He takes his seat next to me.

'Mr Sutton.' We look up to see the smiley stewardess. 'Would you or Mrs Sutton like anything? Perhaps a drink?'

He looks at me. 'Kate – tea?'

'Please.'

The stewardess desperately tries to refrain from staring, but how could she not notice my face?

'Are you comfortable?'

'Luke, I'm fine. Honestly, if I wasn't I would tell you… You have to trust me.'

He arches a brow.

'OK, I deserved that, but things are different now, with a baby growing inside me.'

His lips meet mine, and I feel my body awaken for the first time – another small sign that I'm slowly returning to normal.

While the plane shoots down the runway Luke takes my hand. I watch Russia disappear with mixed emotions – love and hate.

'I feel awful leaving Alexis. I didn't even say goodbye.'

Luke looks straight ahead. 'I told you, she was asleep.'

'I know, but she's alone.' A feeling of tremendous guilt washes over me. 'We've abandoned her.'

'I understand.'

I wait for him to look at me. 'Luke.'

He turns to me.

'She played no part in what Philip did. I know what she did to Ollie was wrong, but she saved my life, and now I've left her in a strange country. Even you must feel guilty.'

'Honestly? No. I'm grateful she helped you, but she has no impact on my life, Kate.'

'That's a bit harsh! If it wasn't for her, Philip would have raped me. Christ, he was choking me when she hit him with the chair.'

I glance at Luke's clenched fist.

'I will always remain indebted to her, but never throw this at me to win an argument.'

'Luke, that's not why I said it…' I take a deep breath and look down. Maybe I did. Crap, I know I did!

He turns my face to his. 'You need time to get over this,' he says, and seals his mouth over mine. Slowly his tongue slips inside my mouth. His warm and tender strokes are just enough for my body to surrender to him before he releases me. Battered body or not, it would seem that I will always yearn for him.

'As for Alexis, I have arranged for a nurse to come here from the UK.' He looks at his watch. 'She should have arrived, and she will stay with Alexis until she is strong enough to fend for herself, not just in the hospital, but when she returns home to London. '

'Oh – you never said.'

'You didn't give me the chance.'

'I'm just worried.'

'She's making progress. It won't be long before she's home.'

'I'm going to help her when she's back in London. She'll need lots of support.'

Luke nods, but he looks beat so I drop the subject.

'Oh crap.' A realisation hits me. 'Our honeymoon – it's in a few days… I can't go looking like this.'

'I've already postponed it. The only place you'll be is in bed.'

I giggle.

'To sleep…'

Our private jokes will always make me smile.

By the time we arrive at City Airport, it's late evening. I feel a sense of peace as Max drives us through the streets of London, my head resting on Luke's shoulder. The sight of the black front door of our South Kensington home sends my emotions into meltdown. The palace – the name I gave it when I first worked for Luke, due to its size – is where I feel happiest. I wipe my eyes before Luke sees; he's exhausted himself.

'Straight to bed, Kate.'

I turn to Luke.

'It's late and you need to rest.'

'I'm not arguing, but I'm hungry.'

'OK. Let's get you settled then I'll get you some food.'

Within ten minutes Luke has helped me change into his T-shirt – my choice of nightwear – and has tucked me into bed. Even though I'm hungry, my eyelids close the moment Luke leaves the room.

I wake feeling uncomfortable and hungry. I peer around our dark bedroom. I check the time on my phone, it's three o'clock in the morning. Feeling clammy, thanks to Luke's body radiating heat next to me, I roll onto my side. Taking a deep breath, I manage to sit upright. Pain shoots through my body. With my feet firmly on the floor, I grab the edge of the nightstand and pull myself up. Ten minutes later, I enter the kitchen – my kitchen, the room where Luke took over my heart and my entire existence.

The only light comes from the opened fridge, which I scan. Nothing looks appetising. Next stop is the larder, but suddenly I feel weak and overwhelmed. I sink to the floor, drawing my legs to my chest, crying uncontrollably.

'Hey.' Luke's voice echoes from the doorway. He comes over, kneels and takes me in his arms. 'Shh, it's OK,' he says and lifts me carefully into his lap.

'I'm sorry,' I mutter.

'You have nothing to apologise for.'

I look up to his face. 'I do… I might have killed our baby.'

His strong arms tighten their grip. 'You haven't, Kate.'

'I'll never forgive myself. I didn't want a baby and now I do.' I try to breathe between sobs and broken words. 'I bring shit to your life… You were happy, then I arrived… You should divorce me.'

Luke lifts my face and wipes away my tears. 'My beautiful wife, are you feeling sorry for yourself?' He smiles tenderly.

'I'm not beautiful. I look like crap…'

My head rests against his bare chest and I listen to his heartbeat.

'Neither of us knows what will happen with the baby. I have arranged an appointment for a scan in a few days, so let's wait until then.'

I nod against his chest.

'But whatever happens, you have not killed our child – never think that.'

No matter what he says, I know how I will feel.

'So, you're hungry? The larder was a giveaway.'

'I was, but not now.'

Luke helps me to my feet.

'So what would you like to eat, other than me?'

I can't help but smile. 'You read my mind.'

He kisses my nose.

'I don't know. I can't think straight.'

'In that case, may I suggest a super-strong cup of tea and a biscuit? I know you're trying to keep McVitie's in business.'

'Are you offering me world peace?'

'Bet your arse I am.'

Next day, I wake with a pounding headache. Luke's side of the bed is empty. It's time to face the day.

My body feels a little stronger this morning – I manage the stairs easier than I did last night. I head for Luke's voice, which I hear in the kitchen, and am met with a stunned silence from Rosie and Jerry. They are Luke's housekeepers, they are part of our history and today is just another memory – what goes on in the palace stays within the walls of the palace.

'Oh my goodness.' Rosie moves to me. 'I can't believe what I'm seeing. Luke said you were in a car accident, but…' Shocked tears come to her eyes.

'It's OK – it's mainly bruising.'

Jerry comes to my side and gently cuddles me.

'What have you been up to, flower?' His warm Northern Irish accent makes me cry – again. 'There, there, you're OK.'

For the record, I suspect neither of them buys the 'car accident in Sandbanks' story. They know about the adoption, and that Luke rescued me from Russia the first time, plus they were both caught up in the explosion, but they will also remain loyal and won't question either of us about it.

I lift my head. 'Sorry, Jerry – I wasn't expecting that,' I say through sniffs.

Luke makes his way towards me. 'You should be in bed.'

'I need to get back to normal.' Instinctively, I lean against Luke.

'Luke's right, Kate, you should be resting. How about I make you both something to eat? I won't take no for an answer.' Rosie heads to the island and the cooker.

I look up at Luke. 'Have you told them?'

He frowns.

'About the baby?'

'No… I thought we should wait.'

'Either way, Rosie will be here for me. I won't be able to hide it from them, plus Max knows anyway.'

'Fair point.'

'You tell them,' I say.

'We have some news,' Luke says.

'I found out yesterday,' I pipe up.

'It better be good news, Luke.' Rosie continues to beat some eggs.

Luke pulls me closer. 'Kate is pregnant.'

Rosie almost stops breathing. 'I can't believe it.' She runs over to us. 'A baby in this house… I think I'm going to cry.' She hugs us both and gently touches my stomach. 'I am so happy for you, my darling.'

'It's early days. I just hope everything is OK – because of the accident.'

'You'll be fine,' Jerry says. 'You're one of the strongest people I know.'

'I hope you're right.' I honestly can't cope with more bad news.

'Sit down, the pair of you. Oh, Kate, I'm sure I read that you're not allowed eggs,' Rosie says.

'Why?' I ask.

'I can't remember – maybe salmonella. I've probably got it wrong.'

'As long as they're well cooked, they're fine,' Luke says. 'No soft cheese, pâté, alcohol or caffeine.'

I look at him in amazement.

'I took the time last night to read up about pregnancy.'

I lean in for a kiss. 'Of course you did. I love you, Mr S.'

'Back at you.'

By late afternoon I feel exhausted, and lie on the sofa in Luke's office, which is the room we spend most time in. The familiar background noise of him working and the crackling of the fire are perfect. The last few days almost feel dreamlike. I know it happened and I know the dream was in fact a nightmare. And the nightmare will need addressing, but not now.

Thankfully Luke gave Rosie and Jerry a couple of days off, and Max is on standby. Waking from a snooze, I channel-hop and get distracted by some mindless TV while drinking more tea. The front door opens.

'Oi, Princess Harper?' Barney shouts from the hall as he lets himself in. I love my best friend with all my heart, but today I could do without his visit.

Luke immediately gets up and goes into the hall. 'Barney,' he says.

I listen from the sofa.

'All right, Sutton, how's it going? Bloody cold out… Where's my girl?'

'She's—'

Before Luke can answer, Barney appears in the office.

'I've been calling you! Where have you been?'

'Nowhere.'

Within seconds he's standing in front of me.

'Holy fucking Mother of Mary, what the hell has happened to you?' He crouches beside me.

'Car accident,' I respond. Luke arrives at my side.

Barney looks at Luke then at me. 'A car accident? Where was this?'

'Sandbanks,' I say.

'In your car?' he asks.

'Yeah.' I struggle with making eye contact, especially when I'm lying to my best friend.

'Your car, the black Bentley with the marry me number plate? The very same car that's on the driveway, looking pristine?' He stands up and looks at Luke. 'What the fuck happened to her, Sutton? Did you do this?'

'What! Barney, no! Luke would never hurt me. I can't believe you just said that.' I try to stand. 'Argh… Shit.' My hand goes to my wound. 'It would kill me if you thought Luke would do that. Jesus, you know what he's like.'

'Kate, sit down.' Luke takes my arm and guides me back to the sofa. 'Barney, if you think I would hurt Kate, then you need to leave.'

'Forgive me for pointing out the fucking obvious, but I smell bullshit. What did you expect me to think? She looks like she's done ten rounds with Mike bloody Tyson, and let's face it, Luke, you can be a little – no, a lot – hot-headed and a pain in her arse. Whether you like it or not, she means the world to me.'

'OK, enough! Barney, go and put the kettle on,' I almost yell.

The men glare at each other, protecting their territory. Barney stomps off to the kitchen, leaving me with a pissed-off husband.

'You don't need this stress,' Luke says.

I pull at his arm to join me on the sofa. 'I know, but I can't lie to him. Mum and Dad, possibly, even Rosie and Jerry, but he knows me too well. I need to tell him the truth. Besides, I don't want him thinking you would hurt me.'

'I don't give a fuck what Barney thinks.'

I stroke his cheek. 'He cares about me. I'm his family, you know that.' I lean towards him and kiss his lips.

Then Barney returns and sees our display of affection.

'Fuck it. Sorry, Sutton, I owe you an apology. I know you think the world of her. I'm just a bit shocked. She looks like shit… and…'

'Thanks, Barney.' I smile, grateful for his words. 'Your critique is a bit harsh, though!'

'Honestly, babe, you look rough.'

As Luke stands up, Barney pulls him to his chest. 'Sorry, mate, I saw red.'

'It's OK.'

'Oi, hands off my husband.' I laugh and pray the mood has lightened.

'I might go in for seconds. That felt good, Sutton, or was it just me?' Barney responds.

Half an hour later, Barney picks his jaw up from the floor. Silence is rare from him. I should make the most of it.

'Jesus Christ, babe... And to think I helped you by giving Max an empty box. I bet I was popular. Sorry, Luke, if I had known I wouldn't have helped her,' Barney says, keeping a tight grip of my hand.

'Believe me, if I had known, I would never have gone to Sandbanks,' I respond, feeling guilty.

'Stupid question, but how's Harry taking the news that her father is a sick fucker who murdered her mum and tried to rape her sister? Fucking hell, Kate, just saying it sends shivers down my spine. Poor Harry.' Barney looks as devastated as I feel.

'I don't know. She hasn't spoken to me, but she's agreed to have a DNA test. I'm just praying I've got it wrong.'

'She needs time to process the news,' Luke says, trying to soften the blow.

Once again I cry.

'Don't get upset, she'll be in touch soon. You two are so bloody close, there's no way this will come between you,' Barney says, wiping my cheeks.

'I hope so, Barney.'

'So what have you told your mum and dad? I don't want to put my foot in it when she pops in for a cuppa.'

'Nothing, and I want it to stay that way. They went through so much when me and Harry found out about the adoption. Besides, Luke said Harry doesn't want them to know either.'

'My lips are sealed. Car accident, you said, at Sandbanks.' Barney winks. 'Treacherous roads down that way!'

Luke looks at me, already regretting telling him. But I trust him with my life.

'Who would have thought the superbitch would be your friend? What a bloody mess.'

'I know! Imagine how odd it was for me, knowing she saved my life and might be Harry's half-sister.'

'Life moves in mysterious ways, babe. Well, your life does… Sutton, what the hell have you taken on?'

'Nothing I can't handle,' Luke replies.

'I can see that.'

'Actually, we do have something to tell you.' I take a breath. 'You're going to be an uncle.'

'Fuck me gently.' His hand rushes to his mouth with shock. 'You're knocked up.'

I nod and giggle. 'Yep.'

'Bloody hell, out of something so shitty you have the best gift. Boy – no, I think a girl – definitely a girl.'

'No one else knows yet, so don't say a word. It's still really early days.'

'Are you joking? With parents like you two, controlling, stubborn and obsessed with each other, Christ, you should sell your DNA to the military – of course this baby will be fine!'

That night, I leave Luke working. I can hear him discussing the hotel he is building in Dubai and I assume he is talking to Bradley Taylor, the architect Luke employed to take over from Zhan. I wonder what Bradley will say to the news of my pregnancy? Luke will gloat, that's for sure, but then Luke has me and always will, unlike Bradley. Wrong time, wrong place, wrong woman.

I slip under the duvet and make myself comfortable, then Luke enters the bedroom.

'Do you think I'll have a nightmare? Flashbacks?' Last time I had a nightmare it was after the explosion at our home, but I did think Luke was dead, which was my most haunting memory.

He strips and slides his naked body in next to me. 'Your body deals with every trauma differently. I think you're too tired. Try not to worry about it.'

'Maybe.' I roll to my side that doesn't hurt. Instantly my lips are drawn to his. It's been the same since the day we met: I'm addicted to him. My hands travel to his hair and for the first time since Russia our kiss deepens.

He pulls away and our eyes lock: dark and compassionate meet dark and grateful.

'I know I'm nowhere near ready for sex, but I miss how close it makes me feel – does that sound stupid?'

'It doesn't. Although I would like to think there's more to our relationship than sex... But when you're under me I know where you are.'

I take a deep breath.

'What is it? Tell me,' Luke asks.

'Philip Cooper.'

Luke brushes my hair away from my face.

'I can't help wondering... if he had raped me, then what... It would have affected us, I know it would.' My eyes close as I battle with my emotions. 'When he was between my legs…' I shudder at the memory.

Luke leans towards me and seals his mouth over mine, his soft tongue gently stroking mine. As he pulls away, his gaze stays with me. 'Thank God, he never touched you, but if he had we would have dealt with it together. When I married you it was forever – there's nothing in the world that could alter how I feel. I love you.'

'I wanted to die, Luke. When I was naked on the bed, I begged for Katenka to take me.'

He just looks at me.

'I didn't want to leave you, but I couldn't bear for him to touch me.'

'I understand,' he says and closes his eyes for a moment. 'You're so strong, Kate, stronger than you realise.'

'I don't feel it.'

'You handle me.' He smiles, trying to lighten the mood. 'And when you're ready we will take it slowly. We have all the time in the world. Besides, I need you to get stronger. After all, you're carrying my heir!'

I can't help laughing. 'Your heir…'

'I need to leave the Sutton legacy to someone.'

'OK, let's hope you don't pass on your stubborn, controlling and irrational behaviour to your child!'

'Maybe our child will be lucky enough to be born with a verbal filter.'

'Don't make me laugh, it hurts… I don't care, he or she can have everything we have, good and bad. I just want the baby to be OK.'

He kisses me goodnight. 'Sleep, baby.'

The next morning I manage to shower and dress myself. I walk into the office with two mugs of tea. I'm proud of this small achievement. This also proves to Luke that small parts of me are returning. I also want to fend for myself.

I put his mug on the desk. 'What are you working on?'

'Various acquisitions, and of course the hotel… How are you feeling? I see you showered. May I ask why?'

'Because I wanted to, and obviously I am capable … and look.' I manage to open my bad eye – not for long, but it works.

'Kate, don't rush everything. Your body needs time to heal. Please listen to me.'

'I hear you, husband. But I think we need to get back to normal… So, as of tomorrow I want you to go back to work.'

'It's too soon.'

'For you or me? Besides, you know it's a good idea – we need this. Yes, I love having you around, but it's not real life.'

'I'll think about it.' His hand wanders to the edge of my T-shirt and slips under it to stroke my clean, naked skin. Of course his fingers head towards one of my nipples. He squeezes gently then lets go.

'Ouch – they feel sensitive.'

'You're pregnant, Kate.'

'How much did you read on the internet?' I shake my head, but at least one of us is prepared.

'Enough.'

I return his hand to my breast. 'They're only slightly sensitive. I still like you touching me.'

He pulls away. 'Not yet.'

'I just want you to touch me, that's all. It makes me feel safe.'

'Do you need a job?'

I scowl at his distraction tactic. 'I don't know, do I need a job?'

He shifts me from his lap and guides me to the sofa, bringing various folders with him. 'I was going to ask you before Russia.' He sets the folders on the coffee table.

'What are they?'

He sits next to me and opens a file.

'You have a good eye for design, and I trust your judgement more than anyone.'

'You do?'

'Yes, and I need some answers, ASAP.'

I scan the pictures. 'This is your hotel.' I'm still blown away that my husband is building a hotel in Dubai!

'Right – that's what I need you to look at.' He lays drawings and mood boards on the table. 'I want your honest opinion on colours, materials, et cetera. I want you to cast your eye over the designs, Kate.'

'You really want my input?'

'Yes. This hotel is for all of us, and I want you to be a part of it.' Tenderly, he touches my stomach.

'Got it, boss.'

'That's music to my ears – you would fit in perfectly at Sutton Global.'

'I already work at Sutton Global, in case you've forgotten. Which reminds me, I need to message everyone as they think I'll be on honeymoon soon.'

'Harper Jones wasn't what I had in mind. Sutton Global would be better.'

'You love that I'm there; you just don't love fashion.'

'True. There is a slight rush on these files. Will a week give you enough time?'

'I think so. You're definitely trying to keep me busy.'

'I wanted your input anyway, and I can see you're bored.'

'Before I start, have you heard from Ivor and Alexis? I was going to call Harry, but I think you're right about her needing time.' What if she doesn't want to speak to me?

'I haven't heard from Harry or Ivor. As for Alexis, she is due to return home tomorrow. The hospital called me this morning.'

One out of three!

We work for most of the day. Luke's buying several businesses he can add to his growing empire – and mine. After a few hours, I drift off to sleep.

'Kate.' I feel a gentle stroke on my face. 'Kate.'

I open my eyes in disbelief. 'Harry?'

'Careful, let me help you.'

'I'm fine.'

She sits next to me on the sofa.

'How are you feeling? And don't tell me what you think I want to hear.'

'Better than I did… What about you? I've been so worried. Harry, I'm so sorry.' I start to cry, as I knew I would. All I want is to protect my sister.

'Don't, Kate.' She starts to cry too.

Raymond and Luke walk into the office, carrying mugs of tea.

'Kate, how are you?' Raymond, Harry's French husband, asks, sitting close to Harry.

'Better.'

'Luke said you were badly hurt, but I didn't expect this,' she says.

'I'll be fine. The bruises are fading and I can almost open my eye.'

'Bloody hell, Kate, I can't believe what happened to you. I should have come to see you straight away.' Harry looks at her hands, lying loosely on her lap.

'You needed time.'

'I couldn't face you, that's the honest truth… Finding out who my real father is, and finding out how I'd been conceived, was a real shock. It made me question everything. But knowing that he nearly—'

'He didn't. I wish I could change things and make it better for you. Besides, we don't know if he's—'

'We do,' Luke says.

'It's true, I am his,' Harry says.

I take Harry's hands.

'I don't know what to say. When did you find out?' I look across at Luke. *Why didn't he tell me? Harry's my sister. Why does he keep me in the dark?*

'I called Harry a couple of hours ago,' he says.

'What? Thanks a lot, Luke!'

Defensively, he holds his hands up.

'Kate, I asked him not to tell you. I wanted to tell you myself.'

'Raymond, I want you to look at this artwork for the hotel,' Luke says, giving Harry and me some space.

'Kate, I don't blame you for any of this; it's just a bloody

81

shock. Your dad shot my dad… Jesus Christ, you couldn't make this up.' She takes a breath. 'Luke said Alexis is flying home tomorrow.'

I run my thumb across Harry's knuckles, trying to reassure her.

'So now I have another sister. How do you feel about that?'

'Fine. Besides, she saved my life, I can't thank her enough.'

'Bloody hell, I'm related to the superbitch. This just keeps getting better.'

'In the grand scheme of things, we got off lightly, Harry.'

'How so?' Harry asks.

'Philip has raped Alexis since she was twelve.'

'Holy shit.' Her face falls with the realisation that maybe she is the lucky one. 'How did you find out?'

'The moment he touched her, something seemed bloody odd, then she told me.'

'Sick bastard… Poor Alexis. What about her mum?'

'Apparently she died in a mental institute when Alexis was ten.'

'Well, there's a surprise, being married to that sick bastard would make anyone go nuts.'

'Luke said you don't want Mum and Dad to know?' I say.

'God, no, they've only just got over the fact that we found out we were adopted. I can't go through that again. Besides, they don't know him. As for Alexis, I'll figure out a way to introduce her.'

Harry reaches for my mug and passes it to me.

'What if they find out?' I ask.

'They won't, and if they do I'll cross that bridge when I come to it. I spoke to them yesterday. They think you're still at Sandbanks. I told Mum not to call as you needed some time alone with Luke – a sort of mini-moon, because Luke had to cancel Bora Bora due to work. Perhaps you'll have a minor collision today?'

'That sounds like a plan – not literally. I'll tell Luke the same. She did message me to say she hopes we're having a good time. I want Luke to call and tell them about the accident. I know I should, but I hate lying to them.'

'I don't blame you. Let Luke tell them.'

'You seem OK, sort of,' I say.

'Oddly, I feel OK. There's nothing I can do but be angry – but with who, our dead mum or my dead dad? I never met him, and I hate what he did to you.' She takes my hand. 'I have to dust myself down. It's all I can do, Kate, or I'll crumble.'

'I understand. I'm trying not to think about the what-ifs. I said to Luke, what if he—'

Harry squeezes my fingers. 'Luke loves you, and there is nothing in the world that would change that. What about Alexis? I mean, what now?'

'I'm going to see her as soon as she's home. I owe her for what she did. We can go together if you want.'

She nods. 'I would like that… Do you want to hear something funny?'

'Oh God, yes please.'

'Raymond brought the picture of me home to finish…'

'You mean the naked picture,' I say and can't help laughing.

'Yep.'

'The joys of being married to a French artist,' I say.

'Handy, right? Anyway, he put it above the fireplace to surprise me. After a few days I forgot it was there – until Mum and Dad came over for dinner and saw it!'

'No! I assume it looks like you.'

'Totally.'

'Tell me, how graphic is it?'

'Not quite porn!' Harry laughs. 'I could have died, it was so embarrassing.'

'Harry, I'm pregnant…' I blurt.

'Hang on a minute! You're pregnant? Luke!' Harry bellows. 'You're having a baby.'

He beams at the news. 'I know.'

'Kate – you're having a baby.' She pulls me in for a hug.

'Careful – that hurts.'

'Sorry. But I can't believe you're pregnant.' She looks at me. 'Holy shit, you're going to be a mum. Kate, I'm so happy for you – a bit shocked but so happy for you both.'

'Believe me, I never planned this. I still can't work out how it happened.'

Raymond chuckles. 'Kate, you are funny.'

I rub my head. 'Harry, it's been a whirlwind… Anyway, Luke said I may lose the baby.'

'What!' Harry looks at Luke for an explanation.

'I never said that. Kate has been through a lot, and it's still early days.'

'Shit, no. When can they tell you? Have you done a test?' She takes my hand.

'We have a scan booked, so I'll know more then. Harry, I'm so overwhelmed with everything and I'm scared. I guess part of me doesn't want to do a test just in case…'

Luke sits next to me. 'Don't be scared. We can do this, OK?'

5

My hand slides across the empty space. Luke's gone to work. Back to normal. There's a note on his pillow.

Dear Kate, my amazing wife

I listened to your request and have decided to work at Sutton Global today – please do not make me regret this decision. I understand your need for normality, and I agree with you.

Max is with you, and Rosie and Jerry. They will look after you.

I will call your parents as promised, and tell them we are home and that you're OK after the car accident.

Love you forever, Luke x

I love our notes. Some days I wish we were back to being boss and cook. I smile as I recall the notes we used to hide in the fridge. My hand rests on my stomach. Already I feel the need to protect my baby.

I shower and dress fairly quickly today, and the stairs are a breeze.

'Hi, Rosie.'

She looks up from the sink as I enter the kitchen.

'How do you feel?'

'Better today.'

'You look brighter, and your eye's better.' She looks more closely.

'It almost opens. Anyway, I need distraction, so any news from Adam?'

'Yes – sit down and I'll make you a cup of tea.'

'Rosie, it's fine.' I head towards the coffee machine and fill my mug. 'Carry on. Adam.' I sit down and begin to drink. 'What is wrong with this coffee?'

Rosie laughs.

'What?'

'Luke changed the coffee to decaf this morning.'

I frown. 'Oh my God, he's going to be so overbearing – worse than usual, if that's even possible.' I head towards the fridge. Taking centre stage on the shelf is a note.

'Listen to this.' I wave a sheet of paper in the air. '*Dear Kate, here is a list of food you must avoid. Your folic acid tablets are next to the kettle.*'

Rosie's face says it all.

'See what I mean? Overbearing.'

'Oh, I think it's sweet.'

'This isn't sweet, this is Luke's normal behaviour – except it's not normal, is it?'

'Let's look at the list,' she says.

I opted for cheese on toast – extra-strong mature cheddar cheese. Apparently it's not on the list, so I guess I can eat it.

Later, the phone rings.

'Hello?'

'Good morning, and how did you sleep?'

'Really well. Thank you for the note – actually, both the notes. I assume you've spoken to my mum and dad?'

'I did. We had a brief chat, and I mentioned the accident, but they're going to come and see you this afternoon.'

'OK. Thanks for calling them, I just can't face it. Anyway, I do have a question for you. Just how overbearing are you going to be now I'm pregnant?'

I hear his breathing alter, and I know he's smiling.

'You thought I was bad before – now I will show just how bad I can be.'

'Woo-hoo, I'm such a lucky girl. I miss you – come home.'

'You told me to go to work.'

'Yes, and I told you not to be overbearing but you didn't bloody listen – yet today you listened.'

'You sound on form today… My Kate is back.'

'Be careful what you wish for. So, tell me in great detail what is happening in the world of Sutton Global.' I walk towards his office with another mug of tasteless decaf that I will have to learn to love.

'The usual – meetings, a few holding companies that I'm selling and—'

'What are you wearing?' I interrupt.

He laughs. 'Sorry, am I boring you?'

'Yes, you lost me when you mentioned "holdings" and "companies"… To be honest, I'm not really interested. The man running the operation is what interests me, so I repeat, what are you wearing?'

'Black suit, white shirt and—'

'Stop there! So you look hot.' I sit back and rest my feet on his desk. 'You know that suit kills me. I mean, it gets me every time… A bit like how you feel when I sink to my knees and slide you in my mouth.' I giggle. This is what happens when I get bored.

'So you called me to make me hard.'

'Actually, you called me. I suppose I should let you continue your long, hard day. How I remember lying across your desk while you explored various parts of my body.'

'Thank you. I will now be late for my meeting.'

'You know what your problem is, Luke? No self-control. You're a great disciplinarian, yet you can't control your dick.'

His silence is the perfect response. I'm not strong enough to have sex yet, but knowing he needs me is good enough.

'Goodbye, Luke. I love you.'

Looks like I just found myself a new hobby!

I continue working on Luke's project, taking each room of the hotel and looking at every aspect of the design, from fabrics to colour schemes and lighting. Shortly after lunch, the intercom buzzes. I open the door to see a very worried Mum and Dad.

'Darling, why didn't you call us last night?' Mum walks past me. 'Luke said you'd be sleeping all morning and not to come over until the afternoon.'

I kiss her cheek. 'I haven't been up long.' Another lie – I'm going to burn in hell. 'Tea?'

'You sit. Dad will make it.'

'Kate, what happened? How did you crash?' Dad asks.

'I was caught off guard, the car clipped—'

'I thought Luke was with you in the car?'

Crap – what has Luke said? 'Look, do you mind if we don't talk about it? I'm fine, I'm all in one piece. I just want to forget about it. Anyway, what have you both been up to?'

'You girls sit and I'll bring in some tea,' Dad says.

'How was Sandbanks? Harry said you and Luke needed some time together. What about your honeymoon?'

Shoot me, someone!

'Luke postponed it because of work, and Sandbanks was fairly relaxing.'

It's lovely to see my parents, even though it feels like the longest afternoon of my life. Mum fusses over me, and I nap while they watch a film. Part of me feels guilty, but I agree with Harry: their reaction when we found out about the adoption was one of the worst times of our lives. If they knew the next chapter in our bizarre lives, I can't think what they would do. I don't tell them I'm pregnant. It feels wrong to deliver the news of them becoming grandparents without Luke by my side – besides, I want proof first.

After they leave, I do some more work on the last of the rooms on the south side of the hotel. Then the phone rings.

'Hello?'

'Good afternoon.' His silky voice washes over me.

'What can I do for my gorgeous husband?' I look at my watch. It's four o'clock.

'How are you feeling?'

'OK. I'm pleased I got Mum and Dad out of the way. She wanted to know how Sandbanks was!'

'They were fine this morning when I called, just worried.'

'It's done now. Obviously, I didn't tell them about the baby. I wanted us to tell them together so I told them we would see them over the weekend.'

'OK.'

I need to change the subject. 'So, has your day been hard?'

'I need to fuck you – when you are well and back to normal.'

'Good, I love it when you talk dirty.' I laugh.

'You love it when I need you… I can read you, Kate Sutton.'

'I'm not hiding from you, Luke.' I lie on the sofa. 'Let me think.'

'About what?' he asks.

'My favourite time with you. I think Sandbanks in the cold was pretty hot – what do you think? Or maybe your three-grand blow job – that was fun too.'

'My wife has too much time on her hands.'

'I know. Remember the red lipstick marking my territory?'

'Have you finished?'

'No. When will you be home?'

'In about five minutes.'

We laugh.

'And that night in London – you pushed me to a point that I could have come again and again… Twice in the back of the car was not enough. I have never needed anyone as much as I needed you that night. I'm addicted to you, Kate, and always will be.'

Fuck. My game highlights our obsession for each other; our mutual need. I want to cry. This is ridiculous; I'm bloody ridiculous.

'Please come home soon – I miss you.'

I think about all the times we have spent together – whether they were times of lust, need, or just simple greed, they are ours alone. I need a diversion, so I head to the kitchen to cook.

I scan the fridge for ideas, but I have no appetite. What would the boss want to eat? Sausages – it has to be toad in the hole.

While I wait for Luke, I glance over the work I've done for him. The phone rings again. I know it's him.

'Are you stalking me, sex god?'

'Brave words – it could have been my mum calling. I thought you would have learned?'

'That's my problem – I never learn, besides I don't regret saying it.'

'It's almost five o'clock – I'll be leaving shortly. What would you like for dinner?'

'I've made dinner.'

'I think making dinner may fall into the "not resting" category.'

I chuckle. 'Good evening, Mr Irrational Sutton, I wondered when you would make a guest appearance.'

Luke chuckles. 'Mr Irrational Sutton will be home in thirty minutes.'

'Good. I've missed you.'

'Missed you too, baby… And remember Venice? When my glass hit the floor and I kissed your mouth for the first time, I knew you were mine. I'd never felt like that before. It was definitely a high point for me.'

The dial tone rings in my ears, along with his words. The memory of Venice and my ball gown brings a grin to my face. God, he's right – after that it was us facing the world together.

'Kate?'

Startled from my daydream, I turn. 'Hi, Max.'

'Just checking on you.'

'I'm fine.' I sit on the stool at the island. 'Has Luke said anything to you? Do you think he's all right now?'

'He was fine when we left Russia, Kate. You both need time to get over it.'

'I guess. Toad in the hole for dinner. I'll bring it through when it's ready.'

'I can cook, Kate.'

'I know, I just like cooking. Actually, can I ask you something?' I place the muffin tray in the oven.

'That sounds ominous!' Max says.

I turn to face him. 'Cynic.'

'Spit it out, Kate.'

'How do you feel about dating?'

'Bloody hell, Kate.'

I raise my hand. 'Don't dismiss the idea, just listen for a moment.'

'It's not for me.'

'That's rubbish – you're a good-looking man with a lot to offer. I want to set you up on a date.'

He turns on his heel and waves his hand in the air.

'Don't walk off – I have a plan.'

'Goodbye, Kate,' he bellows from the far side of the kitchen.

'Watch and learn, Max,' I mumble, plotting how to get my other victim to agree – Valerie.

Just after five thirty, the front door opens.

'Hi – just in time,' I yell.

Luke enters the kitchen and walks towards me, his eyes on my lips.

'Something smells good.'

'Thank you! Sit down.'

I dish up. Luke eats hungrily, but my appetite fades as soon as I sit down. Luke sits back on the stool and stretches his arms above his head. 'I need to go for a run. You look tired, and you've hardly eaten anything.'

'I feel sick. I'll have something later if I feel better.'

'Alexis is home,' he says.

'Have you spoken to her?'

'Yes.'

'Can we go and see her?'

He shakes his head. 'Give her time. I've spoken to her nurse, plus my doctor dropped by to see her.'

'How did she sound?' I stand and begin to clear the dinner plates.

'Tired, but pleased to be home. She asked after you. I had to speak to her – tomorrow is Philip's funeral.'

My hands grip the worktop. 'You never said. Are you going?'

'No! And neither is Alexis. I offered for someone to take her, but she declined.'

'I know you want this cover story, but won't it look suspicious if she doesn't go? Of course I don't blame her.'

'Her PA has released a statement that Alexis is too devastated to make a public appearance. She will mourn in private.'

My hand goes to my neck. I can feel him.

'Kate, look at me. It's just us, he's gone.' Luke lifts my chin.

'Just his name – it…'

'I had to tell you.'

'I know. But poor Alexis, it must hurt even though he was a sick fucking bastard.'

'I know. But I'm more worried about you. How was your day? Honestly, how are you feeling?'

'Fine – look at my eye. It's beginning to open.'

He comes closer. 'I love you, Kate Sutton.'

I link my arms around his neck. 'I love you too. Are you going for a run now?'

'Yes – I'll take the quick route tonight.'

'It's fine, I'm not going anywhere.'

He shoots me a look. *Fucking right you're not going anywhere!*

With Luke off for his run, I shower and change into comfy clothes, then come face to face with Luke, who has returned. He's dripping with sweat. When does this man ever not look hot?

'Enjoy your run?'

'I needed it.'

'Frustrated?'

He gives me a quick peck.

I'm exhausted. I slide into bed and surround myself with magazines. Within a few minutes Luke appears, a towel wrapped around his waist, and slips into a pair of shorts. He lies beside me.

'What are you reading?'

'Fashion mags. I wanted to ask your opinion on something.'

'Go on.'

I sit up slightly. 'It's about Max.'

He looks confused, but I have his undivided attention.

'Nothing's wrong. Do you think he's lonely?'

'I can't say I've thought about it.' His brows shoot up. 'You've got that look in your eyes, Harper – it's screaming that you're up to no good.'

'Sutton, remember!' I playfully tap his arm. 'Anyhow, Max is a good-looking bloke, right?'

'Where are you going with this?'

'Listen and you'll find out. I think he should have a companion. When was the last time you saw him with a woman, or the last time the poor sod had a shag?'

'Jesus, Kate!'

'You're a man – take pity on him. I think he needs a life that doesn't involve me or you. He needs a girlfriend.'

'Go on. I know you have someone in mind, this hasn't come out of thin air.'

I clap. 'I do – Valerie!'

'You mean Harper Jones's Valerie?'

'Yes. Before you answer, think about it. They're both single, Max is early fifties and Valerie is mid-forties, I think! Max is tall and burly and she's feminine and petite. He would love to take care of her, I know he would. And when they danced at our wedding, they looked perfect for each other.'

'Kate, when you meddle the outcome is seldom, if ever, good.'

'That's not true. Ollie and Scarlett are together.'

'My brother was a one-off. Anyway, Max is old enough to decide who he wants to date, and I don't think he will appreciate you setting him up.'

'I asked him.'

'And did he agree?' Luke smiles, knowing full well Max would never agree.

'He didn't say no.'

Luke tries to speak, but my finger reaches his delicious lips before he can utter a word. 'I just think he needs a gentle nudge.'

'If he asks for your help, that's fine. Otherwise, back off.'

Of course I'm not going to back off. Luke must understand that I've already launched my mission to meddle.

The next morning my eyes open to a bright room. Luke is moving around, dressed in his signature black suit and ready for global domination.

'Morning. I didn't want to wake you.'

'What time is it?'

'Seven thirty.' He perches on my side of the bed. 'Your eye looks a little better today.'

'It doesn't hurt as much.'

'Another day resting for you – it seems to be helping.'

'I guess.'

'Be good. I'll call you later.'

'OK. Love you.'

'Back at you.' He gives me a quick peck and leaves the room.

I stretch my arms high above my head. 'Argh!' *When will this pain be gone?*

I stand in my dressing room dealing with my crazy 70s hairstyle – some things never change. I dry and straighten my hair. So long, Roller Girl, see you tomorrow morning! What shall I wear? I decide on soft black faux leather leggings, a long black T-shirt, black blazer and black Converse. I lean towards the mirror, saving the hardest task until last: make-up that will cover my bruises. I decide that dark glasses will be the best tool for the job.

Max and I head towards my car. He looks disapprovingly at me.

'I need some fresh air. Besides, I'm only going to see Luke.' I don't want to mention my visit to Alexis – I will save that little surprise.

I slide into the seat next to him and he drives.

'He'll be pleased to see me, trust me.'

He sniggers at my choice of words. 'Trust you?'

'You can't keep throwing Sandbanks in my face.'

'You let me run around London for you – with an empty bloody box,' Max says.

I change the subject. 'So, any more thoughts on dating?'

'No!'

'Let me fix you up on one date, that's all. If you hate it, I will never ask again.'

'No.'

'You can't keep saying no. It will be fun. We could get Mr Jones to make you a new navy suit, and what about a pale blue shirt?'

'Jesus, Kate, you're like a dog with a fucking bone.'

Twenty minutes later we arrive at the glass skyscraper that is home to Sutton Global. It's one of many buildings Luke owns – he wasn't lying about leaving a legacy. Max parks the black Bentley in my parking bay.

Max and I step out of the lift at the fortieth floor. Knowing how I look, I bow my head slightly and walk straight to Luke's office, which is opposite my office. Stella looks up from her post outside Luke's room and comes over to me.

'Kate, you poor love. Luke told me about the car accident. I wanted to call you yesterday but he said you were resting. Are you well enough to be out?' She is Luke's right-hand woman and she and I have a strong friendship – after all, she was the one who offered me the job as Luke's cook!

'No, she isn't, Stella,' Max says. I prefer the silent Max as my sidekick.

'I'm fine! Besides, I'm going stir crazy at home and I have some files for Luke.'

'He's in a meeting, but I'll tell him you're here.'

I lift my dark glasses and sit them on my head.

'Oh my goodness, your eye.' Her hand flies to her mouth.

'It's a lot better today.'

'Well, it looks dreadful.'

I guess my make-up wasn't particularly effective after all.

'Is Tanya here?' I ask. Tanya is an ex-employee of Luke's and she has been at my side since I inherited the Bagrov and Cooper shares.

'Yes. I'll let her know you're here.'

'Thanks.'

'Kate, call me when you want to leave,' Max says.

'OK.'

I open the door to my office. It feels good to be back in my safe haven. My office is completely out of place at Sutton Global. It's simple and feminine, a far cry from Luke's masculine workplace. First, I check my emails then I call all the Harper Jones crew, requesting a meeting next week to go over our future plans. My door opens.

'Kate, I didn't expect to see you. How are you?' Tanya says.

'Not too bad. Bored with my own company.'

She smiles warmly and walks towards my desk. We have become extremely close since Luke insisted that she take the role as my personal assistant.

'Are you sure you should be here?'

I point to my eye. 'Looks worse than it feels!'

'Really? It looks bloody painful.'

'I'm good. So, what's been happening here?'

'Not too much – except for Philip Cooper's shooting accident. Apparently the funeral is today.'

'Yeah, Luke mentioned it.' Sick fucking bastard. His name alone makes bile rise to my throat.

'Bagrov and Cooper will change with Philip gone. It might be more bearable... Sorry, that sounded dreadful. I didn't mean to speak ill of the dead.'

I reach across for her hand. 'You and I both know what he was like.' *He's a murderer! I can't hide how I feel.*

'There was something ... off about him. I can't quite put my finger on it.'

'Let's not talk about him.' I fold my arms and lean on my desk. 'As my honeymoon has been postponed, we need a meeting to run over the charity fashion show for Mrs Gold. I know she's inviting various designers. No pressure, then.'

'Her charity ball was definitely the right place for you to wear your dress. It looked amazing.'

'Us all being together too – it was a good night. Christ, a fashion show!'

'Exciting times ahead, Kate. I was looking over the designs yesterday, and Mr Jones sent over some more pieces too.' She points to the corner. 'It's amazing to see the drawings come to life.'

For the first time since my wedding, I feel excited.

'I want to get everything booked – hotels et cetera. Luke has changed our honeymoon, but it won't affect the show. Stella will have the dates.'

'I'll get them from her. I saw your sketches.'

'Did you like them?' I ask.

'Yeah. It's bizarre, but you and Mr Jones are on the same page, so to speak.'

'Wow, that means a lot to me.'

'Smart, but edgy smart. Is that a fashion term?' She smiles.

'Get you and all your fashion lingo! You must miss working for Luke?' We are both new to the fashion industry; we're learning as we go.

'Of course – shares, acquisitions, mergers.' We giggle. 'What can I say, you're definitely my favourite Sutton.'

'Good, I wouldn't let him have you back now anyway.' This moment of ordinariness feels good.

The door opens and Stella appears. 'Kate, Luke's guests are leaving. Thought I would let you know.'

'Thanks, Stella.'

I stand up and join Tanya.

'I'm not sure when I will be back. Maybe in a few days.'

'Just make sure you're ready, OK? And I'll make a start organising the New York schedule.'

'Perfect,' I say.

She leaves my side and I head for Luke's office, carrying all the hotel files. I open the door with caution.

'Hi.' I walk towards him and put the files on his desk. 'All done. I've made some adjustments. Let me know what you think.'

A perfect Sutton smile spreads across his face, a green light for me to slide onto his lap.

'That was quick.'

'It was fun. Anyway, I needed to get out.' I lean against him.

'The fresh air will probably do you good.'

I look up at him. 'I thought you'd be mad that I left the house.'

'Kate, I'm not a tyrant!'

'I did want to talk to you. I want to see Alexis, and I thought I would speak to you first.'

He smirks.

'Plus, I need her address.' I raise my brows. 'You're OK about me seeing her?'

'Do I think you should be at home resting? Yes. But I understand you need to talk about everything that happened.'

I nod. 'She must be feeling so alone, especially today.'

'I'll get Stella to write down her address.'

'This is odd, us agreeing on something.'

He arches a brow. 'I'll enjoy it while it lasts.'

I stand, then straddle him. 'My other question is, when are we going to have sex?'

'When you're strong enough.' He lifts up my top and peels back the dressing. 'It looks good. After you see Alexis, please go home. Remember, it's not just you now.' He places his hand against my abdomen. 'Are you still feeling sick?'

'Off and on,' I say.

'As for sex? Soon.'

'Soon, as in tonight? I think I'm ready.'

He takes my face in his hands. 'Why the rush? Kate, you've been through so much.'

'It's simple. I need to feel close to you.'

Soon after leaving Sutton Global, Max and I are greeted by the doorman at Alexis's building. We take the lift to the top floor. This feels bloody odd!

Her nurse greets us both.

The apartment is stunning: floor-to-ceiling windows run the length of the apartment, with a view of the River Thames. The furniture is smart and modern, as I would have expected.

'Would you like tea?' the friendly nurse asks. It suddenly dawns on me that we might be Alexis's first visitors.

'Thank you, that would be lovely. Where is she?'

'She went to the bathroom. Go through to the living area. She won't be a moment.'

'Kate, I'll wait here.' Max sits at the kitchen table.

I hear footsteps and turn to see Alexis. I go over to her and take her arm. 'Lean on me.'

She lowers herself to the sofa.

'OK, are you comfortable?' I ask.

'I'm fine. How are you doing? How is your wound?' Alexis says.

'It's healing well. How do you feel about today?' I get straight to the point. 'I know he was evil, but he was your dad.'

She looks down at her lap and takes a deep breath.

'Sorry, I didn't mean to upset you.'

She raises her head. Her green eyes look empty, but mostly sad.

'I'll be fine… I have to be. I couldn't face going to the funeral – not just because I can't face anyone, but I'm far too weak.'

'It would have been too much for you.' I take breath. 'You're the only one who knows how I feel, Alexis. What we went through together will stay with me forever.'

She nods.

'Let's try and help each other,' I say.

'I see him. When I close my eyes, I see him.'

'I understand.' *I feel him too,* is what I want to say.

'I don't just mean what happened in Russia, but—'

'Alexis, I can't begin to know how you're feeling.'

She looks broken.

'What can I do to help?' I ask.

'Kate…' She takes a breath. 'I appreciate your offer, but…' She trails off and looks away. I want to save her, but I honestly don't know how to.

'You can tell me anything,' I say.

'Thank you.'

'I mean it. I will never let you down.'

'I believe you, Kate. It feels odd to have someone in my corner. I've never had that before.'

'Times have changed, and you're not alone. I won't let you face this on your own.'

Her eyes shimmer with tears.

'It's odd being here. Probably feels the same for you too.' Her silence is enough of a response. A diversion is needed – food.

'OK, so what do you like to eat? Let me cook for you.'

'Ladies, here are your teas.' The nurse places white mugs on the coffee table.

'Thank you,' I say.

'Kate, you don't need to cook for me.'

'I know, but it's what I do… Feeding people always makes the hardest days more bearable.'

'I know about Harry,' she says.

I nod, forgetting that Alexis had no clue that she has a half-sister.

'Who told you?' I pass a mug to Alexis before I take my own.

'Luke told me this morning. How is she?'

'Fragile, but coping, if that makes sense. She avoided me for a while.'

'It's not your fault… I can't believe my dad raped your mum. What am I saying? Of course I can believe it. I'm sorry for you all.'

'I know you are, but it's not your fault. Anyway, we've spoken and she wants to meet you, her half-sister.'

'I would like that.'

'Alexis, I'm pregnant.'

Her expression freezes, then she reaches for my hand. 'I'm really pleased for you both.'

'Thank you. To be honest, I'm scared.'

'You will make a wonderful mum. Have you seen a doctor yet?'

I shake my head. 'I have a scan in a few days... I'm dreading it but I'm also excited.'

'It will be fine.'

'I was shocked when Luke told me, but the news has sunk in now,' I say.

'Kate.' I turn at Max's voice. 'You need to rest.'

'I really appreciate you coming to see me,' Alexis says.

'I'll be back tomorrow – I promise.'

'No, it's fine. Look after yourself.'

'I'll just drop off some food for you then go home, and I'll speak to Harry. Perhaps we could come round on Friday if you're up to it.'

'OK, but wait and see how you feel.'

'Listen, if you want to visit your dad's grave I'll take you.'

She shakes her head. 'No.'

'OK, but when you do I'll come with you. Alexis, he was still your dad.'

'I know, but I can't forget what he did. He raped me. He shot me.'

'But he was trying to shoot me! You just got in the way. He would never have killed you.'

'He did that years ago, Kate.'

A single tear rolls down her cheek, and I wipe it away.

I change the subject. 'So, now you have an empire to run!'

'I know. I spoke with my lawyer today.'

'Before all this happened I was going to sign my shares over to Luke, but not now… I think strong, independent women should run the show.'

Her eyes widen. 'I had no idea.'

'After the incident in Philip's office I – well, I asked Luke to take over the shares. I couldn't face seeing him again.'

'I was there too.' She shakes her head, guilt-ridden again.

'He grabbed me, you didn't. Look, that was then and this is now, OK?'

'I can't think about work yet,' she says.

'You'll get there.'

Max appears again at my side. 'Kate.' He holds his hand out.

'I'll see you tomorrow but call me if you need anything.' I reach in my bag and offer her my business card.

'I will. Thank you for coming.'

Back at home, Luke and I sit together at the kitchen island, but again I'm not hungry.

'You're quiet,' Luke says, finishing off my meal too. 'What's on your mind?'

'Seeing Alexis today. I felt so bad for her.'

'You can't change what's happened.'

'I know.'

'Neither of us can understand what she's gone through,' he says and takes my hand.

'I prepared some meals for her this afternoon. I'll drop them off tomorrow.'

'Just don't—'

'Overdo it. I hear you. Actually, Harry is going to come with me on Friday. She wants to meet her – properly.'

'The three of you need time to adjust.'

I nod.

'I was impressed with your design work. You raised some valid points regarding the costs too,' Luke says.

'Really?'

'There's a job if you want it.' Gently, he pulls me into his lap.

'I already have a job, but thank you.' Our lips make contact, and my tongue begins to dance with his. I break away. 'Luke, I want to have sex. Can we at least try?'

After showering together, we lie naked on the bed. I hope the next part of his plan is to make love to me. Am I ready?

He lies between my legs. I freeze. Memories unravel in my head, images of Philip in the same position as Luke.

'Kate, look at me.'

My glazed eyes meet his.

'I said you weren't ready.'

'No, Luke,' I whisper. 'I need this… I want you to help me get rid of the images in my head. Only you can do that. Please, I can't let him take this away from me too.'

He changes position and we lie side by side. His soft lips begin at my jaw and move to my mouth, and his hand glides across my body, skimming my breast and moving slowly across my pubic bone. His touch sparks a yearning inside me. At last, he gently strokes my clit. His mouth breaks free of mine and he looks into my eyes – dark and protective meet dark and apprehensive.

'Stay with me,' he whispers. At no point does he stop tantalisingly stroking my clit. Occasionally he dips his fingers inside my sex. 'Feel me touching you.'

I nod.

'Take hold of me.'

I never argue with him in bed, and tonight I need him to take control. My hand moves to his erection, which rests against my hip.

'This is what you do to me. Jesus, Kate, I will always want you. Work me, OK?'

My grip tightens and I slide my hand up and down his thick shaft. His mouth returns to mine with passion. My breathing quickens – and so does his hand. I'm close. I'm losing myself to him. He pulls away from my mouth.

'I know you need to come, then I'll slide inside you.'

My eyes rest on his. I can think of nothing else but him: his sexy, raspy voice and my need to come.

'Oh God, Luke.' My hand loses the ability to grip him.

'Give it to me, Kate.'

'Yes…' is the only word to leave my lips. My eyes close and my body tenses as the shockwave of my orgasm rocks through me.

Luke is already kneeling between my legs. I feel him slowly sinking inside me. He waits for my body and mind to relax.

'Kate, look at me. Are you OK?'

I bite my lip and nod.

'I love you,' he says.

One hand is under the cheek of my arse, and he uses the other to support himself, ensuring he doesn't make contact with my wound. My hands slide up his back towards his hair. I need to maintain as much contact as possible.

It's Luke – no one else.

He maintains his pressure and speed, brushing the sweet spot inside me. Surprisingly, I am almost there. With a few more thrusts, he has me for the second time.

'Luke, I need to come.'

'I'm with you.'

Luke pumps harder and loses himself inside me. Afterwards, we remain still and locked together, not just physically but emotionally. Tears fall from my eyes.

Luke slides out of me and pulls me into his arms.

'Shh, it's OK,' he says.

'I'm sorry.'

'That was a huge milestone. I'm proud of you.'

I look at him. 'I needed you.'

'You always have me, Kate.' He smiles and kisses my nose.

'Promise me, Luke?'

'I'm never letting you go, baby.'

6

By the time Friday arrives, I feel almost human. My eye opens, although not fully, and my bruising is beginning to fade.

'Are you OK?' I ask Harry as we sit at the boardroom table in my office at Sutton Global.

'I've been trained to hate her, and now she's my half-sister,' she says.

'I know it's crazy, but she told me yesterday she's looking forward to seeing you.'

My office door opens and Luke strides towards us.

'Hello, Harry, how are you?'

'OK. But nervous about today.'

'You'll be fine,' he says, then turns his attention to me. 'Kate, I'll wait for you outside Alexis's apartment at four o'clock, OK?'

'Four o'clock, got it. Crap, I feel sick.'

Soon, we are sitting around Alexis's coffee table. I feel awkward.

'How was the shepherd's pie?' I break the silence.

'It was lovely, thank you. All your meals have been lovely.'

'You'll get used to Kate feeding you. It's what she does,' Harry says.

'I'm starting to see the bigger picture.' Alexis smiles. 'How are you, Harry? I know that seems a ridiculous question, but…'

'Some days are better than others. I've gone from Malcolm being my dad, then to Ivor, then back to Malcolm followed by no dad, and now Philip Cooper, who's dead. My sister's dad shot my dad!'

'Christ, Harry! You know how to break the ice,' I say.

Alexis chuckles. 'Sorry, it's not remotely funny but—'

'Laugh or cry, right?' Harry says.

'You're absolutely right. Is there anything you want to ask me about… him?'

'No! I know he was your dad but I don't want to…' She stops.

Alexis reaches across for Harry's hand. 'I understand.'

'It sounds cold, but knowing what he's done… To be honest, I'd rather just get to know you. Now you're Alexis my half-sister, not the superbitch!' Harry says.

'Apparently so.' Alexis smiles.

'I think it's time to put that pet name to bed, but you were a pain in the arse.' I try to exonerate myself.

'Kate, you were new, and I could see how much Luke was into you.' Alexis throws me a revelation. 'I believe you told me to crawl under a rock when we first met.'

I chuckle. 'God, that feels like a lifetime ago.'

'I had never seen Luke look at anyone that way, not even Maddy. So when you turned up with him, people were curious about you – the woman who had made Luke Sutton settle down.'

At four o'clock exactly, Max escorts me to the foyer of Alexis's apartment. As we make our way to the parked Bentley, I see my delicious husband sitting in the back of the car. Thomas, Luke's driver, hands the keys to Max.

I open the door. 'Hi.'

'How was it?'

I slide towards him, needing to feel close.

'I think it's going to be OK. I've left them to it.' I look at him.

'Good. How are you feeling?' He squeezes my hand.

'Nervous… Really nervous. Actually, I'm shitting myself.'

'We'll deal with the outcome together.'

Luke is on his phone for the entire journey. I'm grateful to be alone with my own thoughts, not just about this afternoon, but also about the baby. After half an hour, Max pulls up outside a clinic in Harley Street.

Luke helps me out of the car. I follow him up the stone steps.

He presses an intercom. 'Mr and Mrs Sutton,' he announces.

The door unlocks and we walk in.

'Good afternoon, Mr Sutton, Mrs Sutton.'

I scan the room, which looks more like a business than a doctor's waiting area. Normal for him, another first for me!

'Good afternoon. We have an appointment with Dr Jacob, followed by the obstetrician.'

'Yes, that's correct. If you would like to take a seat, I'll call you when Dr Jacob is ready for you.'

'Thank you,' I say.

We sit on a tan leather sofa. We're the only people there. Luke rests his arm along the top of the sofa, allowing me the space to be close.

'Would you like a drink?' he asks me softly.

I shake my head.

The receptionist comes over. 'Mr and Mrs Sutton, Dr Jacob is ready for you.' She smiles. 'Would you like to follow me?'

'That won't be necessary. I know the way,' Luke snaps and stands up. Why is he being so arsey? I wonder. Maybe he's anxious.

'Ready?' he says.

No!

We arrive at a door and Luke taps against the wood.

'Come in,' a voice calls.

Luke opens the door. I enter first. Dr Jacob stands. She's maybe in her late thirties, tall with dark mid-length hair, wearing a tight-fitting grey suit with a white shirt. Although we briefly met at Luke's parents' house on Valentine's night, I didn't realise how attractive she was.

She holds out her hand. 'Hello, Kate.'

I shake her hand. 'Hi.'

'Please take a seat. Luke, how are you?'

'Well, and you?'

She offers a friendly smile. 'No doctor wants to be busy, but I am… Read into that what you will.' She sits in the black swivel chair, placing her hands neatly on her lap.

'Kate, I have known Luke for some time so please call me Samantha.'

'OK.'

'I have read your notes and of course I have spoken to Luke throughout the week. Everything you tell me stays within these four walls. Patient confidentiality – OK?'

I nod.

'Good, so how are you feeling?'

'Better now.'

She smiles warmly. 'So – no pain?'

'Not any more.'

'Can you hop onto my couch so I can have a look at your wound? I know Luke has been attending to you, which means you have been in good hands.' She undoubtedly has history with him. I wonder what wounds she has patched up for him.

I remove my black shirt and lie on the couch. Samantha cleans her hands and begins to check my cut.

'Please tell me if at any point you feel pain.'

I nod. I watch Luke as she examines both sides of my stomach, paying particular attention to my wound.

'Argh… That's sore.'

'You still have some bruising, which will take time to heal.' She removes the gauze. 'Good, it looks clean. I think you should leave the dressing off at home and allow some air to circulate to the area. The stitches have almost dissolved. Luke has been taking good care of you.'

'Can I have a bath? I'm fed up with showers.'

She smiles. 'I don't see why not. OK, get dressed. I'll check your eye and blood pressure.'

After a full check-up, we take our seats again.

'Your blood pressure is good and your eye is healing well… You're not ready to run a marathon or lift anything heavy, but within another week or so you should be feeling almost back to normal.'

'The pregnancy?' Luke cuts to the chase.

'Yes, the pregnancy. Dr Karen Jenkins is waiting for you in the ultrasound suite.' She looks at me. 'Kate, Luke said that you were worried about the pregnancy.'

'I'm just worried about the baby being healthy.'

'Let's not get ahead of ourselves.'

Luke takes my hand and squeezes it tightly.

'Right then, let me take you to Dr Jenkins. Kate, please try to relax.'

Relax – is she kidding?

Luke and I follow Samantha Jacobs to the rear of the building. She opens the door to a low-lit room.

'Karen, this is Kate and Luke Sutton.'

'Hello, pleased to meet you both. Kate, if you would like to take a seat on the bed, we can have a chat before I begin.'

Once again I nod.

'Luke.' She gestures for him to sit on a chair next to me.

'I will leave you both in Karen's capable hands.'

'Kate, this will be painless, I promise.'

'I'm really nervous.'

'Of course, that's natural. Right then, I need to ask you some questions before we start. When was your last period?'

'I'm not sure.'

'Dubai, two weeks ago,' Luke says, offering my cycle chart.

I take a deep breath. 'I bled for a day, then it stopped. Normally my period lasts for a few days. I thought maybe the stress of getting married was to blame.' I watch Luke's expression alter; he knows there could be another reason for my bleed. Him.

'That's fine. I will do a transvaginal scan.'

I swallow.

'Kate, could you slip on a gown and remove your trousers and underwear, then lie down on the couch.'

Silently I step behind a screen and follow her instructions. I sit on the bed.

'Samantha said that you were in an accident.'

'Yes,' I say.

'We are worried that the accident may have had an impact on the baby.' Reassuringly, Luke takes my hand.

'Let's take a look. Kate, lie back and place your feet in the stirrups.'

Again I follow her instructions while Luke watches her closely. She slides on a pair of latex gloves and picks up the scanner. The colour drains from my face.

'Kate, it won't hurt, but it might be a little uncomfortable. If at any point you want me to stop, just say, OK?' Dr Jenkins says.

'OK.'

My eyes dart to Luke's as his gaze flits between Dr Jenkins and me. My heart is thumping. I almost hold my breath while she inserts the probe and looks at the screen. The wait is killing me. As ever, Luke reads my mind. He leans down and presses his lips to my forehead.

After a while she clears her throat. 'OK, let me show you.'

'Is there something wrong?' I blurt.

She turns the screen towards us and enlarges a grainy image. I can't quite make it out – a grey area with two smaller circles.

'Kate, you are definitely pregnant.'

Luke kisses me and wipes away the tear that runs down my cheek. He looks the way I feel – relieved and excited.

'I can't believe it, Luke.'

'Kate, I'm so happy.'

'Here you can see a very small flicker next to this circle – that's the yolk sac. Kate, you're seven weeks and four, maybe, five days pregnant.' She uses her pen to tap the screen. 'There are two small flickers. I'm pleased to say you are expecting twins!'

'Holy—' I stop myself. Twins!

'Twins,' Luke says. 'How accurate is that?'

'Very accurate. The heartbeats are strong, and there are definitely two. Kate, I think the blood loss you experienced was some spotting. Many pregnant women experience this.'

'Will I bleed again?'

'Not necessarily, but if you do then contact me immediately. Have you had any more bleeding since?'

'No.'

'Well, don't worry.'

'But you didn't listen for a heartbeat.' My lack of knowledge is obvious.

'It's a little too early for that. I want to see you in three and a half weeks, when you're around eleven weeks. We will be able to see a clearer image then. I will also need to run some blood tests. Nothing to worry about. But we will monitor you closely, as twins can bring problems. Once again, this is quite normal.'

Oh, crap. I've just realised that I will have to push two out!

'Twins,' Luke repeats.

'Yes, Luke, twins.' She laughs. 'It will be fine.'

Dr Jenkins lifts my feet out of the stirrups and returns the couch to an upright position.

'Kate, this pack is for you.' She sits a folder next to me. 'It contains various pamphlets that should answer any questions you may have, and a list of dos and don'ts. Do either of you have any questions?'

'Am I allowed to lock my wife up to keep her safe?' Luke smirks at me.

'I understand your worries, Luke. Obviously, Kate, you need to take care of yourself – no skydiving or anything that may put you at risk, but Luke, remember that Kate is pregnant, not ill. There is a difference.'

'With twins.'

That's the third time he's said that. He's obviously shocked.

'Can we still have sex?' I blurt.

'Of course. Quite often women's sex drive increases during pregnancy.'

I look across at Luke. I don't think that's possible, given the fact he makes me melt – constantly.

'It won't damage the baby?' God, I feel stupid.

'No, not at all. Babies are well protected. Just carry on as normal.'

Luke takes my hand as we exit the building and silently walk down the stone steps. I'm still in shock. I have no idea what to say.

Max opens the door for us. 'Everything OK?' he says.

'Twins,' I blabber.

Max chuckles. 'Seriously, did everything go OK?' He looks at Luke.

'Twins,' Luke repeats.

'Bloody hell.' He whistles.

My brows shoot up. 'I know, we're in shock.'

'I'm so happy for you both.'

'The Sutton family is about to grow, Max. I hope you're good at night feeds?'

I slide in first, closely followed by the father of my babies... Holy crap, babies?

Luke takes my hand and squeezes my fingers. 'Are you OK?'

'I guess. What about you? I don't think we're ready for two babies... Bloody hell, I've just accepted I'm pregnant, and now there is more than one.'

He looks blank. 'Why didn't you tell me about your bleeding in Dubai?'

'I told you my period was due – I assumed that was it.'

I know his memory of that night still haunts him, and probably always will. The sex was rough and intense, but I knew what he needed and I allowed him to use me.

'Clearly it wasn't your period. It was my fault.' He looks out of the window, rubbing his hand along his jaw. 'You were already pregnant, and taking you the way I did...'

He turns to me: dark and repentant meet dark and forgiving.

'Luke, it didn't even occur to me I was pregnant. I bled for a day. Honestly, I thought it was just a weird period. A lot has happened since that night. A night that I played a part in. Please let's not go over it again. So you were a little rough and I bled. Anyway, the babies are fine.'

His lip curls with a hint of a smile.

'So, are they girls or boys? I hope they're boys. If they're girls you'll drive them mad.'

His brows arch. 'I'll lock them up with their obedient mother.' He chuckles.

'May I suggest you find her first?' I can't help laughing too. 'Can we stop and get your mum a birthday present?'

'I sent her flowers, plus a spa voucher.'

'How thoughtful of you,' I mock him.

'Every woman likes flowers.'

'But she deserves something personal,' I say.

'OK! I have an idea. Max, could you pull over?' Luke says.

Within half an hour we arrive at Moor Park, Luke's childhood home. Declan's car is already on the driveway. We step out of the car; Max throws the car keys to Luke and leaves with Thomas, who's already here.

Luke takes my hand and I carry Livy's gift – literally!

'Do you think they'll ask me about the car accident?'

He looks at me. 'Yes, but I'll shut it down.'

'What about today?'

'Later.'

As predicted, Luke's mum asks me about the accident, then his dad gives me some road safety advice, while I listen obediently.

Thankfully, Ollie arrives, the youngest of the Sutton clan, in his new car, which becomes the hot topic. Luke disappears for a test drive. This is the first time Luke has seen Ollie since he found out Alexis took advantage of his younger brother during a difficult time in his life.

I sit at the table with Declan, while Livy and Edward begin to prepare dinner.

'So, what have you been up to?' I ask.

'Not much. This and that... You know how it is,' Declan says, sounding pissed off. He takes his wine glass and swirls the burgundy liquid. Why is he being arsey? Is it to do with Kiki? His 'relationship' with my best friend is anything but serious.

'Kiki is still in LA, right?' I ask.

He nods. I know hostility when it slaps me in the face. His eyes meet mine. 'I'll tell you what I haven't been doing, Kate, shall I?' He fires his words. 'I've not had the pleasure of visiting Alexis daily! Let's be honest here.'

Oh crap – how the hell did he find out? The dining room is a fair distance from the kitchen, so we can't be heard by Livy or Edward.

'Is that why you're being arsey with me? It's not what you think.'

He rests his elbows on the dark oak table.

'You know what she did to Ollie? She ripped his fucking heart out.'

'I know, but—'

'You call yourself a Sutton? Brown-nosing that bitch.'

'Please, Declan, I have my reasons.'

'Back-stabbing reasons.' He leans back in his chair, downing his wine. 'I never saw you as weak. Fuck, you can handle my brother!'

'I don't deserve that. I think the world of Ollie.'

'Bullshit. How do you think Ollie will feel, knowing you're being all pally with Alexis?' Declan stands up. 'I fucking trusted you, and now you've shown your true colours.'

'Don't talk to me like that,' I say, trying to stop myself from crying.

'I can't bloody look at you.'

'I would tell you what's going on if I could. You have to believe me.'

'Believe what? More bullshit?' he says.

'I can't do anything about what she did to Ollie, but she helped me.' When I turn my head, all eyes are on me. Luke is back.

'What the hell is going on?' He looks at me, then at Declan. I wipe away my tears.

'I'm waiting.'

Livy comes in. 'Someone needs to explain to me why Kate is crying. Declan?'

'Don't ask me, ask her,' Declan shouts.

'Declan Sutton!' Livy bellows.

'It's fine, Livy. Please, this is your birthday,' I say.

'This is all your fault, Kate,' Declan hisses.

Luke pulls his arm back. I grab it, knowing what he's thinking.

'Declan, do not ever talk to Kate like that again, do you understand me?' Livy points at his face.

'Luke.' Edward stands in front of his eldest son, in command. 'For Christ's sake, take it down a notch, boys.'

'Would someone please tell me what the bloody hell is going on?' Livy says.

'Ask her why she's been visiting Alexis every day.' Declan waves his arm in my direction.

'Why is that a problem? She's just lost her father,' Livy blurts.

'Declan, I'm warning you, this is not the time or the place. Just drop it,' Luke hisses.

But I know the look in Declan's eyes. He won't give up. He needs to know more.

'Please listen to Luke,' I implore.

'No fucking way. I'm not my brother's puppet.'

'Let's calm down.' Ollie stands by my side. 'Kate, I think you should relax.'

'How can you stand next to her knowing she has been brown-nosing Alexis Cooper?'

'For Christ's sake, Declan, she saved my life. I don't know what else to say. Yes, I hate what she did to Ollie, but I don't hate her for stopping her dad from raping me.' I take a deep breath. *Fuck – I didn't mean to say that.*

'What did you say?' Livy looks at Luke. 'What the hell is going on?' She reaches for my hand. 'Sit down, Kate – and I'm not asking you, I'm telling you.'

She guides me to a dining chair and sits at the head of the table.

'Declan, I fucking warned you,' Luke shouts across the room.

'Luke, please.' I tug him to sit next to me.

'Enough!' Livy shouts. 'I suggest you all take a seat. We

123

need a family discussion – and, yes, Declan, that does include Kate. She is your brother's wife. What's our golden rule? We protect each other. Do I make myself bloody clear?'

Silence envelops the room.

'Ollie, go and get the brandy. I have a feeling I will need it.'

'Sorry, this is all my fault.' I can't stop crying. Luke pulls me close to his chest.

'Nonsense. Obviously you have not been in a car accident and Luke has been feeding us bullshit. Well, no more.' Wow – Livy commands her Sutton boys well. She takes her glass of brandy and downs it in one. 'I'm warning you, do not lie to me!' Her stern voice echoes around the room, silencing the Sutton men. 'Ollie – something happened between you and Alexis?'

Ollie looks across the table. 'Mum, I don't want to talk about it.'

'This must have been some time ago?' she asks.

Oh crap, this is too painful to watch.

'Does this have anything to do with Jeremy's death?' Jeremy was Ollie's childhood friend. After his death, Alexis took advantage of his vulnerability. She took his virginity – and heart, leading to Ollie's attempted suicide.

'Yes, but…'

'You and I will chat later,' Livy says. Ollie looks relieved – but not nearly as relieved as I am. 'Declan, you have been a pain in the arse since the day you left my womb. Of course I love you with all my heart, but you need to grow up, stop sleeping with every girl you meet, and focus on your life.'

Wow, Livy is on form this evening.

'Luke, where do I begin? With your tales of working in a bank before you set up Sutton Global, and being posted all around the world, arriving home with various minor injuries, I assume they were from a stapler?' Livy raises her brows at her firstborn. I've always wondered how on earth they believed the story Luke told them.

'Do I want to know what you were up to? No. Why on earth do you think your father and I got married so quickly?' She points to Luke. 'Yes, I got pregnant. Your grandmother went mad. As parents we have had our fair share of dramas, so please don't treat us like idiots.'

'Mum.' Luke reaches for her hand.

'I understand you have your reasons for not telling us things, but your father and I are here for you. We want to see you all happy. So, the Coopers… Why do I not believe Philip was killed in a shooting accident?'

'He wasn't. My birth father shot him.'

Luke glares at me in disbelief.

It takes half an hour for Luke to explain the true reasons for my injuries and to tell everyone about my Russian birth parents. All the Suttons remain quiet throughout, even Declan. Livy holds my hand, as any mother would do, offering strength as I watch them find out that a man they thought was a close family friend was in fact a child molester and murderer.

'To think I paid my respects to him! Edward, I feel sick.' She takes a swig of her drink. 'What that poor girl, Alexis must have gone through. And they visited us over the years. Why did I not see anything?'

'Christ, I went to school with the man. He was always devious but never violent… Or so I thought. It just goes to show, you really don't know people. Kate, maybe you should be at home,' Edward says.

'I'm fine, honestly.'

'Luke, I'm cross with you. You should have told us – we could have helped Kate. This is too much for her to bear, and Harry! Oh my goodness, how is she, and your parents?' Livy squeezes my hand. I appreciate her empathy.

'As I said, this information stays in this room. We haven't told Kate's parents about recent events – which is what Harry and Kate decided. Malcolm and Susan have been through enough.'

'Of course, when the poor man was attacked,' Livy says.

'Honestly, this would break them. Harry and I couldn't cope with another blow to our family,' I plead.

'You have our word. Boys?' Livy says and looks at Declan and Ollie.

'Sure,' Declan says – his first word since Luke began the story.

'Goes without saying.' Ollie holds his hand in the air.

'Luke, what about the authorities?' Edward asks.

'It is not quite that simple, Dad, and what you don't know won't get you into trouble. All anyone needs to know is that Philip was shot while hunting and Kate had a car accident at Sandbanks.'

'Ollie, I'm sorry,' I say.

'Jesus, Kate, it was a long time ago. She saved you. I think we can draw a line under it now. Right, Declan?'

Declan shrugs. He's still pissed off. What a surprise – another Sutton who can hold a grudge!

'This has to be the most bizarre birthday.' Livy tries to smile.

'I think it's time for some champagne.' Edward heads to the kitchen.

I lean towards Luke. 'Where's the gift bag?' He leaves the room and returns with a white bag.

'Happy birthday, Mum – we hope you like it.'

'You two! Honestly, the flowers were beautiful, and my spa day. There's no need for anything else.'

'I wanted to get you something personal, but for obvious reasons I haven't been out,' I say.

Edward returns and places a silver tray on the table, plus six champagne flutes and a bottle of Bollinger. Livy removes the gift, which is wrapped in white tissue, and unwraps it. She looks at Luke, then at me.

'I don't understand.'

She holds up two white baby-grows. Luke gives a smile that would melt any mother's heart.

'Are you telling me you're…' Livy says.

'Pregnant.' The word that has caused me so much panic leaves my lips, but today I know it will bring delight to someone.

'Oh my goodness, Edward, look at these.' She leans to me and kisses my cheek. 'Kate, I'm so thrilled for you both! How are you feeling?'

'I'm OK.'

'Luke, this is just what you need, come here.' She holds him close.

Edward pulls me to him for a hug, then Ollie does the same. I can't help feeling that Declan remains cold. Have I really hurt him? We all sit back down. Luke and I are aware that the penny has not dropped!

'So Mum, you like to think you're quite astute…'

'I have to be, dealing with my boys.'

She watches Edward pour the champagne.

'How many baby-grows were there?' Luke says.

Edward stops pouring and chuckles. 'Oh my word... they're having twins.'

'That's it, I can take no more... Ollie, go and get the Chinese takeaway menus and bring the grappa with you.'

Declan stands and leaves the room. Luke stands too.

I stop him. 'He's cross with me – let me speak to him.'

I wander into the lounge, which is empty. So now Declan is playing hide and seek. I climb the stairs and check a few rooms before I find him in a bedroom; I assume it must be his old room.

'Hi,' I say.

He looks up.

'I'm sorry about this business with Alexis.'

'Why didn't you tell me? Instead you let me rant like a fucking madman.'

I perch at the other end of the window seat.

'Luke didn't want anyone to know.' I reach for his hand. 'I would never hurt you or Ollie – please believe me.'

He looks out of the window. 'I've been a prick.'

'Nothing new, right?'

'I deserve that.'

'So, how do you feel about babysitting? It's part of your uncle role.'

He smiles. 'God help those babies... with my brother as their dad.'

'He'll be a nightmare – I know from first-hand experience.'

'Actually, you'll both be great.'

'Have you forgiven me?' I ask.

'There's nothing to forgive.'

'How did you find out about me visiting Alexis?'

'A friend lives in the same building as Alexis. She told me.'

'I took her some food. I feel bad that she got hurt.' I look out of the window. 'I told her we were pissed off about what she'd done to Ollie.' I look at him but his eyes remain on the garden. 'Declan, she was sorry, and I think she was also incredibly young when it happened.'

'I can't forgive her – not yet.' He looks at me. 'My brother nearly died.'

'I can't imagine how painful it was. Listen, it's your pain and hurt, you put it to rest when you're ready.'

'I assume Kiki doesn't know about the baby? Sorry, babies.'

I shake my head. 'I haven't spoken to her since last week. She doesn't even know I was attacked. Don't tell her about the babies. I'll speak to her as soon as she lands.'

'She lands at eight tomorrow evening. I can't believe Luke is going to have kids… Jesus, Luke with a baby. I never saw that happening.'

Me neither!

We arrive home around nine thirty. Luke heads out for his usual run and I run a bath – my first bath since Russia.

After a while, Luke saunters into the bathroom, already taking off his clothes.

'What are you doing?' he pants.

'Obviously, I'm having a bath!'

'I thought we agreed a shower would be a wiser choice.'

'No, you said that. Anyway, I wanted a bath. Besides, your friend Dr Samantha said I could have a bath.'

He gauges my words. 'My *friend?*'

'Yeah, I thought she seemed… overly familiar with you.'

'Kate Sutton, are you jealous?' He removes his running shoes and joins me in the bath.

'No.' Maybe. Probably!

He watches me closely. 'I've known her for a while.' He takes my feet and begins to massage them. 'She's healed a few of my war wounds.'

'I can imagine!'

He grips my feet. 'Hey, she's just a doctor I trust.'

An attractive doctor. 'Honestly, I don't care. That foot massage feels like heaven.'

'What a day,' he says.

'Holy shit, we're having two babies. I can't believe it – can you?'

'No… Not many situations shock me, but today!' He whistles.

'You're going to be a dad! Does it make your head spin?'

'Yes.' He laughs. What a joy it is to see his face light up. He looks ridiculously happy.

'I want to scream, and cry, and bloody panic – holy shitting hell, Luke.'

'Holy shitting hell indeed.'

'Two babies.'

For a moment we are silent, thinking about our babies: a double helping of parenthood, a Sutton surprise neither of us expected.

'Sorry. I didn't mean to blurt out my double life.'

'It's out and contained. I would rather it not be…'

'I trust your family, Luke.'

130

'They're your family too.'

'Your mum never believed your story about working in a bank!' I laugh.

He smirks. 'She never questioned me.'

'Was it your choice not to tell them about your 007 life?'

'Jesus, what is it with you and 007? And yes, it was my choice, plus there was too much red tape, things I would never be able to discuss. It was easier to keep them separate.'

'I'm pleased you didn't hit Declan.'

'He came close. When you're threatened I see red.'

'What about Russia?'

His eyes close and he sucks in a sharp breath. 'Red is an understatement.'

'You don't want to talk about it, do you?'

'There's nothing to say. When you called me from Sandbanks, I've never felt so helpless. I've had countless missions – both to protect and to rescue people. I treated the person as a job. You stay focused and alert and you take them to safety. But when it's someone you love, the job alters… It's hard to remain professional when it's personal.'

'Have you ever lost someone – on the job?'

'The ones you lose you never forget.' He takes a breath. 'I've been trained to deal with dangerous situations, but I failed to protect my wife.'

'No, don't say that, Luke. You didn't let me down.'

'Soon I'll have three of you to protect.'

'Does that worry you?'

'Yes.'

'Can I ask you something army-related?'

'Go ahead.'

'I know you run Sutton Global, but have you done a job for – whoever it is that you worked for with James and Scott – since we've been together?'

He remains silent for a few seconds before he blurts. 'No.'

'When I was in hospital and you were there dressed in your black 007 outfit, you looked like you. I mean, you were made for that job.'

'It was – I repeat, was – a huge part of my life. The truth is, once you've been part of a team like I was, you're never truly free.'

'What? They own you?'

'No, but I would never turn my back on them. We're loyal to each other.'

'James said I keep bringing you out of retirement.'

'True!'

I can't think about it. Thankfully Luke's phone rings. He steps out of the bath to answer the call.

'Yes?' he says rudely, grabbing a towel to wrap around his waist, which is a shame! 'Give me five minutes and I'll call you back.' He puts the phone on the marble top and holds out a towel for me.

'Mrs Sutton, you are officially clean.'

I giggle and stand up. 'Thank you.'

He holds me close. 'I need to make a phone call.'

'OK.'

I gaze at my naked body in the bedroom mirror. Firstly, my bruising, which is slowly fading. I hope that means Russia will also start to fade from my memory. My wound is almost healed and will probably leave a scar. My eyes fall to my stomach. Do I look pregnant? My breasts are bigger and feel more sensitive. This is bloody madness.

Dressed in my usual Abercrombie T-shirt, I head towards the office. From the doorway I watch him. God, I crave him – always. I walk towards the desk and straddle his lap while he continues to talk on the phone. Life is most definitely getting back to normal in the Sutton household. I slip my T-shirt over my head and Luke cautiously observes my naked body. Whether he wants to play my game or not, his erection presses through his shorts. I love that he fires up so bloody quick.

He holds the receiver away from his ear. 'Baby, give me a minute,' he whispers.

Really – did he just ask me to wait?

My lips begin at his jawline, while my hand disappears inside his shorts and I wrap my fingers around his hardness. Fuck it! My desire takes hold of me. Like I have a choice! He knows I yearn for him. Wet and ready, I rise up and very slowly let him sink inside me. His eyes close and his breathing becomes laboured. He seems lost for words, so I take the phone from his hand.

'Say goodbye, Luke,' I whisper.

'Kate… You…'

My mouth covers his and slowly my hips begin to work. He groans and the sound vibrates through my core, almost like a mating call. I pull away, not only to breathe but also to watch his face.

'We both need this,' I say.

He grips my hips, taking charge of our rhythm, and kisses me hard on the mouth. I feel a sharp pain in my side.

'Argh!' I say, wincing.

'Jesus, Kate, it's too soon.'

'No, it's not. Please, Luke, I need this. Normality is what's saving me from crumbling.'

He lifts me onto his desk and gently lowers me so I'm lying across his paperwork – which I always seem intent on fucking with!

'You have to be honest with me. Tell me if it hurts…'

'I promise.'

He stands between my legs. In one thrust, he buries himself deep within me. His movements are slow to begin with, but gradually quicken – thankfully.

'Is this OK?'

'Yes,' I whisper.

He continues to thrust as his fingers work their magic on my clit: a Luke Sutton hand job has to be the most rewarding treat.

It takes no time for my body to climb; I was turned on after our bath. My orgasm arrives in an intense rush. I can't stop it.

'Luke.' Sensation washes over every part of my body and goose bumps erupt over my skin. This is what he does to me. I have no idea if he needs to come, as I'm still high on him. I needed my Sutton fix. He drives himself into me with power until he comes.

After his orgasm, he lowers his head to my stomach, pressing his lips gently on my skin. He slides out of me and takes my hands, he helps me sit up.

'Do you feel OK?' he asks.

'Better, and you?'

'I just had sex with my beautiful wife, what do you think? I'm not sure Bradley Taylor appreciated you ending our call.'

Oh, crap – that's not a name I want to hear while I'm still dripping with passion from my husband.

'Tell him it was a booty call.'

'I think the words "fucking" and "Bradley Taylor" should never be used in the same sentence – especially by my wife, who he wants to—'

'Er, please, your children may hear.'

'Are you really going to throw that at me?' He nips the end of my nose.

'Too bloody right I am.'

'As much as I love having sex, I do think you need more time to heal.' He lowers his face to my abdomen. 'I don't know if you can hear me, but Mummy needs to rest.'

His words make me cry.

'Baby, why the tears?'

'I love you and now I love our babies growing inside me. This is it – this is our life now, and nothing will ever be the same again.'

'I agree, it is overwhelming.'

'What do you think – boy, girl? Do you want to know? Actually, let's not find out. This is the one thing neither of us can control.'

7

I reach for my phone. It's four o'clock in the morning, yet I feel wide awake while Luke sleeps peacefully. After twenty minutes of staring at the dark ceiling, I know I won't get back to sleep. I get up and make my way to the landing, stopping at the spare room across the hall. As I stand in the doorway, memories of my first night at the palace come flooding back. I think we could change this room into a nursery!

The house is peaceful. I sit at Luke's desk and sip my tea. Something woke me: I could guess at various reasons. Ivor springs to mind. Why hasn't he been in touch? How long do I give him before I ask Luke to track him down? Which he won't, of course. The last time I sat alone at Luke's desk was the day after I met Matthew Williams and pissed Luke off. It was also the day I fled to Sandbanks. I have a thought! A brilliant plan forms in my mind. I prepare a small hamper containing enough food for a few days – and potentially some bribery material.

'Luke.' Tenderly, I stroke his face. 'Luke.' He stirs, then slowly opens his eyes.

'What's wrong?' He props himself up on his elbows and tries to focus.

'Nothing. I know it's early, but I have a plan.'

He looks at his watch. 'It's five in the bloody morning, Kate…' His head returns to the comfort of his pillow. 'You should be asleep, not planning.'

'I've been awake for a while. That's when my brilliant plan hit me.'

He groans. 'The words "brilliant" and "plan" coming from you at five in the morning worry me.'

'You know what my brain is like.'

'Unfortunately.'

'Stop moaning and drink your tea. So, the plan is Sandbanks.'

'What?' he says.

'It's Saturday, we can go for one night.'

He sits up. 'I thought we were going to see your parents today? You told Harry about the twins yesterday. I think they should know.'

'We can stop and tell them on the way home tomorrow. Besides, I've already texted Harry not to spoil our double surprise.'

He runs his hands through his hair.

'I woke up with something on my mind. Alexis and Harry are OK, sort of, and Ivor – well, who knows where he is? And last night when we made love Philip Cooper didn't enter my head – thank God.'

'Good.' Luke touches my cheek.

'I think it's Sandbanks. That house means so much to me – our first Christmas, your proposal. I don't want to think about the men who took me from there. I've packed some food, so all I need is my delicious husband to take me.'

'How much further to go?' I ask.

Luke gives me a sideways glance. 'You made this journey yourself, alone! You should know the route.'

'That's unfair.' Defensively, I fold my arms and look out of the window.

He squeezes my thigh. 'Forty minutes.'

Whatever, Luke!

'Kate.'

Silence from me.

'Baby, look at me.'

I turn my head to view his stunning smile.

'I wasn't trying to upset you.'

'You know I feel guilty, especially when you throw shitty comments at me. I put us all at risk.' I cradle my stomach.

'I hate to admit it, but Philip Cooper would have taken you wherever you were that day. It just so happened that you were alone, which made it easier for him.'

'Don't try to make me feel better.'

'As much as I love telling you when you're wrong, it's true.'

I feel confused. 'How do you know?'

'Sullivan and Parker hacked into his home and office computers. They were full of details about you. He'd been watching you and knew your routine.'

'Jesus Christ, he was watching me? When were you going to tell me?'

'He's dead, and Ivor is dealing with his own things. Why would I worry you?'

'Worry me? Luke, don't keep me in the dark, it pisses me off!'

'Kate, you have enough stress at the moment.'

'Shutting me out stresses me, Luke. Anyway, have you heard from Ivor?'

'No.'

'If you say so.'

'Don't get arsey. I haven't spoken to Ivor.'

'Do you know what amazes me?'

'Tell me,' he snaps.

'The weasel was watching me, and so was Ivor!'

Luke looks at me.

'And of course my devoted husband's security team was watching me, but no one saw each other… There must be some seriously hot contenders for the hide and seek winner!'

Luke laughs. 'Fair point – an oversight that I have dealt with.'

'Are you still watching me? I don't mind if you are.'

'I don't watch you. I simply monitor your movements.'

'Really! That sounds like a posh way of saying you're watching me.'

Finally, we arrive at our beautiful beachfront home in Sandbanks. Luke opens the front door and switches off the alarm.

'Ready?'

I shake my head. 'I don't think I can go in.' Unexpectedly I begin to cry. 'This seemed such a good idea earlier and now…'

He pulls me to him. 'Let's take this one step at a time.' Gently, he lifts my chin and looks deep into my eyes. 'Trust me.' Surprisingly, he lifts me in his arms. 'Close your eyes.'

I link my arms around his neck and lean my head against him while inhaling his Sutton scent. He walks inside and kicks the door shut behind us. I hear his shoes against the wooden floor, then he stops and lowers himself, but keeping me firmly on his lap.

My mind is in a state of turmoil. I tremble in his arms.

'Baby, look at me.'

I shake my head. 'I can't.'

'It's just us. Kate, please look at me.'

His words and soft tone coax my eyes to open, but I can't move.

'I'm sorry, this is was not how I planned it.' My heart pounds against my chest. Luke must feel it too.

'Give yourself some credit – returning here is not an easy task.'

I look up into his eyes.

'Take some deep breaths.'

I mirror his action, and my heart rate begins to slow. I look around. 'The doors?'

'Repaired, with extra security.'

'Oh.'

I get off Luke's lap and leave him sitting on the stairs.

'Fuck.' I look out of the window. 'This is so fucked up.'

'You're right this is fucked up, but it's still our home.' He joins me and takes my hand.

'I was standing in this exact spot when I called you. Alexis was over there.' I point. My eyes flit to the back doors and then the front door. 'The men… Two, no, I think three, were on the decking and…' I take a deep breath. 'I remember the sound of the front door, there was a really loud bang, and then I think there were more of them.

That's when we ran upstairs.' I walk towards the stairs, taking Luke with me. We reach the next level and stand at the bathroom door. My fingers skim the woodwork, which looks as good as new.

'They smashed through this door.' My hands feel clammy and my mouth is dry.

'I can still hear your voice telling me to stay alive and that you love me.'

No more. I can't take any more. I crumble into Luke's arms and cry with such force that I can barely breathe. Again he scoops me up and carries me to our bed, where he simply lies with me as slowly I forget about the world.

For the second time today my eyes open. This time I am met by a stunning view of the sea. Reluctantly I get up from the warm bed, but as I reach the last step I see him outside on the raised decking. I could stare at him all day, but he turns – he always sees me no matter where I am. Luke opens the door, bringing the chilly air in with him.

'How do you feel?' He seals his words with a cold kiss.

'Like a complete lunatic. Christ, I can't remember the last time I cried like that.'

'You look better. I have been waiting for you to let go. You made the right call coming here, this was the key.'

'I hope so.'

Luke looks at his watch. 'It's one o'clock.'

'Bloody hell, is it?'

'You needed the rest.'

'Lunch?' I link my arms around his neck. 'What do you fancy to eat? And, yes, I'm on the menu.' I smile and take a deep breath. It feels good.

'Well, in that case I'll take my wife and her hamper.'

'Good choice.'

We eat in our new kitchen, which is the only room that is decorated. After I clear away our lunch, I join Luke on the decking. He slides the door closed and locks it. The weather is chilly, but the sun beats down. I link my arm through Luke's as he guides me down the wooden steps and onto the beach. The wind is invigorating, blowing away my awful memories – I hope. The beach is empty apart from a few locals. We walk along the sand until I can barely see our house.

Luke stops and pulls me into his arms. I rest my head against his coat and we silently look out at the glistening sea.

'I love you.' His words pierce my heart.

I gaze up to his face. 'I love you too, always.'

'Good. Let's get you all home for a nice warm bath.'

True to his word, he holds my hand as I step into a warm bath filled with bubbles. Right here, right now, the house is beginning to feel like our home once more. The bath has an amazing view of the sea. As I turn around, another amazing view is also on offer. A naked Luke Sutton steps into the water. It's official: I will never tire of looking at him.

'I've been thinking.'

'Twice in one day? Careful.' He smirks.

'Oi!' I splash some water over his face. 'Watch your back, Sutton, this could be dangerous.' I laugh. 'Seriously, the spare room opposite our bedroom in the palace.'

'The palace? I think you can drop the nickname and just call it our home.'

'It'll always be the palace to me. Anyway, I think we should turn it into a nursery. What do you think? I'm sure the twins would like to be together.'

'That makes sense.'

I pause and look out at the sea before I look at Luke, who is watching me closely.

'I wanted to ask you what happened to the evil scumbags who took me. I mean, are they still lurking in a bush somewhere?'

'Unlikely.'

'But you don't know that.'

'I do. Drop it, Kate.'

'How do you know?'

His dark eyes lock on mine.

'Shit – is it bad?'

'This conversation is over and it will never be spoken of again. Understand?'

'No! You're shutting me down again. It's the same when I mention Ivor's name.'

'What do you want from me, a detailed report of all the people who worked for Philip? You won't like the truth.' His tone is raw. 'When I say trust me, I mean it. As for Ivor, I have intel that he's still in Russia, but he hasn't contacted me. Our agreement was that when he feels the time is right we will set up a meeting.'

'Oh.' I digest his statement. 'Thank you. See, little bits of information are all I need.'

'Let this conversation be the last.'

'One last question, Luke.'

He shakes his head.

'Joseph Morley and George Williams?'

Luke remains guarded.

'I know there's more to it?'

'We discussed this in Russia.'

'Not really. You said don't go there.'

'I said let's not kick the hornets' nest. If we investigate either man it could be damaging for us, and for what? They're not likely to implicate themselves, Kate.'

'I know, but they could be involved and they shouldn't get away with murder.'

'They may not be involved in her murder, but they might involve themselves in Philip's death. Ivor could go to prison for killing him. It could also affect me as I was there too. Is that what you want?'

'Of course not. It just feels unfair.'

'Kate, if they were involved Philip would have had great pleasure in telling you.'

He turns and looks out of the window. Of course he has a point.

'Are you grumpy?' I ask.

His eyes connect with mine. 'No.'

'Good. I think we should relive a Christmas tradition: you should cook dinner from your cookbook.'

'Pour in some more stock, but don't let the risotto stick.'

'It is sticking.' I see a hint of panic on Luke's face – what a novelty.

'It will be fine. Pour in the last of the stock and carry on stirring. You're good with your hands, so this should be a walk in the park for you.'

His eyes dart to me. 'Maybe I should reserve some energy for later.'

'Don't worry, we have mine.' With that my hand wanders to the waistband of his jogger shorts. I know he is commando – and horny. The evidence is in the palm of my hand.

'I assume you want to eat tonight,' he says.

'Why, are you offering extras?'

He roars with laughter. 'Thank Christ, I have my wife back!'

We take our plates through to the lounge to eat. I managed to make a small comfortable area using blankets and cushions in front of the crackling fire. Note to self: buy some bloody furniture.

'Luke, this is lovely.'

He nods. 'It tastes the same as when you make it.'

'It does, well done… Do you really hate cooking?'

He shakes his head. 'My prick-teasing wife makes it fun.'

I giggle. 'I love it when you need me.'

'Twenty-four seven, Kate.'

Afterwards, I'm clearing away the last of the crockery when I hear Usher and 'Scream' echo around the house – the exact slowed-down version that was played at our wedding. It's our song. I head to the lounge and there he is, in all his glory, completely naked. Christ, I need him. Dr Jenkins said that my libido might increase when I was pregnant, but where do you go from nymphomaniac?

He walks towards me, holding out his hand. 'Would you care to dance?'

My body is bound to his request. 'I would love to dance with my naked husband.'

'I thought I'd dress for dessert.'

'I won't mention cream!'

We fall into each other's arms, laughing.

Luke slips my T-shirt over my head. 'Sorry, baby, but you're completely overdressed.'

He slides his hands down my body and cups my arse, drawing me closer to his erection. His lips meet mine and I run my hands through his hair. The spark between us matches the fire – an undeniable heat.

He breaks away. 'Christ, if anything happened to you, I...'

'Don't, Luke. I'm here – we're here.' I take his hand to my stomach. I look up into his eyes, then guide him to the makeshift bed in front of the roaring fire. With no lights other than the flickering flames and the stars shining in through the large windows, this has to be the most romantic of settings. Luke lowers me to the blankets strewn across the floor.

Automatically, I pull him towards me and kiss him with purpose. We have resumed our sexual journey and have fallen into our natural rhythm. He leaves my lips and slowly works down my body, stopping at my nipples.

'They're really sensitive, Luke.'

He gently sucks and caresses them with his soft tongue until he hears my breathing alter. Tenderly, his lips cover every inch of my skin, being extra-gentle on my wound and on my stomach. He works his way down my legs, showering them with kisses, and spreading them wider the further he goes.

The touch of his tongue against my clit almost makes me come. My body erupts and buckles with every flick of his tongue, but he holds my legs in place. The circular movements of his tongue are enough. I can hear myself panting. Finally it arrives, like waves crashing against rocks.

'Luke…' I manage. His mouth continues to work until the last tremors of my orgasm slowly fade away.

I come round from my delirious state to see my sex god moving between my legs. His mouth meets mine. At the same time, he drives into me.

With each thrust, he buries himself deeper inside me. My hands slide down his back and my fingers almost claw at his skin, which makes him bury his hardness deeper, touching me where I need it. I know where I'm heading – and, more to the point, so does Luke. Soon he cannot hold back any longer.

'I'm with you.'

'Christ, Luke.' My mouth is dry. Ironically, I want to 'scream' to the song that's on repeat.

'Fuck, baby,' he whispers as he comes. I watch his chiselled face.

Tonight my orgasm feels more intense, for some reason.

Gently Luke frees himself and lies next to me, allowing his breathing to settle. 'Are you OK?'

'Hard and fast, just the way I like it. A perfect dessert,' I say. 'It felt like making love.'

'I like making love to you.' Luke stands and switches off the music. He rejoins me on the floor and pulls a blanket over our naked bodies.

I roll onto one side. 'Argh. Sex was painless but lying on my side hurts like hell – this is shit!'

'Patience!'

'I'm all out of patience,' I say through a yawn.

'Shall we go to bed?'

I look at the time. 'It's only eight o'clock.'

He stands and takes my hands to help me up. 'I'll watch TV – and you – in bed.'

'How exciting for you.'

He taps my arse as I climb the stairs in front of him. 'Bet your arse it is. You'll be quiet for a change!'

I wake to hear my phone vibrating on the floor. My eyes reluctantly open. Caller ID – Harry.

'Hi,' I say.

'Hiya, where are you? I tried calling the palace,' she says.

'Sandbanks.' I rub my eyes awake and turn to see Luke lying on his stomach, asleep.

'Sandbanks? Bloody hell, you're brave.'

'I know. I had a massive meltdown yesterday, and I mean a full-on iceberg meltdown…'

'Well, I'm proud of you, that's a huge hurdle,' Harry says.

'Have you spoken to Alexis since Friday?'

'Yeah, I took Raymond over there yesterday. You don't mind, do you?'

'Of course not, she's part of your life.'

'I'm ringing for a reason. First, bloody twins! I couldn't stop laughing.'

'Thanks for the sympathy.' I giggle.

'Oh my God, Mum and Dad will go mad… I mentioned it to Alexis, I hope that's OK, she won't say anything.'

'That's fine, and we're going to see Mum and Dad later. Harry, Livy and Edward know.'

'Of course – why wouldn't they?' Harry says.

'Not the babies, I mean they know about everything: Alexis, Mum, Ivor.'

'Oh!' She takes a breath. 'That's not like Luke, Mr Secret Agent!'

'Well, it wasn't him.'

'Do you need a gag for your birthday?'

'Declan saw me leaving Alexis's apartment. Look, I'll explain when I see you, but they know what happened to me, and you, and – I'm really sorry.'

'It's fine.'

'I feel bloody awful, but it just came out. Anyway, they won't breathe a word to anyone, especially Mum and Dad.'

'OK.'

Shit, I can tell she's pissed off.

'Harry, I trust them with my life. They won't say anything.' God, I feel bad.

'If you trust them, that's good enough for me. I just don't want to talk about it – some day, but not today, because I'm calling you for a reason at nine o'clock on a Sunday morning.' She pauses. 'Molly's gone into labour.'

'Holy shit.' The first person in our friendship group to have a baby! 'Is she OK? Hang on, she's early, right?'

'About a week, but she's been ready to burst for the last month. Anyway, Danny called me an hour ago. You'll see missed calls on your mobile.'

'Sorry. We were exhausted last night. Luke's still asleep.'

'He's had a lot of shit to deal with, he's probably shattered.'

'I worry about him so much, Harry.'

'He'll be fine. Christ, with all that 007 training I'm sure he'll be OK. So, tell me, how are you feeling, yummy mummy?'

My free hand sweeps across my stomach.

'Fat. I think I'm expanding.'

'You're not fat,' Luke says.

Shit, how long has he been awake?

'I'll text you with updates,' Harry says.

'OK.'

She goes, leaving me feeling excited for Molly and Danny, although the actual thought of pushing a baby out causes my legs to close – tightly!

Luke pulls me towards him and nuzzles my neck.

'Molly's gone into labour,' I say.

He raises his head. 'Good news… How far dilated is she?'

I frown. 'What? I haven't got a clue. Are you reading up on labour?'

'Yes.'

I laugh. 'Really? Are you joking?' I meet his dark eyes. 'Christ, you're not joking.'

'No – and I have a set of books for you.'

'Jesus, what am I going to do with Mr Control Freak Sutton?'

I have no time to conjure a plan as he captures my mouth.

'Hi – any news?' I ask.

'No. How long does it take to push a baby out? I tell you what, Kate, don't you take this long,' Harry says.

'I'll do my best, but remember I have two babies to get out.' Once again, my legs cross.

'How long before you're in London?' Harry asks.

'I don't know.' I look across at Luke. 'How long before we're home?'

'Put it this way, we've driven about ten miles since the last time you asked.' His brows arch with a degree of frustration.

'OK.' I scowl. 'Sorry, Harry, my personal sat-nav seems a little grumpy.'

'Hang on, I've got a text from Danny.' She's silent for a few seconds. 'Apparently everything's OK and she's seven centimetres dilated. I think she needs to be ten centimetres. I'll Google it.'

'Don't bother, Luke seems to be in the know.'

'What?' Harry laughs. 'Why am I not surprised?'

I look across at Luke. 'Harry said Molly is seven centimetres – it's ten and then the party begins, right?'

He smirks. 'Now I'm useful.'

'Occasionally. Well?'

'You need…'

'Wait, I'll put you on loudspeaker.' I press a button. 'Harry, you're on loudspeaker. Dr Sutton will provide you with the information.' I laugh at myself.

'Hi, Luke.' Harry's voice echoes around the car.

'Harry.' His tone is stern. 'When she's ten centimetres dilated the birth canal is fully open. The uterus contracts, finally pushing the baby out… She could potentially have another three hours before she is fully dilated.'

What? I stare at him in disbelief.

'OK, thanks Luke.' I can hear the shock in Harry's voice.

'Jesus, Luke, how many books have you read?' Fuck me!

'Enough. Goodbye, Harry,' he says gruffly.

'Bye,' she says.

I end the call. 'You're not the full ticket, Sutton.'

'Is that right?' he answers, keeping his eyes on the road.

'Yes!' Oh my God, I am literally speechless.

'I want to know how pregnancy will affect you.'

'In that case it seems pointless me reading about it. I may as well ask you.'

'Ignorance is not bliss. If you can prepare for a situation, then you should.'

'Oh, whatever. I think you should have been a lawyer or something. You exhaust me with words.'

My phone rings just as we enter the outskirts of London. Caller ID – Harry.

'Hi.'

'It's a boy.' Her voice cracks.

'Oh my God.'

Luke looks at me.

'It's a boy,' I mouth to him.

'Danny said they're both OK. Apparently Molly just had a few stiches.' I swallow. Oh shit, that will be me at the end of the year. 'Grayson Daniel Hall, six pounds.'

'I can't believe it.'

'Danny said we could visit once she gets onto the ward.'

'OK. I'll see you later.'

With my phone resting on my lap, I take a deep breath. Luke takes hold of my hand and squeezes it.

'Luke, I think it's just hit me that I have to do this twice.'

Luke and I enter the Chelsea and Westminster Hospital. We take the lift to the postnatal ward, where we meet Harry and Raymond. Kiki and Barney are yet to arrive. Danny soon appears and takes us through.

I'm not sure which one of us cries first watching Molly cradling her son. Luke and Raymond take it in turns to hold him, which starts Harry and me off again. Both men leave the room, taking Danny with them for a coffee break.

'Molly, he's so beautiful. You've done so well.'

'Kate, Harry told me what happened. Are you OK?'

I look at Harry. 'Which part?'

'She knows everything. I needed to speak to someone apart from you and Raymond.'

I hold my hands up. 'I'm OK. We're getting there – right, Harry?'

She nods.

'Just don't tell Luke. Christ, this has to be the worst kept secret ever.'

Molly reaches for my hand. 'You have my word.'

'I know. Tell me, how was it?'

Molly begins to give a blow-by-blow, stitch-by-stitch account of her labour. Why did I ask?

Then the door opens. 'Where is he?' Barney walks through with Kiki behind him.

'Oh my God, Molly,' Kiki says as she perches on the bed.

'Let me hold him,' Barney says and sits on the chair, cradling the newest member of the pack.

Kiki comes to me. 'Kate.' She pulls me into her arms. 'Declan told me about Philip Cooper,' she whispers and pulls away. 'Why didn't you call me? I would have flown home earlier.'

'There was nothing you could do.'

'Jesus, I can't believe what you've been through.' She looks away. The shock seems to be affecting everyone. 'He said Livy's birthday meal was eventful. He feels really bad, Kate.'

'It's fine. I get it. I just want to forget about everything.'

'I would feel the same. But as long as you're all right.'

'Listen, while we're alone, it seems everyone knows about the latest Harper twist – like I said, the worst kept secret! But it stays in this room – forever. Right?' I look at Harry. 'Plus, we've decided that Mum and Dad don't need to know what's happened. You were all with us when the shit hit the fan with all the adoption business. I mean it – this is where it stops.'

'Not a word,' Kiki says.

Barney holds his hands up. 'Russia, guns – I don't know what you're talking about.'

I point to my face. 'Sandbanks – car accident!' I say.

They silently accept my story.

'Good, but I do have some news you can talk about – well, not until tomorrow as I have to tell Mum and Dad this evening... I'm pregnant.'

'Holy shit, really? Declan never told me,' Kiki says.

'I asked him not to. I wanted to tell you myself.'

'Congratulations, Kate,' Molly says. 'Oh God, I just gave you a graphic recap of labour. Crap, you should have stopped me.'

'Actually, it gets better. I'm pregnant with twins.'

8

I scan the clothes hanging in my dressing room. I have a Harper Jones meeting today, and it's important that I bring my own style and flair to the table; as the only member of the team with no fashion credentials, I need to sell myself. I decide on a black faux leather high-waisted skater skirt, a white shirt and a fitted black crew-neck jumper. The look is completed with black tights and flat suede over-the-knee boots. I pull my hair into a smart ponytail and apply make-up to cover the last of the bruises.

My appetite still hasn't returned since Russia, plus I feel nauseous. I don't know if this is due to pregnancy, or stress. I scan the fridge. Nothing jumps out at me, but I have to eat: granary toast and fruit for three.

'Morning, Kate,' Rosie sings. 'How were your mum and dad?'

'Excited about the babies, and concerned because of the … accident.'

'I'm sure they were.'

'They cried, which set me off. Anyway, talking of babies.' I look at my watch. 'Eight hours and counting.'

Eight hours until Rosie's son Adam arrives.

She comes to my side. 'I can't believe he's arriving today.'

'How's Jerry this morning?'

Adam is gay. He and Jerry had a huge argument when Adam came out, and they haven't spoken since. Jerry is still at war with his own demons: he can't change that Adam is gay, but he can change his mindset. Rosie never believed the day would arrive when her son and husband could be in the same room without arguing.

'Quiet. Keeping busy.'

'Coffee?' I ask.

'Please.'

I pour three mugs of coffee, the third for my delicious husband who is missing in action. He's probably buying a small country, locked away in his office.

'Jerry will be fine. I have planned the perfect meal for tonight.'

'I know he's dreading it.' Rosie is devastated that her husband and son are at odds.

'We'll all be here to make things easier. Besides, when Barney is around everyone seems normal. Jerry will count his blessings.' We giggle at Barney's expense, though he would agree.

'You're my saving grace. Honestly, I would be lost without you.'

'We all would.'

I turn at the sound of Luke's voice. He's sitting on the stool at the island. Christ, that man has stealth in his DNA.

'Breakfast.' I pass him his plate and coffee. 'Luke, don't forget Adam will be here for dinner tonight.'

'I have a late meeting. I may not make it,' Luke says, reading paperwork.

'What?' I snap.

He glances at me.

'Kate, I need to get on. Call me when you're home and we can prepare dinner,' Rosie says, not looking remotely worried about Luke's announcement, and disappears in the direction of the laundry room.

I take the stool next to him.

'Are you seriously not going to be here tonight? I promised Rosie. Don't let her down, Luke.'

'I have a meeting that could run over. I will try to make it, but I can't promise.'

'Then you shouldn't make promises you can't keep.' Feeling sick and irritated, I stand.

'Have you already eaten?' he asks.

'Yes.' No! I head to the office and gather the new drawings I have been working on. Luke follows me and goes to his desk, where he picks up his black blazer and briefcase.

'Ready?' I can feel him watching me.

'Yes,' I reply and head to the hall, where I put on my black riding coat.

We make our way outside. Max is waiting alongside the Bentley. I slide into the rear as Luke follows me.

'Kate, don't sulk,' he says.

I turn to face him. 'I'm not, and for your information I'm choosing not to speak. There's a difference.' Of course I'm sulking! Christ, he brings out the worst in me.

'Fine. I'm a great fan of silence.'

Bastard. Of course he is.

The journey is fairly quick – and quiet. When we arrive at Sutton Global, Luke and I step out and walk into the building. Fortunately Luke carries some books for me, so there will be no hand-holding today. We arrive at the fortieth floor in silence, which is killing me.

'Hi, Stella,' I say.

'Morning, Kate, Luke.'

'Stella,' Luke says sternly. Boss-man Sutton has entered the building.

I head straight into my office and slam the door. I remove my coat, place my books on the table and begin to pace. It's no good. I need to clear the air. Ever since Russia, I struggle with unfinished business. That's what made me flee to Sandbanks in the first place – oh, and speaking to Matthew Williams. Not only is he George Williams' son, who may be involved in Katenka's death, but he also had an affair with Luke's ex-fiancée!

I burst into Luke's office. He is leaning against his desk, looking at his watch.

'Not bad, baby – you waited four long minutes.'

'What? Oh my God, you infuriate me.' I turn on my heel, refusing to indulge him.

'Stop!'

Of course I stop.

He takes my arm and walks me to the sofa, pulling me to his lap.

'I'm teasing you.' He smiles.

'No, you weren't… You did actually time me.'

'Yes, and you were four minutes.' He chuckles. 'Like I said, I have a meeting tonight, but I will try to finish early. Please don't undermine me in front of our employees.'

'Oh, for Christ's sake, Luke, Rosie is not an employee! She treats you like a son. Seriously, you need to remove your head from your arse.'

'Do I now? Thank you for pointing that out.'

'You know what I mean. They're not just employees. If anything happened to either of them, how would you feel? Besides, I asked you about the meal before I planned it, and you told me you were available.'

He holds his hands up in defeat. 'As I said, I will try. You have my word.'

'Fine!'

'Kate?'

'What?'

'Are you OK?'

'I feel sick,' I announce.

'Did you eat this morning?' He runs his hand up and down my nylon-covered legs.

'No. I wasn't hungry.'

'I asked if you had eaten, and you said yes.'

'And I asked you to dinner and you said yes.'

'Kate, drop it. I said I will try. I love you,' he says. 'You need to eat something, OK?'

I nod.

'I have some good news.'

'What?'

'Our honeymoon is booked for the end of next week,' he says.

'Is it?' I smile.

'I thought that would please you. I checked your

schedule with Tanya as I wanted to surprise you. We fly next Thursday.'

'Am I OK to fly, Luke?'

'Yes. We need some time alone.' His hand rests against my stomach.

'Perfect. I can't wait.'

'Your next scan is when we return.'

'Good. Oh my God, I need to think about packing – I need lots of bikinis. Luke, I want to tell the Harper Jones crew about the babies, but we should tell Stella first.'

'I agree.'

'I'll go and get her.'

'Not yet. Kiss me, baby.'

When we tell her our news, Stella looks at us with tears running down her cheeks. She must have mixed emotions. Stella is infertile, and it must still weigh her down.

'Stella, I said two babies… I'll need your help when I come to work. Just don't tell Luke that I've stolen you.'

He looks at me, understanding I'm trying to involve her.

'I think we need a crèche.' Luke takes my hand.

'I am so thrilled for you, although I am surprised,' Stella says.

'That makes two of us. So not only will you be Luke's PA, my friend, but you will also be Nana Stella at work.'

'Oh Kate, I can't wait.'

'Remember, ladies, I am trying to achieve global domination here…' Luke smiles.

'Luke, you make me laugh… I can't wait to see you walking around with a baby in your arms.'

'You might need to brush up on your multi-tasking skills,' I say and lean over to kiss his cheek.

'You never normally complain.'

Bastard!

'OK. So, lunch in my office, Stella. The Harper Jones crew will be here and I know I'm far more interesting than my husband.'

Finally the Harper Jones team are back together. Today feels even more special in light of recent events. I love watching Mr Jones brim with delight as we deliberate his sketches and turn them into reality. After a two-hour discussion we make a unanimous decision on the direction and the pieces we will create for Mrs Gold's charity fashion show in New York: a summer collection that captures timeless elegance using updated versions of Mr Jones's designs.

Though we are using Jones Tailors to create the pieces, Mr Jones also has orders to fulfil for his personal clientele. As we have so much work ahead and a tight deadline, we've taken on two new seamstresses and a tailor. Maria informs us that our website is up and running, and she will keep it updated. Valerie contacts models in New York she has previously worked with, to check their availability. I plan to ask Barney if he's willing to model for us. He is a dancer and he has a perfectly chiselled face. Being over six foot, modelling is already part of his repertoire.

Tanya and I confirm hotels and flights. We'll take Luke's private jet and he's asked that we stay at the Four Seasons. Luke will be in Dubai so I'm going solo – well, sort of. Max will chaperone me. Since Russia, I really don't mind. I've requested adjoining rooms for Mr A. Maxwell and Miss V. Simmons. Tanya smiles. Perhaps she agrees with me that they'd be good together.

When lunch is delivered, everyone stops for a much-needed break, and, as agreed, Stella joins us. I drag Luke in so he can announce my pregnancy. As predicted, emotions run high. The team are delighted for us, although they are concerned for my well-being, especially after the car accident at Sandbanks…

I look at my watch. Two o'clock. The only people in my office are Mr Jones and Valerie. However, I decide to send Valerie home with much more fashion paraphernalia than she can carry. She will need help with it. I call in Max to save the day on his black stallion – actually, my black Bentley. He can give her a ride home.

Closing my office door behind me, I sit on the pink sofa with Mr Jones. Whenever we are alone I remember just how much I miss our time together, and I think back to when I worked for him. Pre-Luke, of course. How simple my life was back then.

'You look lost, Mr Jones.' I slump in the chair next to him.

'Not at all, perhaps lost in amazement. We both seem to have achieved our dreams.'

'Good things come to good people. Besides, you're super-talented – and what a crime it was to see your artistic talents locked away. I still remember the day you showed me your collections of books – it feels like yesterday.'

'So much has happened since you left Jones Tailors, Kate.' He takes my hand.

162

'I know. I'm so excited. Every time I pick up one of your books, I find a new design I love.'

'I want to know how you feel, truthfully,' he says.

'About the fashion show, or the fact I'm pregnant?'

'The pregnancy and the accident.'

'Shit-scared.'

He flashes his best Mr Jones glare.

'You know what I mean. I didn't plan this, so to say I was surprised would be an understatement. I was shaken up after the… accident. And I was worried that it would affect the babies. I have my twelve-week scan booked for when I get back from my honeymoon, just before we fly to New York. It sounds crazy, but I'm too frightened to get excited.'

'You will be fine. Mother Nature is marvellous. I can still see some bruising on your face, though.'

'It's almost gone, and my eye doesn't hurt. You should have seen the state of me.'

'And you should have contacted me so I could have helped you.'

Oh, crap! 'To be honest, I slept for days. There was nothing you could do, but what we're doing now is exactly what I need.'

He smiles.

'I'm going to be a mum,' I say.

'You will be fine. You and Luke are strong individuals. I think your babies will be fortunate to have such interesting parents.'

'Interesting – really? Luke and I are far from interesting. You know he drives me mad. How the hell will he cope when our children push his buttons?'

'Yes, but you testing him and a child pushing boundaries are very different. First, you should know better and, second, pushing boundaries is how children learn.'

I reach for his hand. 'Why do you always make sense? I could do with a Jones book on how to solve dilemmas. OK, so we do have a couple of things to discuss for the show.'

'Tell me. '

'I thought at the end of the show when we make our grand entrance we should both wear a black three-piece Jones Tailors suit – what do you think?'

His face comes alive. 'I like the idea very much.'

'Good. We also need a suit for Barney. I'll send him to the tailors to get measured. Last, I'm planning a scavenger hunt for Luke's birthday. Any chance you can make him a new suit too?'

'A scavenger hunt?' He smiles. 'And I assume he will be looking for you?'

'Spot on. What do you think?'

'Ingenious!'

I've thrown up in the bathroom. Early pregnancy is the pits. I lie on the pink sofa and close my eyes for what feels like a few seconds.

'Kate?'

My eyes open. Luke crouches beside me.

'Are you OK?'

I sit up. 'I'm tired.'

'You look pale. Did you eat lunch?'

'Only crisps. I couldn't face anything else, and I was sick earlier.'

'Crisps! You need to eat more than that.'

I read his dark eyes. 'What's wrong?'

'I have something to show you.' He holds his hand out. I take it and stand.

He flashes a warm smile at me.

'I know that look, Sutton.'

'Trust me.'

He walks me across the hall and opens the door to his office.

'Ivor!'

'Katarina.' He comes towards me, his arms out. 'How are you?'

'OK. What are you doing here?'

He folds me into his arms and I rest my face against his chest. My dad is with me – why does this feel so right? We barely know each other, yet there is a connection between us. Ivor releases me and gestures for us to sit. Luke joins us.

'When did you get here?' I look at Luke. 'How long have you known that Ivor was in London?'

'Ivor called me this afternoon,' Luke says.

'I arrived this morning. I wanted to speak to Luke before I made contact with you, as we agreed. We had some matters to discuss.'

'Like what?' I snap and look across to Luke.

'Your safety,' Luke fires back.

'Is that right? So what happened in Russia with that Chekhol man? Is there still a bounty on my head or did you kick his arse? I know you wouldn't be here if—'

'Kate, leave it.'

'What?' I glare at Luke.

'You look better than you did when I last saw you.' Ivor deflects the question.

165

'I feel better, but what happened to him?'

'Some things are better left alone,' Ivor says.

'This is one of those times you need to back off, Kate.' Luke watches me closely.

'Remember our "don't shut me out" conversation? This is one of those times,' I reply.

Luke rubs his jaw then stands and walks to his desk. He returns with a brown envelope and places it on the coffee table, then sits facing me.

'If you want to remember conversations, then perhaps you will recall that I told you the truth was ugly.'

'Luke—' Ivor tries to defend me.

'No!' Luke looks at Ivor. 'Your daughter does not like to be told no.'

I sit back and fold my arms.

Luke slides the envelope towards me.

'You have two options: you either trust me and put this to bed or you look in the envelope, but once you look you can't take back what you see. Do you understand me?'

'How bad can it be?' I ask.

'Imagine the worst, Kate, and times it by ten.'

I hesitate. Do I trust him? What does the envelope hold? I can't take any more. I make a decision, and silently slide the envelope back to him.

'Ivor, we have some news.' Luke looks at me. I'm still speechless. 'We are expecting twins.'

Ivor laughs. Oddly, it's the first time I've heard him laugh.

'Katarina, this is wonderful news.'

'I'm still getting used to the idea.'

'How long are you planning on staying in London?' Luke asks.

'Until tomorrow morning.'

'Oh.' One bloody day!

'I only visited to see how you are, and to talk to Luke, but I will return.'

'When?' I ask.

'I have business in Russia that needs my attention, and you need to rest… Katarina, I would like to meet your parents. Luke agrees with me.'

'Oh, did he? Looks like you both have it sorted. Was this during a male bonding session?' I'm pissed off. Is Ivor trying to get Luke on his side?

'I want to be involved in your life, not hidden from your parents,' Ivor says.

'Kate, we have our own family coming into the world. It's not fair to bring them into a family of lies,' Luke says.

'I guess.'

'I will make contact with them soon,' Ivor says.

'Wait! Mum doesn't know you're not Harry's dad. As you know, we thought Malcolm had an affair with Katenka, which wasn't true, but we decided to bury the story. So, she'll assume you're Harry's dad… now there's a whole new world of lies.'

'We need to safeguard Malcolm and Susan,' Luke says.

'I will stick to your story unless you tell me otherwise,' Ivor says.

'Thank you. So, since you're only here for the day, does that mean you can come over this evening for dinner?'

Ivor looks at Luke.

'Oh, Luke won't be there. He has a meeting.' Poetic justice, Sutton.

'Yes, I would like that.'

'Good.'

He runs his hands through his silver hair. 'You are like your mother in so many ways.'

'I miss her. That's stupid.' I take a deep breath. 'I wish I could touch her hair… See her just once. Oh my God, I sound crazy.'

Ivor takes my hand. He understands it's the simple things you miss, even if you never had them.

'Kate, why don't you show Ivor your collection for New York? Your daughter is quite the designer,' Luke says, giving me time to recover.

'Katarina, you are a resourceful young woman.'

'I agree,' Luke says.

Ivor follows me to my office. Luke watches from the doorway before he closes my door.

'Please.' I point to the sofa.

I sit next to Ivor. 'This is all a bit – I'm sorry, but you being here seems like… well, I've been waiting for you since we met.'

'It was not the right time for me to enter your life.'

'I suppose you had your reasons… So, what shall I call you?'

He looks completely relaxed in my company. 'I used to call my father Papa. What would you like to call me?'

'I don't know.' *I always knew you as my birth father, who abandoned me.* 'I guess Papa is good. At least I can call Dad, Dad without confusion.'

His smile warms my heart. 'Your office is feminine. May I look?'

'Go for it.'

He walks around the room, slowly absorbing my tastes and choices, items that make me tick as a human being.

'You look happy.' He points to the large prints of Luke and me.

'This was taken when we first met. I'm sure you must have a copy.' Even today, remembering the gallery of photos of me at all stages of my life at Ivor's house in Russia leaves me feeling cold, knowing that he hired people to take the pictures.

He chuckles, understanding what I am referring to. 'No, but perhaps I can have a copy.'

'Maybe you would like a photo of us – together?'

'I would like that very much.'

I stand and head to the board table. 'Here, these are our collections for the show.'

He stands next to me.

'I know nothing about clothes, but these look impressive.'

'Thank you.'

The door opens. 'Kate, a word in private.'

'Luke, it is fine. I do have somewhere to be,' Ivor says. He looks at me. 'I will see you this evening.'

I nod. 'Dinner will be at seven, but you can come over whenever you want.'

'I have your address.' He passes me a business card. 'My numbers for you.'

'Oh, thank you.' I plant a kiss on his cheek before we walk towards the door.

'Luke.' Ivor hold his hand out. 'Thank you.'

Luke takes his hand, but remains guarded. 'Ivor.'

I blink and my father is gone.

'I need to leave for my meeting. Are you going home?' Luke asks.

'Yeah, I'm waiting for Max to get back.'

'Where is Max?'

'He took Valarie home. She had quite a lot of books to carry.'

He gives me a one-sided Sutton smile. Fuck it, I need him!

'You're meddling. I said to stay out of Max's business.'

'Actually, she did have a lot to carry and Max didn't mind. I can't help it if they are attracted to each other.'

'Kate, you're playing with fire.'

'They look perfect together.' I draw him closer. 'Care to take a wager on it?'

'You're that confident you want to challenge me?'

I link my arms around his neck. 'Oh, it's not a challenge, Luke. I'm right and if I win, which I know I will, let me think. What shall I bargain for? A day driving around in your pride and joy.' The other baby in his life is his Aston Martin.

He whistles. 'And if I win, your arse is mine.'

'I suggest you get your keys ready,' I say.

My arse belongs to him anyway!

By early evening the house smells amazing – I'm cooking roast beef and all the trimmings. Today has been bizarre, but incredible. I still can't believe Ivor has just walked into my life, although what scares me the most is, will he stay?

Standing at the island preparing the last of the meal, I watch my houseguests. Ivor seems fairly at ease talking to them. Surprisingly, Max is trying to engineer a conversation between an incredibly quiet Jerry and Adam. I want to shake Jerry. *Your son is amazing. Get over the fact that he's gay!*

I hear the front door open. Luke!

Swiftly, he walks to his office. I follow him.

'You're early.' I head towards his desk.

'Yes, I altered my meeting. I know you wanted me here,' he says, sorting out some paperwork.

'And this has nothing to do with Ivor? This morning you were adamant that your meeting was far too important, but now you're here.'

'I altered my meeting, end of conversation.'

I shake my head. 'End of conversation! Are you practising talking to your children? I can read you like a bloody book.'

He looks at me with a vague smile. *Caught you, Sutton.*

'Is that so? Then maybe you should check the chapter on how to be subservient to your husband,' he jokes, and laughs.

I chuckle. 'No way! But there is a chapter called "do not feed your wife bullshit".'

He steps towards me. 'I'm here, does it matter why?'

Before I can answer him, his lips meet mine. I understand Luke's reservations regarding Ivor, so I need to accept this level of protection. I know Luke may never trust Ivor.

Rosie carries the food to the table while I make the gravy. The front door opens again, and this time the light of my life arrives – Barney.

'I was getting worried. Where were you?' I say.

'Sorry, babe, the tubes have packed up, so I got a cab – but the traffic was horrendous.'

'I should have warned you. Anyway, come and meet Adam, your roommate for a couple of weeks. Ivor is here too.'

'Fuck – no way! When did he turn up?'

'This afternoon.'

'Are you pleased?'

'Yeah, I think so… No, I am, but it feels odd.'

I take Barney's arm and lead him into the kitchen. 'Everyone, this is one of my best friends, Barney.'

An hour later the plates are all empty and the atmosphere is relaxed. Tonight has been a success. Ivor is chatting to Luke, and Jerry appears to be making an effort with Adam. As for Barney – well, he's my trump card and offers all the entertainment you could possibly want. Not one for resting, I begin to clear the table. Weirdly, Barney offers to help.

'Christ almighty, Kate, that meal was painful.'

'What?' Not only did Barney clear his plate, but he asked for seconds.

'Not the food, babe! Why didn't you tell me Adam was hot?'

'Oh no you don't. The last thing I need is for you to upset Jerry.'

'Cheers, babe.'

'You know what I mean. Let me think, what is your motto: oh yes, fuck and run.'

'Sometimes.'

I pass him plates to load in the dishwasher.

'Anyway, I don't know what you expect me to do, he's staying with me,' Barney says.

'Not literally – he's in the spare room.'

'Under the same roof.'

'Barney, no! Keep your bloody trousers zipped up, do you understand me?'

'Yeah, yeah, but you have to admit he's hot.'

I look across at Adam. Barney's right. He is handsome: tall and blond with piercing blue eyes that match Jerry's.

'OK, he is good-looking, but on this occasion please don't make a pass at him.'

Barney leans against the worktop. 'What if he makes a pass at me?'

'He is here to mend some seriously damaged bridges with his dad.'

'I'll make you a deal.'

I stop wiping the worktop. 'Bloody hell, what is it with people making deals with me today?'

Barney raises his brows and sniggers. 'What deal has Sutton made? Babe, he can give me a deal any time.'

'You know your problem? You have a one-track mind.'

He cracks up laughing. 'I know. Christ, babe, you've heard of the bounty hunter – now meet the cock hunter.'

I slap his arm. 'Shh – they may hear you. You're supposed to be on your best behaviour this evening.'

'Fine – but that's my deal. I promise not to make a pass unless I'm invited.'

'OK, but don't flirt or walk around naked.'

'As if I would.' Barney heads towards the table. 'Adam, can you dance?'

Barney, you little shit, I know flirting when I see it!

When everyone has gone, I feel exhausted. It's been a long, strange day. The door to Luke's office is ajar. I walk in to find him at his desk.

'Hi.'

His eyes scan me. 'You look tired. Tonight was too much for you.'

'I won't argue with that.' I head towards his chair and sit on his lap. 'Luke, today in your office…'

He stifles a smile. 'You had the option to look in the envelope.'

'I know, but what did Ivor do? Was it violent? It must be or you wouldn't have gone all Commander Sutton on me.'

'I wish you would trust me. Not everything is about control; this is about protecting you.'

'And Ivor, do you think he's violent?' I ask.

'He made a promise, which he kept. He promised to safeguard you from further harm.'

'So now you're buddies!' I mock him.

'Don't push it.' He runs his hands through my hair. 'Bed.'

'Yes please, Mr Sutton.'

9

'Kate!'

'Shh. I want to.'

Luke frowns, but I keep a firm grip on his hardness, sit astride him and align myself to the crown of his erection. I gently slide down his length until I have all of him. 'I'm fine. Don't look at me like that.'

'At least allow me to help.' He grips my hips and sits upright, leaning against the headboard. 'You're not strong enough for this.'

'Just let me try.' I follow up my request with a hard-hitting kiss.

Giving him no time to argue, I set the rhythm. It's pain-free, but it's not my usual hip-grinding action. The early sun filters through the shutters, showering our bedroom with a soft glow. Our dark eyes lock.

'Touch your clit, baby.'

My hand slides between my legs and gently brushes against the sweet spot. I try to increase the speed, but Luke takes control, angling himself away every time I try to slam against his body. The climb begins and my body has no time to spare as the rippling pulsations inside me make my muscles contract around Luke. The quickness of my hand increases, sparking a delicious orgasm. Judging from Luke's breathing, he's close to coming.

'Kate… Yes.'

His fingers spread wide against my hipbones and he thrusts faster, meeting me as I slide down his shaft. Afterwards, he holds me still.

'I'm fine, stop stressing.'

Luke lifts my hips, freeing us. A sharp pain makes me flinch.

'I told you it was too soon… Jesus, Kate, you never bloody listen.'

'Of course it's going to be tender, but I'm fine.'

'From now on I'm on top. And it's not up for discussion.'

'When I say I'm fine, then I'm fine, OK?' I get up from the bed. He follows.

'Don't be arsey, Kate.' He finishes his statement with a light tap against my arse.

'Oi!' I turn and glare at him as he follows me to the en suite.

'Smile. If you don't I will slap your arse again.'

'Really?' I turn the shower on.

'Are we going to have one of those days?'

'What days? My husband testing me? That's every bloody day.'

He moves closer and I take a step back. 'What am I going to do with you?'

'Gag me.'

He backs me into the corner. 'It will be my pleasure, but first, what's on your mind?'

'Nothing.'

'Baby, I know you. What's up?'

I loop my arms around his neck. 'I just want my body back to normal, plus I have a Bagrov and Cooper meeting today. I'm a bit nervous.'

His hands slide down my back. 'We haven't spoken about your shares.'

'I know. I want Alexis to run the show.'

'It's your choice.'

'That's what I want to do. It's just, the last time I was there Philip grabbed me. Christ, and I thought that was bad!'

'I think you're expecting too much of yourself. You've been through a traumatic time. Let yourself heal.'

'If you mention again that I need more time, I swear to God, I will cause you some harm.'

Luke cups my wet breasts. 'I love that these are bigger,' he says, then lowers his head and gently uses his tongue to tease my nipples in turn.

'You're so easily distracted.'

'You're standing in front of me naked!' He sinks to his knees and kisses my wound. I watch him closely as he looks up. Christ, he is stunning with water running off his face. How did I get so lucky? I have no time to think as his mouth makes contact with my clit. Fuck, I'm aroused again. My head falls back against the shower wall. Round two!

After starting off the morning with a double helping of Luke, we travel to Sutton Global. He leaves me with Max and I wait for Tanya in the rear of the Bentley. I watch her walk through the revolving doors and head towards the car.

'Hi, Tanya.'

She slides in next to me. 'You look a lot better.'

'Thank God for make-up!'

'The Harper Jones meeting went well. I can't wait for New York.'

'Me too – watching the pieces come to life is surreal.'

'I've emailed you all the times, et cetera. OK, so today…' She looks through a file. 'There's not too much. Mainly a company they want to sell.'

Even now I feel overwhelmed by my inheritance, which was given to me on my twenty-seventh birthday – Bagrov and Cooper shares from my mum, who I will never meet.

'I spoke to Alexis last night. She'll be there today. I didn't think she would be able to face it, with Philip dead and…'

'Kate, can I say something?'

'Sure.'

'This seems a little bizarre. I mean, you and Alexis – are you friends now?'

'We've cleared the air. It's early days but I guess we have to work together, and I hate bad feelings – life's too short.' My eyes make contact with Max's in the rear-view mirror. He understands why I'm lying to Tanya.

'You never know. With Philip gone, things might change.'

'Maybe.' Sick bastard.

Within twenty minutes we arrive at the Bagrov and Cooper offices. I feel more settled. We are taken to Alexis's office, which I have never seen before – normally we are shown to the boardroom. It looks how I imagined: modern and perhaps a little too cold. She sits at her desk in a black suit with a red shirt – very elegant and very Alexis.

'Hi,' I say.

'Kate, Tanya, how are you?'

'Fine.'

'Please take a seat.' She points to two chairs in front of her desk.

She looks well. She has no visible injuries. But her eyes remain empty – some wounds will never heal.

'I am sorry for your loss,' Tanya says sincerely.

Alexis manages a soft smile, which speaks volumes. 'Thank you.' She clears her throat.

'Are you sure you're ready to face the world?' I want to reach out to her, but I don't want to appear too familiar in front of Tanya. It was only a few weeks ago that I slapped Alexis's face in Dubai!

'I need to keep busy. Tanya, has Kate signed all the relevant paperwork?'

'Yes.'

'Good. Could you go over everything with my secretary? I'm sorry, but my mind is all over the place. Let's just say I need some help at the moment.'

'That's fine – I'm happy to help.' Tanya looks at me, waiting for my approval.

'I'll come and find you.'

We are left alone – two women who must try to understand how their worlds have been turned upside down.

'Being here must be bloody hard. Are you ready?'

She leans on the table. 'To be honest, I don't know, but I couldn't sit around at home. It was driving me mad. I also dismissed the nurse – I need my own space.'

'Well, you look good.'

'Thanks. You seem brighter, Kate.'

'I have good days and bad days,' I say.

'I want the bad days gone.'

'And they will. I'm here whenever you want to talk – or scream.'

'Thanks, Kate, but that's the problem. I don't know what I need. So, I'm here.' She leans back in her chair. 'I can't allow what happened to take over my life.'

'Definitely not! Look, today may be OK, tomorrow might be shit.'

She smiles.

'But you've won. I mean, you're here at work, you look fantastic and the world is now in your hands, and he's not here to control it or you.'

I watch her eyes glaze over. Crap – too much, Harper.

'Won? You think I've won?'

I nod. 'Yeah I do, and every day you live for you, you've won. You're not a victim; you made the choice to say fuck you!' I reach across the table and take her hand.

'Maybe.' She shakes her head.

'You can take off the armour now and breathe. He's not here.'

She closes her eyes for a moment. 'I'm trying, Kate.'

'And you're doing bloody amazing.'

'Thank you.' She smiles. 'Let's change the subject. I have had enough of the past. I want to take you to lunch. I hope you don't mind, but I asked Harry too.'

'Oh – what did she say?'

'Yes. Twelve o'clock at Marshalls – it's near her office. Actually, I wanted to speak to you both.'

'Is everything OK?'

A knock at the door interrupts us.

'Come in,' Alexis calls.

Alexis's secretary appears at the doorway. 'Your next appointment is here.'

'Thank you, Sally. Show them to the boardroom.'

'Go, we can talk at lunch,' I say. We stand and she slowly comes round to join me, holding on to the edge of the table for support. 'It still feels strange, right? Not hating each other.'

'It does.' She smiles, but I sense she could also cry.

I draw her close. Awkwardly, she holds me. I can feel her heart beating. We remain silent. I wonder how often she was hugged as a child. I pull away.

'Sorry – I hope that wasn't too much.'

'This is all very new for me.' Alexis smiles and takes my hand.

'You'll get used to it. Harry's the same.'

'I have a lot to learn.' She leans against the table, visibly in discomfort.

'This might be too soon? Not just physically.'

'Probably, but I'm not leaving.'

'I understand. OK, I'll see you in a few hours. I'm going to see Molly.'

'Harry told me your friend had a baby.'

'Molly and Harry are really close. She is a sweetheart – you'll love her. We'll introduce you to her.'

After a few hours I wave goodbye to Molly, who is holding baby Grayson. As predicted, she has adjusted to motherhood well. She is incredibly practical – plus Grayson is adorable. I would gaze at him all day in amazement if he were mine.

Max begins the short journey to Marshalls – my lunch date.

'Look at these.' I show him photos of baby Grayson on my phone.

Reluctantly, Max looks. 'Very nice.'

'He's so cute.' I scan the pictures. 'I can't believe that will be me by the end of the year.'

'That's the plan.'

'I am a worried about how we'll cope. Luke and I have trouble dealing with each other, let alone bringing someone else into the world.' I look at Max for some words of wisdom, but he is silent. 'Has Luke said anything to you – I mean, about being a dad?'

'No.'

'Deep and meaningful conversations aren't really either of your styles. Deep and silent is more like it.'

'We don't need to talk about everything in life – unlike you.' He looks across at me. 'And for the record, when Luke told me you were pregnant, he was happy. Believe it or not, he does want a family. I know it's one of his goals.'

'Luke's goal is to have a family? Was that before or after he shagged all of Chelsea?'

'Kate!'

'It's true. Declan told me what he was like before he met me. Actually, the day I met him, when I dropped off his shirts, I thought he was an arrogant arsehole who loved himself.'

'I don't understand women. Luke has a past – so what? Everyone does.'

I shrug petulantly, knowing full well Max has a valid point. Why do I keep bringing up the past and Luke's long list of fuck buddies? Even now I question why he is with me. Maybe it's the fear of losing him.

'Luke idolises you. Christ, he's put a ring on your finger, which I am still surprised at.'

'Cheers, Max, am I not good enough for him?'

'Here you go again. If you were to shut up and let me bloody finish…'

'Knock yourself out,' I say.

'As I was saying, I was surprised. Before he met you, he never bothered with long-term relationships. He worked hard—'

'And played hard,' I mutter.

He shakes his head. 'Back then he wasn't ready for a wife, let alone kids. But he is now. He fell in love with you. As for having a family, I think he will make a great father.'

'But he's so controlling.'

'He will give them the world – he does the same for you.'

'I don't need the world, just him. There's a difference.'

'That's why he married you. Kate, you make the difference.'

Bloody hell, we've gone from looking at pictures of Grayson to discussing my marriage…

'So, have you thought any more about the date?'

'No. Drop it.'

I can see Marshalls up ahead. I have Max alone for about a minute.

'I think you should just let me set you up – just once. Luke thinks it's a good idea.'

The car comes to a stop.

'Don't bullshit me. Luke would never agree. I'm quite happy, thank you.'

'We shall see!'

As soon as I enter Marshalls I spot Alexis in the far corner – alone. The restaurant is heaving. It's trendy and super-expensive; Kiki and Henry brought me here for my birthday a couple of years ago.

'Hi.'

'How was your friend – Molly?' Alexis asks.

I sit down. 'She's fine. Look.' I whizz through the twenty or so pictures on my phone.

'He is lovely.' Alexis smiles but I sense babies are not her priority. Come to think of it, they weren't for me until last week.

'Do you want kids?' I pour some sparkling water into my glass.

She shakes her head. 'Honestly, I've never given it much thought.'

'Me neither, but now I have to.'

Alexis chuckles. 'I think it's a bit late for that. I can't believe you're having twins.'

'Tell me about it.' I raise my tall glass of sparkling water. 'Here's to us.'

'Well, well, well.' We turn around. There's Charles Morley, a good friend of Alexis. 'Afternoon, ladies. Kate, Alexis told me about your car accident. Are you well?'

'I'm fine, thank you.'

'Good to hear. Apparently you have decided to bury the hatchet.'

'Life's too short.'

He takes the seat next to me and gently squeezes my hand.

'How very admirable of you, Kate. I know how testing the superbitch can be.' He winks.

I hold my finger up. 'Let me stop you there. We don't use that name any more.'

'I'm not sure about this.' He leans back in his chair. 'No, I much prefer the catty rivalry.'

'Would you like us to have a girl-on-girl fight just for your entertainment?' I offer.

'I would pay good money to see that.'

'Charles, you're supposed to be my best friend,' Alexis snaps.

'Of course, sweetie, but Kate did offer.'

'Dream on, Charles, dream on.'

'I shall. Kate, how did your investigation work out?'

Investigation. Oh crap! The investigation went well: your best friend's father killed my mother.

'I haven't really looked into it. I've been really busy with work. Harper Jones has a charity fashion show in a few weeks for Mrs Gold in New York.' I hope I've diverted him.

'How exciting,' he says.

'I'm sure you know Mrs Gold?'

'Yes, I know her quite well, and I will get a ticket.' He looks at Alexis. 'Shall we make a weekend of it? I think it will do you good to get away.'

'I'll think about it. Come round for dinner tomorrow. Bring wine,' Alexis says.

'Absolutely, we can have a sleepover. On that note, I must dash. So long, ladies.'

'I haven't told him you're pregnant.'

'It's fine. Next time you see him you can drop it into conversation; he loves a bit of gossip. What about Philip's story – the hunting trip to Russia?'

'I haven't said a word. I've only told him the story that everyone knows, but he smells a rat. Plus I told him that I had my appendix removed. I needed a reason to be bedbound.'

'And he believed it?'

'I'm not sure, but he has seen how poorly I have been, and he agreed I was too fragile to face the world. I know he is brash and—'

'I like him. I always have. It's weird, but I trust him,' I say.

She nods and takes a sip of water. 'The truth is, I am dreading his reaction when I tell him what my father did. I don't want pity. I just want to bury the past and move on.'

'Of course, but you might need someone too. Just make sure he keeps what you tell him to himself, and maybe keep Katenka out of the conversation. After all, Joseph Morley was involved in what happened to my mother. I'm not sure what part he played, but this isn't Charles's problem.'

Five minutes later, Harry arrives at the table. I sit with my new – and old – family. It doesn't take long for us to feel comfortable. Soon general chit-chat is flying around.

'Kate, I wanted to ask how you would feel if I bought out the remainder of the Bagrov and Cooper shares.'

'What, from the other shareholders? Can you do that? Have you asked them?' I have only met all the shareholders once, in New York.

'Yes, most of them. I have already made them an offer way above the asking price.'

'Oh!'

'I don't want to buy your shares, that's not what I'm asking, but I do remember you telling me that you asked Luke to take them over. Are you going ahead with that plan?'

I sit back in my chair. 'No.'

'Good, as I have a plan that involves all three of us. As I said, I have already offered the shareholders a very good price, and they have agreed to sell – they would be mad not to. Philip's estate will all come to me, therefore I may as well use it.' She looks at Harry. 'I want to give you some shares.'

'I don't want your shares or anything to do with... Look, I don't want to offend you, but I really don't want them.'

'I understand, but I thought all three of us could run the business – girl power, you know?' Alexis sips some water before she continues. 'I know you have a fantastic job. Maybe you could bring some of that to the table.'

'Insurance and art... Not really an interest of Bagrov and Cooper,' Harry says.

'It could be. Kate has a good eye for interiors. We could work together. My aim is to grow our hotel chain and buy additional companies. We could branch into art – we can do whatever we want. Besides, we won't have a man telling us how to work.'

'I like it. Harry, this could be fun. We could work together – give the men a run for their money. Let me throw my shares into the pot. Let's go for an equal partnership – a three-way split,' I say.

'Girls, please. Shares and taking over the world, how the bloody hell did we end up here?' Harry is right – how the hell did we end up here?

Alexis leans on the table. 'Think about it, Harry, please. Not for my father, but for me. Please give me a chance.' For the first time, Alexis looks settled. 'I have no family except you. I just wanted to share it with you.'

Harry takes Alexis's hand. 'You don't need to buy our friendship. We don't work that way.'

'Harry, please, I didn't mean to offend you,' Alexis says.

'I need some time to think about things. This is huge, actually it's bloody massive. I can't deny it sounds exciting.'

'There's no rush to give me an answer.'

'I didn't want to bring it up, but have you visited the cemetery yet?' I ask suddenly.

All three of us have reasons to despise him, but he was Alexis's father and she lived with him. She will need to put his death to rest.

Her eyes close. 'No… I haven't been able to face it.'

'You don't have to do it alone. We'll come with you when you're ready.' I look across at Harry for backup.

'Of course,' Harry says.

'What about now? I mean, after we have eaten,' Alexis says. 'Sorry, my timing isn't great. Forget I asked.'

Now? Crap! Am I ready?

'There's no time like the present. I'll call my boss and tell her there's a family emergency,' Harry says.

'Well, that's sorted. Max is outside. He can take us,' I say.

I stand at the kerb with Max and watch the girls slide in the back of my black Bentley.

'Are you sure about this?' Max always queries any destination that has not been cleared by Luke.

'Yes. Alexis needs to say goodbye, and I think it will do Harry good.'

'And you? I'm not sure Luke will want you to go.'

'Fine, I'll call him,' I snap at Max.

I search for 'Boss' on my phone.

'Kate.' Luke's raspy voice sends a shiver through my body.

'Hi.'

'Are you OK?'

'Yeah, I'm fine. I've agreed to take Alexis and Harry to see Philip's grave.'

There is silence.

'Luke.' I look at Max, who pre-empted Luke's reaction.

'Let me speak to Max,' he says.

'Fine.' I pass the phone over. 'Mr Control Freak wants to speak to you – maybe you should tell him to buy me a leash.'

Max takes the phone. 'Yes.' He listens, then after a couple of seconds he hands me the phone. 'He wants to speak to you.'

'Hello.'

'I'm happy for you to visit the grave, but please be safe – all three of you. Max is with you not only because I pay him but he also cares about you. You mention restraints, be careful what you wish for Mrs Sutton.'

'Funny – ha bloody ha.'

'I love you and I can't wait to see you later, as I have a strong need to take you.' Music to my ears.

'Love you too, and don't disappoint me later.'

I end the call, leaving him with a challenge that will grow all afternoon – literally!

Max begins the journey to the other side of London and the private cemetery where Philip has been laid to rest. I think hell is the most suitable resting place for him.

The girls chat in the back of the car but Max and I are quiet. Am I ready for this? Although he's dead and buried, it doesn't make it any easier.

Within half an hour we have arrived, and Max waits by the car as we make our way to plot two hundred and three. We can see the fresh soil and wreaths surrounding the grave, and we all slow down, as though he is here in person. Finally, we stand at the foot of the grave.

'Fuck! This is madness,' I say. Harry glares at me. 'What? I don't know what to say. He tried to kill me.'

'It's OK. Kate can say what she wants, and he did try to…' Alexis's words trail off. 'Harry, is there anything you want to say?'

'Er, no.'

'What about you?' I ask, but Alexis's eyes remain fixed on the ground. 'Do you want to say anything?'

'No…' She inhales deeply.

The silence between us lingers. Perhaps we do have questions, but we are hesitant about voicing them. I remember the moment I kicked him – not only for Katenka, but also for Alexis and me.

'Why?' Alexis blurts out. Startled, I look at her.

She falls to the ground and begins to dig at the earth. 'Why?'

Dirt flies up as she rakes the soil with her fingers, trying to unearth the man who ruined her life.

'Jesus, Alexis.' Harry and I join her on the ground.

'Alexis, stop,' Harry pleads.

'Why? Tell me why!' She continues to claw her way through the soil. 'Tell me, Daddy, why did you hurt me? Tell me!'

Her voice is a howl of pain, and tears layer her face, which is covered in mud.

'Alexis, please.' Harry tries to pull her. It's no use. She seems to have found some inner strength, and she continues to dig.

'Harry, take her arm.' I try to take hold of her other arm. She almost knocks me flying.

'Kate, step back! She might hurt you,' Harry hollers.

I stand up. 'Max!' I shout.

He runs over towards us from the car. 'What the hell?'

'We can't get her to stop,' I say.

He kneels down and touches her arm. She lashes out with heavy punches.

'Get off me… Don't touch me!' she screams.

'Alexis, it's us… Shhh, it's us… Look at me,' I plead.

She huddles in a ball, her head buried in her knees. 'Please don't touch me.'

Max scoops her up in his arms, rocking her trembling body like a child.

'Alexis, look at me.'

At last she glances up.

'It's us, Harry and Kate. You're safe.'

She nods, but remains curled into Max.

'Look at the bloody state of her. Shit, this has gone royally tits up.' I try to brush the mud off, but I am covered.

Harry joins me. 'She can't go home on her own. Let's take her to mine. Raymond won't mind.'

'OK. I think she needs to see a doctor.' I watch her as she hums a soft tune and tears trickle down her cheeks. I have never seen anyone so helpless.

'I'll message Luke,' Max says.

By the time we arrive at Harry and Raymond's studio apartment, it's late afternoon. The entire journey was made in silence. Max opens the doors. Alexis gets out without his aid but leans on Harry for support.

'Raymond is working late, so it'll be just us… Shower?' Harry looks at Alexis. 'Right, shower it is. Follow me.' Harry takes her through the open-plan living area and into the main bathroom. Within a few minutes she closes the door and joins us.

'What a bloody nightmare.'

I shake my head in disbelief.

'Luke messaged. Dr Jacob will be here in an hour,' Max says.

'What then?' Harry asks.

'I don't know. But she can't be left alone,' I say.

'I agree.' Harry reaches across and strokes my arm. 'Are you OK? You look really pale.'

'I feel sick.'

'Kate, I told Luke that I'll take you home. I think you need to rest.'

I glare at Max. 'I need to stay here. It's not fair leaving Harry to deal with this mess.'

'Kate, Max is right – go home, you look exhausted. It's still early days for you. Alexis can stay here until she's back on her feet.'

'It doesn't feel right leaving you.'

'We'll have a quiet evening and I'll order a takeaway. Maybe she needs normality – which I can do. But…' Harry looks away. 'I can't talk about him. It feels too raw.'

'Of course it does! That's why I can't leave you to deal with her.'

'Harry can take care of Alexis. Dr Jacob will be here shortly.'

'Max is right. I promise to call you when the doctor leaves.'

'Fine.' I turn to Max. 'Looks like Luke's wish has been granted – again.'

The warm water washes over my body, washing away the mud and this afternoon's horrendous events. After spending too long under the heat I step out of the shower, wrap myself in a warm towel and wipe the mirror. I look exhausted and I feel emotionally drained. My scars will heal and fade, but the scars Alexis has will never heal. I hope in time she can find some peace. I have a pounding headache. Sleep is my only option. I slip under the bed covers and close my eyes.

The softness of a hand on my cheek wakes me. Luke is lying on top of the bed in shorts and T-shirt. His hair is wet.

'Hi.'

'How long have I been asleep? What's the time?' Our room is dimly lit by the evening sun.

'Seven o'clock. You were asleep when I arrived home.'

'Oh.'

'It sounds like you needed it.'

I sit up. 'I need to call Harry.'

'She called earlier.'

I frown. 'Why didn't you wake me?'

'You need to rest, and after today, so does Alexis.'

'Luke, please.' I roll my eyes. 'I don't need you to decide what I do and don't need. I've had it up to here.' My hand gestures towards the top of my head.

'I just care about you.'

'I'm not questioning that, but I need to breathe.'

Luke's soft lips tenderly meet mine.

'This afternoon was awful. I've never seen anything like it.'

'Max said she was in a bad way.'

'He was good with her, but Christ, Luke, she was digging at the sick bastard's grave.'

He takes a breath. 'That must have been awful. But my priority is you and our babies.'

He pulls the covers back and lifts my T-shirt, placing his lips on my stomach. 'Is Mummy still grouchy?'

'Oi – I'm not grouchy, I just feel helpless.'

'You're helping Alexis through this difficult period of her life, which is selfless of you, but you can't change what's happened. She is the only person that can heal her wounds.'

'I can try and help.'

'Of course, but I need you to think about yourself too.'
'I know. I know you're just looking out for me.'
His lips glide slowly across my sensitive skin to my ear.
'I'm going to make love to you,' he whispers.
There is no challenge – he has me every time.

10

Thursday arrives and Luke and I sit side by side as the plane soars into the sky. After a stopover at LAX we get on another flight: it's around eight hours before we reach Tahiti. I take a deep breath and close my eyes. I don't like flying. I'm always grateful when I land, but for the next eight hours Luke will hold my hand – I guess that will have to do.

We are offered another plane meal. I feel nauseous – air sickness or because I'm pregnant? Luke turns our upright seats into beds, and we lie facing each other. His eyes close before mine: it's a rare treat to watch him sleep.

'Kate.' I hear my name, followed by a gentle stroke on my cheek.

'One hour left. I've ordered you some tea.'

'Hmm.' I stretch my arms above my head, and a pain shoots through me like a knife. 'Ow – shit.'

'Let me look.' Luke is already lifting my black T-shirt. 'It looks fine. It's probably internal scar tissue.'

'OK, Dr Sutton.' I giggle. 'Actually, you missed a small, yet very painful, area here.' I point to my lips.

'Is that so?' Luke seals his words with a kiss.

I insert my tongue into his mouth, hunting for my delicious sex god. His response is instant. He pulls away, wearing the most fuckable smile – a Sutton smile that gets me every time.

'Are you horny?' he whispers.

'Bet your arse I am, Dr Sutton. Actually, there are a few other areas that need some attention.'

Luke grins. 'I have a feeling the next two weeks are going to be fun.'

The last plane we board is from Papeete, the capital of Tahiti. From here it's only fifty minutes to paradise. The view from the plane window is breath-taking – blue lagoons stretch for miles.

The final leg of our journey from Motu Airport is on board a large catamaran. Paradise is the only word to describe the view: a desert island surrounded by clear turquoise water. We sit at the rear of the boat and the sun beats downs on us. Can life get any better?

The boat moors at a sizeable dock. Once the vessel is secured we are escorted from the catamaran to the hotel reception, where we are greeted with live music and beautiful Polynesian leis. Travelling for so long now seems worth it: for the first time in weeks I start to feel relaxed.

Luke checks in, then we are taken from the hotel lobby to our home for the next two weeks. Although Luke showed me the brochure and various pictures online, I am still overwhelmed. There is not a camera known to mankind that can capture this view. Slowly, I walk to the waiting golf cart, suddenly exhausted.

Seconds later, we arrive at a wooden walkway and are shown to our room, which perches on stilts over the ocean. A member of staff opens the door and Luke scoops me up in his arms.

'Luke!'

'Don't argue with me, Mrs Sutton.'

I giggle and clasp my hands around his neck while he carries me through the doorway and speaks to a member of staff in French, their native language. Win-win for me, fourteen days listening to Luke's sexy French accent. I scan the bungalow.

'Wow, this is amazing,' I say.

'It's perfect.' Luke carries me towards the glass doors and lowers me to the deck.

We are in the last bungalow in a row. Directly in front of us is a private plunge pool and beyond that is the calm turquoise ocean. It's a perfect picture of serenity.

'It's stunning.' I lean against Luke.

'Look.' He points into the distance. 'That's Mount Otemanu.'

'It's huge.'

'It is.'

Leaving Luke, I crouch down beside the plunge pool and swirl my fingers through the still clear water. There's a large, comfortable-looking daybed layered with cushions on a slightly raised deck area with a huge canopy offering shelter from the sun. I am at a loss. Do I jump on the bed or strip naked for a swim?

Feeling hot, I begin to undress. Within a few seconds I am completely naked. Luke watches the show wearing a smile. How long will he wait? I move to the edge of the pool and place one foot in the water.

'Would you care to join me?'

The sun may be warm but the cool water is fresh. The combination is tantalising; my nipples are instantly erect.

'Are you coming in or are you just going to stare?' I wait patiently for a response.

A knock at the door prevents him from answering.

'I suggest you lower yourself into the water. That will be our luggage.'

I submerse myself up to my shoulders. I can safely stand. I watch Luke direct the staff to carry our luggage through the lounge and into our bedroom. Once he has tipped them he comes back outside.

'I think you need to cool down.' I laugh at the sight of the bulge pushing against his trousers.

Silently, he strips and steps into the pool, disappearing under the waterline. Next I'm met with a delicious sensation on my clit: the sweet touch of Luke's tongue. Fuck, that feels good, but I guess he will need to breathe at some point. He pops up in front of me.

'I would have thought, with all your military training, you would be able to hold your breath for a bit longer.'

Instantly his mouth is on mine fiercely kissing me. God, I love a frustrated Sutton. It's clear he needs to fuck me.

Luke's hand slides between my legs and he inserts two fingers inside me. I surrender to him. I grip his erection, which is pressing against my pelvis.

'I need you, Luke.'

His lips respond, kissing my jaw, slowly working towards my mouth.

My hands cup his arse, drawing him closer and my legs automatically link around his torso. At last I feel his erection at my sex. He gradually slides inside me, slowly, inch by inch, until I have all of him.

'Breathe, Kate.'

'I need more, Luke.'

His hips begin to move, not with haste, but each thrust is skilled, making contact exactly where I need it.

Our eyes lock: dark and contented meet dark and delighted.

'Touch yourself. I want you to come quickly.'

'Why?'

He nibbles my jaw. 'Kate, I want to fuck you in every corner of this property, but you're exhausted. So please touch yourself.'

My hand slides down between the lips of my sex. With just a stroke against my sensitive clit I feel almost ready to orgasm. From nowhere it hits me: the rush of heat from within breaks out across my exposed skin, and the coolness of the water has no effect. The water ripples around us. I feel weightless and delirious.

'Oh God.' The first wave is intense. 'Luke, I'm coming.'

'Jesus, Kate, I'm coming hard.'

After a few moments he stops. Yes, I can confirm the plunge pool is a good place for a Sutton fuck.

'I love it here, Luke.'

'Yes, it does have something to offer.' He gives me that Sutton smile that knocks me on my arse every time.

'Are you hungry?' I ask.

'Yes. For food, and you.' His eyes gleam, he looks happy. My legs uncurl and Luke is free.

'So, am I your sex slave for the next two weeks?' I ask.

'Sounds good.'

Luke sinks under the cool water and emerges at the steps. Holy shit, he looks hot. Droplets of water cascade down his perfectly toned body. And he is mine for the next two weeks – this feels like heaven.

He collects towels from the daybed.

'Out you get. I need to feed you.'

'Yes, you do.' I swim across to the steps and Luke wraps me in a large white towel. Exhaustion takes over and I yawn.

'Food, then bed.'

'What time is it?' Although the sun is still up, it is low on the horizon.

'Four thirty in the afternoon.'

We head towards the main living area of the bungalow. 'What time are the restaurants open?'

'I ordered our meal to be served here this evening.'

I look across at him. 'When?'

'When we checked in. I knew you would be tired.'

I follow Luke into the bedroom. 'Why do I have a feeling that you would rather we eat here every night?'

'Perfect idea.' His dark eyes meet mine.

'I'm not under house arrest.' I remove my towel and walk to the window. 'Look at this view.'

'It's stunning, probably my favourite.'

I turn to see him lying on the bed, stark naked, watching my arse.

'Very funny.'

The bungalow is open-plan. It's wood-panelled, with white and cream linens and a pop of colour from the various tropical floral displays. It faces the ocean and has a perfect view of Mount Otemanu. Paradise is the only way to describe it.

I feel compelled to join Luke on the bed. I collapse face down next to him and feel tiredness seeping through me. He lies on his side and slowly runs his fingers up and down my spine.

'Hmmm – I can't move.'

'Then don't.'

My eyes open to see him watching me.

'Are you OK?' I ask.

'Why wouldn't I be? I just had sex with my beautiful wife while looking at the most beautiful view.'

'Kiss me,' I say.

He begins at my neck, making his way down my spine with affection although the bite on my arse causes me to squeal and laugh. By the time he reaches my feet, my body yearns for him to touch me where I need it. As ever he reads my mind. He spreads my legs, allowing his fingers to delve between them. My breathing changes at his touch. Even though I'm exhausted I can't help feeling compelled to accept the waves of pleasure.

Luke flips me onto my back and within seconds his mouth is on me again, continuing what he started in the pool. Working slowly, he holds me in a perpetual state of impending pleasure. My hands grip the cotton bedspread. I hope he will do what I want.

This time his fingers slide inside me while his mouth increases its pressure and speed against my clit. For the second time I'm lost as I climax. Then I feel him slide deep inside me.

'Why do I need you so much? If you ever leave me…' His words trail off, and his hips slow.

'Never, Luke, this is forever, I promise.' His rhythm may be unhurried but the connection between us at this moment is electric. 'I love you.'

'I love you too.'

His hips begin to work and his mouth meets mine. This time our kiss is slow and lingering, as though it's the first time we have kissed. Time stands still as he takes us both on another journey, and as he plunges deeper inside me I feel the eruption of yet another orgasm.

My eyes lock on his as I watch him come. His breathing shallows and his mouth opens slightly. This is the real Luke Sutton, stripped back and mine – forever.

It's early evening. Luke closes the double doors to our bedroom, allowing me to get dressed while our meal is laid out on the table. Once again I hear the sexy sound of Monsieur Sutton speaking French. I take a deep breath and have a stern word with my libido: twice, with jet lag, is enough for any woman! What's the point? I need him again. Shit, the doctor was right: pregnancy has increased my sex drive. Luke may have to tie me – and, of course, my libido – to the nearest palm tree.

'Kate,' he calls.

'Coming.' I laugh inwardly and slide open the doors.

The table looks amazing – not just the food but the candles and flowers. Luke stands holding a chair for me.

'Wow. You look amazing.'

'Do you like it? I've been saving it for a special occasion.' I twirl in my small black lace nightdress. I am not sure I can call it a nightdress, as it's incredibly short – actually, it barely hides my matching knickers. 'Dinner smells good.' I sit down. 'This looks so pretty.'

'I told you, we don't need a restaurant.'

I tilt my head, breaking down his words. 'No, you don't want to mingle.'

'I don't see the point in making idle chit-chat with people I have no interest in. Here I can look at you – and what you're wearing. What would you call that?'

'A nightdress.'

'Baby, that is not a nightdress. There will be no sleeping while you're wearing that. It's a dick magnet.'

'You really need to learn some self-control.'

Mission completed. He needs me again.

It's safe to say we both need a distraction – food.

'There's too much here to choose from. What are you going for?'

'I ordered a selection. You choose first, and I'll have what's left.'

'Good idea.' With Luke's appetite, there will be no food left.

I have the asparagus risotto to start, which is deliciously creamy. I avoid the fish and decide to have the Angus steak. I close my eyes for a second as I chew the steak, and it melts in my mouth. God, I was hungry.

I sit back in my chair, absorbing the first night of our honeymoon. 'This feels perfect.' I gaze towards the decking, which is strewn with lanterns. Everywhere looks incredibly romantic. I could cry.

He nods, his mouth full.

'I know that I'm pregnant but can we have one glass of bubbly – just to celebrate us?'

Luke stops eating and takes a breath.

'I want to celebrate, and one glass won't hurt me.'

He gets up, takes a bottle from the cooling cabinet and fills two flutes.

'Cheers, husband. Here's to our wedding and to many more happy memories.' My free hand sweeps across my stomach. 'For all of us.'

'Cheers, baby. I love you.'

'I love you too.' The chilled champagne hits my lips. 'Wow – this is to die for.'

'Don't get used to it.' He chuckles – but he's serious.

'I'll always remember tonight.' I scan the table. 'We have done quite well.'

'You mean I've done well? You, on the other hand, have barely eaten… I'm watching you. Do you feel OK?'

'I'm full, plus I feel punch-drunk.'

'Jet lag.'

I nod and yawn.

'Bed.'

I yawn again. 'I know I've dressed for…'

'To tease me.'

'True.'

Luke comes over to my chair and scoops me up in his arms. I could get used to this!

'Perhaps you could wear this outfit again another day.'

I laugh and lean my head against his chest. 'You're on.'

We stand side by side brushing our teeth. Afterwards Luke takes my hand and we slide into bed. I close my eyes and listen to the water lapping under the bungalow, and within a few minutes, I hear the perfect sound of Luke sleeping.

My eyes open. For a brief moment I feel disorientated, but then I hear the sound of the ocean slapping against the wooden stilts. We're in Bora Bora. The bed is empty, but I can hear him talking. I slip on a hotel robe and head outside. The sky is still dark, with the vague hint of sunrise in the horizon. He looks up as I pad towards him. I wave, not wanting to disturb his phone call. Soon he ends the call.

'You're working?'

'Not really, just a few calls to London.' He closes his laptop and rests it on the table. 'Did I wake you?'

I shake my head. 'No.' I lean over the banister surrounding the bungalow. 'God, it's so amazing here.' I turn to face him. 'What's the time?'

Luke looks at his watch. 'Four forty. Have you not altered your watch?'

'No, I have you to tell me the time.'

Luke makes room so I can join him on the daybed.

'What time did you wake up?'

'Three thirty, thanks to jet lag.'

'You're going to feel like shit later.'

He shakes his head. 'God, I love your mouth!'

'I know you do. That's why you married me. I'll make a drink – do you want one?'

'You sit and I'll make it,' he offers.

'No, I like taking care of you.'

I came prepared. I brought world peace – that is, tea bags – in my luggage.

I return to Luke, who is sitting quietly. It's strange to see him so rested.

'Here.' I pass him his tea and from my robe pocket I produce a packet of digestives, which I place between us.

Luke chuckles. 'I bring you to Bora Bora and you brought tea and biscuits.'

'Of course!'

He leans across and kisses me tenderly. 'You're just a homely girl.'

We lie in silence, drinking our tea and listening to the ocean. The sky is already lightening in the east. The night sky is losing its denseness and sunrise is fast approaching on what I imagine will be a magnificent day.

I place our mugs on the floor and rest my head on Luke's chest, listening to his heart beating.

'Tell me something about you that I don't know.' I raise my head and look at him.

'There's nothing to tell. You know more about me than anyone else.'

'There must be something.'

'If you're looking for information on my past relationships, forget it.'

I frown. 'That's not what I meant. Besides, they weren't relationships; they were mainly one-night stands, and you can keep those stories to yourself. I still can't believe you used to tie someone up.'

Luke chuckles. 'You can't have an opinion on something unless you've tried it.'

'OK, this conversation is not going to plan. Now I have a very disturbed image in my head.' I sigh. Of course I'm bloody jealous.

'Kate, I didn't have a connection with her… Yes, she was a model but she wasn't—'

'What?' I look up again. 'You never said she was a model.'

'There seemed no point.' He runs his hands through my hair.

'Er, I think there is a point. So you mean to tell me Miss Whiplash was a model? Well, this just gets better. Bloody hell, look what you ended up with – the girl next door who's getting fatter by the day.' Give me a gun!

'Christ, Kate.'

'What?' I bite back.

'Look at me.'

'No.' Petulant Mrs Sutton is lying on the bed.

He laughs. 'Kate. I love you. You're stunning and fucking hot – hotter than any girl I have ever been with.'

'I can't help the way I feel, Luke.'

'It's in the past, Kate. You're my world, you know that. Not just you but our family.'

'I know, I'm being stupid. I get jealous. There will always be a part of me wondering.'

'Wondering?'

'Like-minded people and all that. Am I good enough for the powerful Mr Luke Sutton?'

He runs his hands through my hair. 'I've told you, Kate, I never saw you coming. It's me and you against the world, OK?'

I nod.

'Do you understand how hard it will be for me to watch you parade around in a bikini?'

'Don't be ridiculous.'

'That's my point. You have this power over me.'

'If we're talking about heat, you are burning hot, and you know it.'

'It's not the same,' he says and raises his brow.

'Of course it is. You could have any woman you wanted.' Undoubtedly he has.

'May I remind you that other men find you attractive? Bradley Taylor is a perfect example.'

True! He did want to carry me to his bed.

'I would never be unfaithful to you.'

'That may be so, but he wanted you.'

Jesus. What have I started? I only wanted to know something deeper about my husband.

I move next to him. 'Tell me about Paul.'

Luke takes a breath and closes his eyes. Even now, talking about the death of his best friend is painful. I stroke his cheek sympathetically.

'Sorry, I shouldn't have asked. I just wondered what he was like, and I couldn't ask Max.' How did Max ever get over losing his son?

'The truth is, I don't think about him.'

'Is that because it hurts too much?'

'Maybe. I blocked him from my mind after the incident... And then I was thrown into a completely different world, and I had very little time to think of him or what had happened.'

'The army? And was that the best thing for you?'

'At the time I had reservations. I questioned Max's motives. Christ, I was seventeen. He dumped me at the army barracks in Hereford. I was the closest person he had.'

I kiss him gently. 'Max was protecting you.'

'I know that now. At the time, I was angry with the world.' He sighs.

'You were entitled to be, Luke. Christ, they killed your best friend.'

'Nothing to what Max was going through.'

'It must be awful to lose a son.'

'Paul was a lot of fun.'

'Not like Max,' I say.

Luke grins and shakes his head. 'No, nothing like Max. Well, that's not strictly true. Max would do anything for me, and for you. Paul had the same trait.'

'He sounds lovely.'

'We had some good times and some… interesting times. We got up to stuff, just teenagers pushing our luck.'

'He looked like Max.'

Luke nods.

'He would have loved you. In fact, he would have tried his luck with you. A down-to-earth girl like you would be his type. He hated the Chelsea crowd.'

'I wish I could have met him.'

Luke touches my face.

'The man who owned SGI back then. What was his name… Anderson – right? Where is he?'

Luke looks at me, alarmed. 'Why do you ask?'

'Is it unfinished business, Luke? I mean, he killed Paul – well, not literally but…'

He takes a breath. Have I hit a nerve, or is there something else?

'You don't need to worry about him.'

'Oh. I…' What's up, Sutton? 'Luke, you can talk to me.'

He's silent, but I see something else. It never occurred to me that Luke might be looking for him. Perhaps he wants to settle the score.

'There is nothing to say.' His words float in the air, but I don't believe him.

'Have you got over Russia? I see the look on your face every time I mention it,' I say.

'Baby, you're safe. That's all I need. When I think what you went through, Kate, it crushes me.' He bites his lip. 'You were so brave.'

'I don't think I'm brave. I was shit-scared, Luke… And Ivor's visit?'

'I don't trust him,' Luke announces.

I smile. 'I know.'

'Don't ask me to, not yet. He has to earn my trust. I understand what he means to you, but I need time.'

'I would feel the same if it were you. It's hard to explain, but I trust him.'

★★★

'Come on. You promised me a day with other human beings.'

'We went on a boat trip yesterday and to the town, plus an evening on the beach.'

'Alone, Luke, we were alone.'

'Besides, I never agreed to anything.'

'Yes, you did. Last night, when we got back from dinner, you said we'd spend today on the beach and at the pool.'

'Baby, you misinterpreted my words.' He slips his T-shirt over his head while I wait, a beach bag in my hand, ready to leave.

'No I didn't. We've barely left the bungalow. All we've done is eat, sleep and sunbathe naked.'

'Just the way I like you.'

I open the door. 'I'll go on my own.' I wedge the door with my foot as I wait.

Luke sighs and gives in.

The beach is our home for the day. Luke arranges two sunbeds and a parasol a fair distance from civilisation – and other people. I slip off my cover-up to reveal a white bikini with a glossy cream snakeskin pattern. It's minuscule.

Luke glares. 'Is that it?'

'I've been naked every bloody day. To be honest, I'm feeling a little overdressed, so yes, this is it! Come on, Mr Irrational Sutton, let's go for a swim in the pool.'

We walk hand in hand across the pure white sand, the sun beating down on us, and head to the large pool. It's incredibly tranquil, with guests lazing around sunbathing and quietly swimming. Luke keeping a firm grip on my hand, we step into the water and begin to leisurely swim the length of the pool.

'See, this is not so bad. The other human beings aren't bothering us. They're enjoying their holiday.'

'Give it time. Some arsehole will assume we want to be friends.'

'Cynic.'

'Realist.' His lips make contact with mine, purely an alpha male display. I swim away. He swims after me, pulling at my feet and grabbing my arse, making me laugh.

Having spent most of the day on the beach, after lunch I insist on taking a walk. We head towards the snorkelling area, which is supposed to be amazing.

Having got over the fact I will have to swim with the fish, I immerse my face in the water to gain a greater understanding of marine life. Luke is excellent – I wish I could say the same! Within an hour we are heading back to our sunbeds.

'What did you think?'

'The water was crystal clear, and I swallowed a lot of it.'

'Yes, I'm aware of your love of swallowing,' he says, laughing.

I slap his arm. 'Luke!'

His laugh is contagious.

'I have my moments.'

He leans to me and plants a kiss on my lips. 'Yes, you do… Can you scuba dive?'

'No. Honestly, all those fish.' I grimace at the thought. 'It's not for me. What about you?'

He nods. 'I'm a qualified rescue diver. It was part of my job.'

'Of course.' Why does this not surprise me? 'Actually, I am amazed they never taught you how to cook.'

'That's why I need you.' He snakes his arm around my waist, drawing me closer as we walk.

'Why don't you book a dive?' I say.

'No.'

'Why not? You book a dive and I'll get a back massage.'

No response.

'Luke, I mean it. If you don't book it I'll do it for you.' I yank his arm. 'Luke.' My voice becomes stern. Wow, the Sutton in me makes an appearance.

'OK.'

Shit, it worked. Now I need to remember the tone I used. But I know that Luke would only surrender if he wanted to.

He leaves me alone to book our day tomorrow. I leave a gift for him on the sun lounger. Fifteen minutes later he returns and picks up the gift bag.

'A little something for my controlling husband.'

'Caring.' He sits down and pulls out a book. 'Five thousand baby names. Are you kidding?'

'You seem like you need a job.' I giggle.

His hand skims my stomach then wanders further up, slipping under my bikini top and caressing my breasts. 'I have one.'

'You do?'

'Yes, fucking my wife.'

How can such vulgarity cause my clit to twinge? Jesus Christ, where's that bloody palm tree? I feel I might need to be restrained!

'Kate, Kate.'

My eyes reluctantly open to Luke touching my cheek.

'What time is it?'

'Seven o'clock. I need to leave.'

A wave of nausea washes over me. I bolt out of bed and make it to the bathroom just in time.

'Baby, are you OK?' Tenderly, Luke strokes my back.

I stand up. 'I'm better now.' I go to the sink and brush my teeth.

'I think I should stay here with you, just in case.'

'Oh no you don't. Please go and enjoy yourself, but can you cancel my massage? I'm going back to bed.'

'I'm not happy about leaving you.'

'Luke, you're never happy about leaving me.'

'Promise me you'll stay here and rest. There's breakfast waiting for you in the other room – breads and fruit.'

I kiss him then slip back into bed. 'Go and have some fun. I love you.'

After a lazy morning, I feel a little bored. I decide to visit the pool and have some lunch.

Another day means another bikini: this time it's khaki, with an oversized white linen shirt on top. I leave a note for Luke.

Dear husband,

   Feeling hungry, so you will find me by the pool.
   I hope you had a wonderful time, and I can't wait to
hear all about it.
   Love you,
   Your wife and two babies xxx

I head towards the pool area, which seems busier than yesterday. A member of staff finds a bed for me, and I peruse the menu then order a chicken Caesar salad and a fruit cocktail. While eating I skim through a pregnancy book Luke brought with him. I glance at the birth section and the graphic images but decide I'm not ready for this. I opt for five thousand baby names instead.

As the sun beats down on my body, I start feeling a little too hot. Slowly, I walk into the pool, acclimatising my body before I swim. After a few lengths I sit on the side, my legs dangling in the water, while the sun dries my skin. Nearby is a neighbouring holidaymaker. We make eye contact.

'Hi.'

'Hello,' I respond.

'Another amazing day.' He has an American accent. He's maybe in his early forties. He has dark hair with a generous amount of grey running through it. Just an average man.

'Every day is amazing here.'

'You're British?'

'Yes, and you're obviously American?' I ask. He seems friendly.

'Yeah, from Boston.'

'Oh – I've never been to Boston.'

He offers me his hand. 'Daryl Forrester.'

'Kate Sutton.'

'Let me guess – honeymoon?'

'Yes, and you?'

'Anniversary, except my wife is sick in bed… Too much sun and a little too much champagne.'

'Oh no, I hope she gets better soon. You don't want to waste good weather like this.'

'Where's your husband?'

'Scuba diving. He should be back soon.'

We chat for a while. He has been married for five years, has a two-year-old son, and works for a bank. However, it seems bizarre to explain that I am trying to release a clothing line. I mention that Luke owns a business too.

From the corner of my eye I spot a body slide in the water and swim under the water towards me. Suddenly he surfaces.

'Luke.' How very apt that he should appear like an Adonis rising from the sea of love, with water running down his tanned torso!

'Kate.'

Our dark eyes meet and his lips claim mine. I know him, and the meaning behind the hot, lingering kiss.

'How was it?'

'Good.'

'Sorry. Luke, this is Daryl Forrester from Boston, his wife is ill in bed… Daryl, Luke Sutton, my husband.'

'Good to meet you, Luke.' He holds his hand out to a reluctant Luke.

'You too, Daryl. I'm sorry to hear your wife is unwell. Would you mind if I borrowed mine?'

'I need to check on Zoe. Catch up with you soon.'

'Hope she's OK.'

With that, Daryl gets up and leaves.

Luke has my attention. His firm grip on my hips and his dark lustrous eyes tell me he wants me. Already my body tenses, knowing how this will play out.

'I needed some lunch and a walk.' Why am I justifying myself?

'You could have ordered room service.' He kisses me hard.

I pull away. 'You're crossing over to the dark side.'

He looks frustrated. 'Fuck. I can't explain how I feel.'

'Tell me.'

'Get up. We're leaving.'

'What?'

'Unless you want me to fuck you in this pool, I suggest you move, because I need you now.'

I drape my arms across his shoulders. 'What if I don't want to?'

'Then I will carry you.'

I laugh. 'Christ, Luke, where is your self-control?'

'Move. If I wait any longer, I will fucking come.' His lip curls and his dark eyes are on fire. I control this part of Luke: my finger is on his pulse. He needs me more than anything else in life. Perfect.

A few minutes later we are walking down the wooden path to our door. Our bungalow is secluded so I begin to untie my bikini top.

'What the fuck are you doing?'

I pull Luke to me, allowing skin-to-skin contact, my breasts against his wet bare chest.

'I'm sure this is what you want.'

'Yes, but for my eyes only…'

'I suggest you open the door.' I step away and untie my bottoms.

He unlocks the door, pulls me through and slams the door. Seconds later, his wet shorts are on the floor.

'Fuck, this is what you do to me.' He takes his erection and begins to slide his hand up and down the thick shaft. Stop drooling, Kate!

I clear my throat. 'Self-inflicted.'

'You have all the power, Kate.' He takes a step towards me, closing the gap between us, continuing to play with himself.

'Are you feeling horny?' I ask. My stomach contracts and I feel dangerously close to coming.

He kisses me hard. My body responds to his aggressive touch: my nipples peak and dampness builds between my thighs.

'Fuck, you scare me, Kate. What you make me want to do to you.'

'Then do it. I'm not stopping you.'

He swiftly turns me and takes hold of my breasts, manipulating my nipples, gently squeezing and tweaking them until my breathing hitches. My head falls backwards to his chest and his lips make contact with my ear.

'Promise me, if this hurts your wound, tell me…'

'Shh. Just take me, Luke,' I whisper.

With no further debate he pushes my body towards the table. My bare breasts meet the cool wood. Luke dots kisses down my spine, slides his fingers inside my sex, then spreads my juices to my clit and my arse. *Oh God, my body is on fire. Touch me, Luke – everywhere.*

At last I feel his erection at my sex. One thrust and he's in. Slowly he begins to slide back and forth, going deeper with every thrust. I push my arse closer to him, needing more.

One hand runs up my spine to my neck while the other continues to gently touch my clit before skimming across my arse. Christ, I need more. Again I push my hips back towards him.

'Patience.'

'Patience, my arse.'

'Arse.' He laughs. 'You only had to ask.'

There are no more words. Luke begins to ride me harder, pulling himself out only to slam back into me. His hand continues to touch my clit and the other now plays at the entrance of my arse. I pray for his touch.

Eventually he inserts his thumb.

'Oh, Luke.'

'Does it feel good? Tell me, Kate, or I'll stop.'

There are no words when you zone out with pleasure. Luke removes his thumb and slows down the thrusting. Bastard.

'Luke.' Is that enough?

He leans forward and caresses my spine with his lips. 'Tell me, Kate.' His voice is low and sexy.

'Touch me,' I say.

'Where?'

'Oh, for fuck's sake, you know where.'

'Temper… I sense your frustration.'

I try to move but he holds me – not only physically but also in a state of sexual torment.

'Tell me where and I will touch you.'

'My arse.'

His hand returns, tormenting me.

'Do you like this?'

I try to nod.

'Sorry. I didn't hear you.'

'Yes, I like it.'

'Good.' His thumb returns, slowly tormenting me. 'Like this, Kate?'

'Yes.'

Even though I agree, he removes it.

'Beg, Kate! Beg for an orgasm. Beg for me to touch your arse until you come on my dick.'

I am going to fucking knock him out. At this rate I will come from sheer excitement alone.

'Please, Luke, don't stop. I need to come.'

No sooner have the words left my lips than he starts to thrust, hard and fast. He slides his forefinger and middle finger into my arse, his other hand moving in tantalising circular movements against my clit.

The climb is like no other. Reaching the peak of euphoric pleasure has never been this exhausting. Maybe delayed gratification is why it's so intense.

'Shit, Luke, I need to come – now!'

'I'm with you. Fuck, Kate, I'm going to take you harder.'

I don't care how he takes me, so long as he doesn't stop. Shockwaves ripple out from my core, totally obliterating my senses.

'Luke,' I manage to say. My head feels heavy against the table, and my body remains motionless.

He removes his fingers and continues to slam against my arse. 'Jesus, Kate, your body is on fire… I'm coming.' He does, thick and fast. Moments later, he stops and lowers his head to my back, catching his breath. He slides out. Droplets of cum trickle down my thighs.

He pulls me into his arms, kissing me lovingly. How can he be sensitive and yet so sexually brutal within seconds?

'What you do to me, Kate, I can't explain it. I need you so much. You put a spell on me.' I can't but look at his erection, which remains hard. We have equal parts to play in this possessive relationship.

'Back at you, Luke.'

'Are you OK?'

'Honestly, I'm fine. I just have you running down my leg.'

His lips curl. 'How I love your honesty.'

'It's the only way I can be with you.'

'May that never alter.'

'Do you like it when I touch your arse?

'Maybe.' I close my eyes for a second.

'Baby, look at me.'

My eyes open to his warm gaze. 'I enjoy it. Is that what you want to hear?'

'Kate, I intend to look after all your needs.'

I nod.

'Talk to me, tell me what you enjoy.'

'I didn't know I liked it until…'

He kisses me, but as he pulls away I see something else in his eyes, almost like a dark cloud.

'Tell me,' I say.

'Tell you what?' He touches my cheek.

'What's in your head, Sutton.'

'You.'

'No, there's something else. I can read you, and you had the same look when we were in the hospital and the other morning out on the decking when we were talking about Paul and that man Anderson.'

'I have work on my mind.'

'No. Something else.'

'What we just did… If I lost you.' His eyes close. 'I have never felt like this, Kate, and it scares me.'

'You'll never lose me.' I watch him closely.

'I just want to protect you.'

Yeah, right, Sutton. You are definitely holding out on me.

'OK, so you have three days left to protect me in every inch of this bungalow. I want the full platinum service.'

He laughs, thank God. 'Platinum service.'

'Yep, I mean it. Twenty-four seven Sutton-style protection begins here.' I point to my lips. 'I love you, Luke.'

Again our eyes lock. Dark and withholding information meet dark and I see you Sutton.

11

'You both look well.'

'Thanks, Max. Did you miss us? Two weeks of bliss without us, right?'

'Kate, get in the car, you're getting wet.' There's no mistake we're home – not just because of the miserable weather, but Luke also seems to have left his charm in Bora Bora. Surely that's enough of a reason to return.

The journey from Heathrow Airport took ages due to the busy traffic, but I never tire of London's hustle and bustle. Eventually we arrive at the palace.

Home sweet home – there is nothing in the world quite like it. I walk through to the kitchen.

'Kate, you're home.' Rosie makes her way towards me. 'Let me look at you! You have a lovely colour. Was the resort as beautiful as the brochure?'

'It didn't do it justice. Honestly, it was like I had stepped into another world.' I turn to see Luke enter the kitchen. 'Luke, tell Rosie how magical it was.'

'Impressive.' Short and not so sweet! He turns and

exits the kitchen.

'And how are you all?' She lays her hand across my stomach.

'OK. I had a couple of mornings when I felt sick. Pleased to be home. The flight was really long.'

'You both look rested, which is exactly what you needed.'

'Tell me, how is Adam?' I head towards the kettle. I need tea and the compulsory return-from-holiday bacon sandwich.

'He's fine.'

'What about Jerry?'

She takes a seat on the stool. 'Better than I thought, but Adam goes home in two days.'

'Bloody hell, that's flown by. I guess we've been away for most of it.'

'We had a marvellous day yesterday, sight-seeing in London, just Adam and me, plus Barney.'

I look up from making the tea. 'Barney?'

'Yeah. Oh, Kate, he was hilarious. He and Adam seem to be getting on really well.'

'I can imagine.' I can bloody imagine – but he promised to behave himself. 'Good, I'm glad that you've managed to spend some quality time together. So what now? Has he said anything about coming back?'

'Well, between you and me, he met up with an old work colleague he's known since university, who has offered Adam a job here in London.'

I stop. 'Really?'

'I'm trying not to think about it.'

'Don't get your hopes up, just in case. I mean, it sounds as though he has an amazing job that would be pretty tough to give up.'

'That's what Barney said.'

There's that name again. I wonder what he's been up to.

'Either way, he's back in your life for good.'

Shortly after, balancing two plates and two mugs in my hands, I walk through to Luke's office, but he's already busy.

'Here.' I place the mug and plate on his desk.

'Thank you.'

'I thought you'd be hungry.'

He nods and takes a large bite of his sandwich.

'We've only been home for two minutes and already we seem to be back to normal.'

He looks up. 'Sorry. I have some calls to make.'

'That's fine. I think Sutton Global can have you back. I need a rest.' Which is true.

'Come here,' he says and pulls me to his lap. 'Honestly, I wish we were back in our bungalow. That's a first for me, not wanting to work.'

My arms lock around his neck. 'It's been the best time of my life.'

'Back at you... Listen, I need to go to the office. I thought I would be able to delay it for one more day, but I can't.'

'That's fine.' The back of my hand glides across his bristly face. 'You look tired.'

'I am, so I won't be long.'

'OK. I need to unpack and I'm desperate for a bath.'

'Wait for me.'

'I'll try. I want to call Mum and Harry, let them know we're alive. Make sure you call your parents too.'

I stand up and he joins me, collecting documents from his desk.

'The boss turning up in jeans and a polo shirt, what will your employees think?'

'Element of surprise. They're not expecting me.'

My body sinks into a warm bath. I am officially home, where I feel safe and secure.

'We're home, babies.' I laugh at myself, but strangely talking to my babies feels natural.

I reach for my mobile, feeling the need to chat to Barney. I hit send. It only rings for a few seconds.

'Well, if it isn't my favourite Sutton girl.'

'Hi, how are you?'

'Yeah, good. How was Bora Bora? Did Luke wear you out?'

'Oi, cheeky. Actually, he bloody did.' We laugh. He did, and I have no reason to lie. Barney understands that Luke's appetite for me is a little … off the chart.

'You sound happy, babe. That was just what you both needed. No Russians or sick fuckers, just the two of you and some sun.'

'Thanks, Barney. I know Luke still has issues with Russia, and Ivor.' And possibly something else that he won't talk about.

'You can't blame him, Kate. You really don't know Ivor that well. He seems an all-right bloke, but…'

'I know, Luke is only protecting me.'

'He is, babe, although he's a little controlling for my liking, but if that shit turns you on, then knock yourself out.'

I can't help chuckling at his honesty.

'So, now we've discussed my life, tell me, how is Adam? A little birdie told me about your day out.'

'Rosie grown some feathers since yesterday?'

'No, she's a concerned mother. To be honest, she loves having Adam here, which leads me to ask you if you feel the same.'

There's a silence. I sit up slightly. Barney, silent? This never happens.

'Barney?'

'Shh. I'm moving away.'

'From what?'

'Adam, you dozy cow.'

'Oh.'

I hear him close a door. 'He came with me to the studio. I have some new dancers auditioning.'

'Sounds exciting.'

'Yeah, it is. I've set up a meeting with the string quartet from your wedding.'

'Really?'

'Just something I'm working on.'

'So tell me. Adam?'

'Kate, he's pretty damn amazing.'

I can read between the lines.

'I mean it, he's bloody fantastic. But don't worry, I haven't done anything about it. No chasing, kissing or shagging. I stayed true to my word.'

'No parading naked?'

'Well, not really.'

I sink back into the water. 'But you like him?'

'Yeah, I do, and I'm pissed off that he's leaving tomorrow.'

'Oh, babe. Listen, Rosie told me that his friend wants him to work here in London.'

'She told me the same. But if he wants to work here it has to be for the right reasons.'

'Holy fuck, who are you and what have you done with Barney Curtis?'

He chuckles. 'That is me… But this is different. I really like him.'

'I've never heard you talk like this. I wish I could do something to make it happen.'

'I have to let him leave. If he feels the same, he'll come back.'

'Have you told him how you feel?'

His silence speaks volumes.

'Barney, have you told him?' I repeat.

'No. He might run.'

'Oh, Barney, I don't know what to say. I just want you to be happy.'

'I'll get there.' He takes a deep breath.

'OK, I know I ordered you to stay away from him, but maybe you should come clean and tell him.'

'I'll think about it. Anyway, how are you feeling? Getting fat yet?'

'Luke says no, but I think my stomach is sticking out a bit, plus I've been feeling sick.'

'You'll still look sexy even when you're fat with swollen ankles.'

'Cheers, Barney! Now, New York next week. That'll help take your mind off Adam.'

'I'll be fine. Just getting a taste of my own medicine.'

'Don't say that! You deserve to be happy – maybe Adam is the person for you.'

'Time will tell.'

'I'm at Jones Tailors tomorrow. Make sure you pop in for your suit fitting.'

'See you then.'

After my bath, I change into comfy clothing. The day turns into late afternoon, and I'm hungry. I need something warm and homely: roast chicken.

Standing in the kitchen, I stir the gravy while trying to read yet another pregnancy book. If only I was allowed wine to alleviate the shocking images of birth…

I hear Luke walk through the hallway, which is all the excuse I need to put the book down. Luke ambles in.

'Smells good.'

'Roast chicken,' I say.

'How was your afternoon?'

'OK. Did you sort out your issues?'

'Yes.' He goes to the fridge for a cold beer.

'I'm going to be flat out this week finishing off the collection for New York,' I say.

He nods, swigging from the bottle.

'You know I will be fine in New York.'

His eyes meet mine. 'Kate, I am fine about you leaving. If I can get everything sorted in Dubai, then I will make the show.'

He walks towards me.

'You don't have to. I know you're super-busy.'

'Yes, but if I can then I will.' He looks at the books resting on the worktop. 'Reading?'

'These books should come with a warning: may cause you to pass out with fear.'

He looks amused.

'It's OK for you. I have to give birth twice.'

'We have plenty of time to plan for the day. Samantha called today.'

'Oh.' Is Dr Jacob on speed dial?

'We had a chat about Alexis. She also wanted to make sure you were feeling OK.'

'I spoke to Harry. She said Alexis seems fine – well, not fine, but better.'

'That's good. By the way, I moved your twelve-week scan to Friday. I wanted it before you go to New York.'

'I'm excited.' My hands link around his neck, allowing my lips to make contact with his.

We're exhausted. We eat in silence, though jet lag seems to have no effect on Luke's appetite. Although it's early, I crawl upstairs to bed, leaving Luke at his desk. There's no doubt we're home!

The sound of my phone vibrating on my nightstand wakes me. Our bedroom is in complete darkness apart from the light coming from my phone.

Sleepily I look. Caller ID – Kiki.

'Hello.'

'Kate.'

My brain engages quickly. It's not Kiki, but her dad.

'Henry!'

'Sorry to call you so early.'

'That's OK. What time is it?'

'Four o'clock.'

I'm now fully awake. Henry never calls me. 'Is she OK?'

'No, not really.' He pauses. 'Kate, she's had a miscarriage.'

'Sorry, Henry. I don't understand. I haven't spoken to her yet. I've just got back from honeymoon.'

'She's asking for you.'

'Of course.' I'm already heading to the bathroom. 'I take it you're with her?'

'Yes. We were at a meeting this evening and…' He trails off. 'Well, she started bleeding.'

'Oh God, poor love. Where are you?'

'Chelsea and Westminster, A and E. I think they're moving her to a ward – she was losing a lot of blood and they want to keep her in for observation.'

'I'm on my way.'

I end the call and lean against the marble washstand. Kiki was pregnant? I wonder if she knew. Is Declan the father? My gut instinct says yes, but then this is Kiki, the female shag monster!

I wash my face and brush my teeth, then quickly slip on some jeans, Luke's Abercrombie hoodie and Converse. With my hair scraped into a ponytail, I grab my black riding coat. Before I leave, I write Luke a note.

Dear Luke,

Henry called at 4.15. Kiki is in Chelsea and Westminster Hospital – she's had a miscarriage. I've gone to see her.

Call me when you wake.

Love you,

Kate xxx

The journey is fairly quiet, but it is four thirty in the morning! Now to find a space. Where's Max when you need him, and why is the car park busy at such a ridiculous time of day? When I reach the main reception area I dial Kiki's number, praying Henry will answer.

'Kate.' It's him, thank God.

'I am at reception.'

'OK, I'll come and get you.'

Five minutes pass before I see Henry.

'How is she?'

He shakes his head. 'I'm not sure. Physically the doctors have said she will be fine – apparently it's common. But…'

'I know – it's messing with her head.' Her mum died of breast cancer five years ago – and now this.

He nods.

I take his hand. 'Come on, take me to her.'

We arrive on the fifth floor and I follow him to her room. She looks to be sleeping peacefully, but when I get closer she opens her eyes. Tears stream down her face. I lie on the bed and wrap my arms around her.

'I'm here… It's OK.'

The echoing sound of pain vibrates against me.

'It hurts, Kate, it really hurts.'

'I'm so sorry.'

She nods against my chest.

I look across at Henry.

'Henry, can you get us a cup of tea?'

'Certainly.' He disappears.

'Let me look at you.'

She moves her head slightly. She looks broken. I stand

and take off my coat and shoes, then climb back on the bed. We lie side by side, facing each other.

'Did you know you were pregnant?'

She shakes her head. 'No.'

'I know this sounds shitty, but is Declan the father?'

'Yeah, he is. Or was. There's no baby now.'

'Oh, Kiki.' I stroke her face. 'Henry told me the doctors said it was one of those things. It could happen to anyone. Have you told Declan?'

'No, he's in Germany. How do I tell him that I lost his child? Fuck, this really hurts. I didn't want kids and now I do. I want my baby, the one that's gone.'

'You can try again. That might not be the best thing to say, but you can.'

'I don't want to. I can't go through this again. It reminds me of losing Mum.'

'Will you let me call Declan?'

'There's nothing he can do. Besides, I don't think he would have wanted a baby anyway.'

'You don't know that. I was unsure at first, but you adjust. He would have done the same.'

'I didn't think it would happen – you know what my periods are like, I haven't had one for a few months.'

'I would have thought the same. What did the doctor say?'

'That I might have been a couple of months. I've been really tired and haven't eaten properly for a while, but work is crazy. It never occurred to me that I was pregnant.' She trails off. 'He saw it as a positive sign that at least I got pregnant. Shame I couldn't hang on to the baby.'

'Kiki, don't beat yourself up over this. It could happen to anyone.'

'I can't help it. I just feel guilty.'

'Why?'

'Kate, I fuck everything up. You know what I'm like.'

'Hey, don't say that! You are you – the most daring and confident person I know. One day, when the time is right, you will be the best mum in the world, I know you will.'

The door opens and Henry reappears with a tray of tea.

'Girls.'

Kiki and I sit up.

'Thanks, Dad.'

'Look what I found.' He produces two chocolate muffins from his jacket pocket. 'I thought they might help.'

'Good thinking.' I smile at a very awkward Henry.

'I'll give you girls some time alone.' He leaves us once again.

Neither of us is hungry, but we pick at the muffins.

'So, how was the honeymoon?'

'Amazing. Maybe you and Declan should get away.'

'I was thinking the same. Declan mentioned it before he went to Germany.'

'The break will do you good.'

'Maybe. I hope he forgives me.'

'There's nothing to forgive.'

'How was Luke?'

'He's fine.'

Kiki smiles.

'I have some gossip. I think Barney's in love with Rosie's son, Adam.'

'No shit!'

'Yes! Can you believe it?'

'He is good-looking. Declan and I saw him with Barney last week at Toulouse nightclub.'

'He flies home tomorrow. Barney is going to be like a bear with a sore head next week in New York.'

'Are you ready for the show?'

'No! This week will be super-busy.'

She yawns and sighs. 'Sorry for dragging you out.'

'I have your back, you know that. I only wish there was something I could do to help.'

'There isn't.'

'Time will heal. I'm here for you – always. Now sleep – you look exhausted.'

She rolls over, her back against my stomach, and my arm automatically tightens around her. My eyes close too, if only for a few moments.

Bright sunlight and the sound of someone moving a chair wake me. I raise my head.

'Luke.'

'Kate,' he replies harshly.

Carefully, I sit up and swing my legs round. I look at the clock high above Kiki's bed. Seven o'clock.

Luke watches me as I make my way towards him.

'Did you get my note? I guess you did, otherwise you wouldn't be here.'

He nods. 'Why didn't you wake me?'

'It was early and you were tired last night. Please don't be grumpy with me. I'm too tired to battle with you.'

'Battle with me?'

'Yes. Anyway, Henry called saying that Kiki needed me.'

'I called Declan. I assume he didn't know about the pregnancy.'

My glare says it all. 'You did what? Luke, it wasn't your place to tell him. Kiki was going to call him today.'

'I saved her a job.'

'Is that what you honestly think? Luke, you're out of order.'

'That's where you're wrong. Declan is my brother… Besides, it would seem Kiki needs him here with her.'

'You're pissed at me, but you are out of line.'

'Like I said, she needs him.'

'But it wasn't up to you to interfere!' I say through gritted teeth.

'You're furious… But you promised that you would let me protect you, without question.'

'What?'

'You drove here by yourself. I could have brought you.'

'For the love of God.' I try to keep my voice low, which is difficult when I

want to scream. 'Yes, I drove myself because I didn't want to wake you… and also because I'm a bloody adult.'

He takes a sharp breath.

'So what's the real reason you're behaving like this?'

He remains quiet, once again I've hit a nerve.

I place my palms on his chest. 'Seriously, Luke, you need to let me in. Holding out on me pisses me off.'

He runs his hand through his hair. For a brief moment, I think he will talk to me. No – nothing.

'OK, so when you want to tell me the truth I'm here to listen. But until then, you can't wrap me up in cotton wool. Now I suggest you go to work, as I will leave here shortly and go straight to Jones Tailors... I assume Max is here somewhere?'

His lips fasten on mine, not with speed but with tenderness. I pull away to gauge the darkness of his eyes. Dark and irritated meet dark and dubious.

'Kate, I need to know where you are. Please allow me that. It's not to control you but to keep you and our family safe.' His hands travel to the nape of my neck, causing spontaneous flickers of desire.

'I am listening.' *You're hiding something, Sutton. I know you too well!*

'Good, then listen to me. Please, if you do nothing else at least allow me this.'

'You seriously need some therapy.' I smile.

He suppresses a smile. 'Being married to you does push me. You may be on to something.'

12

Silently, we walk together. As usual, Luke has a firm grip on my hand: the Sutton vice grip he uses when we have had words. After a breakfast in the hospital canteen he still seems ... arsey, or worried. Either way, I give up asking. I can't force him to tell me what's up. I wrap my coat around me, feeling the early morning chill. I see Max waiting alongside my car at the hospital entrance. Leaving Kiki was hard, but she seemed settled – or perhaps just resigned.

Luke pulls me close to his chest and kisses the top of my head.

'I love you,' he says.

I look up to his dark eyes. *Stop hiding,* I want to say. 'I love you too' is what comes out.

Thomas drives Luke to Sutton Global. I slide into the passenger seat and Max starts the car.

'Well?' I say.

He swipes a look at me. 'Get to the point, Harper.' I desperately want to mention Anderson's name, but I don't want to hurt Max.

'What the hell is going on with Luke? OK, I know he has issues with Russia and Ivor, which I get, but I see something in his eyes… I know him. But he won't tell me what's wrong.'

'You know what he's like about your safety. Don't forget he's got another two reasons to stress.'

'Bullshit!'

Max shakes his head.

'I know I'm right. I just wish he'd come clean. Wouldn't it be easier if he let me help? But no, so now I'm playing give us a bloody clue.'

'And you wonder why I don't want to date.' He sniggers.

'Lucky for you, I wouldn't set you up with someone like Luke.'

'No setting up. I've told you.'

'Whatever. And you can tell Luke from me, don't shut me out. It pisses me off.'

We arrive at Jones Tailors. I already feel as though I have run a marathon this morning. As I open the door to the shop I am thrown into pre-show madness. Everyone is on a high of excitement, with the added strain of apprehension. We are all – except Valerie – runway virgins, so the next few days will be filled with checking stock, lists and final cuts.

The shop is a hive of activity. God, this is very different to when I worked here. What have I done to Mr Jones?

Although I turned up looking scruffy, for me, this seems to work out for the best. I get down and dirty, packing clothes, steaming, labelling, making teas, sweeping the floors – the list is endless and incredibly gruelling.

Towards the end of the day the workload eases off. We have achieved a considerable amount in a short space of time. Over the next few days we'll add the finishing touches to the collection to ensure it's ready for the show.

When just Mr Jones and I are left in the shop, he finishes my suit for the runway finale. We have matching black three-piece Jones Tailors suits, although mine is fitted with slimline tapered trousers. The suit feels amazing and fits me perfectly – but not for much longer.

I return to the sewing room, dressed in my original scruffy outfit.

'Kate, tea?' says Mr Jones.

'Thanks.' I take the stool next to him. 'I bet you miss the silence. Sorry.'

'Don't be.'

'Who would have thought, when you hired me, that we would be here today? Mad, right?'

'You could say I am surprised.'

I yawn.

'You look tired, my dear.' He looks at me over his glasses. 'Were you sick earlier?'

'Sorry, I didn't think anyone could hear me.'

'I hear everything.'

'I guess. For some reason, I feel sick later in the day. The same happened yesterday. I thought it was supposed to be morning sickness.' I frown.

'I hope it goes away soon.' Mr Jones reaches across for my hand. 'Tell me, did your friend call you again this afternoon?'

I nod. 'She's home – actually, she's staying with her dad. Poor love. I feel so dreadful for her.'

241

'Mother Nature, my dear – we have no way of knowing what will happen to any of us, or what the future holds. You must not allow her loss to cause you pain, and from what I know of the young lady she would say the same.'

'I know she would. But I think a baby would give her a purpose and someone to love. It would help with the loss of her mum. You may not know, but since she lost her mum she has slept around a lot, and I mean a lot…'

Mr Jones just listens.

'Deep down I think she uses it as a tool to numb her loss. Do you understand what I mean?'

He smiles. 'Yes, and I agree with you. Although I think she needs time to come to terms with this loss before she embarks on another journey.'

'Definitely. Luke called Declan and told him. I was bloody furious – I still am. Kiki should have had the choice to call him herself, but oh no, Mr I Know It All Sutton did what he wanted, as per usual.'

'Blood is thicker than water, Kate. You cannot argue that he protects his family, especially you.'

'No shit.' I look at Mr Jones with an apologetic gaze. 'It slipped out.'

'It usually does.' He smiles.

'Well, I'm mad at him.'

'Don't let things fester. Life is too short. I would like to point out that Luke has not changed. You knew what he was like before you married him.'

'He's worse now.'

'Perhaps he has more to lose now.'

'Maybe. Did you want kids?'

He removes his glasses and rubs his eyes.

'I think most people do at some point.'

'You would have made a fantastic dad.'

'Thank you.'

'No, I mean it. You're so calm and logical. When I'm around you I feel at ease. You're like a therapist with an encyclopaedia under his arm.'

'You should give yourself more credit, Kate. Any decisions you make are your choice. I merely help you to see another point of view.'

'I think Luke should spend some time with you. Actually, you should adopt him. His problems are deep-rooted.'

'He has his delightful wife to help guide him,' he says with a smile.

'I need to tie him up and gag him.' Hmm, that may not be such a good idea. He may like it! 'While we're on the subject of Luke, how is his suit coming on?'

'Almost completed and ready for your scavenger hunt.'

'I can't wait. All my notes are done.'

'Notes?'

'The clues to find me, so you have one, and so do Barney, Stella and his mum.'

'I see. You have planned this meticulously, Kate.'

'Sort of, plus I can tie it in with a trip to France – fabric browsing.'

'I am sure he will be thrilled.'

Trying to switch off from my day I lie in the bath, but my mind is elsewhere: on Kiki, then I make a mental list of everything we still need to do before the show. The pressure is on, which makes me feel alive. I can't deny I am enjoying every second.

My phone rings. I shake my hands dry and pick it up. Caller ID – Boss.

'Good evening, sex god. Please tell me you're alone.' I smile at our private joke.

'Kate Sutton and loudspeakers – a fatal combination. Never again.'

'So, how can I help you? For the record, I'm still pissed off.'

'About?'

'You calling Declan.'

'From what Declan told me, it worked out fine. Kiki was pleased he came home.'

'Just because it worked doesn't mean you're right. Anyway, I'm too tired to argue.'

I can hear the smile in his voice. 'I'll be home late so please eat without me.'

'I've been feeling sick this evening. I threw up at the tailors.'

'Try and eat something. Is there anything you need?'

'Only you.' I laugh, but it's true.

'Good.'

Let me push a Sutton button. 'Besides, if I need anything I'll pop out.'

'Max can get you whatever you need. I can call him now. What do you want?'

'Nothing.'

'Please don't leave the house alone. I thought we discussed this earlier today.'

'No, you told me. At no point did we discuss it. Anyway, I'm going straight to bed.'

'I will leave you to it, then. Please listen to me.'

'All right.'

After the best meal in the world – a Walkers crisp sandwich and a large mug of tea – I head straight for bed. I try to read the books Luke lovingly gave me, but it's pointless, so I try some car-crash TV. By now it's ten o'clock and Luke is still out. I'm too tired to wait up for him.

A noise disturbs my sleep. I roll on to my side.

'Max.'

I feel drowsy.

'Go back to sleep, Kate.'

I prop myself up on my elbows. 'What are you doing?' He's at the French doors that lead from our bedroom to the balcony.

'Just checking the doors are locked.'

'What?' OK, I'm fully awake. Max never checks the doors – or does he?

'It's OK. Luke asked me to check them. He'll be home soon. Please go back to sleep.'

He leaves the room. I'm confused. After a while, I get up and head towards the stairs. At the top step, I can hear Luke and Max talking in the office. I sit down and eavesdrop.

'Ghosts have a habit of reappearing,' Luke says.

What does he mean?

'I'd be happier if we knew more,' Max says.

Me too, Max – please share.

'The new guy I saw tonight is good. James Sullivan gave me his name,' Luke says.

'So he must be good.'

'Exactly,' Luke says.

'OK. The alarms were tested and everything is fine,' Max says.

'They were due to be re-checked anyway.'

'Doors and windows locked, plus your room,' Max says.

'Good. Have you checked the CCTV?' Luke asks.

'Yeah. All clear.'

Clear of what?

'And Kate?' Luke asks.

'She was asleep. I did disturb her.'

'She's exhausted. Drink?'

'Yeah, why not?'

I watch their shadows drift off to the kitchen. What the hell is going on?

Silently, I head down the stairs and into Luke's office. Everything looks the same. I open the couple of files on his desk. He mentioned CCTV: where's the feed going to? Must be the computer. I move the mouse on the screen – password needed. I enter *eatme*. The live video feed appears, showing the security gate, the door, garden, our balcony, plus a few more. I look closely, but what am I looking for?

Luke comes in. I look up.

'Kate.' He comes towards me.

'What's going on? And don't bullshit me. Max was just checking the doors in our room, which is bloody odd, but you already know that.'

'Precaution, that's all.'

'Precaution – against what?'

He leans against the desk.

'Luke, you can tell me anything, you know you can.' I go to him.

He runs his hands through my hair. 'I know. There's nothing to worry about.'

'Has Russia spooked you that much?'

'Possibly,' he says. He pulls me towards him and kisses me gently. 'I need to know you're safe.'

'I am. How was your meeting?'

'OK.'

'What was it for?'

'A new client.'

'Oh, what sort of client?' I ask.

'They sell a product I want.'

'What sort of product?'

His forehead creases. 'You hate discussing my business.'

'That's not true. I'm trying to show some interest.' I'm trying to trip you up, now answer my bloody question! 'So, what product?'

'A researcher. They look into companies I want to buy.'

Bullshit, Luke! You're hiding something, or someone is on the loose.

'I wanted to talk to you about the panic room – or den, as you call it.' What? Now I'm concerned. The room in question is in the basement.

'What about it?'

'I want to show you how to get inside – just in case.'

'In case of what? I'm pretty certain we're not going to play hide and seek, and apparently there's nothing for me to worry about!'

He chuckles. 'You can't hide from me. Just a precautionary measure.'

'There's that word again.'

'Zip it, Harper.'

He takes my hand and I follow him down to the basement. We stand in front of the wine rack.

'This will be a quick rundown, OK?'

I nod.

'Feel here.' He takes my hand. 'There's a switch, yes?'

I nod.

'Press it.'

I do.

'Can you hear that sound?'

'Yes.'

'It's the locks unlocking. Now slide the wine rack across – it runs on hydraulics, so it's fairly light.'

My stomach flips.

'You need a code to open the vault door. It's two, two, zero, eight.' He shoots me a look.

'You're funny. Do you think I have problems remembering numbers?'

'Yes! But not the first time we flew to Venice.'

I shrug. 'Never.'

I input the code and the door opens. Luke enters first, turning the light on. I step into his Aladdin's cave. Nothing has changed since I was in here last. There are piles of documents stacked high, plus piles of money. And weapons.

'Kate, come here, I need to show you something… Please listen carefully.'

I nod, feeling completely out of my depth. Survival skills? They're beyond me.

'Firstly, if at any point you are in trouble or your life is threatened then get down here. Even if it's a false alarm, it doesn't matter, OK?'

I nod. Life-threatening!

'Now you know how to get in, you also have to know how to lock yourself in this room.' He walks to the door. 'Slide the rack across; you need to conceal the entrance.'

'OK.' I slide it across.

'Good, now close the door.'

I push the door shut.

'Type the code in again. That ensures the bullet-proof door is locked.'

I laugh. 'What! Did you say bullet-proof? Luke, you're scaring me.'

'Just a prec—'

'Precaution my arse!'

'A safety measure. Is that better?'

'Not really.'

'As you can see, the room has enough water and food to last a while, but there are some things I want to show you.'

He heads towards a cupboard in the corner and slides two metal doors apart.

'Are you shitting me?'

'Kate, you have seen weapons before.'

'Yes, but what is all this stuff?' I pick up a small box.

'I'll take that – it's a detonator with a tracker built in.'

I laugh. 'What? Could that go off?'

'No. Please listen.'

'This has to be your perfect toy cupboard.' I chuckle in disbelief. 'Seriously, where do you get this stuff?'

'That's irrelevant.'

'It always is, Luke.'

'When you're quite finished…'

'OK.' I hold my hands in the air. 'I'm making light of the situation… You're showing me things like detonators and guns and expect me to not ask questions? That's unfair, and before you say it, that's not protection. That's called keeping me in the dark, like showing me how to get inside this room and Max checking the doors in our bedroom for no reason.'

'I can't give you answers all the time. You have to trust me.' His eyes burn into mine.

'Go on.'

'The gadgets, as you refer to them, are no use to you, but this phone is.'

'It looks like a normal phone – or does it turn into a plane or something?' I smile at myself.

'For fuck's sake, Kate, I'm trying to keep you safe.'

'Fine.'

'This phone can't be traced. It's a satellite phone.'

'Traced, as in hacked?'

'As in no one can track you. It's got various numbers saved to it: all of mine, Max's, plus Sullivan's and Parker's.'

My arms fold, guarding my body.

'So basically, you have another phone if I need one.'

'You know how to contact someone in case of—'

'An emergency – got it.'

He closes the cupboard doors.

'Thanks for the insight into your crazy world – again.'

He looks away. I know he'd prefer not to disclose this part of his life. He would rather this part of his past remained buried.

'So listen, Sutton. I am in here for a reason. You say nothing, and I say bullshit.'

He peers at me from his great height.

'There's something niggling – and I don't think it's Russia.' I poke his firm pec. 'I think this precaution' – he takes a breath – 'your word, not mine, is down to you. Something or someone in your past is chasing you. Anderson?'

'What?'

'Don't what me, Luke.'

He bites his lower lip. 'There's nothing for you to worry about.'

'I love you with every bone in my body, and whether you like it or not I know when you're lying.'

His silence fills the air.

'Trust me – that's all I'm asking, Kate.'

'Fine. I don't want to be in here. Let's go to bed.'

We leave the secret den. Although we arrive at our bedroom in complete silence, I can hear Luke thinking.

'I'll just take a shower,' he says.

'OK.'

I climb into bed, feeling wide awake and restless.

Five minutes pass and his naked body slides into bed next to me. I inhale his scent.

'Have you been sick this evening?'

'No. I feel OK. I had a sandwich and crisps for dinner.'

'You need to eat more than that.'

'I really enjoyed it. Actually, I have a thing for ready salted crisps – you need to hide them from me. Besides, the babies are telling me to eat them.'

His face softens with his best Sutton smile. 'Is that right? Why do I have a feeling you'll use this excuse until they arrive?'

'Bet your arse I will, after knowing what I will have to go through to get them out.'

I close the distance between us: not just the physical gap but also the emotional void, which I always feel when he holds out on me.

'So, Sutton, I'm wide awake, and fed up with feeling pissed off at you, so what are you going to do about it?'

'I'm pleased you're no longer pissed off at me.' He lands a cheeky smacker on my lips.

'It's taken most of the day, but that leads me to think you need to make it up to me.'

'Any suggestions?' he says, wearing a smile that warms my heart.

'I have a few, but just as a precaution…' I chuckle.

'You're hilarious,' he says.

'You're banned from using that word – ever! And if you say it again there will be consequences.' God, I love teasing him.

'Go on.'

'Well, for starters I will silence you.' His lips meet mine with heat and passion. I can feel his erection growing against my hip.

'Like this.'

'It's a start.'

He pulls my T-shirt over my head and begins to tease my nipples.

He continues to my stomach, then floats across my pubic bone. As I take a breath his soft tongue touches my clit. Oh God.

He looks up.

'Don't stop. I'm still pissed off with you.'

'I thought you were over that.'

'I changed my mind. I'll get back to you. Now stop talking and start working.'

As his tongue sweeps across my clit again my body surrenders to him. Fuck. I don't care about anything else.

13

It's been the busiest week of my life, but we're finally ready to go. Luke and I stand in the lounge at City Airport.

'Please try to rest when you can,' he says.

'I wish you were coming with me.'

'You'll be fine.'

I nod. 'I feel so emotional. Yesterday blew me away. Honestly, I think I'm still in shock.'

He places his hand against my stomach. 'Not many situations leave me speechless, Kate.'

'I couldn't get excited before, but now it feels real – we've seen them and heard their heartbeats.'

He wipes the single tear that trickles down my cheek.

He reaches inside his blazer. 'Here.' He passes me two laminated scan pictures.

'Look at our babies,' I say.

'They're perfect.' He beams with delight.

'God, I feel so lucky, Luke.' He knows I feel bad for Kiki.

'We are.' He tenderly plants small kisses on my lips. 'Please take care of yourself and our babies. Promise me that you'll rest.'

'I promise. I just hate feeling sick.'

'Eat little and often, even if it is crisps, OK?'

I laugh. 'OK.'

He folds me into his arms.

'Excuse me, Mr Sutton, Mrs Sutton, the plane is ready for you to board.' A member of the flight crew interrupts us.

'Thank you,' Luke responds. She walks away.

'Shit, why do I feel so nervous?'

I look around the small room, which is full of the Harper Jones workforce, plus Max and Barney.

'You'll be fine, and you will be pleased to know that I have given Max strict orders to make sure you rest.'

'Thanks for the heads-up.'

Luke and I look across the room to where the man in question is chatting to Valerie. I can't help feeling smug.

'Max is here to protect you.'

'They are drawn to each other – and for your information, I haven't even mentioned Valerie's name to him.'

'Go. Remember this is a business trip.'

Well, the word 'business' has a very different meaning to me. Besides, Max and Valerie's happiness is my business!

'You OK, babe?' Barney asks.

'I'm fine. I just hate take-offs. Luke normally holds my hand.'

He takes my hand and squeezes it warmly. 'Well, you have me. I know I'm not Luke, but…'

I rest my head on his shoulder. 'You're a close second.'

The aircraft is packed with the Harper Jones crew. The atmosphere is excited. Even now I can't believe we're on our way to showcase our collection.

Once we reach cruising altitude I make a point of changing seats so I can speak to everyone. Max and Valerie have been deep in conversation since we set off. This has to be a good sign. Max usually has very little to say, so he must feel comfortable in Valerie's company.

Last, I sit next to Mr Jones.

'This is mad, right? Are you excited?'

'I think I'm anxious. Don't get me wrong – I have faith in the designs and the work we have produced.'

'This is your dream. Your creations are coming to life and now they will be shared with the world – at least, with the people of New York.'

He smiles. 'Our dream, and our creation. Harper Jones through and through.'

I take out the pictures Luke gave me. 'Here, look at these, we got them at the scan yesterday.'

'How incredible – Mother Nature at its best. And you, do you feel OK?'

'I can't believe they're growing inside me.' I shake my head in disbelief. 'I'm fine, just tired, and my waistline is beginning to disappear – you might need to add some fabric to my trousers for the finale.'

Mr Jones chuckles. 'A small price to pay.'

'My babies are priceless.' I can't help staring at the

laminated pictures. 'What do you think, boys or girls? They're sharing a placenta so they'll be identical.'

'What about healthy? How marvellous would that be?'

'The best.'

Luke has arranged for limousines to meet us at JFK Airport. Soon we are safely at the palatial Four Seasons – which Luke also requested. The hotel has allocated us a function room to store the Harper Jones collection, which will double up as a workspace. The show itself will be in the trendy Tribeca area.

Barney and I are sharing the penthouse suite Luke and I previously I stayed in. It's so big, it's more like an apartment than a suite.

I open the door and urge Barney to walk through first. I want to see his reaction.

He's silent for a few moments, then he gives a long drawn-out whistle. 'Fuck me gently, I have died and gone to hotel heaven. I've never seen anything like it.'

'It's amazing, isn't it?'

'Amazing? It's the fucking dogs bollocks.'

Barney walks around, exploring. The full-length windows lure you towards them: the views are breath-taking.

'I feel a bit shell-shocked.'

'I did too when Luke brought me here.'

'I'll give it to him, Sutton certainly knows the best suites. Bloody hell, I bet this is more than three grand a night.'

I shrug. I can't allow myself to think about the price tag.

'Go in the master bedroom and look at the bathroom.'

He leaves me alone in the lounge. I look out. Even though this is my second visit, I'm still captivated by the sight – and my favourite view of Central Park. I could just sit here and watch the yellow cabs go by, and the tourists taking carriage rides.

'Bloody hell… The view,' he shouts.

He saunters towards me.

'I need a cup of tea.'

'I need a bloody whisky.'

'I think the next few days will be fun,' I say.

'Too bloody right, babe. I won't want to leave!'

Later we all meet in the foyer of the hotel. We're jet lagged, so we agree to have an early dinner at the hotel. After refuelling our tired bodies, we venture into the function room and unpack the clothes ready for tomorrow. By six o'clock we have done all that we can. Tomorrow will be mad, but at least we are prepared for it.

Max is by my side. 'You look beat.'

'I'm tired,' I say and yawn. 'I've had enough. I'm going to my room for an early night, and you can report that to Luke.'

'Don't worry. I will.' He smirks.

'I'm off to bed, everyone.' I call. 'Valerie, can you and Max lock up? Max, can you hold on to the keys?'

'Sure,' he says.

Fab, they will have to spend five, maybe ten, minutes together – alone, I hope.

'Barney, I'm going.'

'OK, babe, I'll join you. PJ party.'

'You're on your own. The only party I'll be having is with my pillow.'

He walks towards me and takes my hand. 'Come on, sleeping beauty, let's get you in the land of Zs.'

'See you in the morning, everyone. Max, will you make sure Valerie gets to her room? If she's the last here, I'll worry.'

'OK. Our rooms are next to each other.'

I know! 'Oh, that's handy.'

Barney and I head to the lift.

'What are you up to, Harper?'

I look up at him. 'What?'

'Don't what me! Max and Valerie sitting in a tree…' he sings.

'I have no idea what you mean.'

'Bullshit. Besides, I asked Tanya and she laughed. You've been caught.'

'Fine. I think they look good together, and they're both single, so what harm can come of it?'

'Actually, they look well suited. What does Sutton think?'

'He doesn't.' We arrive at our floor. I step out first. 'You know what he's like. Besides, he has zero interest in Max's sex life.'

Barney tilts his head. 'No, I don't suppose he does. Good job Max has you as his little match-maker.'

'Yes, he's bloody lucky.' I open the door. 'Any news from Adam?'

Barney stops in his tracks.

'Not yet.' He walks through to the lounge area.

'You poor love. I never saw this coming and now I feel bad.'

'Bad? Bloody hell, babe, you introduced me to someone that I could spend the rest of my life with. Shit, and I haven't even shagged him yet.'

'That looks good, Mr Jones. I think pin the hem another inch higher, so we see just enough flesh without looking—'

'Vulgar,' he says.

'I was going to say slutty, but vulgar works.'

He pins half an inch of the black lace skirt on the model, and we stand back. 'Better, my dear – a good call.'

'Yeah, I agree.'

'OK. Thanks Olivia, you can get changed now.'

The tall, slender young model walks away and another model arrives, wearing a different outfit, this time a modern twist on an evening gown – the sexy ensemble of the showcase.

After a few more hours the last outfit has been pinned and labelled, and hair and make-up have been discussed with the freelance hairdresser and make-up artist. At last we are ready for our dress rehearsal tomorrow. All that remains is for Barney, Mr Jones and me to try on our black Jones suits.

'Bloody hell, we look like the cast from *Reservoir Dogs*.' We stand shoulder to shoulder and Barney examines his suit in great detail. 'Mr Jones, this is amazing. You are one talented geezer.'

'I love them. What do you think?' I gaze at my colleague in the mirror, full of admiration. 'The extra panel feels better. At least now I can do up my trousers.' I lift my shirt to reveal the smallest bump – my precious babies.

'I believe we are making a statement, Kate.'

'Don't mess with us.' Barney flashes a seductive smile while striking a sultry pose.

I look at Max. 'What do you think?'

He smiles. 'They look good.'

'Take a picture for me so I can send it to Luke.'

Max rolls his eyes.

Our first full day and evening passes. I beg Barney to go out with Maria and Tanya. I need to rest. This is my decision, not one made in honour of Mr Control Freak Sutton. I've thrown up a few times and my wound is aching. An early night is my best option.

I lie in the bath enjoying some much-needed peace and quiet. My phone rings, I pray it's him. Caller ID – Boss.

'How can I miss you this much? Sutton, what have you done to me?'

'I miss you too.'

'What are you doing?'

'Dealing with contractors, plus trying to sort out the air-conditioning nightmare.'

'Tell me, how are the interior plans working out?'

'Good. I did have to argue over one or two adjustments you made.'

'Luke, I'm not an interior designer. You should listen to the people you employed.'

'Not if I disagree with them. Bradley also liked your suggestions.'

'Oh.' Why do I feel awkward whenever his name is mentioned?

'How are my babies?'

'OK, I'm just tired, plus Mr Jones had to add fabric to my trousers. I'm expanding, Luke.'

'I wish I was with you.'

'Me too. Actually not today, today has been a little challenging.'

He laughs. 'What do you mean?'

'I've been surrounded by models all day, all five foot ten and slender... Do models really have to look like that?'

He laughs again. 'I prefer five foot five myself.'

'Bloody good job. But let's not forget your encounter with a model – and, knowing you, I'm sure there was probably more than one. I bet you had a threesome...' I pause. 'Have you ever had a threesome?' Oh my God, I want to scream. Why am I asking this? Do I want to know?

'Jesus, Kate, are you on a self-destruct mission?'

He didn't say no.

'It just popped into my head. Well, have you?'

'Does it matter?'

I bolt upright in the bath, spilling water over the edge. 'Holy fuck, you have.'

'I'm not discussing this with you.'

'But you haven't denied it.' I hate feeling jealous!

'Kate, please, this is not the time or the place. I want to hold you and I can't.'

'Me too.'

I lie back down and sink into the water.

'Thank you for the picture. Very clever to end with matching suits.'

'I thought it would be fun, and now I have my very own suit.'

'Max said you have been behaving yourself, and how is Barney?'

'Sad. He's missing Adam, and I mean really missing him.'

'Missing Adam?' he says, sounding confused.

'Yeah, Adam. Jerry and Rosie's Adam. He really likes him.'

'What is it with you, setting people up?'

'This time I didn't. I actually told Barney to stay away, but he really likes him. They haven't even kissed or shagged yet, and Barney has never waited before.'

'Thanks for that image in my head…'

I giggle, swirling the water with one hand.

'Are you in the bath?'

'Yes – stark naked and in need of my husband.'

'Now I'm hard.'

'Just think of Barney. That'll help.' I laugh.

'It's working.'

'OK, from the top again! Girls, listen to the beat. It's not difficult: watch me then follow.' Barney looks at me, shaking his head. 'I think starvation has affected their fucking hearing.'

I laugh as I watch him climb on to the runway then walk through the steps and turn – again.

After a couple of hours, everything seems to fall into place. It's time for me and Mr Jones to walk the finale. I take his hand and we walk along the runway to the beat of the club music that is echoing around the room.

'Again, Harper, this time with more energy, yeah? Can we get Kate some heels? Take off those bloody Converse.'

'Stroppy,' I shout. I've never seen or heard Barney behave so assertively.

Barney helps me remove my Converse and exchange them for a pair of killer heels. Thank God Mr Jones is walking with me. I need his support, physically and emotionally.

'Let's try this again, shall we? Oh, and Harper, tell your face you're enjoying it, yeah? Now walk like you mean it.'

We walk again, and again. Actually, this has to be the sixth or seventh time.

'Really?' I say and look at Mr Jones, who stifles a chuckle.

'I never saw a perfectionist in Mr Curtis.'

'That's makes two of us.'

'Kate, concentrate,' Barney yells again.

We walk the runway again. This time at the end I break out into my alter ego and perform the best slut drop I can muster.

'Very bloody funny, Harper,' Barney belts out.

'I aim to please,' I say and curtsey.

From a distance I hear a whistle followed by enthusiastic clapping. With the spotlights shining on the runway, I can't see where the noise is coming from.

I shield my eyes with my hand. No clue. Within a few seconds I hear the sound of footsteps coming towards me until the surprise guest is revealed. It's Bradley Taylor. What the fuck? We met briefly in New York, where he was the architect for Bagrov and Cooper, and Luke exiled him to Dubai to work on his hotel.

'What are you doing here?'

'I'm getting a complex. You say that every time I see you,' the tall, good-looking American says.

'Sorry, I'm just surprised to see you. I thought you were working in Dubai.' Does Luke know he is here, not in Dubai?

'I was, but I'm signing over a building here in New York, plus I wanted to see my family before I head back to Dubai.'

'Oh.'

He comes closer to the stage, holding his hand out. 'Let me help you down.'

'Thanks,' I say and step towards him. However, I misjudge the edge and almost fall into his arms.

'Good job I was here.' He jokes, but his eyes gleam with delight.

'I'm a lucky girl.' Crap! It wasn't long ago that he told me he wanted to carry me to his bed – his exact words.

My feet make contact with the floor. I look over Bradley's shoulder and see Max watching me like a hawk. He's on his phone. One guess who he's talking to.

'Coffee?' I ask.

'Yeah, sure.'

He follows me to the corner of the room and the refreshments table.

'How much did you see?' I ask.

'Enough. Nice dance moves.'

'Funny!'

'The designs from earlier – I recognise a couple of them from your office.'

'Yeah.' I'm shocked he remembered the drawings from when he visited me a few months ago in London.

'It looks like your sticking and gluing has paid off.'

'I hope so.'

We sit, and I finally slip off my heels.

'It's good to see you, Kate.'

'You too.' Unnerved, I look away. He does this to me every time I'm in his company. I couldn't live another day without Luke and that will never alter, but in a different time and place, maybe I would have taken Bradley up on his offer.

'Can I say I missed you?' he says.

'How can you miss me? You really don't know me.'

'Maybe, but I still missed you. I hear you got married.'

'Luke told you?'

'No, I heard it from Zhan Abdul. He visited me, making sure I was doing a good job for Luke.'

'I forgot you knew him. Small world.'

'Architects know other architects. He designed the hotel so the project is personal to him.'

'I guess.' I ponder for a moment and take a deep breath. 'Did you know I'm pregnant?'

He nearly spits his coffee out.

'Sorry!'

'What, for choking me or for being pregnant?'

'I don't know, can I say both?' I laugh, hoping to lighten the mood.

He sighs and looks down at his hands. 'Fuck.'

'I don't know what to say, Bradley.'

'You don't need to say anything.' He reaches across and tenderly strokes my hand. 'I'm happy for you.'

'You don't look it.'

He tries to smile, but he looks shocked. 'I won't lie, this was the last thing I expected you to say. Luke hasn't mentioned it.'

'It was a surprise for us too.'

He leans across and kisses my cheek. 'You'll make a good mum, I know you will. I guess I always thought…' He stops and brushes his hands through his mousey wavy hair. 'Jesus. You affected me, there's no other way to say it.

I know how much you love Luke – Christ, it's clear… But when I saw him and Alexis together in Dubai, part of me was hoping…' He gazes at me, looking sad.

'I know how you feel. I love Luke, that goes without saying. But had I met you first – well, things could have been different.'

'Why do you always want what you can't have?'

'I know, right? Do you know how much I love regular coffee, not this decaf crap?'

We both laugh.

'Thanks for comparing my feelings to coffee… That's what I love about you.'

Change the subject, Harper – now.

'How did you find me?'

'I knew you were here. Luke mentioned it, plus I have my sources. You're not difficult to track down.'

I giggle. 'Please tell me I stand out for the right reasons.'

'You know you stand out.' His eyes locks on mine.

'Oi, Harper.' Thankfully, Barney comes over.

'Barney, do you remember Bradley Taylor?'

'Yeah. Ivy League boy, you were at my birthday bash, right?' Barney holds his hand out. 'Good to see you again. It's time for food, babe, we're all bloody starving. There's a sports bar down the road serving big fat burgers and beer. Bradley, join us, mate.'

He shakes his head. 'I have to be somewhere.'

'Yeah, you do – with me, or should I say us. Besides, I won't take no for an answer and I'm hormonal, so you don't want to upset me.' I can't give him anything other than friendship and I need the awkwardness to disappear.

We arrive at the sports bar, which is only a five-minute walk away: a noisy venue where we fit in rather well, especially with Barney there. Mr Jones opted to return to the hotel for room service.

We all squeeze into a large corner booth. Bradley being there does nothing to change the Harper Jones crew. More by luck than anything else, Bradley sits next to me, and Barney the other side. Max is on the edge of the group, watching me closely, no doubt on his boss's instructions.

After what must surely be the biggest meal ever, I am almost ready to burst.

'I can't eat any more. Anyone?' I offer my plate.

'Yep, pass it this way.'

I slide the plate towards Barney.

'Kate, have you eaten enough?' Max bellows.

'I'm fine,' I snap.

'How have you been? I mean, with the pregnancy?' Bradley asks.

'OK. Anyway, tell me about Dubai – the hotel, how's that going? Have you been on any hot dates?'

'Dates!' He swigs from his bottle of beer. 'Building your husband's hotel keeps me pretty busy. The only dates I have are meetings with contractors.'

'You should make time for yourself. Everyone needs some fun, and that includes you.'

'Does that mean you're coming to visit me soon?'

Playfully, I tap his arm. 'No. You need someone available.'

'That would make life far too easy.' He shakes his head.

'You and I are probably quite alike: leave a do not enter sign out and sure enough we will go in.'

'Am I supposed to read between the blurred lines here? Are you leaving a door open for me?'

'No. I'm not. Besides, I'm pregnant.'

'That doesn't matter to me.'

'Seriously?'

'Actually, I've never been more serious.'

'You need a woman, not me.'

'I'm not allowed to tell you what I need, am I?'

'No. Keep it to yourself.'

Max is glaring across the table. I wonder if he heard Bradley's confession.

'Right, who wants to go on to another bar?' Barney asks.

Max stands up from the table. 'Kate, I think you should go back and rest.'

Really? I nudge Bradley. 'You up for another beer?'

'Kate!' Max says.

'Max, feel free to join us… If not, you can go back to the hotel.'

'Right then, let's go, boys and girls.' As ever Barney is in charge of the party.

We put on our coats and get ready, then follow Barney towards the exit. Max stops me and pulls me to one side.

I look up to him. 'What?'

'You know what. First, you and I both know Bradley likes you, so if he tries it on I will fucking knock him out. And second, you should be resting. Going to a bar is not resting. That's my opinion. It has fuck all to do with Luke.'

'I would never risk the safety of my children, and for your information we are friends. Do you think he's really

269

interested in his boss's wife? Of course he's not.' Of course he is!

'But you're not resting.'

'I'm pregnant, not ill. You need to trust me. When I'm tired, I'll leave.'

'One drink and then back to the hotel.'

'Let me be the judge, OK.'

Eventually we catch up with everyone and go into another bar. The night is young: Barney is being entertaining, which includes him singing, dancing, and telling endless jokes. Bradley seems a little shocked, but amused, which is the only way to take Barney. By now our rowdy group has attracted some extra male guests, which pleases Maria and Tanya. Meanwhile, Max is enjoying another beer and talking to Valerie.

'Kate, Barney is crazy.' Bradley downs his beer, looking baffled.

'He is, but I'd be lost without him.'

'I guess he keeps you entertained. What does Luke think of him?'

'He doesn't have a choice. I told him I came with baggage and Barney is one of the pieces.'

I yawn again.

Bradley brushes his hand against my face. 'You look tired.'

'I'm exhausted.'

His hand wanders down my arm, finishing at my hand, loosely touching my fingers.

'I'd better leave.'

I know he doesn't want to; maybe it's self-preservation.

I nod. 'I need to go too. Actually, Max will be over in a few seconds dragging me back.'

'Luke has quite a team.' I know that's a polite way of saying Luke is deranged!

'Me and Max have been through quite a lot – he's family to me.'

'He thinks a lot of you. But I can see how easy that is.'

'Thank you for coming to see me. It was a good surprise.'

'Yeah, it was. I nearly didn't come.'

I squeeze his fingers. 'You know I make a bloody good friend.'

'In that case, friend, I will leave you to it.'

He kisses me. I wonder if it's a 'goodbye forever' kiss.

'Night, Max.'

I shut the door to the suite. At last I am alone. Feeling tired, I decide to take a quick shower and slide into bed. The day certainly changed course with the arrival of my surprise guest. I begin channel-hopping and eating the overpriced chocolate from the hotel fridge.

Ironically, I stumble across *The Bachelor*. Perfect – now there's a man who wants to be set up! Lost in a love life where I am allowed to air my opinion, the sound of my phone ringing causes me to jump. Caller ID – Boss. Shit – I know Max will have told him about Bradley joining us this evening. I'm surprised he didn't call earlier.

'Hi.'

'How is my wife?'

'Tired, and how is my husband?'

'Missing you.'

271

'Good – what time is it with you?'

'It's time that I spoke to you.'

'Which is the best time of the day.'

'What are you wearing?'

I giggle. 'What would you like me to wear?'

'Hmm – nothing.' He seems calm and not at all vexed. A visit from Bradley Taylor normally equals a pissed-off Sutton. Odd.

'In that case I'm lying in bed, completely naked, thinking of you.' My description could not be further from the truth: I'm in Luke's T-shirt and the hotel robe, covered in blankets and eating chocolate M&Ms.

'I thought we could have phone sex.'

I sit up slightly, almost choking on the chocolate.

'Phone sex!'

'Yes, baby. I need some action, and you're not here.'

'That means you'll have to do it.' Why do I feel so shocked? I love watching him touch himself.

'Yes, and I want you to make yourself come.'

I clear my throat. 'I'm not sure I can… On my own, it feels wrong.'

'Baby, have you never masturbated in between lovers or at the very least used a vibrator?'

'Luke!'

'It's a simple question – you shouldn't feel embarrassed.'

I am! My cheeks are burning.

'I'll tell you if you tell me if you had a threesome.'

He laughs at my negotiating skills. 'If you really want to know, I'll tell you.'

Holy fuck. I sit up, fully awake. I've suddenly lost my appetite. What a shame he didn't call me a few minutes ago. It would have saved me five hundred unnecessary calories.

'But then I want you to touch yourself and I'll do the same.'

I shake my head in disbelief. Do I really want to know?

'I don't know, part of me does and the other part doesn't. You're shit hot and sexy, of course you would have done it. Have I masturbated?' Oh my God. I fall back on the pillow, my hand over my face. 'Yes…'

Luke takes a long breath. 'That turns me on. I only wish I was there to watch you.'

'You were.'

'I was? How?'

'Well, not physically, but in my head.'

'So you touched yourself while thinking of me… Fuck, Kate, I need you now.'

'I can't believe you've made me crumble. You're such a shit.'

'Tell me, were we together or was this when I was chasing you?'

'You never chased me. You pissed me off – frequently. It was in the early days, before I knew any better. Actually, this conversation has ended and I don't want to revisit it, understood?'

'OK… Back to the matter in hand.'

'Very bloody funny.' I laugh.

'I think we're both in need of some self-gratification.'

'You have no self-control.'

'Bet your arse I don't. But I haven't seen you for a few days.' His voice changes. I sense his frustration. This could be fun.

'So, you want me to touch myself? Fine, I'll do it if you will.'

'You will?' He sounds surprised.

'Yes,' I whisper. Hell, no, I'm going to lie through gritted teeth while sucking on the second packet of M&Ms with the TV on mute and my blankets firmly tucked under my chin.

'Let's start.'

'Together, or are you going to start? I've never done this before.'

'Together. Gently massage your clit, not too quick. I'm so hard.'

Crap, this is going to be tougher than I thought. At the sound of his voice my body begins to respond, damn it.

'Kate.'

'Yes,' I whisper – not because of my fingers, but because of the M&Ms.

'Tell me how you feel.'

What the hell? I never speak while we have sex because I can't, and now I really can't because my mouth is full.

'Hmmm.' This chocolate is fabulous.

'Sounds like you're enjoying yourself.'

'Yes,' I whisper again, holding back a hysterical chuckle.

'Keep going, increase the speed and tell me when you want to come.'

'OK.' I hold the empty packet up. Shit. Two bags of M&Ms gone – that must be over a thousand calories.

'Kate?'

'Yes.'

'Are you hungry?'

I frown. 'Not especially.'

'I guess two packets of M&Ms would fill you up.'

'What?' Frantically I turn my head – and see Luke emerge from the doorway, laughing.

'Holy shit, you've been here the entire time.'

'Most of it. I let myself in.'

I throw a pillow in his direction.

'Baby, you don't seem to be masturbating.' He raises his brows.

I link my arms around his neck. 'You're in trouble, Sutton. No, I haven't touched myself and neither have you.'

'Looks like my beautiful wife has given me a job.'

'God, I've missed you,' I declare.

His mouth covers mine passionately. I'm now turned on and need him quickly. His kiss deepens and our tongues wrestle together. I slip off his jacket and begin to unbutton his shirt, loving the sight of his exposed torso.

Luke unties my robe then slips the T-shirt over my head. He pulls away and begins to remove the remainder of his clothes.

'Fuck, I need you.'

'Me too.' This time I whisper due to lust, not chocolate.

He moves me up the bed and begins to kiss my legs, spreading them apart. Finally his mouth brushes against my sensitive clit.

'Shit, Luke.' It hits me, his tantalising touch that causes my body to shudder with delight.

This evening his touch is fast and determined.

'Luke, I need to come.'

He offers no words; the only communication is the relentless action of his aggressive tongue. My mind leaves my body as I come hard.

He moves further up my body. I reach up and taste my orgasm on his lips. He's between my legs. I try to flip him so I can also give him some attention.

'I need you.'

'Yes, I know, but I want to kiss you all over first.'

He smiles and allows me to flip him onto his back.

My lips start at his mouth and jaw, followed by a nip on his earlobe. I work slowly down his body, caressing every inch.

At last I reach his erection, which stands to attention, almost begging for my touch. I gently lick his head before I lower my mouth over his hardness, slowly absorbing his length. My speed is slow but my grip is tight, and as soon as I hear his breathing alter I increase my pace. He groans and I taste pre-cum – a sure sign he will not be able to withstand me for much longer.

'Kate, stop. I want you.'

I stop and straddle him, feeling the crown of his erection slip inside me with ease. I need him. Normally I take this slowly, allowing my body to adjust, but not tonight.

I start to ride him. Luke pushes me back slightly, allowing his thumb access to my sensitive clit. I have no control. My body reacts instantly to his touch.

Christ, it arrives quickly. 'I need to come.'

His thumb does not relent, his tantalising touch tipping me over the edge. Not giving me a chance to recover, Luke flips me onto my back. He kisses me and enters me at the same time. He holds my arms high above my head and drives himself harder and deeper into me, taking what he needs. The tale-tale signs begin to map across his face: as his breathing grows shallow and his jaw clenches, he spills warm fluid deep inside me.

'Sorry, baby, did you want to come again? I couldn't hold back any longer.'

'No.'

He lets go of my arms and kisses me before freeing himself.

It's official – I am now exhausted.

'Well, that was a surprise, my phone sex becoming a 3D experience,' I say.

'I think we should discuss your wandering hands.'

'Oh no we don't. That discussion is closed for good, so don't even think about asking me.' I roll onto my side, propping my head on my hand. 'Besides, I thought you were in Dubai. I'm thrilled you've made it in time for the show tomorrow. You never said you were leaving.'

'I said if I could make it then I would.'

'Well, I'm glad you're here. How is the hotel coming along?'

'We're making excellent progress. Actually, the entire operation is running perfectly. Bradley Taylor was a good find.'

Shit, there's that name again. I wonder if Luke knows he's here in New York.

'That's good. Talking of Bradley, he's here, in New York.'

Luke nods.

'You knew?'

'Yes.'

'Oh.'

His eyes bore into mine. What's he not telling me?

'When did you find out?'

'Yesterday.'

'He came to see me at Mrs Gold's venue today – but I guess you already know that.'

'Yes.'

I smell a rat!

'Right then, Mr Control Freak Sutton, tell me the truth.'

'About my threesome?'

Is he trying to distract me?

'No, not your threesome, I'm talking about you, flying halfway round the world to follow Bradley Taylor. Why did you do that? Because you thought he might come to see me? That's why you're here.'

'No, it's not.'

'You didn't come to surprise me, you came to keep an eye on me! Admit it. Did you leave as soon as you found out he was heading here? You must have.'

His hand caresses my breast before fingering my bare nipples, which instantly stand to attention. It doesn't seem to matter that I am cross with him.

'I told you that I wanted to try and make the show.'

'Bullshit! Luke, tell me the truth.'

He begins to laugh. I grab a pillow and throw it at him.

'Oh my God, Luke bloody Sutton, you're a nightmare.'

'Kate, stop.'

'No! The only reason you're here is because of Bradley Taylor.'

'OK.' He grabs the pillow, then my wrists. 'But I was ready to leave.'

'You're unbelievable – and not in a good way.'

He yanks my arms, pulling me to him, resting one of his legs across mine, ensuring I have no room to escape.

'What can I say, other than I want to protect you at all costs. Not just you but also my babies.' He gently touches my bump. 'You know I hate being away from you. I don't see this as an issue.'

'No, you wouldn't, because you're a lunatic.'

'Jesus, Kate, I'm hard again. Get on all fours. I need to take you again.'

'No way – you can kiss my arse.' I don't mean it; I am wet and ready too, and no doubt I will be on my knees in seconds.

'Is that so? Do I need to change your mind?'

'You can try.'

'Fuck, baby, you know I love a Harper–Sutton challenge.'

The madness started as soon as the sun rose and continued until the afternoon – and the start of our runway show. Thank God, as a team we are organised. Our theme is black and white with tan accents – stunning black and white silk suits, bias-cut and asymmetric-hemmed skirts, lace shirts and flowing silk tops. The entire collection is cohesive with a hint of Parisian flair.

The music begins. Barney ensures the girls are ready while Mr Jones and I cast our eyes over the clothes, one last time. Suddenly the models begin to walk the length of the runway, then pose and turn at the end. The next models are waiting to go. Backstage is complete madness, perhaps organised chaos, which doesn't ease up until our last piece is ready to go – an evening dress.

'Barney, you look handsome,' I say, checking his tie is straight.

'I know, babe, but look what I'm wearing.' He winks. 'Ready, Saskia?' he asks the model wearing our full-length black evening dress.

The music echoes around the stage and he sets off. I could cry. I can't believe we have pulled it off.

I look across at Luke leaning against the wall. He's been silently watching me all day.

'We need to walk,' I shout at him over the music. 'Me and Mr Jones.'

He weaves through the models until he reaches me.

'I have to walk now. Shit, I'm nervous.'

'Don't be. I'm so proud of you, Kate.' He presses his lips against mine. 'Go and strut your stuff, Mrs Sutton.'

'Kate, they're calling for us,' Mr Jones says and holds his hand out to me.

'Here goes.'

We stand side by side at the entrance to the catwalk. I link my arm through Mr Jones'; he tilts his head towards me.

'In case I haven't told you, there's no one else I'd rather stand here with.'

'Likewise, Kate. Ready?'

'Ready, Mr Jones.'

14

'You look tired. Are you OK?'

Mr Jones removes his glasses and gently rubs his eyes. 'The travelling has affected me more than I thought it would.'

'Jet lag – I know what you mean. My body clock is still on New York time, not London.' I gather the photos of the fashion show from the boardroom table. 'So, we've agreed on these pictures for the website. I'll send these to Mrs Gold, and the same to the magazine. I still can't believe they want to print a spread.'

'Quite unexpected.'

'It still feels surreal. Like Christmas Day and my birthday at once.'

Mr Jones smiles. 'It is definitely a time for celebrations.'

'Mrs Gold sold all the tickets. She was really happy with the pieces we donated for the auction too. Hopefully she raised lots of money for her Alzheimer's charity.'

'A worthy cause.'

'Luke was shocked,' I say.

'Shocked? I would say he looked immensely proud of you. I noticed him watching you from the sidelines. He's not the only business entrepreneur in the Sutton household.'

'Entrepreneur? I don't think so. I'm no fashion mogul.'

'My dear, do not underestimate your ability.'

'Oh my God, he's far too powerful for me to compare myself with. Anyway, I'm just so bloody proud of us. Together, we smashed it.'

'We did, Kate, that we did.'

'Tanya said her phone hasn't stopped ringing since.'

'My mother always said a phone off the hook is better than a deadline.'

'Looks like your mum was right.' I take his hand. 'Let me take you home. I'm going anyway, so I can drop you off.'

'I would be grateful.' We stand and I help Mr Jones with his jacket.

'Everything ready for tomorrow and Luke's birthday?'

'I think so, but I'm worried that he won't play my game. You know what he's like.'

'He may surprise you.'

'I'll be surprised if he does as he's told. Do you have your note?' I ask.

'In my pocket.' He gently pats his jacket.

'Good, don't forget.'

'I'll call you when he collects his suit and his next clue.'

My phone vibrating wakes me. I've had the worst night's sleep, knowing that my master plan begins at the godforsaken time of four o'clock in the morning!

Quickly I get up and head for the spare room to get ready, not wanting to wake the birthday boy. Within half an hour I am ready for France, in black skinny waxed trousers with an elasticated waist, a satin V-necked T-shirt and black dinner jacket, plus black patent Chelsea boots for comfort. I'm ready to embark on my plan, but I need to leave Luke his first clue. Quietly, I creep into our bedroom and leave a note on my pillow.

My dear husband,

Happy birthday to my favourite person in the entire world.

As you might be aware, I am not with you this morning – it's all part of my birthday plan. Your day has been mapped out for you.

This is your first note. It should give you a clue that will help you find your next note. Your birthday treat is a scavenger hunt – and your prize is me (I hope this is not a disappointment).

Each note holds a clue and you must follow all the instructions. I think today may test you a little!

I will meet you later. In the meantime, you will not be able to contact me. Before you hyperventilate, Max is with me.

Your first clue is: eat me… Happy birthday, my delicious husband. I love you.

xxx

Job done, I head towards the kitchen.

'Morning.'

'Kate.' Max looks at me. 'Everything ready?'

I nod and adjust the cake sitting on the counter. It has a note resting on the top, reading *eat me*. Two small words that changed my life.

'Ready?' he asks. 'The cases are in the car.'

'OK.'

Max decides that we should leave through his apartment – less noise. I sit in the back of the Range Rover for the short journey to Valerie's house. Luke's birthday gift is a night away in the stunning Hotel Le Meurice. That was where Luke told me he loved me for the first time, and it was probably there that I knew I would spend the rest of my life with him. This also gave me an excuse to ask Valerie to join me, as we have two appointments with potential fabric suppliers close to Paris. Win-win!

Soon we arrive at Valerie's house. Max gets out of the car to help with her luggage. She slides into the back seat next to me.

'Morning,' I say.

'Hello, Kate.'

'Sorry it's so early. I had to leave before Luke woke.'

'He's in for a surprise when he wakes.'

'I hope so.'

'I'm looking forward to seeing the suppliers.'

'Me too.'

I'm not as thrilled as my inner cupid, who is delighted. I love the fact that Valerie and Max are oblivious to my cunning plan – or are they? I think after a quick tour of the two fabric suppliers I will have a terrible headache and will need to rest, leaving Max and Valerie to entertain themselves.

We arrive at City Airport where we are greeted by Luke's friendly staff. I booked one of Luke's jets under an assumed name, in case he checked. Once our luggage has gone through security, we have a coffee before we board.

My mobile phone pings. Caller ID – Boss.

'Here goes.'

I open the message.

Dear Kate,

   It seems that you have left me alone on my birthday.
   However, it would also appear that you have a plan…
You know how much I love a Harper–Sutton challenge.
   Be safe. I love you
   Your hunting husband xxx

I chuckle.

'Well?' Valerie says.

'So far so good! Rosie said she would call once he's found the next clue.'

Feeling the need to wish him a happy birthday, I send a text.

Dear love of my life,

   I love a Harper–Sutton challenge too.
   Find me, Luke. No cheating – that means you can't use my watch. Besides, I have been planning this for weeks.
   I love you xxx

We board the plane, a smaller aircraft than Luke's personal jet. I sit next to the window, placing my bag on the adjacent seat, leaving the only two remaining seats opposite me. I wish Luke was with me holding my hand. To distract me,

I retrieve a baby book from my bag, to discourage Max and Valerie from talking to me. I hope they will take the chance to talk to each other.

After the short flight the plane descends and lands smoothly at Orly Airport. Max acts as our baggage handler, wheeling a trolley with our luggage to the waiting limousine. Our first appointment is a forty-minute drive away, and the second appointment is much closer to the hotel. As we drive, I call Rosie.

'Hello?'

'Rosie, it's Kate – how did it go?'

She begins to laugh. 'It was hilarious. He told me your note said eat me. At first he looked in the fridge, then he asked me.'

'Really? I thought he would have guessed.'

'No, he didn't. I nodded towards the cake.'

'And?'

'I told him he had to eat it, and he thought you meant the entire cake!'

'I'm sure Jerry was on hand to help.'

'He was! Anyway, he cut the cake and found the note. Good job you wrapped it in a clear bag.'

'Did he seem happy, or was he…'

'No, my darling, he was laughing. Actually, I think he was excited. He couldn't believe you put a note in the cake.'

'Good, I was praying he would play the game.'

'He bounced out of the house.'

'Bounced?' Does Luke ever bounce? 'Thanks, Rosie. We've just landed in Paris.'

'OK, have a lovely time.'

'Will do. Bye.'

I look across at Max and Valerie. 'He laughed at the note in the cake. First one done, just the rest to go.'

'You're bloody mad, Kate. Actually, the pair of you are bloody mad,' Max says.

'I'm madly in love with him. I know that sounds cheesy but I don't care. God knows how he's going to take Barney's note.'

'I think it's sweet,' Valerie says.

We arrive at a large glass office building in the middle of nowhere. I'm here to see a company called International Fabric Distribution, IFD. We are greeted by two members of staff who speak perfect English. They show us around the manufacturing area, then give us a tour of the showroom, which is filled with the most stunning materials, from lace to faux leather.

They give us some fabric samples and a price list. It surprises me that they have heard of Harper Jones. Not only were they aware of the ready-to-wear collection we took to New York, but they are a fairly new business and want to invest in an equally new fashion label. Harper Jones seems to fit the bill.

The three of us return to the car after our tour, delighted.

'I'm shocked,' I say.

'I never saw this coming. The show was only last week, but the feedback has been incredible.'

'I'm so pleased for Mr Jones.'

My phone rings. Caller ID – Stella.

'Kate, how are you?'

'Good, Stella, and you?'

'I'm very well. So, Luke came to the office.' She goes silent. 'Sorry, Kate, just checking he can't hear me. Well, anyway, he arrived an hour ago. I wished him happy birthday, he frowned at my gift – you know what he's like.'

'I do.'

'Immediately, he asked me about a note. He showed me the one from the cake, which I thought was hilarious, telling him he had to go in search of world domination.'

'I always say that to him.'

'Anyway, I handed over the note addressed to 007 from Cinderella. He found it highly amusing. I reminded him that Cinderella stated he must leave the office no later than twelve o'clock... Oh – hang on.' Silence once again, but this time I can hear his voice in the background. 'The plan is on target.'

'Thanks, Stella, I owe you.'

'Have fun and look after those babies.'

'I will. See you soon.'

My shoulders relax and a smile washes over my face.

'I take it the plan is working.' Max shakes his head in disbelief that Luke is going along with it.

'Yes, Mr Cynical. Stella gave him her note. I addressed it to 007 from Cinderella.'

'Where does he have to go next?' Valerie asks.

'Barney's studio for a dance lesson.'

Max and Valerie break into hysteria.

'No way will Sutton go along with that.'

'He will if he wants the next note. I did tell him that today might be challenging.'

We arrive at the second meeting: Garcia Morel, a much smaller establishment. They too make us feel welcome and – of course – speak fabulous English. This makes me feel completely inept for the second time today. I wish I'd paid more attention to my French teacher. The fabrics they offer are higher-end, with matching price tags, which would affect our customers. The two companies seem to be polar opposites: IFD is a new business that wants to take over the world of fabrics and Garcia Morel is a family-run business that has been passed from generation to generation, not too dissimilar to Jones Tailors.

After a couple of hours we leave, armed with another set of samples and price lists – homework for the Harper Jones crew. Feeling exhausted after the early morning and two meetings, I need to sleep.

My phone rings. Caller ID – Plus one.

'Did he do it?' I blurt.

'What do you think?' Barney laughs. 'I tell you what, babe, I nearly pissed myself laughing.'

'So he did?'

'All I can say is, ask him how to do a shuffle ball change.'

'No! He didn't!' I giggle.

'When he turned up with his note from Stella he knew there would be trouble ahead, or at his feet… What did your note say?'

'First I called him 007.'

'Cheeky, but on point, babe.'

'Exactly, and then I wrote "put on your dancing shoes and ask my plus one for some moves".'

'OK, so he arrived with a face like a busted arse. I knew straight away there was no way he was going to dance.'

'Was he miserable?'

'Not really. He did laugh once we came to an agreement – hence the shuffle ball change.'

'I can't believe he's going along with it.'

'Knowing his prize is you?'

'Do you think he's enjoying it?'

'Bloody hell, what Sutton doesn't want to be the centre of attention?'

'Thanks, Barney – I owe you.'

'Yeah, you do. I'm stocking up, babe. I'll hit you with a massive IOU.'

'Bye.'

Twenty minutes later we arrive at Hotel Le Meurice. What a building – not only for its beauty, but also for the history it holds for Luke and me. It was here he told me he would always be with me – which he meant literally when he gave me my beautiful birthday gift: a watch with a tracking device!

It's uncanny, but Max and Valerie's rooms are next to each other. Max, of course, escorts Valerie to her room, then me. We agree to meet in an hour. Alas, I fear the start of the headache from hell…

I lie on the bed wearing a white robe, perusing the room service menu. A telephone call is in order.

'Kate?' Max answers abruptly. I'm beginning to think Luke got his charm from Max.

'Hi, I'm too tired to go out and I feel sick. Would you mind meeting Valerie? Explain to her that I'm exhausted.'

'Do you need anything? I can come and sit with you.'

What? Now I feel guilty.

'No, the early morning has caught up with me, that's all.'

'OK.'

'Also, I don't want Valerie to be on her own tonight. I've made a reservation in the restaurant for you. Make sure you wear your navy suit and pale blue shirt – it makes your eyes look stunning.'

'Kate!'

'Sorry, Max, I'm going to be sick. Have fun and don't leave Valerie alone in a strange city. Bye.'

I know he's on to me. Oh well, they still have lunch and dinner together – fingers crossed that one of them makes the first move.

After my bath, and feeling full from the delicious room service sandwiches and French pastries, my phone rings. Caller ID – Mr Jones.

'How did it go?' I ask.

'I could ask you the same question, young lady.'

'Really well. Oh my God, the first company, IFD, knew who we were and had photos of our collection from the fashion show.'

'Impressive.'

'I know, Valerie and I were floored. They really want our business. They love that we are new and quintessentially British. They want to attach their name to our brand.'

'That sounds positive.'

'The other company, Garcia Morel, was really quaint – you would have loved it. It reminded me of the stories you told me about when you travelled through France.'

'It sounds like you've had quite a day. I shall look forward to our meeting next week.'

'Me too. So how was the birthday boy?' I ask.

'Agitated, but also excited.'

'Good. Did he tell you Barney taught him a shuffle ball change?'

'He said that visiting Barney was the most challenging task.'

I laugh. 'So, how hot does he look in his new suit?'

'Refined and exquisite.'

'Perfect. I can't wait to see him.'

'Without a doubt he feels the same. However, he did seem quite taken aback with the lining of the suit.'

'I know it's cheesy, but I do love him.'

'Yes, you do, and the silk lining also loves him.' We laugh.

'So he understood the note from Barney?'

'I think quoting "damsel in distress" was a clear clue as to where his next note would be.'

'Good… Did you read the note I gave you?'

'No, he read it aloud… "Go to the very beginning of your life".'

'His mum and dad – I knew they wanted to see him today.'

'How thoughtful, and, yes, he understood. Have a fabulous evening. I'm sure you will.'

'Thanks, Mr Jones. Love you – bye.'

Though I was deceitful to Max, there's an underlying truth: I feel exhausted. Waiting for Luke, my eyelids are already beginning to close.

The sound of my phone ringing stirs me. I feel disorientated. Caller ID – Livy.

'Hi.'

'Kate, my lovely, I have called you a few times.'

'Sorry, I fell asleep.'

'Oh, I didn't mean to disturb you. Are you feeling OK? And my grandbabies?'

'A bit queasy. It's worst this time of the day.'

'My boys made me feel nauseous at all times of the day!'

I yawn. 'How was Luke?'

'Amused. You have been a busy girl.'

'What do you give a man who has everything?'

'I understand, although today he does seem surprised.'

'Good surprised or stroppy surprised?'

'No, good surprised. When I gave him the box to open, he looked at me rather strangely. I explained that he had to complete the surprise then he could have the last remaining envelope.'

I laugh. 'How did he do?'

'Well, the Lego jet I thought was a marvellous idea, and of course he made it in record time. I then gave him the last envelope, which made him laugh: his passport and a ticket. Very clever, Kate, it was plain to see that he was taken back by all the notes. He showed them to us.'

'I thought it would be fun. I wanted to show him how much he means to me.'

'He knows, my darling, he knows. Kate, I don't think you realise what you bring to his life.'

'Thanks, Livy.'

'He left about forty minutes ago. I assume he must have boarded the flight or at least he's waiting to board.'

I lie on the bed and wonder what he's thinking. I have one more call to make.

'Stella Trevant speaking.'

'Hi, Stella.'

'Kate, I was just going to call you. Luke took off about five minutes ago.'

'Thanks.'

'Has it gone to plan?'

'So far so good. Have you spoken to him?'

'Not for a while. Now have fun.'

'I will. Bye.'

I chuckle to myself and kick my legs on the bed. Now I have to get ready for dinner.

I check my reflection in the mirror. I'm wearing a simple bias-cut black dress that skims my bump, but it does resemble a mid-length nightdress – silk and lace! I'm in black Louboutins with poker-straight hair and smoky eyes.

After a brief conversation with his air staff I know he's on his way to the hotel, so I grab my Chanel bag and make my way to the restaurant, where I'm shown to our table. My waiting game is nearly over. The restaurant looks beautifully romantic, exactly as I remembered it, and incredibly busy. I stand out like a sore thumb, dining alone!

I sit with a glass of sparkling water, lost in thought. Suddenly, I feel someone watching me, and I know he's here. I turn towards the doorway. There he stands in his new black suit, looking so manly, so handsome, so Luke Sutton. My heart pounds. I stand up.

He strides over to me, takes me in his arms and kisses me. I respond with tenderness. Eventually he pulls away to read my eyes: dark and enthralling meet dark and thankful.

'You took your time. Happy birthday, Luke. I love you.'

'I love you too.' He holds my chair for me, then lowers his lips to my ear. 'What are you wearing?'

'Your birthday present. I can take it off within ten seconds.'

He sits opposite me. 'Ten seconds – as long as that?'

'I'm pleased you like it.'

'Yes I do, but I'm not alone.'

'Oh, I sense you're a little frustrated.' I slip my foot from my shoe and slide it between Luke's legs.

His eyes close for a second as he takes a breath.

'Just so you know, I have ordered our meal. Since I have been in control of your day, I thought I would extend that to dinner.'

He flashes me his best Sutton smile at my reminder of our first visit to Hotel Le Meurice.

'This is going to be a long meal. Shall we get room service? I take it we're staying here?' he says.

'Yes and no, we will not be getting room service. I will provide that later.'

Once again he laughs. 'You're teasing my dick.'

'Yes. Happy birthday.'

'Quite the little plan.'

'Have you enjoyed it?'

He tilts his head and smirks at me. 'Yes, most of it.'

'Barney!' I laugh. 'Are you going to show me your shuffle ball change?'

'No, and honestly I nearly left the studio. Let's just say we compromised.'

'I wish I could have been there. Even Max was shocked.'

'Speaking of Max, he told me that you asked him to take Valerie out. He is on to you.'

'About bloody time! I think telling him to wear his navy suit and pale blue shirt was a bit of a giveaway.'

'OK, I admit…' Luke holds his hand in the air. 'He does seem a little more…'

'Cheerful? Perhaps he knows he might get laid.'

'End of conversation.' Luke's brows knit.

'I'm sure he wants to have sex. Can you imagine abstaining for years?'

'No,' he says and roll his eyes.

'Well, you wouldn't have that problem. Let's not forget that half of Chelsea would be queuing up. No dry spell for you.'

'You're probably right.'

My jaw hits the ground. 'What?'

'I love sex.'

'No shit, Sherlock, but remember that's only with me, not with the Chelsea contestants.'

'Baby, you seem a little hot under the collar.'

'I'll show you hot!'

After our fish starter, we have steak, but I already feel full. Good job Mr Birthday Boy Sutton has a large appetite. I excuse myself to go to the bathroom – again. Not only do I have to contend with feeling nauseous in the middle of the day, but now I need to visit the loo every five minutes, or so it feels.

As I return, Luke watches every step I make through the crowded restaurant. I almost collide with another guest. I apologise and the young man places a hand on my arm. Luke stands up, and I move towards him.

'What's up, birthday boy?'

'Complete strangers touching you piss me off.' He runs his hand through his hair.

'Come back to the light, Luke,' I say and smile.

'I need you – now.' Perfect, Luke.

He signals to the waiter, who arrives instantly. Luke chats to him in French, then stands and holds his hand out for me. 'We're leaving.'

'We haven't had dessert.'

He lowers his face to my ear. 'If we don't leave I will be fucking you on this table. You choose.'

'Fine.' I collect my bag from the table and slide my hand in his. He pulls me to him, kissing me fiercely, taking my breath away.

As we leave the restaurant and enter the magnificent foyer, we come face to face with Max and Valerie. And Max's arm is around Valerie's waist!

'Hi.' I greet them both, feeling the need to cartwheel – internally, of course.

'Luke, happy birthday.' Valerie says. 'Kate, are you feeling better?'

'Much better… Max, you look lovely. I love that blue suit on you. Don't you think it looks lovely on him, Valerie?'

'Say goodnight, Kate,' Luke commands and walks on.

'Bye, see you in the morning,' I shout over my shoulder.

Luke continues to hold my hand firmly as we wait for the lift.

'Problem, Mr S?'

'Only my wife.'

'Oh, I'm a problem, am I?'

'Yes, you're like a dog with a fucking bone.'

'And?' I say.

'And…' He doesn't finish. He lets his lips do the talking with a sizzling kiss. The lift arrives, and we enter.

'What floor?'

I push the button and pull at his new black suit. He pushes me back against the wall. This time my mouth devours his. He breaks free.

'What I wouldn't give to fuck you in this lift.' His voice, full of desire, is all I need to hear.

'Do it,' I say.

'There are security cameras. If I stop the lift they will override it.'

My hand gropes the very prominent bulge in his trousers. His eyes close with the need to be buried deep inside me.

The lift stops and the doors open. For a change, I guide him to our room. As soon as we enter, Luke slams the door and pushes me against it. Savagely his lips are on mine and he slides one hand up my dress while the other hand pulls at my straps. The dress is incredible flimsy, allowing Luke to almost tear it from my body. I wrap one leg around his arse, drawing him to me.

'Fuck, I need to be inside you.'

I nod. 'Do it.'

I drop my bag to the floor and my hand works at Luke's zip and he rips my knickers from me. In seconds he is hard in the palm of my hand. Driven mad by desire, I guide him to me. He lifts me and enters me ferociously, pushing me hard up against the door.

'Holy shit,' I mutter.

He stills.

'I'm fine. Just take me, Luke.'

'My greedy wife. How I've missed you today.'

He continues to thrust into me and my internal walls lock around him every time he hits the spot. As Luke thrusts harder, I'm almost at the point of climax. My head falls back against the door as the first wave hits me.

'Shit, Luke, I need to come.'

'I'm with you, baby.'

'Harder, Luke, harder.'

I can feel him smile against my neck. 'Fuck, I need you.'

Moisture released from my orgasm layers the head of Luke's erection as he takes what he needs and drives harder into me until he comes. He stops dead, resting his forehead on me.

'Happy birthday, Luke,' I mutter.

'The best,' he pants.

He lowers me to the floor. 'Bath?' he asks.

I nod.

We lie at opposite ends of the bath.

'Have you had fun?' I ask.

'What do you think?'

'You're a bloody nightmare to buy for.'

'The notes were very clever.'

'Everyone wanted to help me.'

'Yes, I can imagine.' He strokes my feet. 'Thank you for the suit.'

'Did you laugh at the lining?'

'I assume it's unique and I'm the only person with a lining that reads *I love Luke Sutton*?'

'It's a one-off, handmade for you.'

'Good.'

'I'm pleased you're here. Pathetically, I was missing you.'

'Honestly, I was disappointed to not see you this morning... You have some making up to do.'

'I thought I just did.' I giggle.

'I'm due more than a quick fuck against the door.'

'So you're horny again? At least wait for me to give you your presents,' I say.

He looks a little confused. 'I thought you were my present.'

'I have a couple of extras.'

We lie in the bath for as long as possible before Luke stands and wraps me in a towel. We sit on the bed in matching white robes. I pass him his gifts.

'I really do not need any presents.'

I reach for his lips. 'Yes, you do… Just because you're rich doesn't mean I don't want to buy for you.'

'OK, what shall I choose first?'

'Here, this one.'

I pass him a present. He removes the grey bow and lifts the lid off the box.

'I know it's silly but…'

Luke chuckles and takes a bite out of a flapjack. 'Hmmm, my favourite.'

'That's why I made them – with extra chocolate chips.' I reach in and take one.

He opens the remainder of the presents. First, he opens a black Aston Martin lightweight jacket.

'Thank you.'

'Do you like it? I thought you could wear it at the weekends.'

'Of course I like it! Why do you doubt your choices for me?'

He opens another box. I know this will make him smile. He puts the black Aston Martin baseball cap on his head.

'Well, do I look fuckable?' He smiles at his own question.

'Always.' I remove the cap. 'Look at the back.'

He smiles at me. 'Where did you get this?'

'From the Aston Martin shop. I got *Daddy* embroidered on the back… your first gift from the two dots growing inside me.'

'Jesus, you get me every time.' He takes a breath, obviously feeling overwhelmed.

'OK, this is your last present.'

He opens the box and removes a snow globe. Automatically, he shakes it.

'The car in the globe?' I raise my brows, wondering if knows what the globe represents.

'Aston Martin.'

'Right. I thought about ordering you a new car. But for two reasons I didn't: first, I can't accept the price tag, and second, I don't have a bloody clue what extras you would like.'

'Agreed. I would sooner choose it myself.'

'So I booked you a trip to Lapland, although it's not until February next year, so you'll have to wait. You get to drive an Aston Martin across ice.'

He looks surprised – really surprised. 'That sounds incredible.'

'Look under the tissue paper – there's some information about the trip. Though the babies will be here by then, but you can take someone else if you want to.'

He shakes his head. 'No, we'll go together as a family.'

'I thought it looked amazing.'

'I have never heard of it. Thank you for all the gifts.'

He reaches in the box and takes another flapjack.

I remove all the gifts from the bed while Luke wears his cap and shakes the globe.

'Did you get this made? The car has *eat me* on the number plate.'

'I did.'

'Come here.' He hugs me. 'I can't remember the last time I had a birthday like this – probably never.'

'I know you're a controlling gazillionaire, but you deserve happiness and surprises.'

'Thank you – I think.'

I giggle. 'Lucky for you I'm partial to a controlling gazillionaire.'

'Lucky me.' His smile warms my heart.

My hand sneaks under his robe and glides across his chest. 'Did you wonder why I brought you here?'

'Your watch. It was the first time I told you I loved you.'

I look up at his face. 'Yep, and that was the first time I knew I could never be without you.'

My mouth meets his. Flapjack kisses – perfect.

15

Tenderly Luke kisses his way down my spine before he gently bites my arse. Of course I laugh. God, I love a playful Sutton.

'I know we only got back yesterday, but I need more than one night in France. Let's take a sickie and stay in bed.'

'Kate Sutton, you're nothing but trouble.' Luke rolls me onto my back.

'I love being at home with you.'

'Good, but I have to work and you have a meeting today.'

Luke's mouth hovers over my bump. 'Mummy is going to be trouble today. Watch out, babies!'

'Oi. I'm fine, I just want to stay here. Is that a crime?'

'No, but if we both stay here there will be a crime committed against my wife, thanks to my need to fuck her.'

Great, I'm now turned on – again!

Luke and I take our seats in the Bentley. I shuffle across to his side and swing my legs over his. I need to feel close to him today. I need him. He puts his arm around my shoulders and lowers his lips to my head.

'If you're tired, call off your meeting.'

'No, I'm fine.' I take his hand, which rests on my shoulder. 'Let's have a lazy night in front of the TV.'

'I have a meeting late this afternoon and a workout booked.'

'Am I not keeping you fit?'

He laughs. 'Yes, but I need more.'

'You always do.'

'Have you thought about baby names yet?' he asks.

'No. Have you?'

'Only our mothers' names if we have girls, and my name for a boy.'

'OK… Just a heads-up. I love our parents, but not necessarily their names.'

'It's tradition,' he says, sounding amused.

'Maybe in the nineteenth century.'

'You surprise me. I thought you loved tradition.'

'Not passing down names!'

He lifts my face. 'And my name?'

'It suits you – not our children.'

His smile spreads. I love it when he is this happy. 'Are you saying you don't like my name?'

'It belongs to you. Besides, I gave you a book of five thousand names, so why would you use a name that someone already has?'

'Fair point.'

'Why don't we compromise and use family names for middle names?' I say.

'Middle names it is,' he says.

That was easy.

Tanya and I sit at the boardroom table reading through magazine articles about Mrs Gold's charity show.

'Well?' Tanya waits for a response.

'This is really encouraging,' I say, utterly amazed.

'I know.' She reaches across and takes my hand. 'I'm so pleased.'

'Me too, even more so for Mr Jones.' I sit back in the chair and clasp my hands over my bump. I'm convinced it's bigger than yesterday. 'I'll never forget the day he showed me the cupboard in his shop... His design books were stacked high.'

'What a waste.'

'I know, and now he's finally receiving the recognition he deserves.' I look at my watch. 'Right, the crew should be here soon. Have you spoken to Alexis?'

She nods. 'Yeah, while you were in France. Kate, I must admit I'm a little shocked that Harry is coming on board Bagrov and Cooper!'

'Oh!' Tanya has no idea that the evil fucker was Harry's father. I take a breath. 'Listen, I have something to tell you but it has to stay between us. If Luke finds out I've spoken to you, he'll do a Sutton code red!'

She tilts her head.

'Trust me, it's not pretty. Why am I saying that? You probably know exactly what a Sutton code red is like – you worked with him.'

'He's not that bad, maybe a bit hot-headed.' She smiles.

'Er, I beg to differ, but we have to work together and there's this huge bloody elephant in the room.'

'OK,' she says, looking confused.

'Promise you won't breathe a word, not even to Harry and Alexis, even though it involves them? I haven't got a clue how this will all pan out. Shit, I really shouldn't…'

'You have my word, you know that,' she says.

'I trust you – completely.'

She squeezes my hand, encouraging me.

'OK, so life for me and Harry changed last year when we found out…' – I take a breath – 'we were adopted. Hence the business.'

Tanya remains silent.

'Anyway, you know Ivor Varizin is my birth father.'

'The Russian guy.'

'Yep, well, he's not Harry's dad. We've known for a while but kept it quiet to protect Mum and Dad. We will never tell them.'

'Malcolm and Suzanne,' she says looking a little puzzled.

'Right. Philip Cooper – may he burn in hell. I hate him more than you will ever know. He… raped my biological mother.'

'Oh my God.' Her hand covers mine. 'Kate, I'm so sorry. I don't know what to say.'

'It gets worse. Harry is…' I swallow acidic bile.

'No way? She's his? She can't be,' Tanya says. She looks the way I feel.

I nod. 'She was conceived when he raped my mother. Look, we've only just found out.'

'That explains why you and Alexis have signed over shares to Harry. I'm so sorry, and of course you have my word this will go no further.'

'Thank you, and sorry for landing this on your lap.'

'It's fine – at least it all makes sense. I couldn't get my head around Alexis being your friend after how rude she's been to you. But I guess you had to make peace for Harry's sake.'

'Yeah.' Oh, and she saved my life. 'As I said, this isn't public knowledge.'

'I totally understand, and I would never hurt you or Harry.'

'I know you wouldn't,' I say.

'It goes no further than this room, I promise. I hope it all goes well for the three of you.'

'Thank you, we're all still processing it.'

'Oh my God, Kate, it'll take time for all of you,' Tanya says.

I take a breath and nod.

'Shall we change the subject?'

'Please,' I say gratefully.

'OK, on a lighter note I have some info that I know will make you happy. I spoke to Valerie last night.'

'And?'

'She has a thing for Max. Who would have thought it – except the person who set them up?' Tanya raises her brows.

I clap. 'We bumped into them in the hotel foyer and Max had his arm around her waist. What else did she say? Do you think she's on to me?'

'I don't think so. She never mentioned it. Apparently, they're meeting for dinner tonight.'

A solitary tear rolls down my cheek. I wipe it away with the back of my hand.

'God, look at me.' I laugh. 'I just want him to be happy. Did she seem excited? Oh – what about France? Did anything happen?'

'All she said was they had a wonderful evening and a lovely day walking around Paris. She did say you were tired and Max looked after her. As for action…' Tanya looks away. 'I have a feeling something did happen. Valerie is not the sort of woman to kiss and tell, but I saw a sparkle in her eye.'

The day continues. 'From a marketing point of view, IFD would be on board with advertising, et cetera, but obviously you have history with Garcia Morel.' Maria makes notes.

'OK, we still have our UK suppliers, but my gut instinct says IFD would be more accommodating of our ideas. After all, they want something exciting to get their teeth into – why not let that be Harper Jones?' I'm amazed that I can hold my own. If only Luke could see me. I look across the table. 'Mr Jones?'

'It's a double-edged sword, my dear. However, IFD would be my choice, merely because they seem hungry for the challenge.'

Eventually we decide that IFD is our best option – also, they offer the best prices. Valerie and Maria make arrangements to return next week for further discussions. Lunch arrives and thankfully we get some time to switch off. I sit next to Valerie – I want to hear all the gossip.

'Have you recovered from France?' I ask.

'I loved every minute. What about you? Max said you're tired a lot lately.'

'It's the sickness. It drains me.'

Valerie takes my hand. 'You poor love, hopefully it will ease soon.'

'Sorry I ditched you in France.'

'Actually, Kate, I wanted to say something, but I'm not sure if this is the best time and place,' she says.

'We're friends; the time will always be right.'

'In that case, it's about Max.' She looks away for a second.

'Go on.'

'It's just … I like him.'

'He means the world to me and Luke.'

'I know, and he thinks of Luke like a son.'

'I just want him to be happy – and you too.'

'I didn't want you to hear it from someone else but Max is taking me out this evening for dinner.'

'I'm so happy for you both. Valerie, he will protect you and look after you.'

'I know.' She places her hand over her heart – in relief, I think. 'I'm so pleased I spoke to you.'

'I want you to be happy.'

My inner cupid is having a party. I can't wait to tell Luke… Bring it on, Sutton!

At the end of the day everyone leaves, except Mr Jones.

'Are you pleased with how things are going?' I remove my shoes and curl my legs on the sofa.

'Shocked,' he replies.

'You did it – this was your dream.'

'We did it,' he replies.

'The new collection will be stunning, and better – in a good way.'

He nods and sips his tea.

'Are you OK? You look a little pale,' I say.

'I'm tired.' He places his cup and saucer on the table and loosens his tie.

'Have I worn you out?' I smile.

'Not at all.' He unbuttons his top button, which is not like him. 'It feels rather hot in here. I think I need some fresh air.' He stands and walks away from the sofa.

I go towards him. 'Are you sure you're all right?'

He nods, but he is ghostly white.

'Look at me,' I say. His eyes widen and he tries to swallow.

'You're not OK. Come and sit down.'

He tries to speak, but nothing comes out. He collapses to the floor and his body stiffens.

'Mr Jones!' I drop to my knees and grip his shoulder. 'Mr Jones, look at me.'

But he just lies there, completely still.

'Mr Jones!' I scream.

Nothing.

'Luke? Luke!' I shout.

Within seconds, Stella barges through the door. 'Kate?' She sees Mr Jones on the floor. 'Oh my God.'

'Where's Luke?' I say.

'Marketing!' She almost falls over her words and leaves the room.

I shake him. 'Please, Mr Jones.' Christ, I don't know what to do. 'Come on – wake up, please.'

Stella comes running in again. 'An ambulance is on the way. I've called Luke too.'

'He looks…' I say and swallow my words. *He looks dead.*

Then I hear someone running, and Luke enters the room.

'He collapsed.' I say through the fear that constricts my throat.

'Move over,' he says.

I crawl to one side and give Luke some space.

'Stella – ambulance.' As ever, Luke is in command.

'I've already called one.'

Luke brings his ear to Mr Jones's mouth and rests his forefinger and middle finger against his wrist, searching for a pulse, then starts CPR.

I am transfixed.

This can't be real. Ten minutes earlier, I was talking to him, and now he's just lying there, motionless, in front of me.

'Please be OK… Please, Mr Jones.'

Luke carries on with CPR, but there is no change in Mr Jones. I lose track of time and how long Luke continues CPR. All of a sudden, two paramedics are brought in to my office.

Luke places his fingers against Mr Jones's pulse and turns to them.

'I can't feel a pulse, and he's not responding to CPR. Possibly twenty minutes, maybe longer.'

'OK. Let us take over,' one paramedic responds. 'Does he have any heart-related illness?'

'We don't know,' Stella answers.

'Kate…' Luke says and pulls me to his lap. I bury my face in his chest.

I hear Stella talking to the two men, and the sounds of the paramedics working, but I can't look. I remain with my head against Luke until he pulls away.

One of the paramedics comes over to me. 'Kate, right?'

I nod.

'We are really sorry but…'

'No, carry on… You have to.'

'Kate, it's been too long,' Luke says.

'No! You save everyone. Please, Luke.'

He shakes his head. 'He's gone.'

'No, you're wrong. He said he felt tired, that's all.' Horror explodes across my face. 'Move out of the way, let me try.' I crawl towards him. 'Mr Jones, please.' I push against his chest. 'Come on, Luke, please help him.' I hit his chest again.

'Kate, look at me.'

I glance at the two paramedics. 'Please help him.'

'Kate.' The paramedic places his hand on my arm. 'There is nothing we can do.'

'No!' I collapse over Mr Jones's body. 'Please don't leave me – you can't leave.' I turn to Luke. 'He can't leave me.'

I start to shake with shock.

Eventually they place a blanket over Mr Jones's body.

Nausea washes over me. I scramble up and run to the bathroom.

Luke follows me and gently rubs my back. 'Kate.'

After I've finished throwing up, I rinse my mouth. My eyes meet Luke's in the mirror.

'I need to tell him I'm sorry.'

Luke frowns. 'Why?'

'I did this. It's my fault. If we hadn't started the business, he wouldn't have worked so hard. Luke, I killed him.'

'Jesus.' He rakes his hand through his hair. 'You haven't killed him. Christ, you couldn't hurt anyone.'

'I did, Luke. He told me he was tired. I should have seen it was too much for him.'

'No way! You will not take the blame for something that was out of your hands. It looked like a heart attack.'

'That I caused,' I say and leave the bathroom. In the office, the paramedics are loading Mr Jones's body onto a trolley. 'Stop! I need to see him.' My eyes feel raw with crying. I bolt towards them. 'I have to tell him I'm sorry... Please.'

One of the paramedics looks at me. 'It's fine – take all the time you need.' He pulls back the red blanket.

'Thank you,' I whisper.

His face is pale. I remove his glasses and kiss his soft cheek.

'I never started the business to hurt you. I'm so sorry. I love you so much.' I lay my head on his chest and my tears fall. I have no way of stopping them.

'Kate, they need to take him,' Luke says.

He lifts me and carries me through to his office, where he sits on the sofa and holds me close while I continue to cry.

'That's right, let it out, baby.'

How is it possible to lose him so suddenly? Whenever I close my eyes I see him lying on the ground, motionless.

'A cup of tea?' Stella's voice.

'That's a good idea. Thanks,' Luke says, holding me close.

It feels as though my world has stopped.

'Kate, please drink something.'

I shake my head and tighten my hold on Mr Jones's glasses.

'Baby, look at me.'

I don't want to move. I can't move. I feel cold and paralysed.

Luke pulls me away from his chest, trying to gauge how I am.

'Please drink something.' He slides me off his lap and takes a mug from the table.

I feel the heat against my lips, but no amount of heat can warm the cold, empty feeling inside me. I close my eyes. The last time I drank tea was with Mr Jones.

'I can't,' I whisper and pass him the mug.

'I'm taking you home.'

Right now, Luke could take me anywhere. I am numb to the world.

I hear him talking to Stella and Max.

'Kate, stand up.'

I do as requested. Luke bends down, slips my shoes on, then rests my coat over my shoulders.

'Stella, call me at home.'

'Of course. I'm so sorry, Kate,' Stella says.

Luke takes my hand and leads me out. I stop outside my office.

'Kate, let's go.'

I shake my hand free, walk to the sofa and collect Mr Jones's navy blazer.

I look up at Luke. 'I can't believe he's gone.'

'You're in shock. I need to get you home.'

'Why, Luke? He was one of the kindest people who ever walked this earth.'

'There are no rules. People are taken from us for no reason.'

He slides his arm around me and encourages me to walk away. I leave with Mr Jones's blazer and glasses, knowing I will never see him again.

Eventually we make it home. Luke guides me through the front door. 'I'll run you a bath,' he says.

He helps me out of my clothes and takes my hand as I step into the hot water. I huddle, my knees locked to my chest. Luke gets in behind me, wrapping his legs around mine and his arms across my torso.

'Lean on me.' Luke tries to encourage me to rest my back on him.

Eventually, I lay my head against his chest and sink further into the warm water.

'It hurts so much,' I manage to say.

'I know.' He kisses the top of my head and cradles my stomach.

'He'll never meet our babies.' Hot tears fall.

'I have a feeling he will never leave you. I remember the day you dropped off my shirt and I went rushing to the tailors, desperate to find out who you were. He compared you to silk.'

I smile through my unbearable pain. 'He helped me make your tie.'

'Handmade by Kate, aka damsel in distress. He brought us together,' Luke says.

'He did… I never thought about him like that. How can someone be in your life for such a short time, but have such a huge impact?'

'At least you had that time with him. He loved you.'

'I worked him too hard, Luke. Deep down inside I know I did.'

Luke tightens his hold. 'Please don't say that. You have nothing to apologise for – you allowed his dream to come true. Watching you walk down the catwalk in New York –

I was so proud of you and Mr Jones. What you achieved together was very special. You gave him a life he never thought was possible.'

'Do you honestly believe that? I feel so guilty making him work so hard – not only on the show but also making things for us.'

'Your wedding dress? You looked stunning. And he wanted to make it for you.'

'I loved it.' I try to speak but emotion closes my throat. 'He helped me get ready, zipping me into my dress. Now it seems like the most priceless memory I have.'

'And what an amazing memory. You made his world – please don't forget that.'

'Oh God, Luke, why?' I bury my face in his wet chest as a deep groan is torn from my body. Surely I can't cry any more?

After attempting to eat some soup, I curl up on the sofa in Luke's office. He's on the phone, but I have switched off from the world.

I hear Luke leave the office and then voices echoing from the hall. Luke walks in with Dr Samantha Jacobs.

'Kate,' Luke says.

I look at them.

Samantha walks towards me.

'I am terribly sorry for your loss. A foolish question, but how are you feeling?'

I shake my head and take a deep breath. 'I don't really know.'

'Would you mind if I took your blood pressure, just to check on you and the babies?'

My eyes skate towards Luke's. 'OK.'

She has soon completed her checks, and gives me a clean bill of health.

'Did Luke tell you what happened?' I ask. 'He thinks it was a heart attack.'

'The symptoms do sound like heart failure.'

'He was working long hours – would that have caused it?' My eyes meet Luke's.

'There are many reasons for heart failure, but there's usually a physical cause. For him to die so suddenly, I would hazard a guess that he might have had an aneurysm or sudden cardiac death.'

'Oh! Would work or stress affect that?'

She takes my hand. 'No. Did he have any heart problems?'

'I don't know.'

'There is no positive to his death, but he went quickly and he was with you. Luke said you were extremely close.'

'Yes.'

'I believe he made your wedding dress,' she says.

I smile and look at the charcoal drawing on the wall.

'May I see a picture?'

Luke returns with a photo of our wedding day and passes it to Samantha.

'You look beautiful. He was obviously very clever.'

I nod.

'I will leave you two alone. Kate, call me if you need anything. Time will help you heal – and some rest would help too.'

Luke shows her to the door then returns to my side.

'I should have warned you she was coming,' he says, running his hand through my hair.

'It's fine.'

'Shall we go to bed?'

'I'm scared to sleep. I know when I close my eyes I'll see him. I can't cry any more, Luke, I don't have the energy.'

'How about I read to you in bed?'

'Read to me?' I give the smallest of smiles.

'I was thinking I could read from the book of five thousand baby names.'

'That sounds good.'

We lie in bed. My phone bleeps. I pick it up from the nightstand. I have six messages from Harry, and messages from Kiki, Molly and Barney. I put my phone down, not wanting to speak to anyone other than Luke.

'Shall we start with girls or boys?'

'I don't mind.' I look at Luke. 'Did you know Mr Jones's first name?'

'Strangely, I've never heard you say it.'

'Jefferson.' I return my head to Luke's chest. 'But he will always be Mr Jones to me.'

16

For the second morning running I wake at four o'clock feeling hungry. I am certain that throwing up every afternoon means my appetite kicks in at this crazy hour. With a mug of hot tea and a packet of biscuits, I go to sit in Luke's office.

When a tear traces its way down my cheek I wipe it away, knowing it will be the first of many today. Today is Mr Jones's funeral. Funerals are for who, the living or the dead? 'Keep me strong today, Mr Jones,' I whisper to myself.

It's still dark outside when I wander upstairs and check our suits, which hang side by side. Matching black Jones Tailors suits – Luke's birthday gift and my runway suit. Straight away, I notice my tie is missing, but Luke's is hanging with his shirt. I scurry around searching for it, opening drawers and cupboards, then it dawns on me. The show – I bet it's at the tailors. Shit!

I scrape my hair into a ponytail, slip on some clothes and grab the Jones Tailors keys, but first I leave a note for Luke.

Dear Luke,

Can't find my tie for today – gone to look for it. I won't be long.

Love you,

x

I rest it on his pillow and leave.

Within twenty minutes I draw up outside the shop. The quiet street off Savile Row feels a little eerie: it's five o'clock and the dark sky is starting to lighten. Quickly, I unlock the door and close it behind me. I switch the lights on and turn off the alarm. I shiver in the chilly morning air. This is my first visit to the shop since I lost Mr Jones. When I close my eyes I can hear his voice – and the sound of sewing machines running. I glance across the room to his desk, where he used to sit, looking at me over his glasses. I smile and fight back the need to cry.

'Right, where are you, tie?' I mutter.

I go over to the corner of the room, where we left boxes and hanging rails from the show. I open the lids and clear the mountain of clothes – but there's no sign of my tie.

'Shit. Where the bloody hell are you?'

I'm running out of options. I go to his desk and switch on the lamp. The desk is covered with paperwork, although it looks reasonably organised. He was neat and tidy in every aspect of his life. No tie. I sit in his chair and rifle through the drawers on either side. Nothing, except some sketchbooks and a small leather-bound book that looks like a diary.

First, I open the sketchbook. I touch the charcoal drawings and hold the book close to my chest. Pull yourself together, Kate, I repeat mentally. Next, I open the small brown book. The first page reads *1967*. As I flick through the pages, I realise the book is what I thought: a diary. But diaries are personal, and Mr Jones was incredibly private. Nonetheless, I open it at a random page and begin to read. I realise he's in Paris. I am certain this must be the year he bought the fabric for my wedding dress.

I begin to read his story. As I read, I can picture him and the journey he was on. The story he told me is now coming to life once again.

Suddenly, the present day comes back when there is a bang on the door. I look towards the window and notice the blue sky. Shit, how long have I been sitting here?

Quickly I scurry to the door. Luke stands there with a face like a busted arse. I fiddle with the lock and finally open the door.

'Sorry, I lost track of time.'

'Jesus, Kate, you could have said where you were going. A note with no address is not good enough.'

He barges past me and takes out his phone.

'I found her at Jones Tailors. Come and get my car. I'll drive Kate's home,' he says – I assume to Max. He runs his hands through his hair. 'How many times have I told you not to disappear? I've been calling you.'

I pat my coat for my phone. 'Sorry, it must be in the car. I couldn't find my tie and there is no way I can go to the funeral without my tie.'

'Your tie?' he says with an air of frustration.

'I woke up at four o'clock – again. Then I realised my tie was missing.'

He releases a low breath. 'Tie.' He shakes his head in disbelief. 'I assume you have it?'

'No.'

'Let's look for it together. We need to get ready.'

'OK.'

We begin to search. Actually, Luke looks thoroughly while I move things around randomly, not really looking but mentally taking stock of items that meant nothing and now mean a great deal. Resting on the cutting table is Mr Jones's cloth measuring tape. It has frayed edges and numbers that are barely visible – nonetheless, it was his favourite.

'Kate.' I look at Luke, who is holding up a black tie. 'Is this it? Your name is on the back: *handmade by Mr Jones for Kate Sutton.*'

'Yes.'

'We need to go.'

I nod, fighting my emotions.

'It's OK. Let's get today over with and then you'll feel better.' He pulls back, observing my reaction.

'I'm so bloody mad, Luke. Mad he's left all this and left me. I could scream and hit something, I'm that bloody angry.'

'Then scream and hit me.'

'What? I would never hit you.'

'Then scream. Let it out.'

From nowhere I unleash a scream. Even Luke looks shocked.

'Better?' he asks.

'Not really.'

'You have quite a pair of lungs, Mrs S.'

322

He picks up a long, heavy cardboard tube.

'Use this to hit the wall.' He points. 'Be careful of our babies.'

Without hesitation, I pull my arm back and swing the tube with all my strength. It smashes against the wall.

'God, that felt good.'

'Do it again,' Commander Sutton says.

I hit it again, this time harder, so hard the tube breaks in half.

'Here.' Luke passes me another.

'I am so angry, Mr Jones… So fucking angry.' I hit the wall again and again and again, then suddenly I drop the tube and fall into Luke's arms.

'Ready to go home?'

'Sorry I didn't wake you. I'm not thinking straight at the moment.'

'Nothing new there, baby.' He smiles, trying to lighten my mood.

As Luke drives my Bentley home, I sit next to him and read Mr Jones's diary.

'What are you looking at?' His eyes flit from the road to my lap.

'A diary I found. Mr Jones wrote it while he was in Paris. I'm sure that's when he bought the fabric for my wedding dress.' I look at Luke. 'Listen. *I know I will never be able to have the love I want, but at least G knows how I feel.*'

'Who's G?' Luke asks.

'I have no idea. Mr Jones always told me it's better to have loved and lost than never to have loved at all. I think he was talking about G.'

'Possibly.'

'How sad. He never admitted it, but there was sadness in his eyes when he spoke about Paris.'

Later on, Luke and I stand side by side in front of the large French mirror in our bedroom. He takes my hand. We look identical in our Jones three-piece suits.

'He made good suits.' God, I feel proud of him.

Luke squeezes my fingers. 'We need to leave.'

'I just need to collect the white roses from the kitchen.'

We arrive at the church car park, which is busy. I see familiar faces: the Harper Jones crew, friends, our family. Mr Jones had no living relatives; without doubt I was his family.

Luke looks at me.

'I'm here if you need anything. I'm worried about you.'

'Just stay with me and I'll be fine.'

Max opens my door and I step out. I can feel people watching me. Mum and Barney walk towards me.

'You look lovely, darling,' Mum says and gently touches my cheek. 'Did you manage to eat anything?'

'No. I feel sick, even more so today.'

'It'll pass, but you need to rest later, OK?'

'I will, Mum. Where's Dad?'

'Over there talking to Jerry. The flowers are beautiful.'

'I can't face everyone. I just want to run home,' I say.

'After the service, if you want to leave, you can leave. I can tell everyone you're not up to it.'

'Thanks, Mum.'

'She's right. When you're done in, babe, get Sutton to take you home. Good turnout.'

'Yeah. Your suit looks lovely.' I touch the front of his jacket.

'How could I not honour the man himself?'

I look at Luke, who watches me like a hawk, waiting for me to crumble. It won't be long, Sutton.

Luke guides me inside the church. We sit at the front, ready for the vicar to begin the service. But first the undertakers carry the coffin down the aisle to 'Adagio', which Mr Jones often played at work.

Planning the funeral was harder than I thought it would be, with my sparse knowledge of what Mr Jones liked and disliked – other than tea and fine clothing. So I decided to choose simple hymns and prayers, no fuss and frills. I chose the suit his father made for him to be buried in. He wore it on our wedding day, and I know how much it meant to him. In his pocket I placed a Harper Jones handkerchief, a scan picture of the babies, and a note from me.

Luke continues to hold my hand, and in the other I hold two white roses. After we sing the second hymn, 'Jerusalem', the vicar looks across at me. 'Kate would like to say a few words.'

I stand and walk forward to the lectern, gripping my notes.

'Bear with me,' I say. 'This is really difficult.' Already tears are rolling down my cheeks. 'Mr Jones was a man of quality and refinement, a true English gentleman. I will never meet another person like him. It goes without saying that he was talented, not only as a tailor and a designer, but also with his outlook on life and his words of wisdom, which he shared with me on many occasions.' I take a breath and look at my audience. 'He taught me more than I realised, questioned me when he didn't agree with me, and made me view things in a different light, and for that I will always be grateful.' I retrieve a handkerchief from my pocket to wipe my eyes. 'Was it fate that I worked for him and that he made Luke's shirts? I believe he brought us together.' I glance at Luke. 'He once told Luke I was like silk: treat me well and I would last a lifetime. If not, then I would disintegrate. This got me thinking: what would he be? And I decided on cotton. Reliable, strong and multi-faceted, he was all of those and so much more. I loved him with all my heart, and I feel cheated he has left this world, and me.'

Luke jumps up and comes over to me. Just in time. I crumple into his arms, sobbing. He guides me back to the pew. I can't take much more.

Barney leans towards me. 'Well done, babe. You did him proud.'

I can't speak. I have spoken all I can for the day.

After the funeral service there is the burial. Finally, the guests start to leave and I'm alone.

'Kate.'

I look at Luke, then bend down to place the white roses on the earth. 'These are for you, Mr Jones, from the babies. I – we – will always love you.'

Luke thought it would be best to hold the wake in one of the large meeting rooms at Sutton Global, keeping the palace as our sanctuary and not infringing on Jones Tailors or Mr Jones's flat above the shop. In retrospect, it was the perfect idea.

The caterers have laid out platters of sandwiches and pastries. I requested an afternoon tea. I also made several fruitcakes, as this was Mr Jones's favourite guilty pleasure.

Thankfully, people are chatting without needing too much from me.

'Oi, princess Harper, give us a hug.'

I turn to Barney. He squeezes me tight.

'Good gathering, babe. Mr Jones would have loved it.' He pulls away. 'You look like shit.'

'I still keep throwing up.'

'You poor cow. Looks like you're expanding.'

I look down at my trousers, which I could not do up this morning. 'I know.'

'Have you spoken to Adam?' I ask. I desperately need side-tracking. 'Spill.'

'Yeah, I have. I think he's coming over in a few weeks. But don't tell Rosie just in case it goes tits up.'

I smile for the first time today. 'I'm really pleased. Let's hope you don't fuck it up.'

'There she is, my Harper girl. No bullshit from you.'

Again I smile. Only Barney could make me smile today.

Harry walks towards me with Molly.

'Come here,' she says and hugs me. 'You OK?'

'I'm exhausted, Harry.'

'You looked so pale standing up in the church,' Molly says.

'It's done now, thank God. I can't think about it any more.' Kiki is heading in our direction.

'You did him proud, Kate.' Kiki rubs my arm reassuringly. 'You OK?'

'I'm fine, what about you?' I ask.

'Bearing up, but today is about you and Mr Jones.' Silence falls. Kiki waves at a waiter who walks towards us and hands us all glasses of wine – and orange juice for me. 'A toast.'

I nod and bite my lip, feeling fragile.

'I'll start,' Barney says. 'What a talented bloke, a true gent.' He raises his glass.

'I second that,' Molly says.

'One of a kind – they broke the mould with him,' Harry says.

'Absolutely,' Kiki says and looks at me.

'He was—' I swallow hard. 'He gave me Luke.' We raise our glasses.

'Mr Jones,' we say together.

'Listen, I can't think straight at the moment, but Luke is off to Dubai sorting out his hotel. I thought we could go to Sandbanks for a couple of days. I'll message you dates.'

'Great idea,' Barney says.

Needing some time alone, I collect my bag and slip out of the room. Max catches me at the door.

'Where are you going?'

'Walk with me to my office. I haven't been in there since…'

As Max walks with me, I see Luke watching us through the glass wall.

As soon as Max opens the door, I freeze.

'God, I feel sick…' A cold burst of air covers my skin in goose bumps.

'Maybe you're not ready.'

I shake my head. 'No, I need to do this. Mr Jones would want me to.'

'Then take it slowly.' Max holds his hand out for mine. I take two measly steps forward.

'You're in. You've done it.'

I smile. 'I can do this.'

I walk further into the room. I look at the floor where Mr Jones died.

'Kate, you need time. Believe me, I know.'

Of course he knows… His pain would have been far worse than mine – he lost a child.

'I want to be on my own. I promise I'm not going anywhere, although there's a good chance I might be asleep in five minutes.'

'OK.' He leaves me be.

Feeling mentally exhausted, I sit down on the pink Louis sofa. With silence around me, I remove the diary and tape measure from my bag, feeling the worn fabric. I set it on the table and open the diary to the page I stopped at earlier.

Again, I'm caught up in his story, discovering Paris and him falling in love with G. I continue to read. His writing is amusing; I never realised he was funny.

'Kate.'

I look up to see Luke. He's not alone.

'Hi,' I say.

'This gentleman wanted to speak to you. He is a close friend of Mr Jones.' The man looks to be a similar age to Mr Jones.

I stand and hold out my hand. 'Pleased to meet you.'

'I have heard a great deal about you,' he says.

'Really?' I frown, wishing I could say the same to him.

'I will leave you to it. Come and find me if you need anything.'

'Please, take a seat, Mr…'

'Gerald Watson, but please call me Gerry.'

'So, tell me, how did you know Mr Jones?'

'Jefferson…'

I shake my head. 'He's always been Mr Jones to me.'

'His great-grandfather was Jefferson, and the name was passed down to him.'

'Oh.' It's clear I really don't know much about him. 'I take it you were at the funeral. Sorry, it was a bit of a blur.'

'It was a beautiful service and you spoke well.'

'Losing him has crushed me… I know that sounds ridiculous.'

He takes my hand. 'Not at all. He thought the world of you – he told me that you adopted him into your family.'

I chuckle. 'It wasn't difficult. We hit it off since… Well, probably from when he interviewed me.'

'We met once a month for dinner. I remember him telling me about a young lady who had started working for him, and he told me some of your stories and dilemmas. We would laugh about them.'

'So, you were good friends.' I look away. 'Honestly, I feel guilty that I worked him too hard.'

'No, I think you're being unfair to yourself. When he told me about Harper Jones, he was excited, and for the first time in a number of years he felt alive. Kate, you gave him something he never thought possible – his dream. You must never doubt your decision to go into business together. I hope you will continue in his memory.'

'I don't know if I can.'

'You must. Do it for him – allow his dream to be fulfilled. He deserves that.'

'I stopped at the shop earlier. I couldn't find my tie. It was hard being there without him.'

'I knew you were wearing a Jones creation – and so is your husband.'

'And you?'

'Of course.'

'Although my trousers are too tight… did you know that I'm pregnant?'

'Yes, he told me.'

'Did he?' I say.

'He was thrilled for you.'

'He won't meet the twins.' I shut my eyes for a few seconds.

'Do you know what you are having?' he asks.

'No. I have another scan in a couple of weeks, but we don't want to know.'

'I met him just before you flew to New York.'

'I don't mean to be rude, but he never mentioned you. He kept his life under lock and key.'

'He was a private man.' Gerry picks up the leather-bound notebook lying next to me. 'Where did you get this?'

'I found it this morning when I was looking for my tie. Mr Jones spoke about his trip to France.'

'I remember it like it was yesterday.'

I frown. 'You were there?'

'Yes.'

'Oh. Like I said, Mr Jones didn't really say much. Actually, you may be able to shed some light on something.' I pick up the diary and flick through the pages. 'Here, read this,' I say and pass him the book.

He reads the page and takes a deep breath before closing the diary.

'G – do you know who that was?' Then a thought occurs to me. Shit! 'Are you Gerry with a G or a J?'

'G.'

My mouth snaps shut. 'Oh! But...'

He gazes out of the full-length windows that overlook the historical buildings surrounding Sutton Global.

'Was Mr Jones gay?' I ask.

'Kate, things were very different back in our day.'

'I understand. My best friend is gay.'

'I'm married with two children.'

'So, you're not gay?' I ask.

He shifts in his seat, looking uncomfortable.

'Jefferson and I have been friends since – well, ever since I can remember. He knew he would eventually inherit his family business and I had a job working in a bank alongside my father.'

'Your lives were already mapped out for you – Mr Jones said so himself.'

'Quite right. Most of our friends drifted off to pastures new, but we remained close.'

'Did he ever have a girlfriend?'

'I would say he had acquaintances more than relationships.'

'So you and he never – sorry, I don't mean to pry.'

'No, I understand. We went to Europe for a couple of months. Our fathers thought it would benefit our careers – mine for the language and Jefferson for a history of European fashion. I have to admit, it was one of the best times of my life.'

I reach across and touch his hand.

'We had a lot of fun, too much wine and one night of passion – a passion that would never be allowed.'

'Crap! He loved you. Poor Mr Jones, he lived with this secret for his entire life.'

'He knew it was not something either of us could revisit, and I doubted whether that path was for me… Do you understand?'

I nod. 'But you remained friends?'

'We did. He was the best man at my wedding.'

I raise my brows. 'Christ, poor Mr Jones.'

'We've been friends for years, so nobody was ever suspicious when we met up for dinner.'

'Did he try to meet someone else?'

He shakes his head. 'Sadly, no.'

'Reading between the lines, I think he never got over you. I asked him about the fabric and he mentioned a lost love. He said it was better to have loved and lost than never to have loved at all.'

'That sounds like him.'

'I'm really sorry for dragging up the past. I didn't mean to cause you pain.'

He sighs. 'Bizarrely, I feel relieved to share his secret.'

'I won't tell anyone. I will honour his memory forever.'

'I know, and I know how much you meant to Jefferson. He once said you were like the daughter he never had. That's why he was thrilled you used the fabric for your wedding dress. I know he helped you get ready on your special day, Kate, and that made him happy.'

'Me too.' Tears roll down my cheek. 'I am so fed up with crying.'

He reaches inside his blazer and retrieves something from his pocket.

'I would like to give you this.'

He passes me a white cotton handkerchief. Inside is a pocket watch.

'This belonged to Jefferson's grandfather. He gave it to me many years ago.'

'No, I can't… He gave it to you.'

He covers my hand with his and shakes his head. 'Honestly, I would like you to keep it. My children never had a relationship with him, for obvious reasons. I trust that you will treasure this as much as I have. Maybe you will have a son one day. It would mean a great deal to me if you accept it.'

'I will.' I reach across and pick up the tape measure. 'This was his favourite.'

'See, you understand him.'

'God, I miss him.'

'Me too.' He takes my hand and squeezes my fingers. 'I must go.'

We stand. At the same time, Luke appears at the door.

'Bye, Gerry.'

'Goodbye, Kate. It has been an honour to meet you,' he says and leaves.

'Is everything all right?' Luke asks.

'I want to go home.'

'OK.'

'I don't have the energy to say goodbye to everyone, can we just leave? I'll message Mum and Harry.' I collect my bag and slip the book, watch and tape measure inside it.

Luke takes my hand and we walk past the conference room and head towards the bank of lifts.

'Bath and food… You look exhausted.'

'Mr Jones was gay.'

Luke turns to me. 'What?'

'I know. Holy cow. I wanted to say that earlier, but Gerry – with a G, not a J – probably would not have approved.'

'He's the G from the diary?'

'The very same. I didn't twig when he introduced himself because our Jerry spells his name with a J.'

'How did this come about?'

'I asked him about France and the fabric, which he knew all about because he was there. Apparently they took a trip to Europe years ago, had a great time, and shared a night of passion. A night that would never happen again.'

'Times were different back then.'

'I know. Now Gerry is married with two children. Poor Mr Jones was his best man.'

'That's tough.'

'Can you imagine how bloody awful it must have been for him? He died with a broken heart. He was such an enigma. I feel like I really didn't know him.'

'You did, Kate. You knew him, and he loved you. Everyone could see that.'

'Maybe. Christ, Luke, today has been hard, too bloody hard.'

He reaches across and touches my knee. 'It's over. Now we need to move on, taking his memory with us.'

'You're right. I do feel a bit better. Thank you for everything – I don't know what I would have done without you.'

'We're in this together, remember?'

'I love you – just in case I don't tell you enough.'

'You tell me all the time.' He flashes me his best Sutton smile. 'Promise me you'll never stop saying it.'

'I won't. Life is too short. I'm going to tell our babies every day how much I love them.'

Shortly, we arrive at the palace. I input my code and walk through the door.

'Are Rosie and Jerry coming back today?'

'No.'

'Good.' I loosen my tie and begin to unbutton my shirt. Luke looks surprised.

'I need to take off these trousers and wash the day away.' I hold my hand out for him. 'You promised me a bath.'

We walk hand in hand to our bedroom. I remove the remainder of my clothes and hang my suit in pride of place. I stand back and admire it as Luke enters the dressing room.

'I need to carry on.'

'Carry on what?'

'Harper Jones. This morning I wanted to close the business or give it away to the girls.'

'Give yourself time.'

'Gerry with a G said that Mr Jones was so excited about the business, watching his dream come alive.'

Luke stands in front of me, naked.

'Hmm, just how I like you, Sutton.'

He smiles at me. 'You never cease to amaze me.'

'Back at you. You looked after all our guests today, and I was beyond useless.'

'You just buried your friend.'

'Today is over. I can't talk about it any longer. What I need is you.'

Luke frowns. 'I don't—'

'Shh. This is about love. We're lucky to have each other, Luke. I will never take what we have for granted.'

My lips reach his before he has a chance to say anything. For the first time in days I feel alive: blood pumps around my body and wakes my soul.

I pull away and take his hand, guiding him onto our bed. He kneels in the centre.

'Kate…'

'Don't question me. I want to be close to you; this is what we do.'

His mouth gently closes over mine. I run my hands through his hair, drawing him closer. 'I want to make love to you, Kate.'

This time I reach for his mouth with tenderness and all the passion I can muster. His tongue brushes against mine, and I feel my body surrender to him. I reach down and grip his erection while he slides his fingers inside me.

'I'm ready, Luke.'

He lies down and I straddle his lap. Holding his erection, he slowly sinks inside me. We wait for a few seconds, allowing my body to adjust, before I take him deeper. As I begin to move, Luke holds my hips and gently thrusts, as the head of his erection touches me where I need it.

Soon my rhythm changes and the speed increases: we both need more power to reach an orgasm. Thankfully, Luke continues to meet my thrusting. In no time at all I begin to lose myself to him. I watch his muscular torso tense and he tightens his grip on my hips.

My body responds, feeling the onset of an orgasm, and a rush of sensation overwhelms me. I come hard. Luke follows me; his breathing is laboured and his lips parted.

Our eyes meet with a connection that electrifies us both, an undeniable pull that I pray we will always have.

'I love you,' I manage to whisper as my orgasm continues to roll through me.

Afterwards, I lie on my side and smile.

He runs his hand down my face. 'Do you feel better?'

'Yes. It might be cheesy, but that was beautiful.'

'It's always about love, Kate.' He pulls me close to his chest.

'I let him go to the angels today.' A single tear trickles down my cheek.

Goodbye, Mr Jones.

17

'Luke, stop,' I yell, laughing uncontrollably.

'No,' he says and continues to nip at my ear, then moves across to my jaw, keeping my arms pinned above my head. 'You started it.'

'OK! I surrender.'

His mouth works south towards my ribs and finally my stomach. 'Mummy is happier today.'

'Luke.' I giggle.

He shifts his focus back to my face. 'It's good to hear you laugh.'

I run my hands through his hair. 'Today is a new day.' Four days of resting and sleeping as much as possible since the funeral have helped.

'You could stay at home forever. I told you, this is the only place you should visit.'

'What, our bed?'

'At last she sees reason. I think hormones are helping you make the best decisions.'

'Oh, really?' I push him onto his back and straddle

him. 'You think you're always in control. Sorry, but you're not!'

'That's what I let you think,' he says, laughing

I shift further down his body, scattering kisses across his skin. 'Care to take a wager?' I say, just as I take him in my mouth.

★★★

'Here.' I slide another pancake onto his plate.

'Kate, I'm full. I'm pleased you're feeling better, but you have to stop feeding me.'

'I'm making up for lost time. Besides, I love taking care of you.'

'You did this morning – twice.'

'Very funny.'

He scans my body. 'You look beautiful.'

'You mean, thank God your wife actually got dressed? I needed to make the effort before you ran off with a supermodel.'

He pulls me between his legs. 'Been there, done that.' He flashes me a wolfish grin.

'You're such a shit – but I guess you're mine.'

'I am. Honestly, you look stunning.'

I lift my shirt to show Luke that my jeans just about fit under my bump. 'I aim to please.'

'In that case, get rid of your jeans and shirt. I'm thinking hot lingerie instead.'

'Go to work! Global domination is calling you. Anyway, the Harper Jones crew are arriving at eleven and I want to get your office ready.'

'You could meet them at Sutton Global.'

I shake my head. 'Not yet. I want to spend a day there on my own. I owe Mr Jones that.'

'Whatever you need.'

'I'll have dinner waiting for you – and if you're good I may dress for the occasion. Oh, and think of me when you're at your desk, doing what I did to you this morning.'

His hard-hitting kiss takes me by surprise. Now the day will be long and hard for us both.

'Rosie, can you answer the buzzer?' I remove the cakes from the oven and put them on the counter.

Rosie returns with Valerie and Maria.

'Hi.' I greet both women with a hug.

'How are you?' Valerie asks.

'I've been cooking, and I'm dressed – so, today is a good day.'

'Well done,' she says and smiles.

I look at my colleagues and realise this is what I need. 'I can't wait to hear how your meeting went in France.'

Within half an hour Tanya arrives. We sit around the boardroom table in Luke's office and make a plan.

'OK, so we'll stick to our original idea. Here, look at these.' I open the sketchbook I found in Mr Jones's office. 'He was obviously working on some new ideas.'

'I love them.' Maria passes the book round the table.

'Girls, I have to be honest. Last week I wanted to chuck in the towel. Even now I feel fragile – and slightly disloyal – moving forward without him.'

'Oh Kate, I understand. I was talking to Max about it last night. I wondered whether you would continue.' Valerie reaches for my hand. 'I'm sure I speak on behalf of everyone. Mr Jones will always be here – he is Harper Jones so let's honour his memory.'

I raise my mug. 'Mr Jones.'

This is just what I need: something to focus on for the future, a future that I began with Mr Jones. Today I kick my self-deprecating arse to the kerb and feel mentally ready to chase our dream.

The afternoon continues. We plan where we want to go from here with regards to launching our product line. With a few companies showing interest, we need to make a quick decision. The phone rings.

'Hello?'

'How is my gorgeous wife?'

I smile. 'Fine, and how is my delicious husband?'

'Missing you.'

'Good. Remember our deal for this evening?'

'Every word.' He laughs.

'May your day be long and hard.'

'Argh – thank you for the distraction.'

A chuckle escapes my mouth. 'As much as I love speaking to you, I do have a house full of girls.'

'OK. See you later.'

'Goodbye, love of my life.'

I return to the crew and bring our meeting to a close. This might be the best job in the world.

After I prepare dinner – chicken stew with lentils – I have time to kill. I need a distraction.

'What are you looking at?' Rosie looks over my shoulder.

'Nurseries. Look at this.' I pull a stool out for Rosie to sit and turn the laptop. 'Probably a bit too soon, but…' I need time to adjust.

'There's no harm in looking, Kate. I love that cot,' she says.

'Me too.'

'I spoke to Luke about using the spare room opposite ours for a nursery. What do you think?'

'You'll want them to be near you.'

'We can give them a room each when they get older.'

'It's so exciting – babies in the house, children running around,' Rosie says.

'Be careful what you wish for. They can sleep in with you.'

'I don't mind. Actually, I said to Jerry that I'd be happy to help – but only if you need it.'

'That goes without saying. I still want to run Harper Jones.'

'That's a lot to take on, Kate.'

'Listen, I was going to speak to Luke. This house is a lot of work, right? And I know nothing about babies.'

Rosie giggles. 'You'll pick it up.'

'I hope so. But I was thinking about getting you some help.'

'Here? But we have the cleaners, Kate.' Rosie says, her forehead creasing in confusion.

'Yeah, but I'm being selfish. You'll have more time to spend with me.' I laugh. 'Bloody hell, that sounds awful and like something my husband would say. What I mean is, I'll need help with the babies, especially if I want to continue to work – which I do, and I want them with me all the time.'

'Of course.'

'If we got someone in, let's say for a couple of hours every day, just to keep on top of things, you'll have time to be with me and the babies.'

'A nanny?' she says.

'More like a grandmother. What do you think?'

In answer, tears roll down her cheeks.

'Crap – you hate the idea!'

'No, I'm just shocked you asked. You have your mum and Livy.'

'I know, but Livy works full-time and I don't want Mum to give up her job at the bakery – she loves it. You live with us, the children will know you and Jerry like grandparents. Besides, I trust you both with my life.'

'Of course I would love to help, and I can babysit so you and Luke can have time together.'

'OK, that's sorted. I'll speak to Luke tonight. So, back to the nursery. Shall we go upstairs and have a look?'

'Good idea.'

The security buzzer rings.

I walk towards the intercom. 'Hello.'

'Mrs Sutton, your mother is here.'

'OK, send her in, thank you.' I shake my head and press the button that unlocks the front door. 'She's a bloody nightmare! Four numbers, that's all she has to remember, and they are her birthday.'

Rosie and I make our way to the hall. At the same time, the large black door opens and a woman appears.

The world stops. I can just about breathe. 'K–K–Katenka?'

'Kate! Kate?'

I open my eyes.

'Kate, look at me.' It's Max. 'Rosie, open the door.'

He scoops me up from the floor and carries me to the back of the Bentley. His eyes meet mine and I see fear.

'Max?' I whisper.

'Shh… It's fine. I'm taking you to hospital.'

'I – don't…' I feel disorientated.

'You need to see a doctor,' he says. Rosie slides in next to me and secures my seatbelt.

'Darling, it will be fine.' She touches my cheek.

'I'm fine.'

'I know,' she says without conviction.

I look down.

'No… No!' I scream. My jeans are covered in blood. 'My babies! Max, I need Luke.'

'I've called him. Keep calm.'

'This can't be happening.' Oh God, no.

'Come here.' Rosie pulls me to her chest. This is all I need to make me start crying.

Eventually we arrive at the private hospital where Dad went after he was attacked. Max lifts me out of the car and carries me through the doors. Rosie is already speaking to the reception staff.

'Max, we need to follow that young lady.'

He remains silent and carries me down a corridor and into an examination room.

'Can you lay Mrs Sutton on the bed? Thank you,' the nurse says.

Max gently lowers me to the bed.

'Dr Jenkins is on her way, OK?'

I nod.

'Let's get you out of these clothes and make you a little more comfortable.'

'Kate, I'll wait outside,' Max says.

'No, don't leave me, just turn around. Please, Max.'

He holds his hand up. 'OK.'

Within a few minutes my clothes have been replaced by a gown.

'I'll get you some water,' the nurse says and leaves the room.

'Have they died?' My eyes sting, and tears trickle down my cheeks.

'Let's wait and see what the doctor says.' Rosie squeezes my fingers, trying to give me strength.

'How can I tell Luke our children have died?'

Max wipes away the dampness on my cheeks. 'Stay positive.'

I nod.

'Max… Katenka – my mum – was in our house.'

'What?'

'She was in the hallway, and then… I don't remember anything.'

He looks alarmed, then disbelieving. 'Kate, that's not possible.'

'It was her. I know what I saw.'

He touches my forehead. He apparently thinks I have had a blow to my head. 'Kate, she's dead.'

'I know she's dead, Max! I'm not making it up. Plus, Rosie saw her too.'

'There was a blonde woman there, Max, but I've never seen her before,' Rosie says.

The door opens and Dr Jenkins walks in with a nurse wheeling an ultrasound machine.

'Hello, Kate. Please try not to worry, OK? First of all, let's take your blood pressure.'

I nod.

The nurse takes my blood pressure.

'Do you think they're dead?'

'It's best not to jump to conclusions. Bleeding in pregnancy is not uncommon. Let me scan you. Do you want to do this alone?'

'No, I want them to stay. Luke is on his way.'

'OK. The gel will be cold.'

I don't care how cold it is; just tell me my babies are alive.

She pushes the probe across my bump. 'Take a deep breath, Kate. I'm worried about you. The nurse said you passed out – is that correct?'

'Apparently, but I did have a shock today.'

Dr Jenkins turns the screen around and all of a sudden the volume increases, allowing us to hear what sounds like galloping horses echoing around the room.

'They're alive,' I say and close my eyes for a few seconds before looking greedily at the images of my two babies, to see how much they've changed from my previous scan.

'Yes, they're fine. Look.' She points to the screen. 'Two very strong heartbeats. I need to check the fluid around the babies, and your placenta. As you're almost sixteen weeks, we can get a clearer picture.'

'But what about the blood? Where did it come from?'

'There's no obvious sign. Sometimes bleeding can happen for no reason. You need to rest.'

'They look amazing,' Rosie says, keeping a firm grip of my hand.

I look at Max, who remains silent.

Then the door bursts open. It's Luke.

'Oh, thank God you're here.'

He strides towards me. 'Are you OK? And—'

'They're fine.' Dr Jenkins reassures him.

He turns away, running his hands through his hair. Max takes his arm.

'She'll be fine.' He looks across at Rosie. 'Let's get a coffee.'

'I'll bring you some tea,' Rosie says.

Luke presses his lips to my temple. 'Jesus, Kate…' He runs his hand down the side of my cheek. 'What caused the bleeding?' He looks at Dr Jenkins.

'As I told Kate, I can't find any underlying reason for the blood loss. The placenta looks healthy and the babies' heartbeats are strong.'

I take his hand. 'I heard them.' I look at Dr Jenkins. 'Can you show him?'

'Certainly. Take a seat, Luke.'

She rolls the ultrasound probe across my bump.

'OK. Here's one.' She points to the screen, although it is clear enough. 'And there's the other.'

Luke lowers his head to the bed. 'Thank you.' He closes his eyes with relief.

'Do you want to know the sex of your babies?' she asks.

'We said no. But now…' I look at Luke. 'Do you want to know?'

'If you'd asked me yesterday, I would have said no.'

'It's your decision,' she says.

Luke looks at me. I nod.

'Yes,' he answers.

'As you know, they are identical twins, and I am pleased to say you are expecting girls.'

'Girls,' he says.

'Luke,' I say and laugh.

'Girls,' he repeats. 'Are you sure?' His eyes widen and he looks stunned. Not many things shock him.

'Positive.' Dr Jenkins wipes the gel from my stomach. 'I'd like to keep a close eye on you, Kate, OK?'

'What can we do?'

'Luke, there is nothing to do other than to ensure Kate rests. Her blood pressure is slightly low, but she did say she had a shock today, which might explain the low pressure and fainting.'

Luke looks puzzled. 'Shock?'

'Kate, you already have an appointment next week, so I'll see you then.'

'OK.'

Dr Jenkins leaves the room, followed by Luke. Then Rosie comes in, holding a tray of tea and sandwiches.

After a few minutes, Luke returns, still looking puzzled. He sinks into the chair next to me. 'Max just told me Katenka was in our house. Kate, I think you—'

I wave my hand. 'Oh no, you don't get to sit there and tell me I'm bloody mad.' I swing my legs aside.

'What are you doing?'

'Going home.' Even though I want to leave, I feel too light-headed to stand.

'Calm down.'

'Calm down? You just said I'm losing it. I told you I saw Ivor at our wedding – and I was right.'

'Breathe. Remember what Dr Jenkins just told you.'

'Ask Rosie – she was with me. Better still, check the new CCTV you installed apparently looking for no one.' I fold my arms and look angrily at the blank wall.

'Tell me what happened.'

'What's the point? You don't believe me.'

'Just talk to me.'

I take a deep breath. 'Rosie and I were sitting at the breakfast bar and the buzzer rang. I answered it and the security man told me my mother was here. I didn't read too much into it because Mum keeps forgetting the entry code.'

'Go on.'

'I told them to let her in, and when I walked into the hallway…'

'It was Katenka.'

I nod. 'I know it was her. She looked older than in the photo I have of her, but she looked the same.'

Luke sits back in his chair, looking thoughtful.

'I don't understand. Philip told me he killed her – unless it wasn't her. But I know it was – he took such pleasure in telling me about it, he definitely wasn't lying. And we know she was cremated.' I close my eyes, longing to turn the clock back to yesterday so today could never happen. 'Go on, tell me I'm crazy.'

'I never said that.'

'Who was the woman, Luke? Rosie saw her too.'

'She said that a blonde woman was in the hallway, you

collapsed and the woman ran off.'

'Do you think it's possible it was Katenka? I need to tell Ivor that I saw her.'

'What can you tell him? That a woman stood in our hallway who looked like Katenka.'

'Fuck, fuck, fuck.'

He smiles. 'Do you feel better for that?'

'No.'

'First, you need to rest. Today has been very stressful for you.'

'I think it's safe to say that your dead mother turning up would upset your mojo too.'

'Hey, calm down. Let me take a look at the CCTV footage.'

'Fine.' I lie back. 'I was having a good day – and now this. I want to go home.'

'I'll go and speak to Dr Jenkins. But you need to rest, OK? Don't fight me on this.'

I nod.

Luke leaves the room, and leaves me wondering what the hell happened back at the house. I know what I saw, but how can I explain it? Then Rosie walks in.

'He thinks I'm mad. But you saw her too.'

Rosie sits down next to me. 'I saw a blonde woman.'

'Katenka.'

'I don't know, Kate... I don't know what she looks like, and I'm sure she was wearing sunglasses. Honestly, it's a bit of a blur.'

'Perhaps I'm losing the plot.' I close my eyes, feeling utterly lost.

We finally arrive home. I lie on the bed feeling exhausted, both physically and emotionally. Whenever I close my eyes I see the silhouette of a woman in the hall. Is it Katenka? Who else could it have been? Regardless of who it was, our babies are OK, for which I am eternally grateful. Luke comes in and sits on the bed.

'Do you feel better?' he asks.

'I'm hungry.'

'I'll order a takeaway.'

'I made a chicken stew earlier.'

'Of course you did.' He kisses the tip of my nose.

We sit at the island and consume the stew. The heat and richness are just what I need to warm me.

'How was your lunch?' I know Luke is trying to sidestep the elephant in the room – my dead mum.

'Good. We're going to carry on with our initial plans.'

'Are you sure that's what you want to do?'

'I have to, for Mr Jones. I want this – for him too.'

'I understand.'

'I spoke to Rosie today – pre-collapsing.'

He raises his brows.

'What? I take it you haven't checked the CCTV?'

'I have.'

'And?'

'Eat and then we will look at it together. Carry on. You spoke to Rosie?'

'I wondered whether we should get her some help, here at the house, other than the cleaners.'

'You did?' He smirks.

'Yeah. I thought if we got her some help to keep on top of things it would free up her time to help me. This house will be chaos: two babies equals two feeds, two nappy changes, one pair of hands each time. I know people cope and I'm sure we'll get there, but I thought Rosie would be the best choice to help us. What do you think?'

'A nanny?'

'Sort of. Well, she'll be like an adopted grandmother anyway, won't she? She can come to work with me and if we need to go away on business she and Jerry could come.'

'You've given this some serious thought.'

'I have. The babies mean the world to me, especially after today when I thought…' I take a breath, not wanting to think of any other possible outcome. 'She's the perfect choice and when I mentioned it to her she was really excited.'

'I like the idea.'

'You do? Good. She also said that she can babysit if we want to go out for dinner or have some time alone.'

'A booty call,' he says with a sexual glint in his eye.

'If that's what you want to call it, yes.'

'Have I told you how much I love Rosie?'

Holding two mugs of tea, I walk to Luke's office. I can hear him talking on the phone. I join him at his desk and he ends his call.

'Thanks.' He rubs his jaw. 'Come here.' He pushes back his chair, allowing me room to sit on his lap. 'I want to show you something.'

He presses a button and a video begins to play on the computer screen. It shows the outside of our house: first of all the gated area, then the front door. Then a woman appears in a dark coat, sunglasses and scarf. She looks as if she has tried to disguise herself.

'You can't see her face?' I say.

'No, it could be anyone.'

'But the man at the gate said my mum was here. Why would he say that?'

'I don't know.'

I sit up again. 'OK. Let's look at this with our rational hat on.'

Luke tilts his head.

'Bear with me. As far as we know, Katenka is dead – the slime ball told me that himself, and we have a copy of her death certificate to back up the story.'

'Agreed.'

'So why would a woman turn up here, saying she was my mother? Not Susan, but a blonde woman who looks like Katenka? Answer that.'

He sits back in the chair. 'I can't.'

'Did she come to the wrong address?' I don't believe it.

'Honestly, I don't have an answer. Let me look into it,' he says.

'Like you did when Ivor turned up in Venice and then vanished – you did a great job of finding him.'

'Careful,' he says. 'I've spoken to Sullivan about it and sent him the video footage. He'll see if she's been picked up on the surrounding CCTV.'

'What about Ivor and Harry?'

'What about them?'

'Er, should I tell them?'

'We don't have anything to tell them – apart from that

a blonde woman turned up here announcing she was your mother. I'm all for honesty, but on this occasion I think you should keep quiet until we have hard evidence.'

'OK. My next question is…' I pick up his glass, which is filled with whisky. 'You never drink.'

'It's been a stressful day.'

'Work or me?' I ask.

'You. Work very rarely causes me issues.'

'I was so scared. I thought I lost them.' My hand tenderly brushes over my stomach. 'So, we're having girls…' My eyes widen, waiting for his reaction. 'Is that why you're drinking?'

'Maybe… Yes.' He downs his drink.

'Why?'

'The house will be filled with two more females I can't control.' He runs his tongue along his bottom lip.

I smile. 'Seriously! And that worries you?'

'Slightly. Girls – I will want to protect them.'

'Of course, and if they were boys?'

'I would teach them to shoot.' He gives me a half smile.

I laugh. 'Luke, that's sexist.'

He holds his hands up in defeat. 'Girls will want boyfriends.'

'Well, don't get ahead of yourself. I haven't even had them yet. Besides, they may have your temperament, so good luck with that.'

18

'Luke, harder.'

He stops moving.

'Jesus, Kate.' He frowns.

'I asked Dr Jenkins and she said sex is fine – you were there too, Luke.'

'She said yes to sex – not to me fucking you hard.'

'She didn't say slow either,' I quip, which he finds amusing. 'It's not funny. You saw the scan the other day and the girls are fine, so you either fuck me hard and fast or you get off me.'

'I can't believe you said that.' He stifles a smile.

'Well I did, so bloody get on with it.'

My hands slide through his hair, drawing his lips to mine. My libido has gone through the roof…

Without too much persuasion, he increases his speed and thrusts harder. In no time, a delicious orgasm begins.

'Luke…' I'm lost in my very own delirious world.

He thrusts with power, and I know he's coming – hot and thick.

'Fuck, I'm going to miss you.' Tenderly, he presses his lips to mine.

Eventually he lies next to me. I roll onto my side, propping myself up on my elbow.

'I hate you leaving.'

'You planned this girls' trip to Sandbanks.'

'I know, but only because you're going to Dubai and now I want you to stay. What can I say? You have control over me.'

His brows rise. 'I will never have control over you.'

'At last you see the light.'

'Anyway, how's Declan? Has he said much to you?' I ask. 'About work or about Kiki?'

'Kiki.'

'Nothing, but I know he's upset about losing the baby. I think coming with me will do him good. We can talk.'

'Kiki said he hasn't really left her side since they lost the baby. I can't imagine what they've been through.'

'They seem to be moving on.'

'I know, but I feel bad for them, especially after last week and the bleeding – that could have been us. Anyway, going away with the pack will do her good.'

'I'm sure you will have fun, although I am surprised you invited Alexis.'

'It feels right, what with the shares and the three of us in charge of Bagrov and Cooper. Besides, Harry said she's really excited. The only thing is, I feel bad about – well, if it was Katenka?'

'I spoke to Sullivan last night. No news on Katenka. I wish you could tell them she was here, but we have no proof.' He brushes his hand against my cheek.

'I know you're right, but I hate lying to Harry.'

'You're not lying.'

'OK, but I'm holding out on her. Same thing, really. So, I'm thinking that if it was her, for some crazy fucked-up reason, she might come back.'

'I don't want to see you hurt.'

'Hurt? It's a bit late for that. Anyway, you're my armour, Luke.'

'Ivor called me,' he blurts out.

'What? When?'

'Late last night – you were asleep.'

'And you waited until now to tell me.'

'We only woke up half an hour ago, and you've been … demanding my attention since.'

'Why didn't he call me?' I run my fingers across Luke's taut chest. 'What's so special about you?' I smile.

'I hope a few things about me are special, since you married me.' His brows shoot up. 'Take your time listing them, baby. I have all day.'

'This could take a while.' I laugh. 'Seriously, what did he want?'

'He's arriving in London tonight. He's kept his word and made contact before visiting. I told him you were away for a couple of days and you'll contact him when you get back.'

'And you're OK with that?'

'Do I have a choice? He hasn't given me any reason to doubt him – yet. He did mention that he was going to contact your parents today.'

'Crap. Really?'

'This is their issue – let them sort it out.'

'Thank God Harry and I will be AWOL for few days.'

'I agree. Perfect timing. Don't give Max too many problems.' He tries to lighten the mood.

'I won't – besides, he's invited Valerie to stay with him… Who would have thought they'd work so well together? Oh yes, I did, the woman with the Cupid's bow and arrow.'

'It worked out this time.'

'What can I say? Maybe you should listen to me more often, and feel free to leave your car keys next to my bed…'

'Is that right?' Luke laughs.

'Kate – seat belt.'

'Yes, sir.' I salute.

'Watch it.'

'Did Luke give you a badge – the one that states *I must treat Kate like a child*?'

He shakes his head. 'Christ – I have a two-and-a-half-hour drive with you.'

'Aren't you lucky?'

Max begins the journey to Sandbanks. As Luke needed to visit Dubai, I thought it would be a perfect opportunity to take the pack – except Molly – to see our holiday home. However, we still have no furniture! With that in mind, the back of the Range Rover is full of airbeds and extra bedding. Let the indoor camping experience begin – except for Max and Valerie, who will sleep in the studio above the garage.

'What time will Valerie arrive?' I ask.

'Later. She has an appointment this morning.'

'Oh.' I look out of the window, trying to hide my smile.

'I know what you've been up to, Harper.'

I turn to him. 'Sutton.'

'Pain in the arse, Harper.'

'Not lately.'

'Setting me up with Valerie.' His vision flits from me to the road. 'Did you honestly think I didn't know what you were up to, asking me to drop Valerie home? Not to mention that our hotel rooms were always next to each other.'

'Coincidence.'

'Coincidence, my arse.'

'Do you like her – I mean, really like her?'

'I'm not answering that.' He doesn't need to. I see the look of love written across his face.

'I'm so happy for you.'

'This has nothing to do with you.'

'That's where you're wrong.'

'You really have some balls.'

'You know how much you mean to me and Luke. I want you to be happy, and Valerie is perfect for you. When you danced with her at our wedding... Well, I knew there was something there. Do you love her?'

'Jesus, Kate.'

I hold my hands up. 'Like I said, I just want you to be happy. Do you think you'll get married? Please do it in Bora Bora.'

'There's no stopping you. You're like a dog with a fucking bone.'

Eventually we arrive at Sandbanks and unpack the car. Once all the airbeds are set up in the lounge Max leaves me and heads to the studio.

First to arrive are Barney and Kiki. The house fills with noise.

'I wish Sutton batted for the other side. This house is the dog's bollocks, and to think he gave this to you for Christmas! What will Santa get you this year?'

'Two healthy babies.' Instantly I regret my words. 'Shit, sorry, Kiki. Come here.' I pull her into my arms.

'Kate, it's fine.'

'No, it isn't fine. I shouldn't have said that.'

She pulls away to look at me. 'Don't wrap me up in cotton wool. You're my best friend and I want you to enjoy your pregnancy.'

'And Declan?' We walk into the kitchen.

'It seems to have brought us closer.'

'Christ, life deals you some shit cards.'

'Both of us, Kate! How about your bleeding last week?'

'I guess.'

'Kate, I mean it. I want you to talk about your pregnancy. I have to get over it.'

'I want you to be godmother, and Harry, and Molly, but don't tell anyone.'

'Tell anyone what?' Barney says as he enters the room.

'Nothing.'

He tilts his head and sits next to me. 'I smell bullshit, Harper.'

'I was clearing the air with Kiki – pregnancy talk.'

'Kiki, you'll get knocked up again soon, babe. Loads of my mates have had miscarriages.'

'I wished I lived in his world,' I say to Kiki. She smiles at his candid response.

'Got any food? I'm bloody starving,' Barney asks.

361

'Chimichanga for dinner, but if you can't wait there are snacks in the fridge. Why don't we go for a walk? The others will be at least another hour.'

The three of us walk along the shoreline, our boots sinking into the sand.

'There's nothing like the sea to blow the cobwebs away.' I link my arm through Kiki's. 'This will do you good – a few days away.'

She nods and inhales the sea air.

'Are you sure you're OK?' I say.

'Each day is a little easier.'

'I wish there was something I could do. I know I haven't been there for you lately.'

'Kate, you lost Mr Jones.'

'Ivor's back in London. Apparently he called Luke last night. As part of the deal, Ivor has to check with Luke before he can enter the country.'

Kiki's brows shoot up. 'What the fuck? Luke should work for the government – oh, he did. You sure know how to pick them!'

'Tell me about it,' I say. 'I kind of get it. Luke doesn't trust him – yet.'

'Have you spoken to him – I mean Ivor?'

'No. He told Luke he's meeting up with Mum and Dad today.'

'Ouch! Honourable, I guess.'

'Thank God me and Harry aren't around.'

'What did Harry say about Ivor meeting them?'

'I texted her on the way. We haven't spoken about it. She struggles with the whole Ivor situation,' I say.

'Wouldn't you? I mean, we thought Ivor was bad… You got the better deal.'

'Maybe,' I say.

We stop. 'What the bloody hell is he doing? Barney!' I shout. 'Look at him.' Kiki and I can't help laughing at Barney, who's making sand angels on the beach.

'I told Declan it would be a laugh a minute with him around.'

'Luke said Declan seems OK.'

'Like I said, it's brought us closer… Sounds stupid, doesn't it? Losing our child makes us realise we want to be together. He's been amazing. I never thought it would have affected him the way it has.'

'And you? Do you want to wait, or…'

'Honestly?' She looks at me. 'We're not ready, but one thing is for certain, I want a baby… Not today or this year, but I do want one.'

'And you will have one, and you'll make the best mummy in the world.'

***

Harry claps, delighted. 'I was hoping you were going to cook, but I didn't want you to overdo it.'

'I'm fine.'

'Can I help?' Alexis hovers awkwardly.

'Yeah, can you find a bowl for the salad? Harry, take the napkins and drinks into the lounge.'

Eventually we gather around the fire, surrounded by scatter cushions. A tablecloth has been laid on the floor to serve as our table. We begin to devour our meal.

'Kate, this is lovely. I miss your food deliveries,' Alexis says.

'One guess why Sutton married her,' Barney says with a mouth full.

'My charisma,' I answer.

'Yeah, right? What fucking charisma?'

'Oi…' I throw my napkin at him. 'You're probably right.'

As everyone seems to be chatting, I look at Alexis. She's trying to relax but also remains guarded.

'Is it weird being here?' I say.

She shakes her head. 'It only feels like yesterday.'

'I know it does. Luke and I came down here a few weeks back. I needed to get rid of the memory. This place is our sanctuary. Luke proposed to me here, on the beach.'

'It is a beautiful house.'

'It will be when I get round to buying some furniture for it.'

'Kate, I spent last weekend with Charles and…' Alexis sips her wine – I'm guessing for Dutch courage.

'You told him?' I ask and she nods. 'Everything or everything?'

She stifles a laugh. 'Both – about Russia and my father.'

'You needed someone else to talk to. I know it sounds odd, but I trust him.'

'He likes you, he always has. Are you OK that I told him?'

'It's your news. One thing, though, don't tell Luke.'

'Charles's lips are sealed.'

'How was he – I mean, about…'

'My dad?' she says.

I nod.

'Shocked and…' She looks down. 'Sad.' Our eyes meet. 'He was genuinely upset and angry.'

'And now, do you feel better? That sounds crap, because how can you, but—'

'I know what you mean.'

'A problem shared,' I say.

She smiles. 'He understands that I need to take it slow. Plus, he didn't buy the appendix story. I never mentioned Katenka.'

Oh, crap. 'Best not to. We don't know what the deal is with Joseph Morley and we'll probably never find out. His dad is a powerful man and maybe what we don't know won't hurt us. Luke also said it could open up a can of worms.'

Her eyes glaze over and I reach for her hand. 'You're doing bloody well,' I say.

'Thanks. Anyway, Harry said you had another scan the other day.'

'Yep, everything is fine. I've got another appointment next week,' I say and my hand goes automatically to my bump.

'Good. Have you got over the shock of being pregnant yet?'

I laugh. 'Yes and no. I still can't believe I'm going to be a mum.'

The next day is a lazy one. The only reason we decide to get dressed is to go for a walk – at two in the afternoon. After a long stroll along the sunny beach we return with glowing cheeks.

We're all ravenous – but I have a knot in my stomach: a sense of betrayal towards Harry. Every time I close my eyes I see Katenka again. It was her, I'm certain of it. Either way, I don't like keeping secrets from Harry.

'Kate.' Harry interrupts my tormented thoughts. 'Can I do anything?'

'No,' I respond and slide the chicken pie into the oven.

'What's wrong?'

'What?' I turn to face her.

Harry comes closer. 'I know when something's up with you.'

'I'm fine.'

'You've been on another planet all day.'

'Hormones,' I say and look away.

'If you say so, but I know you.'

I take a deep breath. 'OK, there is something.' Oh crap, here goes. I turn to face her.

'What is it?'

'I don't know where to begin.'

'At the beginning… it's usually the best place.' She smiles, trying to relax me.

'I warn you, this makes no sense, OK?'

'Now you're worrying me.'

'Last week, when I bled. Just before I collapsed…'

'What? You never said you collapsed.'

'I thought I did.'

'Er, no. You just said you had a bleed.'

'My blood pressure was low, that's why I collapsed. Anyway, I was at the house with Rosie, and the security man on the gate said my mother was here – you know she forgets the code.'

'Yeah…'

'So I told them to let her in.' How do I say what I saw?

'Go on.'

'It wasn't Mum.'

'So who was it?'

'The woman was blonde.'

Harry looks confused.

'The woman – she looked like Katenka.'

'What do you mean, she looked like Katenka?'

'Exactly that. I don't remember anything else because I collapsed.'

'She's dead! Christ. Cooper told you so.'

'I know, but who was the woman standing in my hallway? Rosie saw her too.'

Harry begins to pace the kitchen. 'This is seriously fucked up. So you're telling me our mum isn't dead?'

'No. I don't know what it means. Luke and I looked on the CCTV footage and you can't tell who it is. She wore dark glasses. You couldn't see her face.'

'Why am I only hearing about this now?' She fists her hands on her hips.

'There was nothing to tell. I really don't know who the woman was… and Luke thought it might upset you…'

'This has fuck all to do with Luke.' She cuts me off. 'Our dead mum may have turned up at your house and you didn't bother to tell me? You're out of order, Kate.'

'I didn't want to upset you, that's why I never said anything. Besides, I don't know who she was. Like you said, our mum is dead. But… she looked like her.'

I walk towards Harry. She steps backwards.

'Harry, please.'

'No! I'm furious with you. How dare you keep this from me?' Her voice is loud and full of rage.

'Hey, what's going on? I can hear you in the other room,' Barney says.

'Why don't you ask Kate?' Harry spits.

'Harry, please.'

Barney turns to me. 'Kate?'

I look away.

Harry steps in. 'Apparently our birth mum – you know, the one who's dead – magically turned up at Kate's house wait for it – last bloody week.'

Barney looks at me. 'What the fuck?'

'Yes. What the fuck, Kate?' Harry mimics his response.

'I collapsed after I saw her, so I don't remember anything else. It may not be her. Anyway, whoever it was just walked out.'

'But you thought it was? Un-bloody-believable.'

'Harry, please, I didn't tell you because—'

'Kate, you're not in charge of me! You shouldn't have kept this a secret.'

'Even if it was her, I don't know where she went.'

'Babe, Harry is right. You should have told her.'

'Cheers, Barney!' I say.

'At least he's looking out for me, unlike my so-called sister.'

'That's not fair, I would do anything for you,' I say.

'Except tell me the truth? I can't tell you how disappointed I am with you.'

Harry exits the kitchen, pushing past Kiki and Alexis.

'What's going on?' Kiki asks.

'Girls, go after Harry,' Barney commands. 'They've had words.'

Not wanting to relive the last ten minutes, I rush past everyone and head upstairs, slam the bedroom door shut and fall onto my bed, sobbing.

'Fuck, fuck, fuck,' I mutter under my breath.

After a while I manage to calm down. Knowing I can't change things, I grab my phone. I ring Luke.

'Hi, baby.'

'Hi,' I mutter.

'What's wrong?'

'Nothing. I want you to come home. I want to go home.'

'Kate.'

'I told Harry.'

'About Katenka?' Luke asks.

'Yes.'

'And?'

'I've fucked up.'

'Why did you tell her?'

'She knew something was wrong. She's pissed off with you too. I told her you said not to say anything.'

He takes a breath. 'I can take it.'

'Fuck it.'

'Where are you?' Luke asks.

'In our room, lying on our bed. Harry has stormed off, Kiki and Alexis went after her.'

'Ask Max to take you home.'

'I can't leave everyone here.'

'You just said you want to leave.'

'I can't leave Harry. I just told her that I think our mum is alive.'

'You're getting stressed. Think of the girls.'

'I do, all the time. Why is my life so messed up?'

'It isn't. You just have a few issues.'

'Issues! You don't have issues. I don't think you understand. Last year, I found out I was adopted and that the people I thought were my parents weren't. Since then, my real dad has gone AWOL. My sister is the product of a rape, by the man who I thought killed my birth mother – who I know I saw last week! I think it's fair to say that you don't have *issues*. Livy and Edward have never given you a day of grief in your life.'

'OK, I know life is challenging at the moment.'

'Challenging? Is that what you call it? I don't want to be challenged.' I start to cry.

'Baby, don't get upset. I can't hold you.'

'I'll be fine. I just hate myself right now.'

'Let Harry hate me. I told you not to tell her.'

'Luke, it doesn't matter any more.'

'I'll come home on the first available flight,' he says.

'No, don't. I just needed to hear your voice.'

'I'm coming home tomorrow. Let me take you out for a meal.'

'No. Let's stay home and sit in front of the fire, just us.'

'Simple as ever.'

'Always. What I wouldn't give to be back in Bora Bora watching the sunset from our veranda.'

'Me too.'

'Oi, Harper, what are you doing?' Barney shouts through the bedroom door.

'Hang on, Luke.' I sit up slightly. 'Nothing – what do you want?'

'Dinner's ready. Everyone's waiting for you – including Harry.'

'OK.'

'Go and have dinner and speak to Harry. She knows you love her.'

'I hate that I hurt her.'

'You protected her.'

'Well, she doesn't see it like that. I love you so much, Luke.'

'Back at you.'

When I walk downstairs, Harry is sitting on an airbed.

'Hi.'

She looks up at me. 'You OK?' she asks sympathetically.

'Not really. How about you?'

'I feel like shit.'

'Sorry, Harry. I would never hurt you.'

She stands and comes towards me. 'I know. I'm just angry.'

I shake my head. 'I'm sorry.'

'You had your reasons for not telling me.'

I pull her into my arms. 'My only reason was doubt. I can't be sure it was her.'

'But you think it was,' Harry says and walks to the air bed and we sit.

'I can see her face and then I remember nothing except Max holding me… Even then, she had glasses on, but she looked familiar.'

'What does Luke think?'

'Other than I should be carted away?' I shrug. 'What can he say? I told him I saw her and he doubts me – but wouldn't anyone?'

'Kate, my father told you he killed her,' Alexis says from the corner of the room.

'I know. Come here.' I pat the space next to me.

She sits down. 'How can it be her?'

'I don't know! Besides, she was cremated! I can't explain what I saw. But at least Rosie saw her too. Why would she have told security she was my mother?'

'I don't know.' Harry looks across to the window.

'For what it's worth…' Harry and Alexis look at me. 'My gut instinct tells me it was her.'

The weekend turned out to be more eventful than I expected. Thinking your mother is alive can affect your sanity and upset your mojo. Still, getting together with the pack was long overdue. After a few hours' drive we finally arrive home. I feel a sense of relief. As I open the front door my eyes fall to the rose petals scattered on the floor. I can't help but giggle. I follow the trail to Luke's office.

'Hey, baby.'

The man of my dreams stands there, wearing jeans and a dark T-shirt, holding three bouquets of roses: one white and two pink.

'Flowers for all of my girls.'

He places the three bunches on the table.

'Thank you.' I fall into his arms.

'You needed cheering up.' He pulls away. 'You look tired.'

'I couldn't sleep last night.'

He kisses the top of my head. 'You're home now. OK, we have various jobs for this evening.'

'We do?'

'Of course.' He takes my hand and begins to walk with me. 'First, a bath.'

'Good choice.' We climb the stairs.

When I walk into our room I see two parcels on the bed. 'Luke!'

'You reminded me yesterday that life has given you an unfair deal.'

'No shit, Sherlock.'

Luke tilts his head. 'Please.' He gestures to the boxes.

First, I open a gift set: Jo Malone – my favourite infusion of lime, basil and mandarin.

'I love it, thank you.'

'Good, and now this.' He passes me a pink and black box. I recognise the packaging – and I suspect I know what may lie beneath the tissue paper.

I laugh. 'Is this for me, or for you?'

'For you to wear, and for me to remove later.'

'Sounds like stage two of your plan. When did you get time to do this?'

'I got an earlier flight. Stage three is food… Open the box.'

I remove the lid and part the tissue to reveal the most beautiful black silk pyjama set.

'I don't know what to say.'

'I'm glad you like them. I've run you a bath.'

He walks me to the en suite, which looks dreamily romantic. The bath is filled with bubbles and surrounded by candles.

The bath oil coats my skin and leaves me feeling relaxed. What is it about warm water and soft lighting that makes a bad situation more bearable? I hope Harry is feeling happier. It's unlikely; she was quiet last night.

After my bath I slip on my gift. I smooth the fabric between my fingers before I button up the oversized shirt. As ever, Luke has chosen well.

When I reach the last step I am met with a delicious smell coming from the office. When I enter, I see the table is crowded with candles and takeaway dishes from a local Italian restaurant. Perfect.

'You've excelled yourself, Luke. It smells delicious.'

He pulls a chair out for me. 'Dinner is served.'

'Thank you. I'm starving.'

'Good.'

'I haven't heard from Mum and Dad. And I'm too scared to call them. I have Ivor's number, but I can't bring myself to call him either. Have you heard from him?'

Luke nods.

'And?'

'He said it went better than he thought. Apparently Malcolm has been expecting Ivor to contact him.'

'He has? What now? Shall I call them?'

'Not tonight. I'd let them process things and deal with their emotions. It can wait until tomorrow.'

We devour the takeaway steak and vegetables with bread and oil, plus a gooey dessert of fruit and meringue. Afterwards we sit on the sofa full and warm, which is exactly what I have craved since telling Harry about our mother.

The next morning my phone rings. I want to ignore it, but can't. I grab it from my nightstand.

'Hello.' I know I must sound half asleep. My voice is barely coherent.

'Morning, did I wake you?'

'Yes.'

'Do I detect a grumpy Mrs Sutton?'

I smile. 'Tired but not grumpy. Sorry I fell asleep last night.'

'I carried you to bed.'

'I know. I was too comfy to offer to walk.' I laugh.

'Any time. How do you feel today?'

'OK – except my gorgeous husband is not with me.'

'Soon, baby. I need you to sign some investment documents. I'm transferring some shares into your name. Nothing to worry about.'

'Give me some time and—'

'No.' He cuts me off. 'Stella will bring the documents to you after lunch.'

'Thank you. I don't feel like going out today, but I was thinking tomorrow I'll go back to work.'

'It's your call.'

'I need to get back on track.' I stretch my arms above my head.

'Kate, you can't change the past. Mr Jones will always be with you, especially at Sutton Global.'

'I know, and I quite like that – our special place. Luke, I'm going to call Mum and Dad.'

'OK.'

'I just need to clear the air. I'll invite them over for dinner one night this week.'

'OK. Listen, I have a meeting, so Stella will come by later.'

'I miss you.'

'You too.'

What's left of the morning soon disappears. I feel brighter, and today is a new day, a new beginning. I have a long phone call to Mum. Unexpectedly, she seemed OK – perhaps even relieved. Luke said Dad had been expecting Ivor to contact them. Well, it's out there now. I ask them to come round for dinner next week.

Later, I have baked three fruitcakes, two jars of cookies and a batch of cupcakes.

I hear the black door open.

'Kate, it's only Stella.'

'Hi, I'm in the kitchen.'

She enters with her usual beaming smile. 'I can smell where you are… Oh my goodness, you've been busy.'

I pull her into a tight hug. 'Coffee or tea? Please say you have time for one.'

'Yes, I told Luke I wouldn't rush away. Tea, please, Kate.'

'This cake is for you to take home.' I slide it towards her. 'Now, what would you like with your tea?'

'Hmm, cupcake, I think. Is that butter icing?'

'Of course, one hundred per cent full of fabulous calories.'

'Well, in that case I will have one.'

We sit for an hour chatting, mainly about my health. I show Stella the scan pictures. In turn she questions me about Kiki and her loss, then we talk about her own harrowing experience. She still harbours a similar pain to Kiki. She doesn't have what she always wanted – a child.

Just before she leaves we go into Luke's office, where she lays out various documents on the table for me to sign.

'OK, two more. Sign here and here.' Stella closes the various folders. 'Good, I can send these off.'

'Speak to Richard about coming over for dinner.'

'That would be lovely. Luke said you might return to work tomorrow.'

I nod. 'I have to make a start and, like I said to Luke, I know he's there with me. I can see Mr Jones giving me one of his looks. Crazy, right?'

'Not at all.' She smiles. 'And he would give you that look.'

As I stand up from the desk, I see a figure looking through the gates. I step closer to the window.

'It can't be,' I whisper. 'Crap – it is.'

'Kate?'

I dart towards the office door.

'Kate?' Stella calls.

'Call Luke!' I shout. 'My mum is here again.'

'Kate,' she calls again as I head for the front door.

I reach the gate barefoot. 'Open the gate!' I shout.

The two security guards look at me, and then at each other, then open the gate. I can't see her. I stop and look both ways. Some distance away, I notice a figure. I run towards her.

'Stop!' I shout, but my words have no effect.

'Katenka – stop!'

Nothing.

'Mum – please stop.'

Bingo. The figure dressed in black stops dead.

So do I.

'Mum?' I mutter.

Very slowly she turns to face me and her dark eyes meet mine.

19

Time seems to stands still. I can barely breathe.

'It's really you, isn't it?' I say. Her face looks older, but it's definitely her.

'Yes. Hello.' Her voice echoes through my body.

I take a deep breath, feeling physically sick. *Don't cry, Kate, don't cry.*

'I knew it was you.'

Looking ashamed, she lowers her eyes.

'Kate!' Max bellows as he bounds towards me. 'What the bloody hell are you doing? You haven't got any shoes on!'

I look down at my bare feet. 'Max, this is Katenka Bagrov – my birth mother.' I want to cry hysterically – or laugh. Probably both.

'Jesus!' He looks the way I feel.

'Hello,' she responds politely.

'This is bloody crazy.' Thank God I'm not going mad.

'I think we should go home and discuss this there,' Max says.

I hold my hand out to the stranger who gave birth to me.

'Please, come with me,' I say.

'OK,' she responds and slowly slips her hand into mine. I feel the touch of my mum's hand for the first time.

Eventually we make it home and sit in the grey lounge, Max with me and Katenka on the opposite sofa.

Stella walks in. 'Kate, are you all right?'

I nod, but of course I am not OK. My mum is here. *Where have you been for the last twenty-five years?* is what I am thinking. I take Max's hand and hold it tightly.

'I'll make tea.' Stella leaves the room.

'Let's get this straight: you are Katenka Bagrov?' Max is the only person who can speak.

'Yes.'

'I don't understand,' I manage to say as tears roll down my cheeks.

She comes over to sit next to me, and gently touches my face.

'Please do not cry. I do not want to cause you pain.'

'It's too late.' *You did that when you walked out of our lives.* 'Harry – I have to call Harry.'

'Give yourself a minute to calm down.' Max wraps his arm around my trembling shoulders.

'Go and get her, Max. Don't let her get a cab – please.'

'OK.' He stands up.

'Kate!' Luke shouts from the hallway and appears at the entrance to the lounge. I rush to his arms.

Katenka also stands. 'Hello.'

Luke walks to her, holding me close. 'Luke Sutton, Kate's husband.'

'Pleased to meet you.'

Luke looks at me, concerned. 'Are you OK?'

I nod.

'I'm sorry,' he says.

What for? Doubting me?

'Please, sit.' He gestures to Katenka and sits down next to me on the sofa.

'I want Max to collect Harry.'

'Of course, give me a minute.' Luke walks away from the lounge with Max, leaving me alone with her.

'You look pale. I am sorry…' She looks at her hands, which rest on her lap.

I feel compelled to touch her and take her hand. Skin-to-skin contact with my birth mother – it is almost too much to bear.

'I don't know what to say to you,' I confess.

'You don't have to say anything.'

I take a deep breath. 'You're supposed to be dead.'

'I am – on paper.'

'Philip Cooper…'

Her dark eyes meet mine. I sweep her blonde hair from her face. Ivor always said I reminded him of her, and I do. I look like my mum.

'What he did to you – he tried to do the same to me.'

'No, please, God, no. My sweet Katarina.' She takes my face in her hands.

'I escaped.'

She sighs and pulls me closer. I shut my eyes and the world ceases to matter. My mother is holding me. I look up at her and see her face mirrors my emotions: tears of sadness, and maybe some joy, track down her cheeks.

When I turn, Luke is beside me once more.

Stella walks in. 'Here we go, tea. Luke, I will go unless you want me to stay,' she says.

'No. Thank you, Stella,' Luke says.

'OK. I will see you all soon.'

I nod, but can't find any words.

The room is silent. I have so many questions, but where do I begin?

'Katenka, do you take milk and sugar?' Uncharacteristically, Luke becomes the host.

'Milk please, no sugar.'

He passes her a cup and saucer.

'Thank you.'

'Kate, tea?'

I shake my head. 'No, thank you.' I take a breath. 'I'm pregnant.' I want her to know.

She takes my hand. 'How wonderful.' She offers me a warm smile.

'I collapsed the other day, when you were here…'

'I saw your face and… I ran away. Katarina, I am so sorry.'

'You know, I questioned my sanity. I thought I had imagined you.'

'Katenka, I don't want to appear rude, but Kate has questions that need answering.'

'I understand.'

'I think we should wait for Harry to arrive,' Luke says.

'Yes,' Katenka says.

'She won't be too long, as she has been working locally.'

Katenka nods and remains silent.

Once again the silence is deafening, but when I hear Harry talking to Max, I get up and bolt into the hall.

'Harry.' I fling my arms around her and draw her close to me.

'Kate.'

I pull away. 'Max said it was an emergency, but not the babies or you… What's going on?'

'I need to show you something. Take a deep breath and remember we have each other.'

'OK, now you're scaring the shit out of me.'

I take her hand and walk us through to the lounge, where Katenka is standing waiting.

'Jesus Christ!' Harry squeezes my fingers as though her life depends on it. 'No.' She shakes her head in disbelief. 'No way, this can't be happening.'

'Helenka.'

I look at Harry. The colour drains from her face and tears shimmer in her eyes.

Katenka holds us both and I inhale her sweet scent. Harry pulls away but keeps hold of my hand.

'Ladies, please take a seat. Harry, I have called Raymond. He will be here shortly.'

'Thanks, Luke.' Harry and I sit side by side. 'So, you did see her.'

'I know.'

'Am I the only person who's confused?' Harry looks at me, then at Katenka. 'You're dead, but you're here… We know Philip killed you because…' Her words hang in the air. 'He told Kate what happened to you.'

Then Raymond enters the room and goes over to Harry. 'Hi, everyone.' He offers a wave. 'I am Raymond,

Harry's husband.' He leans towards Katenka and takes her hand.

'Hello,' she says.

Harry returns to my side.

'Let me start, if I may,' Luke says.

Go ahead, Luke. If there was ever a time I needed you to take control, it's now.

'We all thought you were dead. I have a copy of your death certificate.'

I give Harry a reassuring hug.

Luke returns his gaze to Katenka.

'We also know you fled to London from New York.'

'Yes,' she says. 'With Katarina.'

'But no one seemed to know that Kate existed,' Luke says.

'No. My husband, Ivor, had enemies in Russia, and was sent to prison for something he did not do. I could not risk Katarina's life; I had to take her away. Russia was not safe, and then there was Philip Cooper... He was – evil. That is why I left New York.' She pauses. 'I moved to London but his threats did not stop. My home was broken into. He terrorised me, telling me he would hurt me, and…'

'You should have gone to the police,' Harry says.

'In my world, they can be as evil as Philip Cooper. I did not know what he would do to me – us, and I was pregnant. When you arrived, Helenka, I became scared and that is why I paid for your details to be wiped from official records. Both girls were wiped.'

'So you were frightened and gave the girls up for adoption to Malcolm and Susan?' Luke asks.

'Yes. Malcolm worked on my house. He was wonderful with Katarina, and then Helenka arrived…' Her voice cracks. 'I had no choice.'

'You could have taken us with you – somewhere, anywhere,' Harry says.

'What life would that have been for you both? How could I have hidden two babies?'

'I don't think Kate would give up her babies.' Harry is not backing down.

'My choice was simple. Let you girls live free of fear, or live in fear with me. I made the right choice! As a mother, your instinct is to protect, even if that means giving away your most precious possessions. I hope one day you will understand that saying goodbye to you was so, so hard for me.'

'Why didn't you tell Ivor? We could have lived with him.' God, I feel so confused.

'He was in prison and surrounded by bad people.' She shakes her head. 'All I wanted was for you to be safe and happy.'

'I couldn't do what you did, but I understand your reasons,' I say. Harry wears a deadpan expression; she's not budging.

'Philip told Kate he visited you in London, and that's where you were – apparently – murdered,' Luke says.

She nods. 'We met in New York. I was only there for a short time, then I fled to London. That's when he tried to kill me.' Instinctively her hand goes to her neck. I know how she feels.

I have no choice: my legs take me towards her. I look at Harry, who comes with me and we sit either side of

Katenka. Carefully I peel her hands from her neck and take hold of them.

She takes a breath – and perhaps she takes some strength from us. 'He did try to kill me. I fell unconscious.'

'And he thought you were dead?' Luke says.

She nods.

'Your death certificate states you committed suicide.'

I watch Luke trying to piece the puzzle together.

'Yes. I do not know what happened after he tried to strangle me. Except, my eyes opened and two men were in the room, talking – Joseph Morley and George Williams.'

'They wrote the reports and George Williams pronounced you dead, and—' Luke responds.

'How do you know all of this?' Harry asks.

'Charles Morley found some unfinished reports in his dad's safe. He gave me a copy just before our wedding.'

'Oh!' Harry glares at me. 'Keeping more secrets from me, Kate?' She looks across at Luke.

'Harry, stop and breathe,' Raymond says.

'It's becoming a regular thing!' Harry bites back.

'Don't be like that, Harry. I don't keep things from you. It was the same report everyone had. Charles just wondered why his dad had kept it. I guessed one day I would ask his dad, that's all.'

'Please, carry on,' Luke says.

'Did they hurt you?' I need to know.

'No, no, never, they saved my life,' she says.

'How?' Harry asks.

'You have to understand that Philip was…' She looks at her trembling fingers.

I will rescue her. 'A sick bastard.'

'He tried to kill and rape Kate too… and his daughter Alexis – he abused her for years.' Harry's rage spews out of her.

'Girls, I am sorry.' Katenka squeezes our hands.

'I assume you know he's dead?' Luke asks.

Katenka nods.

'Is that why you're here?' Once again my husband seems on point with his assessment.

'Yes,' she whispers.

'I inherited your shares,' I say.

'Yes, on your twenty-seventh birthday,' Katenka says.

'Guess what? Philip wanted them. Some things don't change,' I say.

'I could not change your shares. I just prayed that you were OK,' Katenka says and looks down again.

'We all own them now – I mean, Harry and Philip's daughter.'

She looks painfully sad. I take her hand.

'So what happened to you? Where have you been?' I still need some answers.

'Philip called Joseph and George telling them he had killed someone. He had some information on them, and he blackmailed them into helping him. They had no choice.'

'Christ, that's loyalty for you,' Harry says.

'I never asked them questions; I am just thankful they saved me. All I know is that something happened when Joseph and George were young. Philip abused their friendship.'

'They grew up together, my father included,' Luke says.

'It must have been bad for them to agree to cover up a murder.' I would fall on a sword for my friends, but murder? 'It makes sense now why they dealt with your case; they had to cover for you.'

'George saw that I was still alive, but he told Philip to leave and he would deal with the body.'

'Philip knew George could "lose" a body at the mortuary and no one would question the chief coroner…' Luke says. 'Joseph would file the case as suicide, leaving no paper trail.'

'Yes. They saved my life – I owe them everything.'

'Where did you go?' Harry looks as tormented as me.

'Joseph owns a cottage in Wales. They drove me there that night and stayed with me until I had settled in.' She shakes her head. 'Philip was evil. The men knew that if he thought I was still alive, he would try to kill me again.'

'This is bloody madness! He took you away from us.' My hatred for Cooper burns brightly.

'So have you been in Wales ever since?' Luke asks.

'Yes.'

'Charles asked me about an address in Wales. He found it with his dad's paperwork and now it makes sense. Do Joseph and George know you're here?' I ask.

'Yes, they came to see me after Philip died. They understand the pain I have been in since the day they drove me to Wales, and now I can find peace.'

'Could they get into trouble?' Raymond asks.

'I would never allow that – I think they need to find peace too.'

'Katenka, I can vouch for everyone in this room. What you have said will not be repeated,' Luke declares.

'Ivor!' I blurt and Katenka looks at me, surprised. 'He killed Philip saving me.'

Her eyes fill with tears.

'He loves you. You were the love of his life.'

'Is he in your life?' Her face comes alive.

'He is now… Why didn't you contact him?' I ask.

She looks down. 'It was easier to accept my new life – alone.'

'He misses you, every day.' I take her hand.

'What have you been doing all this time?' Harry has no intention of indulging her love story.

'I cook in a local café and care for an elderly woman who has been very kind to me.'

'Why have you never tried to contact us? I know you say it's because of Philip, but I don't understand. Kate is pregnant and she would never abandon her children, I know she wouldn't.'

I can feel Harry's pain – and I agree with her.

'Helenka…' Katenka smiles.

'Harry – my name is Harry…' She goes over and sits next to Raymond. He hugs her.

'Harry, I mean you no harm. I will leave.'

'No.' I look at Harry. *Back off,* I tell her silently.

'Let's all take a break…'

'Luke is right. I think we need a drink and some time to breathe,' Raymond says.

'Can I help?' Katenka asks.

Luke stands. 'Yes, follow me.'

He carries the tray and leaves the room, Katenka following.

I lean against the bookcase. 'How fucked up is this?'

'You both need time,' Raymond says.

'Time? That's a bloody understatement. How much time do you think I'll need to not feel like the booby prize? I'm only here because my dead mum was raped, and guess what? She isn't dead after all.'

'Harry, don't say that! If I didn't have you…' I shake my head.

'I just feel numb, Kate.'

'It doesn't feel real, like we're watching someone's life,' I say.

I have an idea. I head to Luke's office to find my phone. I know Ivor's in London. Caller ID – Papa. I press send.

'Kate?' Ivor answers. I realise this is the first time I have called him.

'Papa.' My voice is faint.

'What is wrong?'

'I need you to come to my house – now. Please.'

'You sound… Katarina, what is it?'

'I'm fine, we're fine, but Papa, please… If you love me, then you'll come now.'

I end the call.

Katenka – the woman he lost – is here. He has to see her.

'Kate.' Luke moves towards me from the doorway.

'I want to cry, and laugh, and scream… Please help me.'

'Kate, I'm worried about you.' He pulls me to his chest and kisses the top of my head before pulling away and framing my face with his hands. 'I just want to make it better. Tell me what I can do.'

'Just hold me, Luke, that's the only place I feel safe.'

He wraps me in his strong arms.

'It feels like a dream. I'm waiting to wake up and realise she's not real.'

'I can see how much she loves you both.' He pulls away, 'She tried to keep you safe.'

I nod. 'I can't take any more. I just want to run away with you.'

'Sounds like a plan, Mrs Sutton.' His warm smile makes me feel safe.

'I'm sorry,' I say.

'Why?'

'Your life was swimming along nicely and then I turned up and…'

'You're my world, Kate.'

'I know, but every turn I take, more shit follows me… We never seem to be free from it.'

'But you're my trouble.'

'How did Katenka seem?'

'Honestly?' I nod. 'She seems sad.'

'I can't imagine what she's been through. Do you like her?'

'I see you in her.'

'Do you?'

'You look like her. Her eyes are warm and honest – like yours. I have no doubt she is your mother.'

Tears roll down my cheeks. 'Luke, you mean the world to me.'

'Good, may that never alter.'

'No – never.'

'We should go back to the others.'

When Luke and I return to the lounge, Raymond is showing Katenka his and Harry's wedding pictures on his phone, acquainting her with our lives. Except there will never be enough storage on our phones to familiarise her with the past twenty-five years.

'Harry, you look beautiful… and look at the snow.' She smiles at a photograph of us. In it, our happiness is evident – unlike this afternoon, when we are both so confused.

'She looked stunning… We couldn't believe it snowed, could we, Harry? Do you believe in angels?' I say.

Harry glances at me. I remember how we lay on the snow and watched the night sky, wondering if Katenka was with us. Harry remains silent. I know my sister, and I know she is hurting.

'So, what now? Please tell me you're not going to disappear again.' I have to know.

'I think you should both decide whether you want me in your life – not just you but also Malcolm and Susan.'

'They've accepted Ivor,' I say. Although I wonder how far their kindness will stretch…

'Kate, let's take one step at a time,' Luke says.

'OK. But they need to know you're alive first,' I say.

Katenka looks away. Is she hiding something? Luke catches it too. He smiles. Is this what I do, maybe?

'What is it?' My hand reaches for hers.

'Malcolm knows I'm alive.'

'What?' Harry takes a step forward. 'Jesus Christ, this day just keeps getting better.'

'I saw him, once… I always visit London on your birthdays. I have cards for you both – birthday and Christmas.'

'Let's get back to the fact Dad knows you're alive,' Harry blurts out.

Jesus, Harry, rein it in. I glare at her.

'I sat on a park bench and a man walked past me with two beautiful girls. For some reason, he stopped and looked at me. We were both shocked. Harry, it was your fourth birthday. You looked adorable running around with Katarina.'

'Did you speak to Dad?' I can't believe he kept this from us! Oh, what am I saying? Of course I can believe he kept this from us.

'Yes. He was very kind and allowed me to watch you play. I told him that someone tried to kill me, and I was in hiding, and never to tell anyone he had seen me. Please don't be angry at him for keeping his promise.'

I am distracted by the sound of the black door opening. It can mean only one thing. I rush out to the hall, where Max stands next to Ivor. I drag him to Luke's office.

'Kate.' He frowns, looking worried.

'You need to prepare yourself...' I take a breath. 'We have a surprise for you. Are you ready?'

'You are not making sense.'

'That's nothing new, Papa, you'll get used to it!' I say and take his hand. Silently, he follows me towards the lounge – and Katenka.

He walks through the door – and stops. It's as if time stands still. Quickly he looks at me, then at Katenka. Cautiously, he walks towards the woman who has been waiting to be reunited with her husband for more than twenty-five years.

Gently he runs his finger down her cheek. She leans to his touch. Their connection is plain to see. Tenderly, he kisses her forehead before pulling her to his chest. They stand, locked in an embrace.

'My beautiful Katenka. I thought you were dead.'

'I am so sorry.' She whispers an apologetic response.

Luke pulls me towards him, perhaps sensing I'm running on empty – and he couldn't be more right.

Eventually Katenka and Ivor sit together on the sofa. At no point does he release her hand. My heart breaks watching them rediscover each other. I understand how they feel. If Luke left me there would be no one else; no one could replace the intense feelings I have for him.

'Ivor, this is a shock to all of us… Kate thought she saw Katenka last week,' Luke explains.

Ivor looks at Katenka.

'I do not understand, but…'

She strokes his cheek.

'Papa, Philip thought he killed her but he hadn't, and a friend helped Katenka to escape – and start a new life.'

'Why did you not find me? I would have protected you from him.'

'I think Katenka and Ivor need some time alone,' Luke says.

'I agree.' Harry speaks for the first time. I guess she feels out of place: my biological parents are together, and this is the first time she has met Ivor.

'I can make some dinner if anyone is hungry?' My instinct is to use food to help mend the souls and hearts of the estranged people in the room.

'I need to go home.' Harry stands up and Raymond follows. 'Honestly, I feel sick. I need some air.'

Raymond takes Harry's hand. 'Tomorrow is a new day, yes?'

She nods at him, but I see the raw pain in her eyes.

'OK. If that's what you need,' I say sympathetically.

'It is.' She hugs me. 'I'll call you later.'

'What about you two?' I look at my parents.

'I think everyone needs some time to digest everything that has happened today.' Luke says.

'Where are you staying?' I ask Katenka.

'I thought I would go back to Wales tonight. I have a return train ticket.'

'What?' I look at Ivor. Is he going to say anything?

He takes Katenka's hand. 'No. You are not returning to Wales – not tonight, not ever. I cannot lose you again.'

Thank God.

'You can stay here. We have a spare room,' I offer.

Tenderly, she touches my cheek. 'You are so kind, but you need time.'

'Actually, I don't… Twenty-five years is enough time.' She looks away, hurt at my clipped response. 'Sorry, I didn't mean it; I'm just scared you're going to walk out on us again.'

'I would like to be part of your lives, if you will allow me.'

'Good, so you can stay with Papa.'

Ivor looks at me.

'Katenka, I will never let you out of my life again,' he says. She smiles coyly. God, I want to cry – happy tears.

Luke comes to my side. 'We can pick up again tomorrow. Harry, is that OK with you?'

'I guess.' She looks at me. I know she's crumbling. *Stay strong, Harry, please.*

After a painful afternoon Luke coerces me into eating, which is pointless as I feel sick again, so I opt for ready salted crisps. After a warm bath I lie on our bed, going through everything that has happened and everything that was said today. The shock is too much for me, and I begin to cry.

'Hey.' Luke lies next to me wearing shorts and with damp hair. Perfect.

'Luke, I just – fuck, fuck, fuck.'

'Let it out.'

'Fuck!' I shout.

'I owe you an apology. You were right about Katenka.' He runs his finger down my cheek.

'Wow, Luke Sutton apologising… I've had more revelations today than I can cope with.'

'I shouldn't have doubted you last week.'

'No, you shouldn't.' I roll to my side. 'Christ, I doubted myself, so you're forgiven this time! Just don't make a habit of it or there'll be consequences.'

'I'll do my best.' He flashes his dazzling Sutton smile.

I giggle. 'Luke Sutton on his knees.'

'Just how you like me.'

I laugh. 'You got it.'

'That's the best sound in the world – a happy wife. Seriously, how are you feeling?'

'Shitty and oddly happy! My dead mother has just turned up from the grave, but other than that life is peachy.'

'You're not as fragile as I thought you were.'

'I feel… I can't explain it. Maybe complete? My mum and dad are together. When I found out about the adoption, I know I had Susan and Malcolm, but it felt like a massive part of me was missing.'

'That makes sense.'

'I know the shit's going to hit the fan when Mum finds out. Christ, Ivor's just made contact with them. I don't think she'll be able to cope with another parent coming out of the woodwork.'

'Give it time,' he says.

'Harry isn't impressed, she's angry.'

'Her father tried to kill your mother, and up until now she hasn't had to face it. It was almost like a story to her.'

'And now it's real, I never thought about it like that.'

'Don't be surprised if she backs away or won't accept Katenka. This is her psychological battle, not yours. She has to work this out for herself.'

'OK, Dr Sutton.' I skim his face with my finger. 'Did you see the way Ivor looked at Katenka?'

Luke smiles. He gets it: they're a mirror image of us.

'It's clear they're still in love,' he says.

'That's what I saw.'

'I don't know how he's coped without her. I've never looked at it from his point of view until this afternoon. He lost his entire family.' Luke's free hand loosens the knot of my robe and he lowers his lips to my bump. 'And how are my two favourite girls?'

I laugh.

He lifts his head. 'I'm bonding with my children.'

'And you have the cheek to call me crazy.'

'Yes.'

His lips go from my stomach and head towards my nipples, which are already stiff.

'I see you're ready for me.'

I smile and roll my eyes. 'My body quakes for you,' I respond sarcastically, but it's the absolute truth.

'Quake? Hmm, maybe a small eruption is on the agenda this evening.'

He shifts between my legs and looks deep into my eyes. I link my arms around his neck.

'Promise you'll love me forever, Luke.'

'Always, Kate.'

Forty-eight hours post-Katenka arriving, we sit in the grey lounge with Mum and Dad. God, I love my husband's ability to take over any situation and help to resolve it. He's told Mum and Dad about Katenka. No mention of Philip or how Katenka came to be in Wales, other than she was fearful of returning to Russia. Luke then suggested that what's in the past, stays in the past. Mum remained silent throughout, holding Dad's hand.

'Mum.' I look at her. 'Say something.'

'I… I can't believe she's alive.' The colour in her face fades. 'How? She's dead, we were told she died. So she lied?'

'We are not entirely sure. Possibly fake paperwork,' Luke says.

Dad looks away. He knows the truth. 'She's here now, and there is nothing we can do about it,' he says.

'Like I said, she wouldn't make contact because of Ivor's past,' Luke says.

'But why now?' Mum asks.

My eyes lock with Luke's, begging him to answer. 'She felt the time was right.'

'How do we know that we're all safe? Ivor is back too,' Mum says.

'Ivor's life is different now,' Luke replies. 'He's kept away for all this time, and they've both agreed to give you all some space.'

'Are they together?' Dad asks.

I shrug. 'It's early days, and they have a lot to work out. But they looked genuinely happy. I think Ivor is still in shock.'

'We're all in shock,' Harry says.

'Of course you are – your birth mum is alive,' Mum says.

'This doesn't change anything, just like when Ivor turned up,' I say.

Mum nods silently. But I can see the pain in her eyes.

'Kate's right, Mum,' Harry says and catches my eye. 'You are my mum. Katenka is a woman who arrived on our doorstep two days ago. I don't know her, and honestly I'm not that bothered.'

'You don't mean that, Harry,' Mum says. 'She is still your birth mum.'

'No, I do mean it, believe me.' I know Harry is speaking from the heart; she is cold at the mention of Katenka's name.

'Dad,' I say and look at him. I want to say, 'Hey, Dad, you knew she was alive.' 'How do you feel?'

'I don't want to see your mum upset, Kate.'

'We don't either. Listen, we're not going to run off and play happy families with her – *you* are our parents. That will never change. You made us who we are. But we need to find peace, one day at a time.' I take Mum's hand. 'I will need your help with these babies, Mum. I don't have a bloody clue.'

She smiles for the first time.

'Kate is right. This changes nothing for me and as far as I'm concerned Katenka has to earn a relationship with me,' Harry says.

'Harry, don't rush how you feel,' Raymond says.

'I'm not. I know how I feel, and at the moment I don't need her in my life.'

'Harry!' Dad says.

'Girls, you have to let her in. Don't worry about me, I'll deal with it. You need to get to know her. Yes, I am devastated, but I was blessed bringing you up. She never had that.'

'That was her choice, Mum,' Harry says.

'Susan, I think Kate is right. Take each day as it comes. Like Katenka is doing with Ivor, trying to figure out her new life.' Luke looks at me.

'I agree,' Dad says.

'I can't change that she's arrived.' Mum takes a breath. 'I should meet her.'

'Mum, we have all the time in the world. Me and Harry are in no rush.'

She touches my cheek. 'OK,' she whispers.

Harry moves over to Raymond. She's in no rush to make any contact with Katenka – ever.

I long for today to be over.

'Right, then. I've had enough of talking about something we can't change and I promised you roast beef.' I use food as a diversion. 'Luke, can you grab a bottle of red wine from the cellar? Mum, I want you to make the Yorkshire puddings, and Harry, you can lay the table.' I stand and leave the lounge, but the pain in my heart is crushing. I feel torn. I love my mum and always will, but I'm instantly drawn to Katenka. Something deep inside me already loves her.

Luke pulls my arm and steers me to the dining room. 'It's done. They can figure it out for themselves, Kate.'

His eyes meet mine.

'I know – it's just shit.'

His smile warms my heart. 'Yes, it is.'

'Thank you for telling them.'

'It's easier for me, and Susan has taken it well.'

'I hope so, Luke. I love her. She and Dad saved me and Harry from…'

'Let me save you, Kate,' he says and kisses me.

He does, every day. He is my saviour.

20

'Luke, breakfast!' I yell from the kitchen, placing a full English on the counter top. Within a few seconds he's there, on the phone.

'It's not my problem – sort it.' He ends the call.

'Everything OK?' I ask.

'Fine.' He begins to eat. Food is the perfect Sutton mood diffuser.

'You think you've got problems?'

Luke stops mid-chew.

'Look.' I walk over to him and raise my top.

He laughs.

'It's not funny. I love these trousers.' I try again, but the zip barely does up halfway, never mind the button.

'You knew it wouldn't be long before your clothes wouldn't fit – especially with twins.'

'I know, but… it just feels a bit surreal.'

'Sit – eat your breakfast,' he says.

'I'm not hungry.' My sulking alter ego is visiting this morning with a suitcase full of maternity clothes.

Luke pulls my stool closer to his. 'There'll never be a time that I won't want to fuck you.'

My Sutton with a silver tongue – perfect. 'We'll see about that.'

'Never. You have my word.'

'Even though you had a threesome and spanked some model's arse?'

'There's no comparison. I will always want you.'

'Did you just admit you had a threesome?' One day the truth will be revealed, but until then I will assume he's lying – purely for my own sanity.

Luke chuckles.

'This conversation is done, forever... Actually, I need to tell you something.'

'Go on.'

'I'm going to invite someone for lunch at Sutton Global.'

Warily, Luke watches me. 'That sounds ominous.'

'Charles Morley.'

'What? No fucking way.'

'Ah – hello, I wasn't asking for your permission, Luke. I wondered if you would like to join us.'

'Have you spoken to him?'

'Not yet. I'll call him soon.'

'We don't get on and never will. I don't see why you feel the need to meet him.'

'I need to tell him his dad saved Katenka.'

'I would rather you didn't have that discussion.'

'He knows everything except that she's alive.'

Luke's brows snap together.

'What? It is what it is, Luke. Alexis told him everything. She needed someone apart from me and Harry. Luke,

403

two weeks ago everything changed when Katenka landed on our doorstep. I hope they changed for the better, and whether you like him or not he did try and help me.'

Luke sighs, exasperated by my need to smooth things over.

'The information he gave me on Katenka could have dropped his dad in the shit, but he gave it to me anyway. Plus he never told anyone. I think he's odd, but he does seem to have a heart.'

'Fair enough. I will allow him to attend lunch at Sutton Global.'

I laugh, pushing the food around my plate. 'How kind of you,' I mock him.

'You're welcome,' he says and smirks.

'I admit the whole situation is completely fucked up.'

Luke scowls.

'Well, it is.'

'Maybe, and maybe you could choose a word other than "fucked"!'

I lean to his lips. 'I like it when you say it.'

'That's different,' he says and gives me a very slow and lingering kiss.

I pull away. 'Guess what I saw this morning?'

'It's too early for games,' he says.

'Guess!'

'No.'

I take a breath. 'You're no fun.'

'Spill, Harper.'

'I saw Valerie leaving Max's apartment and he looked very casual, if you get my drift… He had bed hair!'

'And your point is?'

I tap Luke's arm. 'My point is, Mr I-know-nothing-about-love, she must have stayed the night.' I clap.

'She stayed last week – twice.'

'What? You never told me!'

'Max asked if it bothered me. I told him he can come and go as he pleases.'

'Come, I would have thought!' God, I'm hilarious, but I laugh alone.

'Jesus, Kate.' Luke stands and gives me a kiss.

'It's a love story – get with the programme.' I join him at the sink. 'So, Mr World Domination Sutton, how does it feel to lose a challenge – especially to a girl?'

Luke sniggers. 'Maybe you should have rethought your strategy plan. I know how much you love me paying attention to your arse.'

'Keys,' I say and hold out my hand.

'Fine. You won.'

'I'm thinking a nice Saturday afternoon drive through London, down a couple of narrow streets.' I whistle. 'You know how tight those lanes are.'

Luke cups my arse, pulling me close to him. 'You can drive my car, but if you scratch it I will tie you to the bed and tease you, and when you apologise I may allow you to have an orgasm.'

'I might go and scratch it now.'

Immediately he takes my mouth, swirling his tongue against mine, and my leg hooks around his, leaving no distance between us. I feel him harden. God, he's ready and so am I.

'Kate… Kate?' Rosie shouts from the rear of the kitchen.

I lower my leg and pull away. 'Shit timing,' I whisper.

He looks at his watch. 'I know. But we need to leave.'

I gently grope his erection, which presses against his trousers. 'Five minutes won't hurt. What's the point of being the boss if you can't spare some fucking time? Gotta love a pun, right?' I laugh and begin to walk away from him, but he takes my arm and pulls me back.

'Your mouth needs fucking,' he mutters.

'It does, and I would sink to my knees right now, but I can't,' I whisper and quickly step away. 'Is everything OK, Rosie?'

'It's Adam. He's coming back the week after next for an interview.'

'Really? Oh my God, that's fantastic news.'

'I can't believe it. Can you ask Barney if he can stay with him again?'

'Of course he can.' I look across at Luke, standing in the doorway tapping his watch. 'I need to go, Rosie. I'll catch up with you tonight.'

I slide into the rear seat of the Bentley next to Luke as he goes through some paperwork.

'I bloody hope Adam gets that surgical position. I mean, if he doesn't Rosie will be devastated. Jerry will cope, obviously, but Rosie will be upset.' Concentrating on what he's reading, Luke offers no response. I grab his paperwork.

'Kate, I'm reading.'

'You have all day to read! Anyway, I need you.'

I lay his papers on the seat next to me. I tuck myself as close as possible to Luke, and swing my legs over his.

'Better?' he asks.

'Much.' I relax against him. 'Why don't you take the afternoon off work?'

His phone bleeps. Before he answers me he begins to read the email.

'Luke!'

'You asked me to take the afternoon off. I have back-to-back meetings.'

'Fine.' I admit defeat. I know he's busy but for some reason I need him today.

We remain in the same position until Max pulls up outside Sutton Global. As ever, Luke takes my hand and we walk side by side towards our offices.

'Morning, Stella.'

'Kate, you look lovely.' She stands to greet us both.

'Look.' I raise my top, showing off my ill-fitting clothing.

'Maybe some new trousers might be a good idea,' she chuckles.

'Jogging bottoms! Anyway, I'm inviting Charles Morley for lunch.'

'Yes, I know him. I will tell security to expect him.'

'Thanks, Stella.'

I turn to Luke but he's already disappeared into his office.

At last my office feels like the sanctuary it was when Mr Jones was alive and chasing his dream. An odd feeling, a feeling I can't pinpoint. Sitting at my desk, I search my phone contacts for Charles's number, then press send.

'Well, this is unexpected, Kate Sutton.'

'I know how much you love a surprise.'

'Indeed. There must be a reason for this call?'

'Are you free for lunch today?'

'With you?'

'No, with Luke! What do you think? Of course with me, at my office.'

'OK, what's the catch? Hmm, tell me, does your husband know you are calling or am I your dirty little secret?'

'Yes.' I laugh. 'I told him that you're my friend and for some bizarre reason I like you. Besides, I want to speak to you.'

'I'm intrigued.'

'So does that mean you can make it?'

'Yes.'

'One o'clock OK for you?'

'Perfect.'

'I'll order lunch in.'

'Until we meet again, Mrs Sutton.'

The morning continues. I go through Bagrov and Cooper paperwork with Tanya. The company is thriving: perhaps this is due to Alexis having total control. I feel excited about what the future holds for the company now we own it.

We take a break. I need to talk to Barney, tell him my news, although I suspect he already knows that Adam will be arriving at Heathrow sooner than he thought. I hit send.

'How is my favourite Harper girl? Have you got over the shock yet?'

'Which one? That my mother is alive or that I can't do up my bloody trousers?' I laugh.

'I said you were expanding.'

'Yes, I remember – cheers! I've definitely grown. I actually look pregnant. Anyway, have you seen Harry?'

'Yeah, I saw her yesterday.'

'And?'

'She was OK – a bit arsey and pissed off with the world.'

'She's not particularly chatty with me at the moment. It's been a couple of weeks and she's still the same.'

'Kate, two weeks is no time. Christ, this is not quite the same thing as finding out you were adopted.'

'I guess.'

'If I were to be honest with you…' He pauses.

'Go on.'

'I think she's jealous.'

'God, I hope not.' Maybe she is.

'Babe, your parents are alive and together; she's only here because her mother was raped! Christ, that's pulling the short fucking straw.'

'I know, and I feel guilty.'

'No need. Life goes on. She needs to suck it up, which is what I told her.'

'Did you? Bloody hell, Barney.'

'Too bloody right I did. People are dying in the world. Things could be worse. She can't change what's happened. It's shit, but it is what it is.'

'You're right. Love you, light of my life.'

'Have you seen them again – I mean, Ivor and Katenka?' he asks.

'Not much. I want them to have some time alone. Ivor's waited long enough for her. I'm finding it hard: where does everyone fit in? It's bloody odd, but a good odd, if that makes sense.'

'Don't ask me; my parents disowned me.'

'Their loss,' I say.

'How's Luke been with them?'

'OK. He likes Katenka, and Ivor wants to be with her all the time.'

'Takes the pressure off Ivor wanting to be with you. Sutton's dream, I bet.'

'Probably.'

'Harry said they met your mum and dad. Christ, this is confusing.'

'Yeah. Mum and Dad came to the palace. Harry and I told them the news about Katenka – actually, Luke did all the talking. Raymond was there too. Luke explained that she just turned up one day, wanted to make peace, see us. Obviously, we kept quiet about the whole Philip Cooper story. Some things aren't for sharing.'

'Christ, I wish I had been a fly on the wall.'

'It was OK. Mum handled it better than I thought, and I guess Dad already knew she was alive. To be honest, since then nothing's changed. Harry has made zero effort with Katenka and, basically, it's a bloody mess.'

'Give it time. Let them all figure it out.'

'That's what Luke said, so that's what I'm doing. Anyway, my other news – Rosie told me about Adam arriving. She asked if he could stay with you.'

'He called last night. Kate, I'm so excited.'

'I'm excited for you.'

'I really hope he gets the job.'

'Me too. So what's your plan – I mean with him? Does he know how you feel?'

'Don't piss yourself laughing, but I sent him a really long email explaining how I felt.'

'Wow… Barney Curtis putting his feelings on paper.'

'I know – who the fuck am I?'

'At least he's still coming,' I say.

'That's what I thought.'

We laugh.

'Come over next week for dinner and perhaps we can get together when Adam arrives.'

'Yeah. I have a full dance rehearsal that weekend – I'd love you both to come.'

'I still haven't seen any of your choreography since you've had the studio.'

'Well, you have had some other stuff on your plate. I'll message you the details.'

'Perfect. I'll call you soon.'

Even though I have a busy morning, for some reason I keep thinking of Luke. I need some quality time with him. I grab my phone.

Dear Luke,

   Charles will be here at 1. If you would like to, feel free to join us.

   Love you forever, Kate

   PS. I need you today. I don't know why. I just do.

I hit send, then decide to busy myself with Mr Jones's books. As soon as I walk away from the sofa, it hits me, as it always does: this is where we sat and chatted together so often. But now I take comfort that I was with him when he took his last breath.

'I miss you,' I mutter. 'So, Mr Jones, let's get to work.'

Having got back on track with Harper Jones I decide to go through Mr Jones's collection of sketchbooks, which feels even more special as he left them to me in his will. I search every page, deciding which we can use in our new collection.

My phone bleeps. Caller ID – Boss.

Dear Kate,
  I can't make lunch.
  Love you too x.
  You say you need me – you have me.

He may be near me, but he feels so far away. My fingers respond.

How inappropriate would it be for me to walk into your office and kiss you?

I hit send. Christ, what is wrong with me? Concentrate, Harper. I've just received new fabric brochures from IFD, so I flick through them, looking for materials we could use for Mr Jones's designs. Suddenly my office door bursts open and Luke strides towards me. I stand up. No words are spoken as he claims my mouth with a passion that leaves me breathless. Our eyes connect: dark and longing meet dark and understanding.

'Why today?' he asks.

'I don't know. How pathetic does that sound? Sorry for disturbing your meeting.'

His lips return to mine, persuading my tongue to dance romantically with his. This time I pull away.

'I love you.'

'Back at you, baby.'

'Go to your meeting. I'll come and see you before I go home.'

'OK.'

'Let's do something tonight… At home.'

He tilts his head cheekily.

I roll my eyes. 'Leave it with me. I'll think of something.'

He turns to go, leaving me with the lingering taste of him on my lips, which increases my need for him – and not just physically. I wonder how healthy it is to want Luke this much. But I couldn't stop it even if I wanted to.

A knock at the door disturbs my reverie.

'Come in,' I call.

Stella appears. 'Kate, Charles Morley is here.'

'Crap, is it lunchtime already? I haven't ordered food yet!'

'Shall I let him in?'

'Yeah, of course.'

'And your usual from Margot, times two?'

'You're a star. Thanks, Stella.'

Charles strolls into my office, stopping when he catches sight of the enormous pictures on the wall of Luke and me.

'Hmm, nice photographs. You look stunning and Luke looks – like Luke.'

I join him. 'How are you?'

'Very well, and you?'

'Fine.' I rub my bump. 'I'm pregnant with twins – Alexis must have told you?'

'She did. Sutton will be in for a shock.'

'He's really excited. Come and sit down.' We walk towards the Louis sofa.

'You look well, Kate.'

'Thanks, I feel good. I had another scan the other day.'

'And all is well?'

'Perfect. Now, lunch. I hope you like chicken salad.'

'You can feed me anything.' He raises his brow then scans my office. 'You have good taste.'

'Thanks! Did you think my décor would be—'

'Cheap?'

'Oh. That wasn't quite what I was going to say.'

He offers a warm smile. 'It's a compliment, Kate. I am impressed.'

'I never quite know with you.'

He holds his hands up. 'Sorry. Say what you see is my motto.'

'I'm amazed you have any friends.'

'They're mainly acquaintances, except Alexis – she accepts me for who I am.'

'Arrogant and narrow-minded?' I tap his leg. 'No offence.'

'None taken. It would appear you also say what you see.'

'Yeah – but that's not always a good thing. To say I get myself in trouble would be an understatement.'

'You look better than you did when I saw you at Marshalls.' He looks towards the window. 'Alexis told me about your visit to the grave that day. Apparently she had a breakdown.'

'A breakdown? That's putting it mildly. I've never seen anything like it. Listen, I've spoken to her, and I know that you know. Does that make sense?'

'It does.' He takes a breath. 'I let her down.'

I reach for his hand. 'Oh, Charles, don't say that. Alexis covered up the abuse for years. She didn't tell anyone.'

'He was an evil bastard. I can't believe I didn't guess what was going on.'

'It must be hard for you – you knew him for years, just like Luke did.'

'She's asked me to keep quiet about the whole affair, so my lips are sealed.'

There is sincerity in his eyes. I believe him.

'Good. Honestly, how do you think she is?'

'How can she be after years of abuse? I'm struggling knowing what I can do to help.'

'Just be there for her.'

'It doesn't seem enough, Kate.'

'No, you're right. I wish I could take away her pain. She did seen more… stable at Sandbanks.'

'Hopefully with our support and her therapist she will find some peace.'

A knock at the door stops our conversation.

'Come in.'

'Your lunch, Mrs Sutton.' A receptionist comes in, carrying a brown paper bag.

I take it from her. 'Thank you.'

She leaves and I go over to the board table and lay out our lunch. Charles joins me.

'This feels somewhat intimate.' He holds my chair.

'Maybe we should have some candles and soft music.' I giggle.

'Indeed… I assume Luke is in the building.'

I tilt my head. 'Across the hall.'

415

We begin to eat.

'How is your working relationship going?'

'OK, although he's not involved in Harper Jones. I guess you could say I rent some office space here.'

'Favours for the boss?'

I laugh. 'I'm my own boss.'

'Touché, Kate. I once told you that you have all the control in your relationship, not Luke. Never underestimate a powerful woman.'

'That's right, and don't you forget it.' We laugh and continue to eat.

'Speaking of powerful women, Alexis tells me Harry is on board now. It would seem Bagrov and Cooper is on the up.'

'It's early days. Besides, I don't have a clue what I'm doing, and Harry is new to it too.'

'Watch this space! Alexis is excited. It's given her something… maybe hope,' he says.

'Maybe a family.'

He briefly touches my hand. 'Kate, I'm enjoying our chat, but you asked me here for a reason.'

I nod and sit back in my chair. 'First, I spoke to Alexis yesterday. What I am about to say has something to do with Cooper – may he rot in hell.'

Charles holds his bottle of sparkling water in the air. 'Amen to that. Rot away, and thank God for hunting trips that go wrong.' He winks.

'Here goes. My birth mother, Katenka Bagrov, is… alive.'

He stops, his fork in mid-air.

'She turned up at my house two weeks ago.'

'Fuck. You aren't lying, are you?'

'Do you think I would lie about this?'

He shakes his head. 'Of course not, but after the evidence I found… I don't know what to say.'

'There is nothing you can say. To be honest, we are all in shock.'

He downs some water.

'Let me answer some questions for you. Philip Cooper strangled her. He thought he had killed her.'

He sits back. 'I can't believe this. So how are you dealing with this? Must have been a hell of a shock.'

'Believe me, it was.'

'OK. So Philip Cooper tried to kill your mother. The paperwork… Fuck – my father was involved in this, wasn't he?'

'Yes – in a good way.'

'In a good way!'

'That's why I needed to see you, to explain what he did.'

'Should I be concerned?'

'Not at all. I know you don't have a particularly good relationship with your dad.'

'Kate, there's no way to salvage our relationship. When I was a kid, he fucked around a lot. My mother – well, she likes to drink. I think she drinks to numb the hurt he caused her.'

'I'm sorry.'

'Me too.'

'Look, you say your dad is a bad man, but he did at least one good thing: he saved my birth mother's life. Philip did strangle her – he thought he'd killed her but she was unconscious. He then called your dad and George Williams to help him get rid of the evidence. Katenka said he had some sort of hold over both men; she doesn't know what.'

'I have no idea. My father would walk in the other direction whenever he saw Philip. I know for a fact Philip tried it on with my mother a few years ago, and I wouldn't be surprised if they had an affair, which makes this all the more dreadful.'

'She had a lucky escape. Like I said, I don't know what Philip had on them, and I don't want to know. Maybe saving Katenka gave your dad some peace.'

'Perhaps,' he says.

'The thing is, George realised she was alive, he made Philip leave and they took Katenka to a safe house in Wales. Do you remember the address you asked me about in Dubai?'

'Yes.'

'It must have been the same. Your dad and George doctored the death certificate and coroner's report, and gave Katenka money to live there.'

'And now she is here because Philip is dead.'

I nod. 'She couldn't return. Not only because she wanted to protect me and Harry, but she feared for her safety. She didn't know what Cooper would do if he realised she was alive. She also wanted to protect George and your dad.'

He sits back in his chair. 'Does my father know she has made contact with you?'

'Yes. Your dad and George told her Philip was dead.'

'And that gave her the green light to get in touch with you,' he says.

I nod. 'They didn't have to, Charles, but they did. Anyway, Katenka will never talk about it to anyone. None of us will breathe a word.'

'So my father is in the clear.'

'Absolutely.'

'Next time you ask me to lunch, I will be busy.' He smiles, but he can't hide his shock.

'Sorry… Was I wrong to tell you?'

'No.'

'I wanted you to know that your dad saved Katenka's life.'

'You said Alexis knows about your mother and our lunch date.'

I nod again. 'I wanted to tell you myself, and to thank you for helping me.'

'You're welcome.' He reaches for my hand. 'I may have a wild lifestyle, Kate, but I have never hurt anyone.'

'You're a party boy, not a nasty boy.'

'Alexis needed you, and you were there for her,' he says.

'I'm indebted to her, Charles.'

'And she to you. She's gained a guardian angel in you.'

I swallow the lump in my throat.

The door to my office opens and Luke strides towards us.

Charles shoots me a look.

'Hi,' I say.

'Kate.' He looks at my guest. 'Charles.' He extends his hand.

Charles stands. 'Luke. I hear congratulations are in order.'

'Yes. Thank you.'

'You are a very lucky man. We may have not seen eye to eye over the years, but I do believe Kate is the best asset you have ever acquired.'

'Asset? Cheers, Charles,' I respond, laughing.

'I would like to steal my wife if you have finished your lunch?' Luke says.

'Yes, of course. Lunch was…' He tilts his head, still processing our conversation. 'Entertaining.'

'My wife is the most entertaining person I know.'

'Quite possibly.' Charles kisses my cheek. 'Kate, if you need anything you have my number, and I will keep a close eye on Alexis.'

'Thanks, Charles.'

He walks out of the room.

'Why are you here? Are you making sure he leaves?' I link my arms around Luke's neck and he gives me a quick kiss.

'No. Like I said, I'm here to steal you.'

I frown. 'Why?'

'You asked for some time together. You never ask, and I appreciate that you never complain about the long hours I work. So, now you have me. Let's go.'

'Go where?'

He shrugs. 'Wherever we want to go.'

I laugh. 'What about your meetings?'

'Postponed.' He takes my hand.

'Postponed!'

We stand side by side at the lift.

'Where's Max?'

'He's got the afternoon off.'

'He might meet Valerie.' I can't hide my excitement.

'Or he may have an afternoon to himself.'

'You're shit at playing my game of romance.'

'Yes, I am.'

The empty lift arrives and we ride alone to the basement. Luke holds open the door of the Bentley for me.

As we drive away, I ask, 'Where are we going? You must have a plan.'

'No plan. Where would you like to go?'

'I don't know. The palace? Or is there somewhere you want to go? This feels naughty – like skipping school.'

'You like naughty Luke.' I watch his face come alive as he checks for traffic.

I laugh. 'In small doses.'

'Noted.'

God, I love it when he's playful.

We drive through the streets of London. Luke knows many of the shortcuts, which I love as we pass buildings and townhouses I have never seen. Fifteen minutes later, Luke tries to find a parking space.

'King's Road?'

'Yes.'

He points and I follow his finger.

'Seriously? You want to go baby shopping?'

'Why not?'

'I haven't bought anything yet.'

'So, let's make a start.'

My emotions are fragile today. As I enter Bambino, I feel like I might either laugh or cry. The shop is filled with stunning furniture, clothes, high chairs, cots, moses baskets…

I hold up a pink baby-grow. 'Luke.'

'It's so small.' He takes it and lays it across my bump. 'I think the babies have some growing to do yet.'

'Speaking of growing, I need to buy some maternity trousers.'

Luke cups my growing bump. 'That means our babies are safe.'

'I guess.'

'OK, where shall we start? Nursery furniture or clothes? You choose.'

I feel like a child in a sweetshop: there's too much choice and I don't know where to begin. I have an image of the nursery in my head, so furniture is where we start. Luke walks around, shaking cots, reading about the materials they are made of. He's so protective of our babies, watching him fills my heart with joy.

We agree on white French-style cots, a large changing table and two side units, two cribs, plus bedding sets in white and pink. Once the furniture choices are made we continue to browse. After half an hour, there's a growing pile of baby clothes, plus maternity trousers and jeans for me, on the sales assistant's desk.

'Kate.' Luke holds up a delicate pale pink dress.

'It's beautiful, but we have quite a lot.' I never thought I would be having this conversation with Luke Sutton, the man who builds businesses and hotels! My heart could burst.

He looks at the sales assistant. 'Two of these – in nought to three months.'

I laugh. 'They will never want for anything, will they?'

'Well, not while they're babies, but they will have to work for what they want in life.'

'Agreed.' I pick up the most delicate pink baby-grow with a white collar. 'Luke, look.' I hold it up. 'Why does everything look so adorable?'

Again he looks at the shop assistant. 'Two of these, please.'

'OK, that's enough.'

'Are you sure?'

'I'm bit overwhelmed, to be honest.'

'Let me pay and we can leave.'

I walk away knowing the last hour has cost an obscene amount of money. Even though I have a healthy bank account of my own, I still struggle with Luke's wealth.

'Kate, ready?'

'Yes.'

Luke's arms are full, so the shop assistant helps him to carry bags and boxes to the car. The furniture will be delivered. There's no rush.

I slide in the Bentley. 'That was fun, thank you.'

'It was. I don't shop unless it's for cars or underwear.' He raises his brows.

'I didn't think you were going to stop. But we still have to get a pram and—'

'I've ordered the pram.'

'What?' I turn to him. 'You've ordered a pram? When? And shouldn't we have decided that together?'

He leans across and kisses me. 'I was going to surprise you.'

'Well, you have! Luke, I might not like it.'

'As I see it, a pram is the equivalent to purchasing a car.'

'I don't think so,' I say and sit with my arms folded.

'Let me ask, do you approve of my taste in cars?'

'Yes, but—'

He runs his hand down my cheek. 'Then allow me this. I guarantee you will not be disappointed.'

He looks excited. How can I rain on his parade, even though I'm cross?

'Fine.'

He reaches for his phone and begins to search. 'Here.'

I look at the photo. 'Really?' I look at him.

'I thought you would like it.'

'Do you like it because it's a good sturdy pram or because of the Aston Martin name attached to it?'

He offers me his best Sutton smile. 'Both.'

'I hate it when you're right, but I really like it.' Silver Cross and Aston Martin – pregnancy seems to be opening up a whole new world for both of us.

'Are you hungry?'

'Yes.'

'Good, I know the perfect place.'

We begin to drive through the busy Chelsea streets, and within twenty minutes we're climbing a steep road leading to Primrose Hill. I know where we're heading: Luke's sacred place. It's part of our history. Luke drives into the car park and stops.

'I see you want to wine and dine me this evening.'

'Simple – that's what you want.' He points to the burger van. 'Simple is what you've got.'

'What would you like to eat?'

'Hmm – a cheeseburger with onions, mustard and a coffee.'

'Wait here.'

I watch him walk to the burger van. He looks like a model in his black suit and white shirt, but right now he's just my Luke. He turns to look at me, and I wave. How can I love someone this much? He's undeniably easy on the eye, but the feelings I have for him go much deeper than that. Sometimes I love him so much it's painful.

When he opens the door, I'm met by the smell of fried food.

'Here.'

Luke passes me a yellow box. I open the lid to reveal a huge burger.

'How the hell am I going to eat all this?' I look at Luke, who clearly does not share the same reservations. He takes a bite from his double cheeseburger, and the hotdog he ordered sits on the dashboard.

We sit silently, with the best view in London: iconic buildings stand tall, from the BT Tower to the London Eye. Every time we come here it feels comfortable.

After the burger, Luke begins to eat the hotdog.

'Christ, where do you put it all?'

'I love food.'

I nod with my mouth full. Scrummy burger – definitely a guilty pleasure.

'I can't eat any more. Here.'

I give him the last half of my burger – which means a long run for him later.

'Where's my coffee?'

He passes me a bottle of water. 'They didn't have decaf.'

'Water!' I roll my eyes. 'I think I could manage one cup of coffee.'

'Rules are there for a reason.'

I laugh. 'You just gave me heart attack food and yet you won't give me caffeinated coffee?'

'Yes.' He stifles a smile, knowing I have a point.

I sit back and drink my dull bottle of water.

'We haven't been up here for a long time.'

'No.'

I turn to him. 'Do you still run up here?'

He nods, taking the last bite of my burger.

'Does it remind you of Paul?'

'Not now. But when he died I came up here all the time.'

'What about when he was alive? Did you meet here?'

'Yeah, almost every day. We'd kick a football around, hang out.'

'How old were you when you met?'

'Almost sixteen. He was slightly older than me.'

'Did you both drive?'

'Yes. I learned to drive when I was sixteen. We had a family holiday in Australia and we stayed on a huge farm. I drove a jeep around for the entire time and I came home ready for a car, but I had to wait until I was seventeen.'

I shake my head. 'You've had such a privileged life.'

'Are you referring to money?'

'Not just money but also experiences, which money controls.'

'I can't change my childhood.'

I take his hand. 'Of course not. It just blows me away.'

'You know that you have changed my life, Kate.' He looks at me. 'You see me, not my money.'

'Always. Don't get me wrong: I know money is important. I grew up watching my parents struggle to pay

426

bills, but Harry and I never went without anything. You've never had to worry about money.'

'No.'

'Money doesn't rule my life, but money rules what we can do in life.'

'I understand, and would never take it for granted. You know how hard I work, Kate.'

'You work harder than most. But I need to remain grounded.' I look away. 'It's hard.'

'Dealing with money?' he asks.

I nod. 'It changes people. Even for the babies. We may live in a big house and be able to offer them everything, but I want them to know the value of money.'

'And they will. I remember, when I was eleven I wanted a remote control car.' His face comes alive. 'My mum said if I wanted it I had to work for it – and I did. Every weekend I cut the grass, washed cars – you name it, I did it. I'm sure I invented jobs just to earn extra money. What I'm trying to say is, I agree with you: we will provide our children with the best tools in life, but they will have to carve out their future.'

'OK,' I say.

'They'll be grounded – they have you as their mum. Christ, you keep me grounded.'

I laugh. 'Enough money talk now! How about a bath and French toast?'

'You have missed a small detail.'

'Of course I have!' I giggle at him.

He looks at the rear of the car and laughs.

'I don't think so, Sutton. I can just about move after that burger, and I need to take these bloody trousers off.'

I look at my stomach, which I swear has grown in the last hour.

'Home it is, then. You can bathe, then I will make love to you, and then you can feed me.'

'Perfect.'

21

My fingers swirl through the hot soapy water as I lie back in the bath, the morning sun filtering through the shutters. However, my tranquillity is short-lived, as Luke bursts into the bathroom, panting and dripping with sweat.

'Good workout?'

Luke nods. 'He kills me.'

'Must be an age thing. Martin's how old?' I laugh.

'Younger than me.' He smiles and gives me a damp kiss.

'I'd better tell him to go easy on you.'

'He flies out to LA for boot camp training,' Luke says, stripping. My morning view just keeps getting better.

'That'll knock you on your arse.'

'You're staring at me.'

'You're stark bollock naked, what do you expect?'

Luke steps into the shower to rinse away the residue of a Saturday morning workout. My mind drifts to a different kind of workout – my pregnancy libido is killing me!

'What are you thinking about?' Luke asks.

Sex. 'About my parents,' I say.

'Let the dust settle. They've all met. Malcolm and Susan are OK, so give it some time.' He turns the shower off and wraps a towel around his waist.

'Do you think they will ever be comfortable being in the same room together? I mean, for things like birthdays and Christmas.'

'At some point. I think they'll all get used to things. Ivor and Katenka have kept a low profile so far.'

'They've been missing for most of my life, so yeah I would say they've definitely kept a low profile.'

'You don't need the stress.'

'Well, there's not much I can do about that, is there? I can't change what's happened. Mum and Dad are coming over tomorrow for dinner. It'll be nice to spend some time with them, and Mum wants to go baby shopping.'

'Like I said, they will be fine.'

'She gets excited when I talk about the babies.'

'They're a perfect distraction – for all of you.'

'You're right.'

I get out of the bath and begin to towel myself dry. 'What's your plan for today?'

'Work.'

'OK.'

'What time will Adam be here?'

'In a couple of hours. Barney doesn't want us at the theatre until this afternoon.'

'Good – we have time to play. You know how much I love a Saturday morning fuck.'

'Let's be honest – every bloody morning is the right time for you.'

He takes my hand and walks me to the bed.

'I need you.' He seals his words with an unexpected kiss that sends my pulse soaring and makes my clit scream his name.

My arms link around his neck. He lifts me onto the bed and lowers his lips to my nipples, gently caressing them. Small eruptions of sensation flood my body. My back arches against the bed and my hips sway, needing his touch.

'Luke.' There's no response. His lips and tongue continue to tease my nipples.

'Luke.'

Again, he maintains pressure.

'Luke, touch me.'

His mouth leaves my nipple. 'Where?'

'Everywhere.'

His lips travel to my neck. 'I think you should be more specific.'

'Luke, don't. Not this morning.'

His kiss is strong and his tongue slowly dips inside my mouth. My body aches for him. I tilt my hips towards him. His hand glides leisurely down my body and his fingers skim my hipbone before they slowly brush against my clit. I raise my hips to his touch, but his fingers slide away.

I break away. 'I'm a hormonal pregnant woman. Do not piss me off.'

He smiles and nibbles my ear. 'Would you like me to touch you and let you come?'

I nod.

'Did you say something?'

He will feel my fist shortly. 'Yes.'

He strokes my sweet spot, but it is not enough.

'Luke.'

'Baby. I love it when you lose yourself to me.'

I can feel my orgasm building.

'Would you like it faster?'

I nod.

It's too late.

'Luke, I'm coming.' I say no more as he increases speed and pressure, tipping me over the edge, allowing my orgasm to wash over me.

He moves between my legs, spreading them apart, allowing him the space to place his mouth over my clit.

'Luke… I'm tender.'

'Relax.'

I try to, but my swollen clit is so sensitive. The warm sensation of his moist tongue gently coerces my body to begin another ride – a different path but with the same outcome. He gently sinks his fingers inside my sex, heading straight to where he knows will guarantee the arrival of my next orgasm.

'Pathetically needy' are the only words to describe me. Sensations swirl inside me, even stronger than my previous orgasm.

'Luke,' I murmur.

My legs are locked in place with Luke's arms. All I can do is grip the sheet and ride the shockwave that rocks through me.

My eyes remain closed. With one solid thrust, he immerses himself. I open my eyes. Slowly he begins to work his hips, gradually building up speed, stroking me inside.

'I can't orgasm again, Luke.' I'm spent.

'You can, look at me.'

My eyes meet his gaze.

'Relax. I know your body.'

I nod.

Mr I-know-what-I'm-doing Sutton does know what he's doing as he continues to ride me with precision. I am helpless when I'm under him.

'Luke,' I manage to say as I come again.

'Fuck, you make me so hard. I'm almost there.'

As he plunges into me I know he is close to coming. His jaw tightens and his powerhouse body delivers what he needs, until he stops. His breathing regulates and his kisses the end of my nose.

'Like I said, a Saturday morning fuck is always the best,' he says and lies next to me.

'Mr Romantic.' I roll to my side. 'And stop bloody teasing me.'

'It turns me on,' he smiles.

'You just want me to beg.'

'Begging for me – purely self-indulgent.'

'You're merciless in bed.'

'I make no apologies for wanting you.'

'True.' I yawn.

'Tired?' he asks.

'A bit. Let's lie here until I have to leave.'

'I'll make you a cup of tea and then I need to work.'

'OK. Work in bed.'

He slips on grey joggers and a T-shirt and disappears. I close my eyes for a few minutes.

I stretch my arms above my head and look at my watch. Eleven fifty – shit, Adam will be here in ten minutes. I race out of bed and move towards the stairs, only to hear voices in the office. Adam and Luke. Crap.

'Hi Adam. Sorry I'm running late,' I shout from the landing.

'It's fine, take your time,' he responds.

Quickly I dress in black maternity jeans, a long black T-shirt and a black biker jacket. I put on just enough make-up to make me look slightly awake; however, Roller Girl is most certainly with me. I really don't have to time to send her packing; a scruffy ponytail will have to do. Within ten minutes, I'm in the kitchen.

'How are you?' Adam asks.

'I'm fine. Growing.'

'How many weeks are you?'

I rest my hand on the bump. 'Just over twenty weeks.'

'That's fantastic. Luke said your blood pressure is a little low, and you're tired.'

I smile. That's all I need – another doctor in the house, although at least this one is actually qualified.

'I'm fine. It's been a crazy few weeks, and Luke forgot to wake me up.'

'You had a busy morning,' Luke chips in.

Did he just say that? The little shit!

'You're right, so I'm thinking I need a quiet evening tonight.'

Luke gives me a wink.

'Barney called earlier. He sounds stressed. He asked if we could get him a McDonald's on the way.'

'This will be fun… You haven't met Barney the control freak choreographer! Luke, I would never have said that you and he were alike. Well, Adam, you're in for a treat.'

'Should I be scared?' Adam says.

'No, this is Barney at his best.'

Max appears from his apartment. 'Kate, are you ready?'

'I thought you had the day off?'

'I'm off later,' Max answers in his usual stern tone and begins to walk off.

We follow him.

'Where are you off to later?' I ask.

Max stops next to the front door. 'Out.'

'Out? Out with someone or alone?'

'Just out.'

I smile.

'Cut it out, Harper.' This time he smiles.

My arms link around Luke's neck. 'I love you forever.'

'Back at you. Be good, and don't leave without Max or me, OK?'

'Yes.' I roll my eyes.

'This is serious, Kate.'

'OK, chill. And I won't talk to strangers!'

'Kate, please don't make jokes about it.'

'Ah, but there's nothing to worry about, is there? Just a precaution.'

'Don't leave on your own!' His tone is forbidding.

Max begins the journey to the disused office block that has been renovated into contemporary dance studios, not far from Barney's studio in Covent Garden. After stopping at McDonald's, we arrive.

'Thanks, Max.'

'Call me or Luke – don't leave alone.'

'Yeah, yeah, yeah.' I sigh.

'Kate, I mean it.'

I lean between the two front seats. 'I heard you loud and clear. You know what, Max, it would be so much easier if you and Luke were to actually tell me who the hell is freaking you both out.'

He remains silent.

'Oh no, because you and Luke aren't looking for anyone, are you?'

'Just promise me.'

'OK,' I snap. *What the hell is going on, Luke? Who is scaring you?*

I press the buzzer, while Max watches us from the car.

'Hola!' Barney bellows from the speaker.

My finger hovers over the intercom button. 'Let's wind him up.' I giggle and with a fabulous French accent I decide to tease him. 'Hello? I have a delivery for a Mr Curtain. Two boxes of rose petals.'

'What?' He sounds agitated.

'Are you Mr Curtain?' I look at Adam, and release the button. 'My accent is crap, he's gonna guess it's me.'

The speaker comes alive again. 'No, I'm not, and I haven't ordered rose petals.'

'Kate!' Adam laughs.

'I can't help it.' I press the buzzer again.

'Hello!'

'Can I speak to Mr Curtain? I have two boxes of rose petals.'

'Look, mate, I just told you there's no Mr Curtain here.'

I can just about control my laughter as I press the buzzer again.

'What now?' Barney is about to erupt.

'Is that Mr Curtain?'

'You ask for Mr Curtain one more time, I am going to shove this intercom so far up your fucking arse you'll be able to speed dial with your fucking tongue.'

I laugh so hard that tears roll down my cheeks.

'Kate!'

'Hi,' I manage. 'Someone just gave me two boxes of rose petals.'

'Are you fucking yanking my chain?'

'No, seriously.' I can just about speak.

'Ha ha bloody ha. I have a good mind to leave you on the street. Go and scatter your fucking rose petals for all I care.'

'Be very careful, Mr Curtain. We come bearing gifts that come in brown paper bags. Hmm, can you smell that, Adam?'

There is a click as the door unlocks. When we enter, Max drives away. Adam and I make our way towards the main reception area. Barney strides towards us.

'Hi, Mr Curtain.' I wave his lunch bag. 'My mistake – burger, not rose petals.'

'You cheeky bitch.' Barney begins to laugh. 'I tell you what, I was ready to come downstairs and knock you out.'

I reach up and give him a peck on the cheek.

'Bloody hell, what a morning I've had. If it could go wrong, it has.'

'What can we do to help?' Adam asks.

'There's nothing you can do.' Barney pulls at my T-shirt, allowing him to view my growing bump. 'Christ, babe, you definitely look pregnant now.'

'You know how to make me feel good.'

'You're glowing, babe. Pregnancy suits you.'

'Thank you. Right, are you going to show us your masterpiece?'

'Yep.' Barney smiles with delight. 'OK, so, I've had some technical hitches that have caused—' He smirks.

'Barney the bitch to arrive? Don't worry, I warned Adam, so don't hold back because we're watching.'

'Yep, I want to see the real Mr Curtain,' Adam says.

'Curtain.' Barney shakes his head and walks off, mumbling. 'Fucking Curtain!' He leads us to the seats towards the back of the auditorium.

'You should be able to see everything from here. Right, as you're two of my closest friends…' He looks at Adam. 'I'm asking for complete honesty. Got it?'

'You have our word,' Adam answers, and Barney leaves us alone.

'Barney?' I yell. 'In case I forget to tell you, I'm really proud of you.'

'He's quite a character.' Adam watches Barney disappear.

'I'd be lost without him.' I look at Adam. 'You could do worse.'

'What do you mean?' He shifts awkwardly in his seat.

'How could you not fancy the pants off him? He's stunning, with a great body, but he's also lovely.' He looks at me. 'OK, I'm going to put it out there. I think you like him as much as he likes you.'

'Jesus, Kate.'

'Tell me I'm wrong?'

'I don't know what to say.'

438

'"Yes, Kate, I really like him" is a good place to start. Do you know what, Adam? I've had to deal with some real shit situations, and if there is one thing I've learned, it's that life's too short.'

'I know,' he says and runs his hand through his hair.

'Are you worried about Jerry and what he might say?' I ask.

He takes a deep breath. 'Partly.'

I take his hand. 'Your dad loves you.'

'My mum talks about you all the time Kate. You mean a great deal to mum and dad.'

'They mean a lot to me. They were so good to me when I first worked for Luke.'

With that, the lights dim and the sound of an orchestra playing a modern song echoes around the room. It's 'Blame', a Calvin Harris tune with a classic twist. Then Barney makes his grand entrance. He wears ripped jeans, his chest bare apart from some temporary tattoos. Immediately I'm mesmerised: I watch him dance effortlessly across the stage, using his body to tell the story, emotionally and physically drawing us in. The story is of a lost love and the torment it causes.

It's the interval. Adam and I stand and clap wildly. I can't whistle, but my yelling travels upstage quite well.

'Bloody amazing.' I look at Adam.

'I'm lost for words.'

'I told you he was good. Come on, let's find him.'

We head for the stage and venture towards the wings. Barney is talking to a couple of assistants. He comes over to us.

'Wow! Bloody breath-taking,' I say.

'Truthfully, I'm a bit shocked,' Adam says.

'You thought it would be shit?' Barney says, wiping his forehead with a towel.

'I didn't know what to expect. Let's face it, I know nothing about dancing, but I understood the story. It was brilliantly told,' Adam says.

I nudge Adam's arm. 'Told you. I'll go and sit down. Can you get me a coffee?'

They need some time alone. Perfect. I sit down and reach inside my bag for my phone. I ring Luke. No answer, so I leave a voice message.

'Hi, love of my life. Just thought I would check in. Love you.'

I dial the palace but there is no answer – strange for Luke not to answer one of the phones.

'Here, Princess Harper.' I look up at Barney. 'Sorry, there was no decaf.'

'Music to my ears – don't tell Control Freak Sutton.' I take the paper cup from Barney, excited at the prospect of regular coffee.

'One cup won't kill you,' Adam says.

'You need to speak to Luke about that; he's a bloody nightmare.'

'Babe, he loves control, any control. Those poor babies don't know what they've let themselves in for. OK, ready for the second act?'

'Absolutely,' I say.

Adam and I take our seats. I check my phone. No response from Luke. I send a text.

I tried to call!
I miss you x

The music begins and the dancing commences; once more we get lost in the story. Towards the end of the performance, Barney's character dies. It is completely unexpected. My eyes flood with emotions. I turn to Adam, who looks just as captivated. I think Barney's amazing choreography may have just stolen his heart.

Barney takes a bow. We applaud, blown away by how emotive a dance production can be. He makes his way to us, breathless and exhausted.

'Verdicts, please?' he asks.

'Brilliant – you made me cry,' I say.

Adam shakes his head. 'Honestly?' He pauses. 'Amazing.'

'You look shattered.' I run my hand down Barney's arm.

'I am, babe, it takes it out of me.'

'I'm so proud of you. Oh, and thanks for the warning that you die,' I say.

'I wanted to surprise you both.' Barney smiles swigging from his water bottle.

'You did, in more ways than one,' Adam says.

'I thought it went smoothly. I definitely didn't see any problems,' I say.

'It went better than earlier.' Barney wipes his forehead. 'Give me half an hour and then we can leave.'

'OK, I'll call Luke and tell him to pick us up.'

I take a seat at the front of the stage while Barney and Adam wander off together. Caller ID – Boss. I hit send. Once again there is no response from Luke or the palace, so I call Max. It goes straight to voicemail.

'Kate.'

I look up at Adam.

'You OK?'

'I can't get hold of Luke and I just tried Max. He isn't picking up either.'

'We can get a cab.'

I shake my head. 'No.'

Adam looks confused. 'Kate, we'll come with you. It's not a problem.'

'That's not what I mean. Luke always picks up when I call.'

'He's probably busy. I'll go and see where Barney is.'

I nod. This time I try Rosie and Jerry. The phone just rings out.

Half an hour later, Barney strolls towards me. 'Ready, babe? Where's Luke meeting us?'

'He's not. I'm worried.'

'Why?'

'I can't get hold of Luke or Max.'

'I'm sure he's…'

'What? You know Luke always picks up his phone.'

'Yeah, he does.' He pulls me close. 'Don't stress. There must be a reason.'

A cold wave washes over me. 'Something's wrong.'

'Don't worry. We'll come with you. I'm not letting you get in a cab alone. Sutton will kill me.'

Barney flags down a passing cab and gives the palace's address. In the cab the men sit and discuss the show.

'Hey, babe.' Barney pulls me closer to him. '007 is fine.'

'It doesn't make sense. He told me to call him when I was ready to leave.'

'There must be a good reason,' Barney says.

'Barney's right. I'm sure he's lost track of time,' Adam says.

'He wouldn't, not with me.'

The traffic's busy and it takes what feels like a lifetime to reach the palace. As we pull up, I see the security booth is empty.

'Stop!' I bellow and pass a twenty-pound note to the cab driver before leaping out.

'Kate, wait,' Barney says.

I look inside the empty booth. 'Where is everyone?'

'OK, just calm down,' Barney says, but I run towards the front door, which is open.

'Fuck!' I whisper and push it further open. I turn to Barney.

'Let me go in first,' he offers.

Hell, no! I walk through the door and enter the hall. For some reason the house feels eerie. When I left, the TV was blaring out and the house felt warm, but now there is a scary silence.

Cautiously I walk further into the house. I check the office. Nothing. My gut tells me this isn't good. I move to the kitchen.

'Fuck! Barney.'

22

'Jesus Christ! Rosie.' Rosie is tied to a kitchen chair. I fumble to remove the gag from her mouth, while Adam and Barney try to untie her.

'Shit, this isn't budging. We need a knife,' Barney says, wrestling with the cable ties.

'Mum, it's OK, we're here. Where's Dad?' Adam asks calmly, watching Barney cut her free.

'Where's Jerry and Luke?' I ask.

She swallows. 'Over there,' she whispers and tilts her head towards the sofas.

Adam runs across the room. 'Dad!'

I join him. Jerry is lying still on the floor.

'Oh my God.' I drop to my knees. 'Is he all right?'

Adam's doctor training kicks in. He checks for a pulse. Paediatrics is his usual field – but not today. 'Dad, can you hear me?'

Jerry barely opens his eyes. 'Mum,' he whispers.

'She's OK, Jerry.' I look at Adam. 'Luke has a medical kit. I'll get it.'

I run to the office and slide open the cupboard, grabbing the black bag. I stand and spot Luke's phone on the desk.

'Fuck, where are you, Luke?' I mumble.

I return to Adam and he goes through the contents of the bag.

'Your husband is quite resourceful.'

I nod, and pray that he is today.

'OK, Dad, let me check you over.' Jerry looks at his son, who he once rejected.

I turn when I hear Rosie behind me. 'Oh, Jerry,' she cries.

'Come and sit down.' I guide her to the sofa. 'Barney, get a glass of water.'

'Kate,' she murmurs.

'Shh, it's OK.' I pull her towards me. 'Where's Luke?'

She begins to cry.

'Drink this.' Barney passes her a glass of water. 'Fucking hell, Kate, we need to call the police.'

'No,' I snap. 'Rosie, what happened?'

'We were in Luke's office. Max turned up and…' She swallows hard. 'All I remember is a bang on the front door.'

'Then what?'

'Four men crashed in. There may have been more. They had guns. Kate, it was awful! They hit Max. Luke tried to stop them…' She looks away.

I feel a tightness in my chest. 'It's OK.'

'Barney, come here. I need you to hold this drip,' Adam says. Barney squats at Jerry's side. 'Don't move – I need the fluid to go in.'

Barney nods.

'OK, Dad, let's look at this cut. It may hurt a little, OK?'

'Rosie, look at me,' I say, distracting her. 'Do you remember anything else? What did they look like?'

She closes her eyes, thinking hard.

'I think they knew Luke and Max.' She runs her hands through her hair. 'That was what they said…'

'Good. What did they say? Any small detail may help.' I take her hands and run my thumbs across her knuckles.

'Payback. I remember them saying Luke had to pay. They made me and Jerry go to the kitchen, that's when Jerry fought back, and… Adam, is he OK?'

'He will be. He's got a small cut and maybe a cracked a rib. Barney, help me lift him onto the sofa.'

I go to Jerry. 'Here, let me hold the drip. What's in it?'

'Painkillers, he's going to need them. Right, Barney, lift his legs on the count of three,' Adam says. 'One, two, three… OK, easy does it.'

Jerry groans.

'Well done, Dad, let's make you comfortable. Kate, pass me the drip.'

I hand the drip to Adam.

'Babe, I think it's time to call the police,' Barney says.

I shake my head. 'No.' I turn to Rosie. 'Did they mention any names?'

'I can't remember.' She taps her head. 'Think, Rosie, think… Oh Kate, it's no use. Wait. Andrew – I think I heard the name Andrew… But I can't be sure.'

'Well done, Rosie.' I stand up.

'Where are you going?' Barney looks at me.

'I have to get them.'

'What do you mean, you have to get them?'

'Barney, I can't live without Luke… You know that.'

'I get it, babe, but you don't know where he is. Like I said, let's call the police.'

'No… I need to make a call.'

Working on autopilot, I head for the basement, Barney close behind me. As I stand in front of the wine rack I run my hand down the side, feeling for the switch.

'I don't think you should be drinking, not in your condition,' he says, looking a little confused.

'I'm not.'

I slide the rack across to reveal the hidden door and input my code. The door unlocks. I walk inside Luke's den and switch the light on.

Again Barney follows me.

'Fuck me gently. What the hell is this room?'

'I don't have time to explain. Let me think.'

Quickly I open the cupboard in the far corner – Luke's cupboard of tricks. 'Right, I need to call James.'

'What the hell is Luke doing with all this stuff?' Barney walks around the room. 'Jesus H. Christ!'

I turn to see him holding a bundle of money.

'What the fuck is he into, money laundering? Maybe that's why he's been taken.'

'For fuck's sake, Barney, of course he doesn't – he's a businessman… And you're not helping by talking shit.'

'What do you expect me to think with all this money, not to mention the bloody guns?'

He walks further around the room.

447

'This room has nothing to do with you.' I run my hands through my hair. 'Luke had a very different past. He's a hero. Now shut the fuck up and let me think.'

'OK, chill.' Defensively, he holds his hands up.

'Really? My husband has been taken and you want me to chill?'

'Taken? Are you sure?'

Somehow, I am.

I switch on the satellite mobile phone and search for Sullivan's number. Thankfully, it rings.

'Sutton, what's she done now?' James Sullivan asks.

'She has done nothing.'

'Kate?' James sounds confused. He has the right to.

'Someone has taken Luke and Max. I need you to track him, I know he's wearing his watch. He never takes it off.'

'I'm already doing it. Are you OK?'

'I wasn't here. I came home to find Rosie tied to a chair, and Jerry beaten up.'

'Are they able to tell you anything?' he asks.

'Rosie said the name Andrew, but I know it's Anderson! Plus they mentioned payback. I know it's him, James.'

'Did Rosie say anything else?'

'No.'

'Are they OK?'

'She's OK, just shocked. Anyway, Adam's here.'

'The doctor – her son?' he asks.

'Yeah, how do you know?'

'Luke told me. Who's with you?' he asks.

'Barney.' I stand and begin to pace. 'James, we haven't got long.'

'Stay calm. Panic causes mistakes, trust me.'

'Luke had some new CCTV installed – now it makes sense. He knew, didn't he? Don't bullshit me, James. He knew about Anderson?'

'Luke's always cautious – we have to be. It's part of our job.'

'*Was!* Luke doesn't work with you, remember?'

'There's no "was" in our line of work.'

'Are you trying to tell me that Luke never got out? That he will always work with you and Scott?'

'Not officially, Kate.'

'Please answer one question: have you worked with Luke since we've been together?'

He's silent.

I thought I knew my husband. Now I wonder if I will ever know the real Luke Sutton.

'I'm locating him now. OK, I need you to check the CCTV footage. I'll talk you through it.'

I bolt upstairs to Luke's office and sit at his desk, with a silent Barney next to me. The computer is already fired up. I assume Luke was working when he was *taken* – a word I find hard to swallow.

'I'm ready.'

'Good. There should be an icon on the desktop. Luke would have used something like…' James pauses. 'Maybe a car symbol or a sport.'

'A rugby ball?'

'Yeah, click on that.'

The screen changes. 'There's loads of numbers racing around.'

I look at Barney, who seems just as confused as me.

'That's fine. When they stop you will need to enter a password.'

'Luke's computer password?'

'No, definitely not eat me,' he says in a softer tone. He sounds amused.

'Oh!' The boys must talk more often than I thought. 'OK. It's stopped and the cursor is flashing.'

'Enter the following code, letters in upper-case: NZ345HG9.'

'I've done it. What does the code mean?'

'That doesn't matter. Now you should see footage at the top of the screen. You can alter the time frame. When do you think he was taken?'

'I don't know, maybe three hours ago.'

'Alter the time frame. You can then press the forward button to speed up the viewing.'

I follow his instructions while Barney peers at the screen over my shoulder.

'Kate, stop.' Barney points to the screen.

'Gotcha, you little fuckers,' I say to James. 'OK, we can see them but their faces look blurry. Shit – there's Luke.' His face is clear and so are the brutal punches he receives to his stomach and his face. I feel sick, watching him and Max being dragged away from the house and pushed into a van.

'Hold the mouse over the image, left-click to hold the view and right-click to zoom in.' James has the patience of a saint.

'Holy fuck, it's Anderson! He's pointing a gun at Max's head. I'll never forget his face. I know where Luke is. Why didn't Luke talk to me, James? Jesus Christ, this shouldn't be happening.'

'Anderson has been in hiding.'

'Well, he's not now! Have you got the results yet?'

'Just another couple of minutes. Parker is on his way from Oxford. He should be an hour and a half at the most.'

I stand up from Luke's desk, feeling wretched after watching him being assaulted. My body begins to shake and I feel an intense pressure in my chest. I can't breathe. Where is he now? What if he's dead?

'I'm not waiting, James. I'm going to get them both.'

'Oh no, you don't! You're fucking pregnant,' James bellows down the phone.

'Thanks for the reminder! My children's father could be dead in a few hours, if he's not already... which is precisely why I'm not sitting here waiting. I suggest you call me when you have info from his tracker. Besides, you're in Switzerland! You can't stop me.'

I shut the phone and slip it in my pocket.

'Please tell me you're joking and Luke's army boys will be here any minute?' Barney stands, his hands on his hips.

'Not quite. Scott Parker is on his way and the other is going to talk me through how to get Luke.'

'What? Are you out of your fucking mind?'

'For God's sake, Barney, I'm not going to just sit here!' I take a deep breath. 'The man that took Luke is the man that killed Max's son – well, his bouncers killed him when he was seventeen. He died in Luke's arms.'

'Shit.'

'Long story short: Luke saw to it that Anderson paid, one thing led to another, Anderson got done for possession of drugs at his club, and Luke bought the club for next to nothing. SGI!'

'SGI! No fucking way.'

451

'It was Anderson's club back then.'

'Revenge.' Barney hits the nail on the head. 'Jesus Christ, babe… You think that's where Luke is?'

'He has to be.'

'Call the police.'

'No. Anderson will kill them. I've seen how violent he can be.'

'What? When?'

'Max had a run-in with him. I got caught in the crossfire.'

'I can't believe what I'm hearing.' Barney takes me in his arms. 'The babies, Kate – think of the babies.'

'I am! They need their daddy to be alive. I'm going and you can't stop me.'

'In that case, I'm coming with you.'

I pull away. 'No, you can take me but I'm going in alone.' I take a deep breath. 'I'll just get my gun.'

'Your what?' Barney runs his hand through his hair in disbelief.

'It's OK. I know how to use it.'

'Fucking hell, Kate… Anything else you want to tell me? Sutton has got a lot to answer for when I see him. This day is getting worse. I need a fucking drink.'

I head to our bedroom and input the code to the safe in our closet, then retrieve my gun and some bullets.

Barney begins to laugh. 'You're bloody unbelievable, Kate.'

'Luke taught me to shoot after my first time in Russia – actually, that's not true. He taught me when Max was attacked by Anderson. He wanted me to be able to protect myself.'

'Crazy fuckers, the pair of you.'

The satellite phone rings.

'James?' I say.

'SGI.'

'I knew it – predictable little shit.'

'I can't stop you, can I?'

'No. I need him, James.'

'Fuck it, Kate. OK, if you're doing this then you do it my way, no arguing. Got it?'

'Yep.'

'Good. I might just be able to save the pair of you. I've just got access to the cameras inside SGI, but I need you to grab a Bluetooth earpiece from the cellar.'

'And Parker?'

'Like I said – he'll be an hour, maybe longer.'

'Good.'

'Jesus Christ, Kate, when Luke gets hold of you, he will lock you up. Don't say I didn't warn you.'

'I don't care, just as long as he's breathing.'

'Call me when you're ready to leave. I'm heading for the airfield. And Kate?'

'What?'

'Be safe. If anything happened to you or the girls Luke would… it would kill him.'

I frown. 'How do you know? I mean the sex.'

'We talk every day.'

The call ends. Barney glares at me.

'I thought you didn't know.' Barney places his hand on my bump. 'About the sex.'

'We found out when I had the bleed, but we decided not to tell anyone.'

He folds his arms. 'If Luke told James, then I think I should know…'

'Jesus, Barney, I'm trying to rescue my husband and you're pissed off because I kept a secret?'

'Too fucking right I am. I tell you everything.'

'I know, and believe me some things you should keep to yourself.'

In Luke's den, I look at his toys. What might I need – other than a miracle? First a Bluetooth earpiece, but what else? I pick up a relatively small flick-knife; I guess it might be helpful. There's a small black square device with a switch. It's some kind of detonator, I think. I can't remember what Luke said the other day.

In a few minutes, I stand in the hallway, waiting to leave. Adam bounds towards me.

'Barney just told me you're going to get Luke. Are you mad?' he bellows.

'I'm meeting Luke's friends there. They're well trained, trust me. How's Jerry?'

'He's OK. Kate, this is not normal behaviour, people being attacked and kidnapped. You need to call the police.' He looks at Barney. 'Tell her!'

'I've tried. Anyway, I'm taking her to meet Luke's friends, they know what they're doing.'

Adam scowls at us. 'Good!'

'Ready?' Barney asks.

'Yep. I just need the keys for the club. Go and get Rosie's car keys.'

'We can take your car,' Barney responds.

'Really?' I look at my best friend. 'My Bentley with the marry me number plate? That's subtle. Not.'

'Trust me to have a bloody Ford Fiesta as a getaway car.'

Adam glares at him. 'What!'

'I'm joking! Do I honestly look like a getaway driver?'

We head for Rosie's car in silence. Of course the most sensible thing to do would be to call the police. Barney automatically takes the driving seat and I slide in next to him. My palms feel clammy and my heart is racing. What the hell am I doing?

'You OK?'

I take a deep breath. 'Not really. Why does this keep happening to us?'

He rests his hand on my leg, driving one-handed.

'Do you think they're alive?' I ask and look at him.

'That man will survive anything. He can look after himself,' Barney says with conviction.

'I know, but they may have done something to him. What am I saying? Of course they have.'

'I'm sure he'll get out of this. I don't know how, but he will.'

'I hope so. I really don't want to shoot anyone. But I will to save them.'

'I believe you, which scares the shit out of me… Why didn't I know Luke was turning you into some kind of GI Jane? You make a right pair.'

'I told you – he wanted me to be able to defend myself.'

'He bloody has.' He gazes at my lap. 'What's that?'

I hold up the small square box. 'I don't know. I'm sure Luke said it's a detonator…'

'A fucking detonator! Are you out of your bloody mind?'

'I don't know what it is. It just looks useful.' I look closely at it. 'There's a switch – it must activate something.'

'Don't bloody try it now, for Christ's sake.'

'Of course I won't!'

My phone rings in my lap, which causes us to jump.

'Jesus, Kate! Move that bloody thing.'

'Hello?'

'Where are you?' James Sullivan asks.

'About five minutes away.'

'OK. Get Barney to park on the side street by the club – Walter Street. I'll talk you through the entrance.'

I look to Barney. 'Go to Walter Street. It's the road after SGI.'

He nods.

'I have the keys.'

'There will be a large gold key with the number twenty-two inscribed on it.'

I look closely at all the keys. 'Got it.'

'This will unlock the building adjacent to the club. Luke owns it.'

'He does?'

'Yes.'

'Of course he does, why wouldn't he?' I reply sarcastically. 'What is it, an emergency exit?'

'It has a direct link to the club. Also there are no CCTV cameras on that street.'

'Christ, and I was going to go through the front door!'

'Not today. Listen, you will need to follow my instructions, OK?'

'OK.'

'Good, now put the Bluetooth in your ear and press the button at the side. Give it a couple of seconds and you should be able to hear me.'

He's right.

'Just to let you know, I have my gun, which is loaded.'

'And a detonator,' Barney shouts, sounding displeased.

I look across at him. 'Thanks, Barney,' I mutter.

'What did he say?'

'I've got a detonator, I think… A small black box with a switch at the top.'

'What the hell are you thinking?' James bellows through my earpiece.

'I'm trying to use some forward thinking.'

'Picking up a piece of equipment you don't know how to handle is not forward thinking.'

'Fine!'

'Don't get shitty with me, Kate. I'm trying to protect you.'

'And I'm trying to help.'

Even though it's late Saturday afternoon and Soho is normally busy, today the traffic is fairly light. Barney parks outside number twenty-two.

'James, we're here. Give me a minute.'

'OK.'

I turn to Barney. 'This is it.'

'Let me come in with you.'

'No. It's easier this way. Do you have your phone?'

'Yeah.' He hugs me. 'Thirty minutes and then I'm calling the police.'

I step out of the car. Just before I close the door, I say, 'Barney? The twins are girls.'

23

'From this point, listen to every word I say. Use your eyes and ears,' James says. 'Jesus, you shouldn't be doing this.'

'Well, I am.'

'Ready?' he says.

'As I'll ever be.'

'Use the gold key to unlock the door, and make sure you close it behind you. I'm looking at the blueprint of the building.'

From the outside, the building looks like a disused warehouse, and it's surrounded by similar-looking buildings. The metal door unlocks without any problems, although I could do without the creaking sound its rusty hinges make. I step inside and push the door closed. The creak echoes around the enormous empty room.

'Kate.'

Foolishly, I nod.

'I'm in. Tell me again, why does Luke own this building?'

'That doesn't matter now! OK, you need to veer towards the left. There will be another door, that won't be locked.'

'Are you sure?'

'Yes.'

'It's bloody dark in here.' I walk forward, but I can barely see my hands in front of me.

'Your eyes will adjust.'

'What about the staff? They should be arriving soon.'

He laughs.

'What?'

'You think on your feet. I called the manager; the club isn't open this evening.'

'What, on a Saturday night? I smell bullshit!'

'Exactly.'

'Inside job? Do you think the manager knows Anderson?' I ask.

'Maybe. Concentrate, Kate.'

'It really is bloody dark in here.'

'Stay calm, and take some deep breaths.'

Again I nod and do as he asks. This does have an effect: I feel less likely to scream and more inclined to cry. It gets even darker when I reach the rear of the building, using my hands to aid me.

'I'm in the corner.' My hands skim the wall until I find a metal frame. 'I can feel the door.'

'Open it and close it behind you.'

'Do they know Luke owns this building? I mean, Anderson?'

'It's unlikely. OK, as you go through watch where you walk. There will be some steps in front of you. These will lead you to a doorway to SGI.'

'Shit, we're close.'

'Remember to breathe.'

'Any news on Scott? I feel the need for a partner in crime.'

'He's on his way.'

'Shall I have my gun ready?'

'No!' James blurts.

Slowly I move towards the stairs, which I can just about make out. I begin to climb, counting the steps in my head as I go.

'I'm at the top.'

'Good. Now listen. This door opens onto the stockroom that backs onto the bar.'

'Near the dance floor?'

'No, the VIP bar. Remember, you're now on the first floor of the club.'

'Crap! You're right. I'm shit at this.' I feel completely out of my depth.

'The door will look like part of the wall. Make sure you close it behind you. Leave no trace.'

'Leave no trace,' I repeat.

'The room will be full of boxes, so be careful where you step.'

I open the door slowly and gently close it behind me. The room is full. Piles of boxes and racks of bottles.

'I'm hooked up to the SGI cameras. I can see you.'

'Good,' I say and wave. 'Can you see Luke and Max?'

'No.'

'No? What do you mean?'

'They must be in the basement. Unfortunately there are no cameras down there.'

'His watch?'

'Locates him to SGI.'

'Great!' I shake my head in disbelief.

'You will have to enter the basement blind.'

Is he joking? My bravado deserts me.

'Wait here until I tell you it's clear. Then you need to walk quietly to Luke's office. We're going in the back way, OK?'

'Got it.'

We remain silent. The only sound I can hear is my heart pounding against my chest. My hand automatically rests on my bump, protecting my babies.

'Girls, I love you both,' I whisper.

'Kate. Go now. Remember, quiet.'

Cautiously I open the door and close it behind me.

'Kate, get down now!'

I fall to the floor.

'Stay still! There are two men climbing the stairs from the dance floor. I'll tell you when it's safe to go.'

I nod and try to listen, but their voices are muffled.

'OK, move your arse now: go, go, go!'

I bolt from behind the bar across the VIP area and towards Luke's office, not glancing behind me, just focusing on the door.

'I'm at the door,' I whisper and look at the keypad.

'Input these numbers.'

'Venice, baby,' I murmur and remember the first time I inputted the numbers to this door. I know what these numbers mean to me and Luke.

'What?'

'Venice… That's where…' *We fell in love.*

'I get the picture.'

The code is accepted. I walk through and quietly shut the door. 'I'm in.'

'Move to the corner of the room. There's a bookcase with a picture of an old blueprint of the club. Slide the bookcase to the right.'

It glides across with ease. Luke is a creature of habit.

'There's a door.'

'Open it and slide the bookcase back. Remember, cover your tracks.'

'OK. This is where the fun begins.'

'Fun!'

'Metaphorically speaking. You're on your own now, except for me in your ear.'

'Shit. I can't do this. No – I can do this…'

'If you can handle Sutton, then you can do this.'

'You're right, I can do this.' No, I fucking can't!

'I do know some of the layout, so listen carefully.'

I nod.

'The stairs are hidden. Once you get to the bottom, you can only turn right. There is a section of the wall that opens. You need to push it gently. You will then enter another stockroom that I know Luke keeps full, which hides the door.'

'Why does he have so many bloody hidden doors and false walls? Did he know this would happen, that one day Anderson would get him, or someone else?'

'Forward thinking, Kate, that's all. Precaution.'

Precaution, my arse. 'You definitely went to the same charm school.' I don't buy his words, but I don't have the time to worry about that now.

'What?'

'Don't worry. OK, so I push and slide.'

'This is where it becomes difficult. The blueprint shows a long corridor with four rooms leading off it.'

'You think Luke and Max will be in one of the rooms?'

'Yes. Which one, is the question.'

'What about the men?'

'I've been monitoring them from the club's security cameras. There are five in total. One outside guarding the entrance, two in the lower level helping themselves to drinks.'

'Anderson?'

'I can't see him, or the other one. So there should be one plus Anderson in the basement where you are.'

'Hang on, there's movement.' He's silent for a moment. 'OK.'

I jump.

'You need to be quick. Anderson and his mate have just come upstairs, and the guy out the front has driven off.'

'Oh good, one less to worry about, because that makes all the bloody difference.'

'You're good to go. Quick, Kate.'

I make it down the stairs, and feel for the false wall.

'Kate.'

'What?'

'Is your gun loaded with the safety off?'

I swallow.

'Kate?'

'I heard you.' I pull the gun from the back of my jeans. 'It's good to go.'

'Let's hope we don't need it.'

'What's the chance of this running smoothly?'

'As good as any mission I've been on.'

'Right, on the count of three I'm going out there.' I push open the false door. 'OK – one.'

'I'm out.' Already the building feels cold and eerie.

'You can't count.'

'Element of surprise,' I whisper.

'Keep checking all around you. Kate, Parker is close, OK?'

I nod. *Please hurry, Scott Parker.*

'I'm at the first door.'

'Open it slowly and keep your gun at eye level.'

Carefully I twist the brass handle then scan the dimly lit room.

'Empty.' My heart races to an uncontrollable beat.

'You're doing well. Keep breathing.'

'Shit, James, I thought he would be in here.'

'You must be close. I can still detect his watch.'

'I can feel him. Does that sound stupid?' I whisper.

'No. OK – next room. Remember, gun up, stay alert.'

The door is ajar. I can see the corridor is clear. Silently I step out and close the door behind me, leaving no trace. I creep towards the next door and twist the handle.

'Holy fuck!' I slip inside and close the door.

'What is it?'

'It's Max. He looks…' *Dead.*

'Check his pulse.'

'OK. Come on, Max, please be OK.' He's lying on the cold concrete floor. I crouch down and place my fingers against his neck and feel a slow but steady beat. I close my eyes in relief. 'Yep, he has a pulse. But he's been badly beaten.'

'Fuck! Kate, hide behind the door, you may have a visitor. One man is heading for the stairs.'

'What?'

I look at the door like a rabbit caught in headlights. There's a metal bar lying in one corner of the room and I scramble towards it and pick it up. I tuck the gun in my jeans and hold the bar ready. As the sound of footsteps grows louder my breathing escalates. Holding my breath, I watch the brass handle slowly turn.

A man enters the room and walks over to Max.

'Oi, you little fucker, ready for another round?' He kicks Max, but Max remains motionless. 'You fucking cunt, wake up.'

My heart pounds and my temper rises. It's too late. I'm already striding towards the man. I swing the bar with all my strength. It connects just behind his ear with a dull thud. He slumps to the floor.

'Holy fuck, I think I killed him.'

'What happened?'

'I hit him across the head with a metal bar.' My hand covers my mouth. 'Do you think he's dead?'

'I don't know. You need to keep moving.'

'But he could be dead.' I step closer to the body.

'He may also wake up.'

I peer at the victim on the floor. 'He looks dead. I'm sorry, but…' Bile rises in my throat.

'Kate, keep moving.'

'What about Max?'

'Can you wake him?'

I step over the body lying on the floor and kneel next to Max, gently tapping his face.

'Max, please wake up.'

He groans.

'Come on, Max.' This time I shake him. 'Max, look at me.'

His eyes barely open.

'That's it, come on, Max, it's me, Kate.'

His mouth opens but nothing comes out.

'I need to get Luke. Can you move? Of course you bloody can't. Fuck. James, what now?'

'Keep still. Anderson is heading towards the stairs.'

'What?'

'Just stay where you are.'

My heart pounds so hard in my chest that the sound ricochets through my body.

'Go now. He's back in my view. You need to go now. There are two more rooms. Check them.'

'OK.'

Once again I open the door quietly and check the corridor. I twist the handle of the third door.

'It's empty.'

'Go to the last room. He has to be in there. Quickly, Kate.'

The last door faces me. 'Please be here.' I turn the handle and the door swings open. I can't believe what I see inside.

'Kate, talk to me. What's happening?'

'Oh God, Luke.' I close the door and run towards Luke, who is suspended by his wrists from the ceiling.

'Christ, what have they done to him?'

'Tell me what you see,' he says.

I take a deep breath.

'His wrists are bound together and he's tied to a rafter. He's been beaten and…'

'Talk to him. See if he responds.'

'Luke? Luke. It's me.'

Nothing. Fuck, is he still alive? Tears roll down my cheeks. 'He isn't responding.'

'Does he have any wounds?'

'Yes,' I say.

'Good.'

'What?'

'Poke the end of your gun in the wound – the pain should wake him.'

'I can't do that! Luke, please look at me.' *God, this is killing me.*

'Kate, do it now, we don't have a lot of time.'

'OK.'

I look at his naked torso. He has a stab wound on his abdomen. I close my eyes and poke the barrel of the gun inside the wound. 'I'm sorry, Luke.'

He grunts in pain.

'Luke, look at me.' I repeat the procedure again. 'Come on, Luke, please open your eyes.'

He groans and tries to move.

'Look at me.'

Dark eyes meet mine. 'Kate?' he murmurs.

'I need to get him down.' I look around the room. 'There's a chair.'

'Good, use it to stand on.'

I lift it towards Luke. 'I brought a flick-knife with me – but that rope is thick.'

'Is it one of Luke's?'

'Yes.'

'It'll cut through.'

I stand on the chair and begin to slice through the rope. Success: within a few seconds Luke is lying in a heap on the hard ground.

'Kate?' James says in my ear.

I cup Luke's face. 'Luke, please look at me.' Quickly, I untie his wrists and slide the knife in my back pocket.

His eyes open. 'What the hell are you doing here?' He can barely talk.

I laugh and cry at the same time. 'Rescuing you.'

He tries to smile but winces in pain. I know how that feels.

'Max is out cold next door… I have James in my ear and Scott's on his way.' I hold my gun near his face. 'We have this.'

He rolls to his knees, holding his stomach.

'James, he's in a bad way.'

'Tell him he's had worse,' James says.

'I thought you were his friend.'

'I am, now tell him.'

'James said you've had worse.'

Luke manages to kneel. He looks at me while his middle finger offers a response.

I smile, tears streaming down my face.

'He's unimpressed, but he's moving.'

'It works every time. Give him the ear piece.'

'OK.'

I remove the Bluetooth device and pass it to Luke. 'James wants to speak to you.'

Luke puts the device in his ear as he leans on the chair and tries to stand. I try to help him.

'What the hell is she doing here?' He looks at me while listening to James. 'Agreed, she's a pain in the arse.' He looks away and listens, then holds his hand out. 'You have something for me.'

'What?' I frown.

'Detonator.'

I pull it from my jacket pocket. 'I thought it might help.'

'It will once Parker arrives.'

'What?'

'Detonators don't work on their own, Kate.'

As much as I feel the need to pat myself on the back, this is neither the time nor the place.

He pulls me to his blood-soaked bare chest.

'I thought you were…' I say and trail off.

He releases me and his dark eyes meet mine. I see relief in his eyes. He presses his lips gently against mine and the world stands still, if only for a second.

'Where's Max?' he asks, coughing.

'Two doors down. I think I killed a man with a metal bar.'

'Gun, please.'

I pass it to him. 'Luke, did you hear me? I think I killed someone.'

'I doubt it.' He checks the chamber and safety before returning to me. 'These men will not live.'

I swallow my saliva and read Luke's eyes. Sutton code red.

'Can you walk? You look…'

He takes my hand. 'Remember the rule: silence.'

I nod.

'Sullivan, we're leaving.' Luke listens to James. 'Keep me informed.' He takes my hand. 'Let's go.'

He walks with difficulty. What the hell have they done to him? Quietly he twists the door handle, checking the corridor as I did minutes ago. In seconds we're at Max's room. Luke quickly checks his wounds.

'He hasn't moved since I left him.' I glance across to the man lying on the floor. 'Is he dead?'

'I don't care.'

Luke taps Max's face. Nothing. He lifts Max's shirt. His body is covered in cuts and lacerations, which mirror Luke's. I feel sick watching Luke push his fingers inside a wound, but the sound of Max coming to makes me happy.

'There he is – nice of you to join us. Kate, get out of the way. Let me get him to his feet.' Max is beyond useless and far too weak.

'Luke, you can barely walk, let me help.'

'Move away – try and remember you're pregnant!' he snaps.

'Fine.' I step away, feeling a little hurt.

'Sullivan.' Luke remains silent. I know he's listening. 'OK.' He looks at me. 'Kate, we need to head towards the main club the way you entered, via my office.'

'OK.'

Somehow Luke pulls Max to standing, although he can only just walk himself.

'Max, you need to walk,' Luke almost pleads.

'Yeah.' His voice is barely a whisper.

'Kate, door.'

I open the door and peer left and right. 'It's clear.'

We arrive at the hidden door. Now Luke has to climb the stairs. With a grunt, Luke lifts Max and throws him over his shoulder.

'Luke… You can't.'

'Kate, stop talking and go.'

I do. At the top of the staircase, I open the door and slide the bookcase across. Once inside Luke's office, he drops Max on the sofa then almost collapses himself.

'Fuck,' he says and leans on the desk, trying to get his breath.

'You're too weak,' I plead with him. 'Can we wait here for Scott?'

'Pass me the bottle of whisky.'

I remove the lid and pass him the bottle. He downs a couple of mouthfuls and offers it to Max.

'Take it – numb the pain for a few minutes.'

'Here.' I hold the bottle to his lips as he takes a few sips.

'Speak to me,' Luke says to James.

I look at Luke and then at Max. They're lucky to be alive. Any longer and… I can't think about the possible outcome.

'Once Sullivan gives us the all-clear, we need to get across to the stockroom the same way you came in, Kate.'

I nod.

My hand rests against Max's shirt, which is soaked in blood. 'Luke, he's in a bad way.'

'Tell me something I don't know,' he barks.

'I'm just saying he needs a doctor,' I bite back.

Luke takes Max's wrist and looks at his watch. 'Blood pressure is low.' He feels his forehead. 'We need to get him out quickly. I think he will go into hypovolemic shock.'

Luke reads my confused expression.

'Possible internal bleeding.'

'Oh!' Oh fuck.

'Over,' Luke says. 'Kate, we're going. On your feet, Max, let's get you home. Kate, get ready to open the door and close it behind us. Here, take the gun.'

I take the gun and wait by the door.

'On my count, OK? Sullivan, ready when you are.' Luke waits. 'OK. Open the door… Go, go, go.'

Luke manages to drag Max across the VIP area and into the stockroom I was in earlier. Where the hell does he find the strength?

'Kate, keep moving, you know the way.'

As we reach the building next door, we are in complete darkness.

'Be careful – the stairs,' I say.

'Kate, wait!' Luke commands. 'Sullivan.' He listens while propping Max against the wall. 'No visual.' Luke looks at me. 'Anderson is off the radar.'

'And that means?'

'We don't know where he is.'

'Has he left the building?'

'Sullivan is re-checking the footage. Keep moving,' Luke commands.

Finally we make it to the bottom of the stairs and enter the next-door building. I close the door once Luke is through, and he drags Max towards the front door. Round the door we can see the smallest glimmer of light – freedom.

'Going somewhere, boys?' There's the sound of a match flaring. 'Do you think you can outsmart me?'

Holy shit. Anderson.

'Something about you doesn't add up, Sutton… What's with all these rabbit runs? Anyone would think you're hiding something.'

'Take me but let him go,' Luke offers.

'Shut the fuck up. Neither of you are going anywhere. I want to watch you both die.'

My hand covers my mouth as I cling to the far wall.

'I'm worth more to you alive,' Luke says.

'I don't want your fucking money. I want to watch you suffer like your mate did when my boys kicked the shit out of him. Happy memories.'

Luke is silent, but I know he's furious inside at the mention of Paul.

I hear a click as Anderson steps towards Luke and Max. All I can see are shadows, but I recognise the sound of a gun.

'If you run, I'll shoot your fucking kneecaps.'

No! My heart pounds. Think, Kate. I have no choice. I raise my gun and quietly walk towards the shadows. I can just about make out where the three men are standing. Silently, I keep behind the unsuspecting Anderson. My hand trembles as I get closer. I'm three steps away.

'Don't move, you sick bastard.'

He begins to laugh.

'Drop your gun, or I'll shoot you.'

'So, Sutton, you're not alone. Couldn't manage to escape without the help of your cunt of a wife?'

'Kate.' I can hear panic in Luke's voice.

'Drop the gun now. As God is my witness, I will shoot you.' Amazingly, my voice is strong. I nestle the barrel of my gun in the small of his back. 'I said, drop your gun.'

'Make me, bitch.'

As he takes a step, I pull the trigger. Two sounds whirl in my head: the sound of the shot, and Luke shouting my name.

The weak light from the doorframe highlights Anderson on the ground.

'Oh my God.' I begin to shake.

'Kate.' Luke lowers Max to the ground. 'Kate, give me the gun.'

'Luke, I…' Tears roll down my cheeks.

He crouches in the darkness. 'He's dead.'

'I killed him! Luke…'

'Listen. We need to leave quickly. Sullivan, are you listening?' Luke takes the gun from my hands.

'I killed him, are you sure he's…' I can't finish the sentence.

'Kate, go.'

I nod and watch the shadowy figure of Max trying to get to his feet.

'Kate,' Max says. 'Go now.' He can just about string a sentence together.

'Kate, give me the knife.'

I pass it to Luke, and he bends down to the body.

'What are you doing?'

'Removing the bullet.'

'I don't understand.'

'It's evidence. Just go with Max.'

Max rests his arm over my shoulder and we slowly walk to the door, me supporting him. When I turn the handle, daylight hits my face. There is the welcome sight of Barney sitting in Rosie's Ford Fiesta. He jumps out of the car.

'Fuck me, look at the state of him. Jesus, Max.'

'Get him in the car,' I say. Barney manhandles Max onto the back seat.

'Luke?' Barney looks at me.

474

'He's coming.'

'Bloody hell, babe, are you OK? You're as white as a sheet.'

I shake my head. A motorbike screeches along the road and stops beside us. The rider, who is dressed in black, removes his helmet and strides towards me. It's Scott Parker.

'Kate,' he says.

'Luke's inside.'

Scott takes me in his arms and kisses the top of my head. The first time he's ever shown me any affection. 'You did good.'

Scott disappears and leaves me with Barney.

'What happened?' he asks.

I look up at his face while tears of relief and shock roll down my cheeks.

Within a few minutes, Luke and Scott appear.

'Fucking hell, Sutton, look at the state of you.'

Luke passes my gun to Scott. 'Take this back with you and clean it. It goes in the safe in our room. Barney, turn the car around. Kate, keys to the door.' I pass him the keys. 'Get in the car.' He turns to Scott, who hands Luke some green putty – I recognise it. It's explosive – and a mobile phone.

'Sullivan said to come prepared,' Scott says.

'What are you going to do?' I ask, but I know what he is doing.

Luke doesn't answer. He takes the detonator from his pocket and places it in the familiar block of green putty. He then disappears inside the building with the putty and the phone.

I slide in next to Max and watch Luke disappear. In seconds he reappears, locking the door of number twenty-two. He strides towards the car, jumps in and slams the door shut.

'Drive!' he shouts.

As the car jerks forward, Luke bends over his mobile phone. I close my eyes and begin to count in my head. I can't remember what number I reach when I hear the explosion.

24

'Take a left here,' Luke commands. A silent Barney grips the steering wheel. 'First right, then right again at the end.'

Barney nods.

'Carry on until I tell you otherwise.'

Luke directs Barney home. Instinct tells me Luke knows which roads have no CCTV; there's no other reason for us to take the scenic route. I keep hold of Max's hand and check his forehead with the other. He's clammy.

'Nearly home,' I say, but Max remains silent. 'Luke, he needs to go to hospital.'

'No,' he blurts.

'You said he might have internal bleeding.'

'Kate!' he says, as though I'm irritating him.

'I know you can patch him up, but—' Strangely, the last time I witnessed Luke patching Max up was due to Anderson.

'Just leave it,' he snaps.

What? His coldness is slicing through me like a knife.

Barney glances at me in the rear-view mirror, clearly picking up on Luke's hostility. My eyes sting, but I can't cry, not now. Again I realise that I shot a man. He's dead – gone forever. My mind begins to shut down.

I look out of the window, thinking about the last half hour of my life, and knowing it will never be the same – how can it be? Barney draws Rosie's car to a halt outside the palace. The front door is still ajar. I step aside as Barney and Luke help Max inside.

Adam appears from the kitchen. 'Christ. Let me take him. What the hell's happened?'

'I'm OK,' Luke says.

'You don't look it. Anything I should know?' Adam asks. 'Lay him on the table. On three: one, two, three.' By this time Scott is here too. He walks into the kitchen and helps to lift Max. 'Gently.' Adam looks at Luke. 'I don't like surprises. What am I looking for?'

'Lacerations – he may have internal bleeding. No bullet wounds.'

'I need some scissors,' Adam says.

I grab some from the kitchen drawer.

'Barney, get me Luke's medical bag.'

'How's Jerry?' I ask.

'He's bruised, and just needs rest and painkillers, Kate.' Adam looks at me. 'What about you?'

'I'm fine.' No, I'm not OK.

Luke watches me, saying nothing.

Parker re-enters the kitchen. 'SGI Security are working on the door now. I've called Samantha. She will be here soon,' he says to Luke.

Do they all know Dr Samantha Jacobs? I have so many questions for Luke – when he eventually speaks to me.

Parker looks at his watch. 'Barker will be here in forty minutes tops, plus security. I'll go and clean Rosie's car. I need all your clothes.'

'Good.' Luke heads to the table. 'Have you found any internal bleeding?' he asks Adam.

'No. He's bloody lucky. The knife just missed his left kidney. He's lost a lot of blood; he's probably been drifting in and out of consciousness.'

'Does he need a transfusion?'

'Do you want him to go to hospital?' Adam says.

Luke raises his brows and shake his head.

'He can survive without one. Morphine would help.'

Luke looks across at Parker, who leaves the room and returns a few moments later with two bottles of clear fluid.

'Don't ask,' Scott says.

'I won't.'

'Let's just say I came prepared!' Parker says to Adam.

My legs feel weak. I rest on a stool, watching my home turn into a mini hospital. I can't forget the elephant in the room: Anderson. His blood is on my hands. Barney joins me.

'You OK, babe?'

I look up at him. 'I'm sorry about today. You and Adam needed some time together.'

'It's not your fault.' He pulls my head to his chest. 'I won't forget today in a hurry, that's for sure,' he mumbles.

'Me either.' For obvious reasons.

Across the room Luke offers me a cold glance then turns to greet Dr Samantha Jacobs. They chat and walk towards his office. I wonder what he's telling her – and I wonder how familiar she is with this sort of behaviour.

A couple of minutes later, Samantha returns to the kitchen.

'Kate, can I have a word?'

I slide off the stool and follow her to Luke's office.

'Take a seat.' She gestures. 'How are you?'

I look down at my hands.

'I've had better days.' I say, and remove my jacket.

She smiles sympathetically and removes a blood pressure cuff from her bag. 'I just need to check your blood pressure. I assume you've had no more bleeding.'

I shake my head as she wraps the cuff around my upper arm and inflates it. Physically I am here, sitting and breathing, but mentally I can feel my brain defragmenting, piece by piece, image by image.

'That appears to be normal.'

'Did Luke call you just to check on me?'

'Not just you – although your friend is doing a sterling job.'

I head for the door of the office and come face to face with Luke. We cross paths without a word. He simply closes the office door and shuts me out too. Why?

As I return to the kitchen, Adam and Scott are helping to lift Max from the table and carry him to his apartment.

'Is he OK?' I look at Barney.

'Adam said he's bloody lucky.'

'I'll stay with him tonight. Luke is being a complete arsehole. He's avoiding me. Why is he being so bloody nasty?'

'Give him time. He probably thought he was going to die.'

480

'So did I.'

Scott Parker returns to the kitchen.

'Is Adam staying with Max?' I ask.

'Until Valerie arrives,' Barney says.

'Your cupid plan worked. Max has himself a girlfriend.' Barney pulls me closer.

'I guess.'

Parker walks towards the hall.

'Scott?' I call. He stops. I walk towards him. 'Why is Luke acting like this?'

'Like what?'

'He hasn't said two words to me since I…' My face falls. 'You know what I'm saying. He's scaring me.'

'He has a lot on his mind.'

He turns and walks away. Is that it? Is that really an explanation?

My stomach churns and I know I'm going to vomit. I rush to the toilet and make it just in time. I rest for a few minutes, feeling weak.

Barney taps on the door. 'Kate.'

'Give me a minute.' Quickly I wash my face.

'Luke needs us in the office – apparently it's urgent,' he says through the door.

Jesus, I have nothing left to give. I can't think about anything else. I've just killed a man. What does that make me? I'm a murderer.

Finally I enter the office. Everyone watches me as I take the empty seat at the board table next to Barney.

'We need to go over what happened today. It goes without saying that this discussion stays in this room.' Luke says and gauges our reactions. 'Good. For those of you who don't know him' – Luke gestures to his right at an unfamiliar man seated at the table – 'this is Stanley Barker, my lawyer.'

'Afternoon, everyone,' Stanley responds.

Luke looks at his watch. 'SGI no longer exists. It's been burned to the ground – with the bodies inside.'

'Bloody good job.' Barney praises Luke, but receives a glare telling him to shut the fuck up.

'The CCTV has been wiped, here and…'

I know where he's going with this. 'What about the streets leading to the club? The police will see you and Max arriving,' I say.

'The van drove into the loading bay, away from any CCTV, plus there is no evidence as SGI is no longer standing.' He shrugs.

'What about me and Barney?'

Luke is holding his audience in the palm of his hand, but I feel like I'm slipping through his fingers.

'The road you parked on has no CCTV,' Luke snaps.

'If you're asked, say that you and Barney went for a drive. However, it will not come to that, I promise you, Mrs Sutton,' Barker tries to reassure me. However, I need more.

'What about Adam, Luke? He's not used to this crazy shit – that makes two of us,' Barney says.

Again Luke glares at Barney. 'I am grateful for his help, Barney. I will talk to him shortly and explain what he needs to know. The rest stays in this room. Got it?'

Barney holds his hands up. 'I'm already trying to forget about today.'

'What about me, Luke?'

He knows I am asking about the gun.

'It has been taken care of,' Scott says bluntly. 'I need your clothes, Kate.'

'Why?' I look at Scott.

'To get rid of any evidence.'

'I don't want to point out the obvious, Sutton, but you look like shit. If the police turn up here…' Barney says.

Dr Jacob clears her throat. 'Luke was mugged two nights ago. I have proof of that. He called my mobile asking for medical advice.'

'Looks like you have it all sorted, Luke. You've thought of everything.'

'Barney, you and Adam will need to stay at your house. Jerry and Rosie will also stay with you, and Max is on leave.'

'What about the security guards? Where did they go? What happened to them? And what about your staff at SGI?' I respond.

Luke takes a deep breath, looking frustrated. 'I've dealt with it, Kate,' he snaps.

'What does that mean?'

His eyes meet mine; I see fire behind the glare.

'Or is the truth ugly, Luke?' I blurt.

'It means I have dealt with it,' he barks.

'And Max, isn't he the owner of the club?' I ask.

'What is your point, Kate?' Luke looks at me.

'My *point*, Luke, is if the police come looking for him and he has similar injuries to yours, what then?' I shake my head. 'The same alley two nights ago? That's shitty luck.'

There is an awkward silence. First, I have a point, and second, my husband's harsh tone towards me is obvious.

'He's a silent partner, as you know, Kate. He never visits the club, and you also know why. But your concern is noted.'

Screw you, Luke – make a note of that.

I push my chair back and stand. 'I'll leave you to it, then. Oh, and by the way, the door to your den is still open.'

Anger carries me up the stairs, where furious tears start to fall. I can't hold them back any longer. Barney runs up the stairs after me.

'Kate.'

'Go with Adam. I need some time on my own,' I say, but he follows me in to my bedroomm.

'No, you need me.' He folds me into his arms, which makes me cry harder.

'Shhh – give him time.'

'It's not time he needs.' I pull away. 'You saw how he spoke to me! Why?'

'I don't know, but I'm not leaving you.'

'Yes, you are,' Luke says, silently entering our room.

'No way, Sutton, look at the state of her.'

'I'll take care of her.'

'Will you? How's that, mate? You've been a prick to her since she rescued you. Get your head out of your arse.' He takes a breath. 'You haven't even spoken to her properly.'

'My patience is running thin, Barney, so tread carefully.'

'Tread carefully?' Barney laughs scornfully. 'Someone needs to tell you when you're acting like a fucking nutter – and I'm up for the job.'

Luke scowls. 'I promise to take care of her. Please leave.'

Barney turns to me. 'What do you want me to do?'

'Go and help Adam. I'll be fine.'

'Are you sure?'

I nod.

'OK.' He turns to Luke. 'I'm watching you. Don't fuck with Kate.'

Luke holds his hands up. 'You have my word.'

'Good, don't fucking let me down. I'll call you later, babe.'

Barney leaves. I can't bear the tension in the room. Luke closes the door.

'Get it off your chest, Luke!' I bark.

'I'm fucking furious with you! What you did was—'

'I saved your life!'

'Are you looking for praise?'

'You're unbelievable, Luke. I put myself at risk to help you, and you're acting like this?'

'Yes, you put yourself at risk today. You were selfish – it wasn't just yourself you were risking.'

'Of course you would think I was bloody selfish.'

'It was fucking irresponsible.'

'So what should I have done? You got yourself kidnapped. Next time I won't give a shit. Next time, I'll stay home and make a bloody cake.'

'Yes, you will.'

'Oh my God, can you hear yourself? Do you think I would have stayed here and waited for you to arrive home in a body bag? If that's what you thought, then you have married the wrong bloody woman.'

'For Christ's sake, Kate, you're pregnant! Where were your thoughts for the babies?'

'How dare you say that? I would die for them – and you.'

His expression hardens.

'Just go and finish making up your cover story. Leave me to wonder what the hell I did wrong. I killed someone to save you, for fuck's sake! You're the person I can't live without.'

'I would have got the upper hand. I'd have been able to escape in the end.'

'Really? From where I was standing, you were tied up like a fucking animal. I don't see how you would have got the upper hand.'

'Watch your fucking tone! Believe me, I've had worse done to me. Now I have to deal with you witnessing things you shouldn't have to deal with.'

I laugh through my anger. 'I killed someone, Luke, is that what you mean?' I look at my hands: they knead dough, they cook – yet now they are scarred, tainted with evil.

There's a sudden knock at the door.

'What?' Luke shouts.

'You have ten minutes and then you need to face the music – the police are on the way.'

Scott has Luke's back, that's for sure.

'I hear you.' His dark eyes rest on mine. 'I have to clean up.' He points at me. 'This discussion isn't over. Take off your clothes now.'

Go and fuck yourself, Luke. Right here, right now, I despise him.

He goes into the bathroom. I strip naked, head towards our bed and collapse under the crisp white covers. My body feels empty; I have no more tears to cry. I lie silently and listen to him showering, then dressing. He appears at my side.

'Do not leave this room. The police will be here soon asking questions, and I want you to be in bed, resting.'

Does he think I am going to answer him?

'Do you understand, or shall I lock you in this room?'

I roll over and ignore him.

'Good. Make sure you shower. Maybe you should use this time to think about the safety of our children.'

Oh my God. I want to scream at him. How dare he say that? I grab the pregnancy books from my nightstand. The instant he shuts the door, I hurl the books at the wall.

'I hate you, Luke! Stay away from me, do you hear me?' Of course he heard me. I suspect they heard me two miles away. I collapse on the bed and sob.

I lie on my side, staring at the sky, which has now turned dark, and lose track of time. Eventually I convince myself it would be a good idea to wash the day away, but as the water sluices over my numb body, the realisation of what I have done is too much. I sink to my knees and close my eyes.

'Dear God, please forgive me. I know I don't pray, and as of today I will go to hell, but thank you for keeping my miserable bastard husband alive. And I'm sorry for killing Anderson, even though I'm sure he would have killed Luke and Max.' I never thought I would be able to kill someone.

I open my eyes and rest my head against the wall, wondering if my words are enough of an apology. Are there enough words to apologise properly? I will always have blood on my hands.

Eventually I dress in clean pyjamas and go back to bed, but my mind will not rest.

A knock at the door makes me jump.

'Kate, can I come in?' I recognise James Sullivan's voice.

I sit up. 'Yeah.'

He opens the door.

'Watch your step,' I say, as he steps over the books I threw at my husband.

He walks in carrying two mugs. 'Here,' he says.

'Thanks.' I take a mug.

He hovers by the bed. 'May I?'

'Yeah – sit down.' I pat the mattress.

'It's been a tough day.'

'No shit,' I say.

'How are you feeling? The three of you?'

My hand glides across my bump. 'The girls are fine, but I'm numb. Luke has lost the plot and is behaving like a bloody moron. Let's not forget I killed Anderson, and hit another man over the head, so he's probably dead too. Other than that, things are just peachy. What's with Luke? Why's he acting like this?'

'He's pissed off at us both.'

'You had no choice. I was going in with or without your help.'

'He knows that. Listen, I'm proud of you.'

'For shooting someone?' I shake my head.

'No, not for shooting Anderson, but you kept cool. Not many people could have gone in there blind.'

'I wish Luke would say that – I don't mean for him to be proud, but for him to be thankful. But no, he told me I was selfish and I should have thought about our children!'

'He's in shock. He watched the men torture Max and—'

I shake my head. 'Stop making excuses for him. I love him and he's being an arse. I need him. If he left me—'

'He would never leave you! You're made for each other.'

I nod. 'It kills me when he shuts me out. He turns into this cold-hearted person that I don't know.'

'And that's where you need your strength. Just hang in there.'

'Have the police been?'

'Yes. They left a while ago. Luke had them eating out of the palm of his hand. He said he rarely visits the club, Max is just an investor, and the manager is in control. He told them he was mugged a few nights ago to explain the bruises on his face.'

'And…' I look at him. 'Is he in the clear?'

'The police seemed to think so. There's no evidence to say otherwise. One mentioned the electrics…'

'Can't the police find explosives these days? I mean, how can Luke blame wiring when the explosion was in the other building?'

'Trust me, he'll have left no trace. Plus Parker and Sutton have been at home working and watching TV, while you, his pregnant wife, were resting in bed.'

'Now I'm of use to him!'

'One of the officers could relate; his wife is pregnant too.'

'He played them.'

'He's a master at the game.'

'Of course he is – tell me something he can't do.'

'Luke needs you, Kate.'

'Then why is he hurting me?'

James takes a breath. 'When you train for a mission, your mind is focused on the end result and the safety of your team. It's your job to remain on the ball at all times.

489

When you let your guard down, you make mistakes. I understand how he feels. If you were my wife and turned up in a situation like today… it makes a mission a hundred times worse when it's someone you love.'

'Then he should be relieved that we're all safe, right?'

'Of course, but it would have been a different story if you were caught, Kate. They would have hurt you to get at him. Luke would never come back from that. Plus you shot Anderson, which was another problem.'

'Luke said he sorted it.'

'No worries there – the gun is clean and the bullet was retrieved. But you shot someone. Taking a life will affect you at some point.'

'He would have killed Luke.'

He nods. 'Luke is angry with himself: he thinks it's his fault you were forced into the situation. It should have never happened.'

'I don't know how I feel about it. When I close my eyes I can't see anything. The room was so dark, it's more like a silhouette – and then I hear the gun going off.'

'Images are the hardest to forget. Sounds evaporate over time.'

'Luke knew something was brewing, didn't he?' I look at James. 'I'm not stupid. He installed the extra CCTV, plus he showed me his secret room. But he didn't trust me enough to actually tell me what was happening. That's what hurts the most.'

'You have plenty of time to talk to him.'

'Talk! Are you kidding? I like your optimism.'

'A warning for you: he will probably crumble. That's when he'll need you.'

'What do you mean? He's used to this crazy shit.'

'Anderson opened up a lot of Luke's wounds – memories that will probably always haunt him.'

'What – of Paul?'

James nods. 'Watching Anderson attack Max.'

'He couldn't save him,' I say.

James nods.

'OK, I sort of get it, but he is still being an arse.'

James smiles. 'Good job you love him.'

For the first time today, I smile.

'As I say, he will need you. It could be today, or in a week. Anyway, you're safe, he's safe – let's draw a line under everything. I hope you're hungry. We've just ordered Chinese.'

'I would rather tell Luke to shove his spring roll where the sun doesn't shine.'

When I enter the kitchen, the men are already seated, filling their plates with Chinese food. It smells divine. For the first time today, I'm hungry. Unfortunately, the only seat remaining is next to Luke.

'Pass me the rice.'

James slides a silver box towards Scott.

'Kate.' Luke passes me a box of steamed vegetables with garlic and ginger.

'Thank you.' Manners prevail, but it would be most satisfying to tip the contents over his head. 'Has anyone checked on Max?'

'He's stable.' Short and not so sweet, Sutton.

'Kate, don't worry. Scott and I are staying here for a few days,' James says.

'As a precaution?' I say sarcastically.

'No!' Luke snaps.

'Here, Kate.' James passes me some noodles. Maybe he assumes that I won't be able to argue with my mouth full.

The men talk about issues I have no interest in. James desperately tries to draw me into the conversation, but I would rather pull my own teeth out. Half a plate is all I can manage. I have no appetite.

'I'm tired.' I stand and walk away from the table.

'Kate.' Mr Moody Bollocks Sutton stops me.

What?

'Stay here, I need to sleep.' *Alone, you arrogant arsehole.*

Even though I fell asleep with ease, I wake up feeling restless. I need the bathroom. I catch my reflection in the mirror. God, I look a wreck. As I turn sideways, I see I look bigger than yesterday. Our girls are growing.

I go to the bathroom then slip back into bed. It's two thirty. Enough is enough. I get up and decide to face him.

The house is quiet. Soft light leaks under the entrance to Luke's office. I push the door ajar. Luke sits at his desk, looking desolate and lost. He sees me, and this time he cannot hide the sadness in his eyes. I run to him and he holds me as though his life depends on it.

'Don't shut me out, Luke.'

His arms tighten around me and he buries his face in my neck. I can feel his tears, warm against my skin.

'Please don't hate me. I can't bear it.'

Fuck. I have only ever seen him like this when he told me about losing Paul – and on our wedding day.

'Kate,' he mutters.

'Shhh.' I kiss him.

He pulls away and places his hands either side of my face. 'Kate…'

'Talk to me, Luke.'

'I'm sorry for being angry. I just…'

'I get why you're angry. I know I took a risk. But what else could I have done?'

'And you would do it again.'

I nod. 'Always.' I take his hand and place it over my heart. 'For better or worse, right?'

'Seeing you in that room.' His eyes close and he takes a breath. 'I have never been on a mission and felt utter fear like I did today – never. If anything happened to you and the girls…' He runs his hands down my back. 'Fuck. I'm sorry, Kate. I know I was cold and—'

'A prick!'

He smiles. 'I deserve that, and now I've hurt you for saving me. How many times can I fuck up our relationship before you run?'

My lips immediately make contact with his. 'I will never run, Luke.' I look down at my bump. 'I have our girls.'

'I don't deserve your understanding. Be pissed off, angry, fucking shout at me, but don't leave me.'

'Never. I need you, Luke. I can't breathe without you. Why do you think I came to SGI today? I've told you I don't fear you, I fear losing you.'

'How the hell did I get this lucky?' His hands cradle my bump. 'I married the most beautiful woman in the world. Regardless of my fucked-up attitude earlier, I am so in love with you.'

'We're here, Luke. I can't give in to the likes of Anderson and Philip Cooper. They can't win. Do you hate me because I killed him?'

'Never.'

'I thought because…'

'Listen, you killed the man I have hated for most of my life, and I know you saved me. I know that.'

Tears roll down my cheeks. Luke leans forward and kisses them away.

'James said we were well suited.' I smile.

'Maybe. I guess only you would protect me like that.'

'When we met, I told you I would fall on my sword for my family.'

'I regret calling you selfish.'

'And irresponsible,' I say.

'That too.'

'I don't regret coming to find you.'

'That scares the fuck out of me, Kate.'

'You'd do the same. In fact, you have – twice.'

'I'm trained, you're not.'

'I am.' I smile. 'Sort of.'

He takes a breath. 'Kate, the way I feel about you. I can't describe it.'

'Back at you, Luke.'

'I need you.'

'You have me. That will never change.'

'Let's go to bed.'

I stand up and slip my hand into his. Silently we climb the stairs. I watch Luke strip. He has some bruising across his cheekbone, but it's not too bad. He wears a bandage around his body, covering his stitched knife wound.

He looks at me. 'It looks worse than it is.'

'You look like shit.' I slide into bed.

'Thanks.' He smiles and lies next to me, and pulling me close and gently presses his lips to mine.

I pull away. 'You need to rest.'

'Right now I want you.'

'You're kidding, aren't you?'

His dark eyes rest on mine.

'You're not kidding?'

'Let me love you, Kate. I need to be inside you. It's the same for you – don't look at me like you don't understand.'

'But, Luke, you're hurt.'

His lips find mine in the dark, and we make love.

Afterwards, I lie next to him. 'You're not OK, are you? This was too much.'

He pulls me to him and I rest my head on his chest.

'I thought you were dead,' I say.

'I told you I would have escaped somehow.'

'I don't want to think about it. I can't. Do you think Paul is resting now, knowing the evil bastard who killed him has gone to hell?'

'I hope so.'

'And this is why you've been odd? You knew Anderson was going to try something? All the time you were telling me not to go anywhere alone, you knew. But how? I asked you about Anderson and you said nothing, Luke.'

'I have my sources, Kate, and I knew something was up. There's too much to go into now, and that's not me shutting you out, it's me saying I don't have the energy to explain why today happened. Can you give me some time?'

I remain silent.

'Hey, I'm not shutting you out, but today has been – fuck.' His eyes close and he takes a breath. 'You killed a man to protect me. Not just any man, but a man I have wanted dead for a very long time.'

'How long have you been looking for him?'

Luke's lip curls. 'Kate.'

'I need to know.' After all, I did kill him.

'We heard through different sources that he was looking into me and Max.'

'Fuck! Was he following you, us? Jesus, Luke, he was coming for you.'

'Something like that. Listen, Kate, I just need some time. That's all I ask and then I will answer all your questions.'

I nod.

'I'm still in shock too, Luke. I never thought I could hurt someone. How wrong was I?'

'It was self-defence. He would have attacked you, or worse.'

'I need to ask you something, Luke. I want complete honesty, OK?' I shift slightly to see his face. 'Sullivan and Parker, have you worked with them – I mean, on a job or whatever the hell you call it – since we've been together?'

'No.'

'Is that the absolute truth, Luke? I don't care if you have; I just need to know. I need to know the times you have worked away or when you worked late that you weren't off chasing some lunatic.'

He smiles. 'I have not and will not be chasing any lunatics.'

'What, never? James said you're never really free, and with all the weird shit in your secret room, I didn't know what to think.'

'Firstly, there's young blood taking over where I worked – that's the same for Sullivan and Parker. We're all getting older. But…'

'I knew there would be a but!'

His arm pulls me tighter. 'As I have told you before, our training was unique and sometimes a job needs our expertise.'

'So you're not free.'

'I will make a promise to you. If I am ever called upon to take on a job I will tell you.'

'OK, I guess.' I run my fingers through his hair. 'Why are the boys staying?'

'To look after you. And I need to rest.'

'I'm pleased they're here.'

He gently caresses my cheek.

'You're right, Luke – the truth is ugly.'

'We'll get through it.'

'Maybe.'

'Not maybe, we will. By the way, James told me he spoke to you.'

'He said I had to wait for you to need me. Is that what happened at your desk downstairs? You were crying. I've only ever seen you cry when we discussed Paul, and at our wedding.'

'I don't cry that often.' He laughs. 'Ow, Jesus. I'm bloody sore.'

'I know the real Luke Sutton, the man who is sensitive, caring and passionate – OK, you're controlling and irrational too.'

'Only with you, but you never listen to me.'

Then I feel something. 'Luke!'

'What?' He looks panicked.

'I felt something! It happened the other day and this morning…'

I lie on my back, keeping very still. Seconds later, I feel it again.

'It's like a flutter. Oh my God, I can't describe it.'

'The girls are moving.' His face comes alive and he wears the biggest smile.

After the most terrifying day, the most amazing moment.

Luke presses his lips to my bump. 'My beautiful girls, Mummy and Daddy love you.' His dark eyes meet mine. 'I love you, Kate, and thank you for saving me – and not just today,' he says.

'I love you too. You know, we will always be worlds apart, Luke, but our souls will always be together.'

'Always, baby.'

34 WEEKS AND ONE DAY…

The room is completely dark. I reach for my phone. As predicted, it's three o'clock in the bloody morning, which means two things: I need the bathroom and I need food. Luke is radiating so much heat, he's like a furnace.

I push myself up from the bed. Any movement lately is an effort. 'Come on, girls,' I say playfully to my bump. At my last antenatal check-up, I was measuring 40 weeks, even though I still have a few weeks to go. How much bigger will I get? I'll ask Dr Jenkins on Wednesday at my next antenatal appointment.

After eating a plate of leftover Mexican chicken, I scan the fridge to see what else I fancy.

'I see the fridge thief is at large.'

I turn to see Luke watching me from the doorway.

'Yep – I am large.' I cradle my bump. 'You told me yesterday that I haven't got any bigger. You lied. Jesus,

Luke, I'm ready to burst – literally.'

'You look beautiful.'

'And large!'

'Only for the next six weeks.'

'Actually, it's five weeks and six days, not that I'm counting. That's when I'll get my body back – especially my bladder.'

Luke holds his hands up in defeat.

'You should be asleep – you'll be leaving soon,' I say.

'I woke up and realised you were missing.'

'My body clock is all over the place. I want to sleep all day and wake up bloody early!'

'Tell me,' he leans over my shoulder, 'what exactly are you eating?'

'I've eaten the leftover Mexican chicken – sorry. Anyway, now I've got rocket salad, caramelised onions, grated cheddar and beetroot – and let's not forget ready salted Walkers crisps.'

'Our poor children.'

'Hey – don't knock it until you've tried it.'

'I'll pass.'

'I've been thinking about the girls' names.'

'This sounds ominous.'

'Can I have a drum roll?'

'Get on with it, Harper.'

'Sage and Thyme.'

He laughs. 'Are you joking?'

'I really like them.'

'No way! Where did you conjure them up – in the larder?'

'No, not exactly, but they did come to me the other day while I was cooking. Listen, Sage Sutton and Thyme Sutton… Don't they sound nice? I like them.'

'I don't.'

'You're impossible.'

'Give me names that are real, not names they'll be teased for at school.'

'I never had you down as dull.'

'Bed,' he commands.

'Yes, please.' I stand between his legs.

He understands the look in my eyes.

'I'm serious. I want to have sex. I just feel – you know how I feel. Anyway, I can't control my bloody hormones. It's not my fault.'

'I'm not complaining.'

He slides his hands under my T-shirt. 'How about the same position as yesterday?'

I nod. 'Say it.'

He laughs.

'Go on,' I plead.

'You know I want to fuck you.' With these words, my body is ready.

When I open my eyes, a little light filters across the bedroom. It's a perfect November day. I prop myself on to my elbows, looking for something. Luke flew to Dubai after we made love at three thirty this morning, so the next best thing lies next to me – a note.

Dear Kate

Be good and please relax. I have noticed your ankles are swelling (not fat, merely water retention).

Have fun with Barney. If you need anything, ask Max.

> *Girls, be good to Mummy. Don't give her heartburn*
> *and try not to press on her bladder.*
>   *Luke xx*

I laugh and wipe tears from my cheeks. Stupidly, I miss him. *Get a grip, Harper.* As I pull the covers back, I see my fat ankles, which is the only time I can see my feet. At a glance they look OK, not too large – I think!

Eventually I make it downstairs and head towards the kitchen in my usual grey joggers and T-shirt – the only outfit that still fits me!

'Morning, how are you?' Rosie comes over. 'I think your bump has dropped since yesterday.'

'Really? Feels the same. But my back is killing me this morning.' Too much sex? Maybe!

'Take it easy today. When is Luke home?'

'Later. He won't be there long. He has a meeting then he's leaving straight away. Anyway, Barney is coming over to keep me company.'

'Adam told me,' Rosie says.

'How is he?' I ask.

'He loves his new job. He's off today so he might come over this afternoon.'

'OK. I'm going to make some cakes before Barney gets here.'

'Do you think you should? All that standing around. I'm just thinking of your back.'

'I'm fine, just pregnant.'

After a while I hear Barney singing in the hall.

'I'm in the kitchen,' I call and remove the last cake from

the oven.

'I can smell food.' He walks through. 'Good timing. Christ, look at the size of you.'

'Cheers, Barney.'

He laughs. 'Babe, you're pregnant – it's normal. You've grown since last week.'

'Please tell me it's just the bump that's grown.'

'Turn around,' he says.

I do so.

'From the back you don't look pregnant. Turn around slowly.'

I rotate and Barney begins to laugh. 'Fucking hell, your bump is huge. I'd walk backwards if I were you.'

'Cheers, you little shit.' I laugh and pass him the bowl and spoon, with the remainder of the butter icing.

We sit drinking tea and eating cupcakes. Maybe I over-indulge. Oh well. I have just over five weeks left to eat what I want.

'Sutton called me this morning with his orders.'

'Did he? What orders? I haven't heard from him yet.'

'To be fair, he woke me and Adam up. Anyway, my orders are to make sure you rest.'

I hold my tea. 'This is resting, right?'

'Throw in reality TV and I might fake a pregnancy myself, babe,' he says.

I laugh.

'I want to organise the girls' closet today. You haven't seen the finished nursery, have you?'

'No.'

'Actually, I want your honest opinion on the girls' names.'

'Always.'

'I told Luke and he didn't like them. We can't agree on any names at the moment.'

'Go on – hit me with them,' Barney says.

'Sage and Thyme.'

He's silent as he looks out of the window at the clear, cold day. 'Sage Sutton, Thyme Sutton? Hmm, let me mull them over for a bit and I'll get back to you.'

The phone rings.

'Go and get it for me, I'm resting.'

'So, I'm here to be your lackey?'

'Yes,' I say.

He grabs the phone. 'Hormonal pregnant hotline, how may I direct your call?'

God, he makes me laugh.

'All right, Sutton, your lazy wife ordered me to get the phone. You'll want line one, but no sex talk – she's fragile. Oh, by the way, I love the names Sage and Thyme. How did you think of them?'

'Give me the bloody phone,' I mutter and hold my hand out.

'I've planted a seed! If he thinks they're his idea, he may go for it,' Barney whispers.

'Are you kidding? This is Luke.' I take the phone. 'Hi, how's Dubai?'

'Warm.'

'Well, it's cold here, so enjoy it while it lasts.'

'How are you?'

'Fine. I checked my ankles – they also seem fine.' I laugh.

'You liked your note?'

'I cried.'

'What are you doing other than being entertained by Barney?'

'I've had a bath and made some cakes – plus flapjacks for you. Not very exciting, but my back is sore.'

'Too much sex?' His voice changes, and I know he's smiling.

'Not enough sex! Be prepared: I need to have you when you get home tonight. When will that be?'

'Soon. I told you it was one quick meeting.'

'Good. I want you with me.'

'Please relax. Barney is watching you for me. Oh, and I'm pleased you have one vote for your herb names.'

'Very funny. I love you.'

'Close your eyes.' I take Barney's hand and guide him into the nursery. 'OK, you can open now.'

He silently turns around. 'It's stunning – definitely not what I expected.'

'What did you think it was going to look like?' I feel aggrieved.

'Tacky kids' shit – but this is smart and elegant.'

He walks around the room. I have kept it simple with ivory walls and the palest of pink silk curtains. The furniture and bedding are white, with a couple of pink blankets. My favourite thing is the matching canopies which skim the front of the cots, made of the same silk as the curtains.

'Honestly, babe, it looks stunning,' he says.

'Come and see their closet.'

We enter the closet, which not only houses clothes but all the baby paraphernalia.

'It looks like you're short on clothes!' Barney shakes his head in disbelief.

'Luke bought most of these. Every time he goes out he comes home with more stuff.'

I rest my hands on my stomach.

'You OK?'

'Just uncomfortable. So, I just need to rearrange the clothes in age order.'

'That makes sense. Let's get on with it.'

As the closet is relatively large, we can move around with ease and work quickly. After an hour everything is in order.

'Good job,' Barney says.

'Perfect. I'm ready.'

'I'll put these here.' He collects my hospital bag and leaves it by the door.

'I think you deserve some lunch,' I say. Music to his ears.

Barney consumes sandwiches with even more cake and a few cups of tea – where the bloody hell does he put it all?

'Shall we watch a film? What do you fancy?' he asks.

'Whatever. You choose. Not *Black Swan*, though,' I answer, tidying the countertops.

I've had a nagging pain in my back all morning. Now, the pain increases and there's a tightness across my stomach. I feel peculiar. No sooner do I think this than I feel a warm sensation on my legs.

I look down. 'Holy fuck!'

Barney looks across. 'What?'

'Fuck… No!'

'Kate.' He walks towards me. 'Shit, is that what I think it is?'

'Well, I haven't pissed myself!' I hope.

'Holy fuck!'

'I know! Fuck. I need Luke.'

'Fuck!'

'Stop saying fuck.'

'You started it,' he says.

'Fuck!' I look down again.

Barney scratches his head. 'So what now?'

'Let me think. Get Max. No, go upstairs and get my pregnancy book.'

Barney heads for the hall.

'No, go and get Max.' He turns and begins to walk towards Max's apartment. 'Stop, I need to read what to do.'

'For fuck's sake! Book or Max?' He looks at me with frustration. 'Max!' Barney shouts as he walks past me. 'I'll get your book – problem solved.'

I stand and look at the pool of water on the floor.

'Kate.'

I lift my face and make eye contact with Max.

'I need Luke.'

Rosie comes bounding through the door. 'Oh dear God, your waters have broken.' She laughs. 'The babies are on their way.'

'No, it's too soon… I'm only thirty-five weeks. The doctor said I'm doing well and probably have a few more weeks.'

Barney returns to the kitchen, on the phone. Max and Rosie stare at me.

'OK, I'll tell her. See you later.' Barney looks at me. 'I couldn't find your book so I called Adam. He said it will be a while, so don't panic.'

'Panic!' I laugh. 'I'm not panicking. I'm scared shitless and my husband is in another country. I'm beyond panic.'

'Chill, babe. Let's get you changed, yeah?'

I take a deep breath. 'I am calm – and free from pain,' I mutter.

'That's it. Relax and breathe. Do you want to go to hospital?' Barney asks.

'How is that bloody relaxing me?' I bark.

Barney takes my hands. 'OK, forget I said it. No hospital. Jesus, is this how you're going to be?'

'What?' I frown.

Max is already walking away, his phone in his hand.

'Shit, I need Luke.'

'What about your mum or Harry?' Barney says.

'They're coming back from France today, remember?'

'Crap, I forgot. Well, it's me or nothing, babe.'

'Kate, go and have a nice bath. Adam is right: you're not in any pain. First babies usually take a long time,' Rosie says.

'Listen, we have a plan. A nice bath, some car-crash TV, and before you realise it, Luke will be here.' Barney takes my arm.

'I like that plan.'

After my bath, I return to the bedroom, where Barney lies on the bed reading my *Mother and Baby* magazine.

'Ten positions for comfortable sex – have you done them all?' He turns the magazine sideways.

'We've managed.'

'The bump must get in the way.' He looks at me. 'How are you feeling?'

'The bath helped my back.'

'Good.'

'Any news from Luke?'

'I don't know, babe. I've been busy reading about the ten best positions.'

'Barney!' I guess he is taking my mind off the fact that my waters have broken.

I decide to put on underwear and Luke's grey T-shirt, which just about covers my arse. We return to the kitchen, where a welcome committee waits, which now includes Adam.

'Have you spoken to Luke?' My eyes meet Max's.

'He's already in the air. Do you want to call him?'

I shake my head. 'No, I'll cry and it'll stress him. How long before he's here?'

'Another five hours.'

'Five hours! Shit, that's too long, I'm not delivering these babies without him, no bloody way.'

Adam comes to my side. 'You'll be fine. You'll probably be in labour longer than five hours – besides, you're not in any pain, are you?'

'It's getting worse, but I'm OK.'

'Your doctor called. She's happy for me to keep an eye on you for the time being.'

'Good. So Luke's in the air, I'm not in pain – I can do this,' I mutter.

'Barney, let's go and put a film on for Kate,' Adam says.

It's my choice to sit in Luke's office. Max lights the fire and Barney sets up a distraction: my favourite film in the world, *My Cousin Vinnie*.

Within half an hour, I'm having contractions, and they're getting stronger. Even though I desperately try to ignore them, my face screws up when each one arrives.

Adam sits next to me and takes my hand.

'Deep breaths when a contraction arrives – in through your nose and out through your mouth.' He demonstrates. 'Do it with me.'

I join him but can hear heavy breathing from my right. Barney joins in too. Is he taking the bloody piss?

'I think this does help, babe,' Barney says and inhales deeply.

'Who? Because it's not helping me!'

Sitting is not an option, but pacing is a better choice. I walk slowly around the office as the three men watch. This is not how I imagined my first labour would go, or my choice of birthing partners.

The pain takes my breath away. I hang on to the back of the sofa.

'Jesus…' I blow harder and wait for the contraction to subside. 'Wow – that one really hurt.'

'They're getting closer together,' Adam says. He is timing me.

'You're not kidding!' I reply with too much sarcasm.

'Do whatever feels natural, but I would like to feel your stomach just to check their positions. Are you OK with that? You know I'm a paediatric doctor, but I have trained in obstetrics too.'

I nod and lie on the sofa.

Adam begins to gently press against my stomach.

'Good. Their heads are down.'

'Max, any news on Luke?' I ask.

'No. Thomas is at the air field, waiting.'

Another four hours pass. I have two more baths and now feel a strong need to scream and hit something. Barney is the closest.

'Can you stop breathing like a bloody lunatic? You're not helping.'

He holds his hands up. 'OK! Jesus, Kate, I'm just trying to encourage you, that's all.'

'Don't Jesus me. Holy shit, here comes another one.' I pant and blow. Fuck, it hurts. I have never felt pain like it.

'Kate, I think we should get you to hospital.' Max stands at my side in the kitchen.

I shake my head. 'No, I'm not going anywhere without Luke. Forget it.'

As the contraction passes I walk away and begin to climb the stairs, but halfway up another unbearable contraction arrives.

'Argh… Bloody hell.'

'I've got you. Lean on me.' Barney bands his arm around my waist. 'Max is right. I think you should go to hospital.'

My eyes well up. 'I need him, Barney.'

'I know, babe, but you might not have a choice.'

'Just give it a little longer,' I manage to say.

We make it to my room, where I have another contraction and Adam walks in.

Barney looks across at Adam.

'Kate, I've spoken to Dr Jenkins again. She is on another call at the moment, so will you let me examine you? I know this must feel strange, but just think of me as your doctor, or we can go straight to the hospital now.' Adam looks at Barney. 'Besides, you may only be a few centimetres dilated, in which case this could go on for a while. It's your call.'

'OK. Christ, it's here again.'

'I need some gloves.'

'Luke's office,' I gasp. 'Ask Max.'

Barney disappears, leaving me with Adam.

'Lie on the bed. I'll get a couple of towels.'

'I'm really scared.'

He takes my hand. 'It's normal to be scared, but you'll be fine, trust me.'

Within a few moments Barney is back. He sits next to me and takes my hand while Adam slides on some gloves. He lowers a towel across my bump and slips my underwear down.

'Ready? While you don't have a contraction.'

I close my eyes as he examines me.

'OK, that's great. You're about eight centimetres.'

'No – I can't be. Luke isn't here.'

'You still have two centimetres to go.'

Tears roll down my cheeks. 'But the twins are early.'

'Dr Jenkins is happy with their size, and you haven't had any complications, but I do think you should go to hospital.'

'I don't want to go without Luke. I need him with me.'

'Babe, let's go now and Luke can meet us there,' Barney says.

Adam stands and removes his gloves. 'I'm going to call Dr Jenkins. She can meet us at the hospital.'

I can't speak. Another contraction arrives, taking all my senses with it.

Eventually I get to my feet. Max walks into the bedroom. 'Luke has landed.'

The pain is unbearable. 'I can't do this any more, I can't.' Tears roll down my cheeks.

'Kate, you need to go to hospital. Luke can meet you there.' I can see fear in Max's eyes.

'OK, give me a minute. I feel sick.' I walk into the bathroom, closing the door behind me. I lean over and grip the washstand as another contraction arrives. Barney walks in.

'Luke's on the phone.' Barney hands me the phone.

'Luke, I'm sorry. I didn't want to worry you.'

'Baby, I'm nearly home.'

'Argh, hang on... Holy fucking shit.' I pant.

'Kate!'

'Luke, hurry!' I scream and drop the phone.

Twenty minutes later, the pain is relentless.

'What do you feel?'

I look at Adam. 'Pain,' I reply sarcastically.

'Do you feel pressure, like you need the toilet?'

I nod.

'I think it's too late to go to hospital. Barney, sit on the floor and let Kate lean on you. Kate, I need to examine you.'

Adam puts towels on the bathroom floor and lowers me between Barney's knees. Just as he examines me, the bathroom door bursts open.

'Luke!' I can just about speak.

His face is deathly white. 'It's OK, I'm here. You can do this.' He looks at Barney and then at Adam. I'm not sure he's loving the fact that Barney's boyfriend has his fingers inside me.

'We won't make it to hospital, Luke.' He looks at me. 'Max, call Dr Jenkins. Tell her there's been a change of plan and to come here,' Adam shouts to the closed door.'

'Got it,' Max yells.

'You're good to go, Kate. The next contraction, you need to push.'

'What? No! Shit, it's coming… Luke.'

He leans forward and kisses my head. 'You've done this all on your own. I'm so proud of you.'

'Next contraction, you need to push down, OK? Luke, you may want to roll your sleeves up. Wash your hands. There are some gloves behind you.'

'Dr Jenkins is on her way!' Max shouts through the door.

'Good, I could do with an ultrasound for the second baby.'

I'm in too much pain to care what's going on.

'Mum!' Adam says and Rosie appears at the door.

'Come in and get some towels ready – these babies are on their way.'

'It's here,' I groan and pant ferociously.

'Good. The head is down, now push.'

I push with all that I have, but my body is drained.

'That's it, keep going. Well done. Excellent. Next contraction, you need to do the same.'

I nod and grip Barney's legs.

'God, it really hurts,' I cry.

'You're doing so well,' Luke says.

'Oh no.' I close my eyes as another contraction sweeps over me. My fingers dig into Barney's legs.

'Christ, my legs,' Barney complains. 'Babe, you're pinching me.'

'Are you fucking joking? Oh God.' I push again.

Adam looks at Barney. 'Kate, squeeze his legs as much as you need.'

How long have I been pushing? All I know is that I'm exhausted, but after one more push I can feel something different.

'Kate, keep going… Push, push, push! Stop! Pant, that's it. Let me get the head.'

I pant.

'OK, Kate, tuck your chin in and push.'

With one almighty push I feel a sensation like a slippery fish sliding out of me. Baby number one is out.

Luke stares in amazement. 'She's… perfect,' he mutters.

'Well done, Kate. Mum, towel please. Luke, grab those scissors. I need to clamp the cord,' Adam says.

I have no idea what's going on.

'Here, take your baby.'

Luke takes her, wrapped in a towel. I want to cry watching him, but the contractions don't give me a chance.

'Mum, sit next to Luke and take her when he needs to help me with baby number two.'

Adam pushes down on my stomach. 'Perfect, the head is down. Ready to go again?'

I exhale and nod. There is a gush of water.

'Kate, this one should be quicker. Let's get her out. Luke, give the baby to Mum.'

The bathroom is a whirlwind of activity. Rosie sits next to me holding my first baby. Luke and Adam get ready for the arrival of baby number two.

'Kate, I can see the head.'

I nod and try to breathe. All I can hear is crying. Barney!

'Sorry, babe, I am just blown away. She's perfect.'

'Oh God,' I say as another contraction breaks. I'm too exhausted. I rest my head against Barney's chest.

'Kate, look at me. You're tired but you're nearly done. Don't give up on me now,' Adam says.

I look at Luke.

'You can do this. I promise it's nearly over, Kate... Push really hard,' Luke says.

This time I push with all I have, which is hardly anything, but it's just enough to get the second baby out. Then Dr Jenkins arrives.

'She's out! Well done, let me check her,' Adam says.

'Kate, you've done so well.' I look up to Dr Jenkins. 'Are you OK to carry on?' she asks Adam.

'I'm fine here, if you can check the girls,' he says.

'OK, the first baby, please.'

'She's here,' Rosie says and passes Dr Jenkins the baby. I watch her closely as she checks and weighs her.

My baby girl cries, and the sound makes me cry. I want to kiss her and make it better.

'Luke, come here,' Dr Jenkins says. 'She's perfect. Five pounds, four ounces – a good weight. Here, take your daughter.'

My eyes are glued to them. I have no idea what Adam is doing to me or that a new person has arrived – Dr Jenkins' assistant. I feel delirious as Adam pushes down on my stomach, encouraging my body to deliver the placenta.

Luke sits next to me as Dr Jenkins checks over baby number two in the same manner. She also cries when she is stripped and weighed, but she is soon wrapped in a towel and passed to me.

'Congratulations, Mummy. Another perfect baby girl: five pounds, five ounces.'

'Are they too small?'

'No, Kate, they're fine. Good weights for twins. Now I need to check that you're OK.'

'You did it. I can't believe they're here,' Luke says. He kisses the baby in his arms and then leans across to kiss baby number two. 'Your mummy is the cleverest woman I know.' He looks at me with tears streaming down his cheeks.

'I can't believe they're here, Luke. Look at them.' They are perfect in every way, with little rosebud lips and button noses and the lightest dusting of fair hair. 'But they need names.'

'After what you just went through, I have no say in this. It's your choice.'

'No, we need to choose together.'

He gently presses his lips to mine. 'Herbs it is.'

I giggle. 'Are you sure?'

'Whatever you want. You have totally blown me away.'

'OK, so you're holding Sage Olivia Katenka Sutton, and this precious little bundle is Thyme Susan Bagrov Sutton.'

I look at my watch. It's midnight and the babies are swaddled in blankets and lie in the middle of our bed. They're both perfect. Sage is wearing a white baby-grow edged in pink, and Thyme is wearing a pink baby-grow edged in white.

Luke appears in the doorway with a tray.

'How are they?' He looks at our new family.

'Asleep.'

'And you?'

I wince. Not just because of my stitches, but after eight hours of labour I am physically and emotionally drained.

'The painkillers are helping, but not as much as having a shower. I feel human again.'

He puts the tray on a table.

'For my stunning and incredibly clever wife – tea and flapjacks.'

'Thank you,' I say and take the mug of tea.

He returns to his side of the bed and lies next to me. We can't stop gazing at our two little bundles wrapped in pink blankets lying on our bed.

Tears roll down my cheeks and Luke wipes them away, although I see he feels just the same, and tears glint in his eyes.

'We created these.'

'What a good job we did. I have never been more proud of anyone than I am of you today. Watching what you went through will stay with me forever.'

'They had to come out somehow. God, I was scared. I should have gone to hospital. What was I thinking?' I drink my tea and then place the mug on my nightstand.

'Don't second-guess yourself. You didn't have pain relief – you got by on sheer determination. Jesus, Kate, you're officially a superwoman.'

Sage murmurs so softly that we could have easily missed it.

'Come here, Sage.' Luke picks her up and kisses her.

I pick up Thyme. 'Are you OK with the names?'

'They're growing on me.'

We laugh.

'No pun intended. It had to be your call.' He smiles. 'Adam and Dr Jenkins were pleased with you.'

'Adam was a star. I couldn't have done it without him.'

'You need to sleep; you look exhausted,' Luke says.

'This is it. Life will never be the same again.'

'I like change,' he says.

'No, you don't.' I laugh.

'Some change I can cope with – this is one I can definitely cope with.'

I yawn.

'All my girls are going to bed.'

Luke stands up and walks with Sage towards my side of the bed.

'Are you sure you want the cribs next to you?'

'Yes, I need them close.'

'Sage, kiss Mummy goodnight.'

'Night, my precious girl, I love you.' I place my lips on hers.

He lays her in the first crib.

I kiss Thyme again. 'Good night, my little bundle. I love you.'

I pass her to Luke. 'Come here, Thyme, let Daddy kiss you.'

He places Thyme in the next crib.

'You're safe and sound, now I need to hold your mummy.'

He slides in next to me and pulls me towards him.

'I have my wife back! But I will miss your bump.'

'Oh no, I am definitely not doing this again.'

He laughs. 'Maybe in a few years.'

'I love you, Luke.' Every second I feel the need to tell him.

'I love you too, Kate – forever.'

HARPER
SUTTON

FOUR YEARS LATER

A cold burst of air washes over my skin. I open my eyes.

'Morning,' Luke says and continues teasing my nipples.

'Morning. Are you bored?'

He closes his mouth over mine, demanding my body to wake. It doesn't matter when and where; he has me in the palm of his hands. Leaving my lips he begins to nip at my jaw and then move towards my neck.

'What time is it?'

'Time to play.' He returns to my face. 'We have…' – he looks at his watch – '…maybe thirty minutes.'

'I see Mr Demanding Sutton is with me this morning.'

'Bet your arse I am.'

I giggle at playful Luke. I love him like this.

'I need to fuck you – hard.'

My libido dances with delight. I hold his head firmly, commanding his mouth to take me. When we are together, time stands still. It has been this way from the very beginning.

Luke moves and pulls me with him. 'We need to remove this.' He slides my short silk nightdress from my body. Now we are both naked and horny. As I lie down, his hands skim my body, caressing every inch of my flesh. Slowly he dips his fingers between my legs and slides them gently inside my sex. My eyes close and my breathing shallows as he continues to massage the perfect spot. I slowly begin to lose myself to him – but then he removes his fingers and lies between my legs, the tip of his erection nudging at me.

'How much do you want me to fuck you?' He's on a power trip this morning. God, I love him and the games he plays.

'You don't have time to tease me.'

'I always have time.' Slowly, he begins to sink his hardness inside me. My hands slide down his back. 'Let me enjoy you. Give me a minute before I fuck you hard.'

Yes, please.

Lazily he works his hips, allowing me to adjust to his thickness.

Come on, Luke! I need more. I kiss him hard, flicking my tongue against his. He speeds up, thrusting hard and fast. Perfect.

Just as my body succumbs to his touch he pulls out.

'Sit on me.' He kneels and helps me upright, while his free hand works on his erection, which instantly draws my attention.

He laughs. 'How much does this turn you on?'

I purse my lips. Too much.

'Do the same.'

'We don't have time.' Why does he do this to me?

'Touch your clit, then I'll fuck you.'

I close my eyes and my hand falls between my legs.

'Open your eyes.' His free hand lifts my chin. Dark and seductive meet dark and submissive. 'Good. Do you need to come yet?'

'No.'

'Look at my dick.'

Not a problem. I gaze avidly at Luke giving himself a hand job.

'Work harder. I want you to come.'

'I will when you're inside me.'

'No, now. I want to watch you, and then I'll fuck you.'

Jesus Christ, what did he eat for dinner last night to make him this horny and demanding at six o'clock in the bloody morning?

Moments later, a rippling sensation begins within me.

'Luke.'

'You need to come.'

I nod.

'Look at me. I want to watch you.'

My eyes meet his as he lifts me slightly. The delicious feeling of him inside me is enough to make me come hard.

'Oh God. Luke, I'm coming… Yes.'

'Fuck, you're so wet… Keep going.'

For some reason my orgasm lasts longer than usual. Luke continues to grip my hips.

'Touch your clit again – give me another one.'

The area is sensitive, so I slowly begin to massage. Much quicker than before, the rush begins. Luke is my guilty pleasure, a sexual drug that I will never have enough of.

'Luke.' I ride him fast and enjoy the second rush of sensations.

'Has it passed?' he asks.

I nod.

'Good. I need more of you.'

He flips me onto my back and begins to take what he wants, making no apology for his demands. After all, I am his. His hips work hard. He drives himself deep inside my body, pushing me further into the mattress. I watch his face alter and his pectoral muscles tighten as he comes. I have all of him – and what a pleasure it has been.

'Every time, Kate – I need you harder every time.'

I giggle and link my hands around his neck, pulling him towards my lips and delivering a cheeky kiss. He lies next to me, his breathing slowing. I can't help noticing his semi-hardness.

'I think we need a night away,' I say and roll to my side, running my fingers up and down his bare chest.

'Are you still horny?'

'Maybe.' I laugh, although he is spot on. Round two would not take any great persuasion. 'I want to have you all to myself – no children or work, just us and a bed.'

'I like your plan, leave it with me.'

Suddenly the door bursts open. Luke speedily pulls the cover over us both.

'Daddy, Sage is getting Harper.'

I roll my eyes and look at Luke.

'OK.' He discreetly slides out of bed and slips on his grey joggers and T-shirt. 'Thyme, come with me. Let Mummy get out of bed.' He grabs our baby girl, who's not really a baby any longer. The twins are now four. He leaves to rescue his pride and joy, our beautiful son, who is one today.

I sit up and grab my nightdress, then my matching full-length robe.

'Sage, I've told you not to pick up Harper – you could drop him.' Luke's voice echoes through the baby monitor in our bedroom.

I laugh, listening to him deal with his precocious daughter who has her father's intelligence and, most amusingly, his stubbornness.

The girls may be identical, with long blonde hair and dark eyes, but their personalities are very different. Sage has her father's curiosity about life and Thyme is calm and forgiving, just like me.

'Mummy!' Sage comes bounding towards me.

'Morning, baby girl.'

'I'm a big girl. Daddy shouted at me.'

'He didn't shout and I think you know why he is cross.' I swoop her up and twirl her round. She giggles. 'You mustn't pick up Harper, Daddy has told you.' The corners of her mouth drop. 'Are you ready to give Harper his birthday presents, and the card you made yesterday?'

She wriggles to get free, her sadness forgotten. If only Luke was this easy to side-track!

I hear the noise from the kitchen when I am halfway down the stairs. I walk into a scene of madness. The girls are throwing blue balloons in the air. Luke tries to catch them, Harper in his arms, giggling. He has no idea that he's one today.

'Mummy's here. It's present time.'

I walk towards my two favourite boys in the entire world. Harper stretches out his arms to me. I admit he's a mummy's boy and I love him for it.

'Happy birthday.' I nuzzle in to his neck. He loves my affection, which he laps up just like his father.

Luke disappears to the office, to return armed with presents. He carries one ridiculously large present that I am sure is more for him than for our son.

'The big one, Daddy,' Sage commands.

'Shall we?' He takes Harper from my arms. Luke holds him close to the large present. He only started walking last week, and he's very wobbly on his feet. The girls frantically tear the paper off the parcel as Harper watches.

'Mummy, it's a black car.' Thyme looks at me.

'Yes, it is.'

Luke picks up Harper and sits him behind the wheel.

'Girls, this is not just a car! This is an Aston Martin, founded in 1913.' They look at their father as though he is talking another language – honestly, I agree with them. 'The best car in the world.'

'Thyme.' Sage yanks her sister's arm. 'Catch.' They begin to throw the balloons again, uninspired by their father's automotive history lesson.

Luke picks up Harper and lowers him onto the floor. Immediately he heads for his sisters.

'He loves it.' Luke smiles. We both know I have won the debate on who would love this present more – and it's not our son.

I link my arms around his neck. 'Nearly as much as I love you.'

Luke presses his lips to mine and dips me.

A morning of chasing balloons and prepping food has left me no time to get ready. I slip into a simple black dress, which is fitted and clings to my curves in all the right places.

I hear a wolf whistle.

'Do you have to wear that?' Luke stands behind me. I watch his face in the mirror.

'You're trouble, Sutton.'

'My wife looks fuckable.'

He turns me to face him, allowing his lips to do the talking. Within seconds he fires up and presses hard against me.

I pull away. 'It'll be a long hard afternoon for you.'

'Don't tease my dick. I'll take you right now.'

I reach up and kiss his nose. 'I know, and I would let you.'

'Until tonight.'

'Deal. Now go and make sure your son is ready.'

By the time I return to the kitchen our guests have already started to arrive. We have invited all our parents. Four years on, we can now play happy families.

'Kate?' Ivor calls me.

'Hi, Papa.'

'Mama.'

'Darling,' Katenka says. 'I cannot believe Harper is one.'

I shake my head. 'Me neither.'

Katenka pulls me to her in a warm embrace. I can't deny that we had an immediate connection, an intrinsic bond that I can't explain. Sadly, Harry has not had the same feeling. Yes, they meet up regularly and they have grown closer since the arrival of Nico, Harry's little boy, who is now two, but there is a distance between them, primarily due to Harry.

'Can I help?'

'No, just enjoy yourself. I'd better go and say hello to everyone.'

'Of course, my darling.'

I walk away from my birth parents. I still feel the need to put Mum and Dad before them – for obvious reasons.

'Hi, Mum.'

'Kate, have you seen Harper with the dog I got him? He loves it.'

I place my arm around her shoulder. 'I knew he would – he loves Nico's dog. Where's Dad?'

'He's in the garden chatting to Jerry.'

'OK.' I move away.

'Hi, everyone.'

'Kate.' Livy kisses my cheek. 'Did you know Sage has got changed? I did manage to get some pictures of her.'

'That child will be the death of me. She is so defiant! Without doubt she is her father's daughter.'

'Absolutely.' Livy laughs.

I watch her from a distance playing with Thyme and Nico. She may have changed out of the dress I put her in, but the child has an inherent ability to style herself. Mr Jones would be proud.

'Hi, Edward.'

He pulls me in for his usual hug. I can just about breathe.

'Have you lost weight? You feel thin – smaller.'

I laugh. 'No!'

'You may laugh, young lady, but I would worry if you wanted to get pregnant again…' Edward says.

'Pregnant, who's pregnant?' Luke snakes his arm around my waist.

'Not me!' I blurt.

'Edward!' Livy scolds him. 'Kate, ignore him… He's convinced you will have another baby.'

'Definitely not! My ovaries are on a permanent hiatus,' I bluntly respond.

'They are?' Luke says.

'Yes! Besides, you have your pride and joy. I think we can call it a day now.'

'I thought we'd have one more. I love you when you're pregnant.' He leans to my ear. 'You're always horny.'

'Luke!' I tap his arm. Little shit! 'Er, Harper is only one. I am far from ready for any more children. Anyway, we might have another set of girls.'

'Perfect – they adore me.'

'At the moment,' Livy says. We both know how that scenario will play out in the future.

I look over Luke's shoulder and notice new arrivals. Quite frankly, I have had enough of pregnancy talk!

'I need to mingle. I'll catch up with you in a bit.'

As I begin to walk away, Luke takes my arm. 'When was your last period?'

'Right this second, I couldn't tell you. Why?' I frown. 'Fuck… Do you think I'm—? No. Jesus, what is wrong with us?'

His hand skims the edge of my breast, as though by accident. 'These look a little bigger, and my father is right – you look like you have lost weight.'

'Are you shitting me?' I have lost my appetite and my boobs are little more sensitive.

'No. We'll talk about this later. Go and mingle.'

Mingle – holy fuck! I go over to Harry.

'You look lost. What's up?'

'Luke thinks I'm pregnant.'

'What?' She takes my hand. 'Have you done a test?'

'No.' He thinks my boobs look bigger – but maybe it's the dress. I can't remember when my last period was! I'm sure it was only a few weeks ago.'

'Sandbanks.'

I look confused.

'We took the kids there for a few days… We felt crappy because we both started our period.'

'Thank God. Yes.'

'Has your brain gone to mush, Kate? I've just had another period since then. So you must be late.'

'Oh fuck, I don't believe this. Christ, I don't have time for another baby… Harper Jones is so busy, how the hell am I going to fit another baby in?'

'You're crap at taking the pill.' Harry laughs.

'It's not funny! God, what is wrong with me, Harry?'

'How about you do a test and then panic?'

'Yeah, you're right.' All of a sudden I feel nauseous. I'm sure it's due to fear. 'Where are Raymond and Nico?'

She points to the garden. Even though it's only May, the sun is out and the weather is warm.

'I spoke to Alexis. She's coming, but she's split with her new boyfriend so she's bringing Charles.'

'Oh no! Is she heartbroken?'

'She said he's still hooked on his ex. I think she's better off without him,' Harry says.

'Hey, girls.'

I turn around. 'Hi, Molly.'

'I've just seen the birthday boy. I think he's making me

broody. Actually, Danny and I were thinking we should give Grayson a sibling. What do you think?'

I laugh. 'I think my body agrees with you.'

Molly frowns. 'Are you— Again? Christ, Kate.'

'Shh! Well, I don't know, but I think my period is late.'

We all laugh and automatically link for a group hug.

'Oi, oi, oi, what's this? A group hug without the best ingredient? Make way, girls, is there room for a rose among the thorns? Let me in.' Barney glides to the centre.

'Where's Adam?' I ask.

'Over there with the birthday boy.' I turn to see Adam spinning Harper around, with Jerry's help. 'Where's Kiki?'

'She's here somewhere, and I warn you she's hormonal and moody.'

'Nothing new there, babe. I'll hunt her down and cheer her up.'

We part as I continue to meet and greet: our house is now bursting with all our favourite people.

'Hi Ollie, Scarlett.' I greet Luke's younger brother and his new fiancée.

'I love the car, Kate. If Luke could get in it, he would,' Ollie says.

'I told him that Harper was too small for it!'

'Ollie, come here,' Livy calls him.

'Go on – I'll catch up with you both in a while.'

I continue to search for people I have not spoken to yet.

'Nanny Stella and Nana Rosie, are you stealing cupcakes?' I hug two of the most important people in my life.

'We thought no one would notice.'

I laugh. 'Stella, I could bribe you to do anything for cake.'

'Yes, my darling, you could… Tell me has the birthday boy been behaving himself this morning?'

'He's such a good boy – give me boys any day of the week!' I say.

'Yes, well, the girls are here to test Luke, not you.'

'I think you're right. I need to check the oven. Can I trust you both to guard the cakes?'

'Kiki, look at me. Cheer up,' I say.

'Sorry. I'm just so uncomfortable, and have you seen my ankles?'

'You're glowing!'

'Glowing, my arse! I'm fat and ready to burst.'

'You're not fat, you're pregnant. Anyway, when's Declan getting here?' I ask.

'He's pissed me off again. I told him not to play rugby today, it's your nephew's birthday. But no, off he went.'

'I'm not surprised he chose rugby over you,' Barney says and pulls her close to him.

'Thanks, Barney, you little shit. Now go and get me a drink and another sausage roll – and don't forget the pickle.'

I gently touch her bump. 'Honestly, how are you feeling?'

'Ready to explode, my stomach is so tight,' Kiki says.

'I know how you feel, but either way you will be holding your baby in the next five days.'

She nods and sighs with relief.

'I need to check on the food. Call me if you need anything.'

I slide the last of the hot food out of the oven.

'Hi, Kate.'

I turn to see Fiona carrying a blue gift bag. She's standing with Pete. Even though I stopped working at the bar five years ago, they will always be part of my life.

'Hi.' I give them both a hug. 'Pete, go and help yourself to a drink. Danny was asking for you.'

'OK.' He walks off.

I take her hand. 'How did it go? I wanted to call you last night but Luke said to leave it.'

'I was exhausted.'

'And?'

'Time will tell. I have a scan booked. But you know what IVF is like, plus the first round didn't work, so the second…' She trails off.

'It will. We have to stay positive.'

The fear is evident in her eyes.

'No tears, you know I'll join you.'

'OK.' She smiles. 'I can't thank you enough for this.'

'Listen, you and Pete are family to me. I don't care how much the treatment costs. If I can help you, I will, financially and emotionally…'

'Thank you, Kate.'

'Here, make yourself useful and give this to Kiki. Barney was supposed to give it to her. A warning – she's feisty.'

Then Declan enters the kitchen.

'About time.' I rest my fists on my hips.

'Don't start, Kate. She's driving me bloody mad. Luke said you weren't that hormonal when you were pregnant.'

'She's scared, that's all. Be more understanding.'

He holds his hands up. 'I'll try. Now where is my favourite little man?'

'Here.'

Declan and I turn to see Luke holding Harper.

'Come here, baby Sutton.' Declan takes him. 'Let's go and see miserable Auntie Kiki.' He turns and winks at me.

'Your brother is asking for trouble.'

'Sutton boys always do.'

Luke closes in on me.

'I think my period is late.'

'It is. I checked my phone. I think it's safe to say I have knocked you up again.'

'Oh God. I don't want another baby yet.'

'We will do a test and go from there.'

I take a deep breath. 'I guess.'

'I love you.' He takes my face in his hands and kisses me firmly.

'Put her down, Sutton.'

We turn towards the door.

'Hi James… Francesca.' I love it when James Sullivan visits, and now he's married it feels as though Luke has some friends who are normal – just with guns in their closets!

'Sullivan… Hello, Francesca. Let me get you a drink.' Luke walks away with them.

The buzzer goes. I press the door button. There are only a few people who don't have an entry code. I walk towards the black door.

'Hi!' It's Alexis and Charles Morley.

'Kate, I hope you don't mind me gate-crashing,' Charles says.

'You're not gate-crashing. A word of warning – Luke doesn't know you're here so don't piss him off.'

'I will try not to.'

Alexis taps his arm. 'You will behave.'

'Go and get yourself a drink…' I look at Alexis. 'Harry told me about Damien. Are you OK?'

'I had a lucky escape.'

'Oh well, you have us.'

I link arms with Alexis as we enter the lounge. It's a hive of noise and activity.

Soon all the guests are here. Tanya, Maria and Scott Parker plus his mystery woman are the last to arrive.

Everyone is engrossed in eating and chatting. As the weather is unexpectedly warm, people stand outside, making the most of the beautiful sunshine.

Luke walks towards me. 'Shall we bring out the cake?'

'Good idea.'

Luke takes my hand as we return to the kitchen, collect the cake and light the candles.

'I can't believe you got him a rugby shirt cake.'

'He's a boy.' Luke smiles.

'He's a baby. Besides, he may not like rugby when he grows up.'

'Maybe not. But perhaps baby number four will love rugby.'

'Shut up! I can't believe I might be pregnant. It's official – you're never coming near me again.' After tonight, that is!

'I need to find Harper.'

From a distance I see him dragging a car across the floor, watched closely by Max and Valerie. Without doubt they are my favourite couple.

'Harper, come to Mummy.' He gazes up and crawls towards me. He looks exhausted. I scoop him up in my arms.

'Ready?' Luke asks.

'Yes.'

'Everyone!' Luke bellows.

We all sing happy birthday, while Harper looks bewildered. With the help of the other children, he blows out the candles, to cheers and whistles. Luke lowers the cake onto the table and passes me a glass of champagne.

'Kate and I would like to thank you all for sharing this special day with us. Please raise your glasses to Harper Luke Paul Sutton.'

I sip my champagne. A single tear rolls down my cheek.

'Come here.' Luke pulls Harper and me into his arms.

Just then, Barney and Adam walk over.

'Kate, Luke, we have an announcement.' Barney pauses. 'Adam and I are engaged.'

'Oh my God, that's wonderful news!' I look across to Luke. 'Luke.'

'Yes – good news,' Luke says.

'We're planning just a small ceremony with family and friends.' Adam smiles. 'Dad was a little…'

'Jerry will be fine. He idolises you. Listen, why not have it here in the garden? We can have a marquee like the white party.'

Luke glares at me and takes Harper from my arms, clearly not thrilled with the idea. 'Luke.' I nudge him.

'Of course.'

'Really?' Barney smiles. God, I love that he's so happy. 'Cheers, Sutton. A summer wedding here – perfect.'

'Kate, I want you to give me away, be my best woman.'

'I would be honoured.' I pull Barney towards me.

Barney pulls away. 'It will be bloody fantastic. Tell me, Sutton, how do you feel about swans in the pool?'

'I don't! Yes to my garden, no to livestock!'

'Sage, go and get and the others and tell them we're ready for the balloons.'

'Yes, Mummy.' She runs away, screaming the names of her siblings and cousins.

I wait outside holding the silver foil heart balloons, one for each child. Luke and Harry look at me, knowing today is bittersweet.

'Mummy... Mummy.' Thyme bounds towards me. 'Can I have my balloon?'

'We need to wait for everyone.'

'Are you OK?' Harry says.

I nod.

'Luke, where's Harper?' I ask.

'Ivor has him,' he says.

'I need him.'

'I'll get him,' he says.

I feel emotional, no matter how hard I try to remain calm. Luke arrives with Harper.

'Is everyone here?' I take a breath.

The children cheer.

'Good. So, we all know what day today is, and how super-special it is.'

'Harper's birthday, Mummy.'

'Yes, Sage.'

'Today is also the day we celebrate Mummy's friend, Mr Jones. He was super-special, just like all of you, and he floated up to the sky on this day. Super-special people like balloons. I'm going to give all of you a balloon and when you let it fly you have to make a wish and send it to Mr Jones.'

Tears roll down my cheeks. Even after all this time, I miss him dreadfully.

I pass a balloon to each child. 'This blue one is for Harper – it's his first time to make a wish.' I pass the balloon to Luke. 'On three, let them go.'

'Mummy, I want to keep it,' Thyme says.

'Not today. These are for Mr Jones.'

She smiles at me.

'Ready, one, two, three… Make a wish.'

I watch all the balloons float away, glinting against the blue sky. 'Harper, look at the balloons.' He watches, entranced.

Thyme takes my hand. 'Mummy, does he catch them in the sky?'

I nod. 'He knows they're from you.'

'Who wants cake?' Harry takes charge of the children. 'Come here, Harper.' She takes him from Luke, allowing us a moment alone.

Luke pulls me close. I inhale my favourite scent in the world while I enjoy being in my favourite place in the world – in his arms.

'I love you.'

I look up at my delectable husband. 'I love you, too. I miss him, Luke. How can I still miss him after all this time?'

'Some people make an impact on your life, and he was one of those people. He delivered you to me.'

I nod and lean against Luke's chest.

'Kate.' Barney bounds towards me. 'Kiki!'

I pull away from Luke. 'What?'

'It's started,' Barney says.

I run towards the house.

'She's in the bathroom.'

I take the stairs two at a time.

'Kiki,' I call and tap on the door.

She opens the door and lets me in. I recognise the look on her face, having been there twice before. It's called panic.

'Come here.' I take her in my arms.

'I'm scared, and it already hurts.'

'I know, but you will be fine. Trust me, OK?'

She nods, tears rolling down her cheeks.

'I promise you, in a few hours, you will be holding your baby... Kiki, your baby is on its way.' I smile. 'You're going to be a mum.'

'Can I do it – be a good mum? You make it look so easy.'

'Well, it's not easy and some days are bloody long... But it doesn't matter. I love my babies more than anything in the world, and you will too.' I gently skim her cheek. 'You can do this, Kiki Marlow.'

'I love you, Kate.'

'Back at you. Now, Declan is waiting for you, and I am waiting to cuddle your new baby and to watch my best friend be the best mummy.'

As we return to the kitchen, Declan pulls her close to his chest. 'We've got this, OK, you and me.'

The day disappears, and the evening too. All our children are asleep, but I'm like a woman possessed!

'Bloody hell, where is it?' I mutter to myself.

'Where's what?' Luke stands there, a towel wrapped around his waist, looking far too sexy. Undoubtedly, his looks are the reason I have ended up in this bloody mess!

'Pregnancy test. It's here somewhere. I remember buying two.' I open an old hat box, the last place to check. 'Yes.' I wave it at him.

'Don't stress.'

'I am stressed! I'm not ready for this.' I head to the bathroom.

Luke walks in a few minutes later and watches me pace the floor of our en suite.

'Come here.' He pulls me into his arms.

'This has to be the longest wait of any woman's life.'

He silences me by kissing me, his tongue skilfully dancing with mine. Not content, his hands wander under my nightdress. His touch against my bare skin causes goose bumps to erupt.

I pull away. 'Thanks for the distraction.'

'Any time.'

'You check. I can't look.'

Luke picks up the plastic stick and smiles.

'What? Tell me.'

'Boy or girl, I don't mind.'

'Shit. Are you joking?'

'No.'

I look at the white wand. 'Fuck.'

Luke scoops me in his arms and carries me to our bed.

I cover my face with my hands.

His lips begin at my legs and move up my body, skimming my hipbone as he blows air against my clit, and then heads to my stomach.

'Hello, baby number four. Daddy can't wait to meet you.' He begins to laugh.

'It's not funny.'

He works his way to my breasts and slides the fabric from my body, revealing my erect nipples. He sucks on each of them before moving to my face.

'We need to talk about this,' I say

'What do you want me to say?' His hand wanders between my legs.

'I'm serious, Luke.'

His lips go back to my nipples. As ever, I feel my senses crumble, allowing him to win the game. I'm under his sexual spell. At the same time his fingers ensure I am his.

'Luke, please.'

'Yes,' he whispers in my ear, 'I'm pleased we're having another baby. I love you. Let me give you an orgasm. I can feel you want to.'

God, he's right – the first wave is here. 'Shit. Luke, carry on.' My hips sway to the touch of his hand while he sucks harder on my nipples.

'I love watching you come.'

How can his voice affect me so much?

'I need to – Luke.'

'I'm here, baby. Give it to me and then I'll fuck you hard and fast – is that what you want?'

I nod. My libido is writing a thank-you note, always grateful for his words. 'Yes.' My body stiffens and buckles under the waves of my delicious orgasm.

As I start to come down from the dizzy heights, he flips me onto my stomach. 'On your elbows.'

Then he is inside me, one hand on my clit. I push back, needing him to come at me hard. Almost immediately the small eruption begins. My orgasm arrives quickly.

'Luke!'

'OK.' He slams harder into me as he comes. 'Fuck.'

He holds himself in place, leaving every last drop of his orgasm inside me. No wonder I'm pregnant – again! He withdraws, and I collapse to the mattress.

'You side-tracked me,' I pant.

'Is that what I did?'

'Yes, and you know it. You don't play fair, Luke.'

'Not with you.'

He rolls me to my back and tenderly touches my face.

'Are you really unhappy about the baby?' He frowns. He knows I love our children unconditionally.

'No, of course not. We created it, how could I not be happy? But four children are a lot.'

'It's a family – our family. Besides, you're a fantastic mum. Today it was evident – our children are a credit to you.'

'And to you. I love our babies.' My hand wanders to my stomach. 'All of them. I just didn't think I would have another one so soon after Harper.'

'He's definitely a mummy's boy.'

'Yep, and I love him so much.'

'Besides, you're far more relaxed with him than you were with the girls. This time it will be a walk in the park.'

'Really? You squeeze a baby's head out of your arse and tell me what park you've visited!'

He laughs. 'Jesus, Kate, your mouth.' He pulls me tightly to his chest. 'I love it.' He kisses me.

'Did you ever see yourself with four kids? Oh my God, four kids – what the fuck?'

'No, but I never saw myself married, yet here I am.'

'What are people going to say, other than we have no self-control?'

'We don't, do we? It's been that way since the beginning. I need you more than anything else in the world.'

Later, in the early hours of the morning, my phone wakes me. Caller ID – Kiki.

I bolt upright.

'Hi?'

'Kate,' Kiki says.

'Are you OK?'

'Yes.'

'Thank God.'

'Kate, she's beautiful.'

'It's a girl,' I say, tears falling down my cheeks.

'Yes,' she says.

'I'm so pleased. How are you feeling?'

'Shell-shocked that I have a baby, but pleased it's over.'

'I know – it's surreal. How's Declan?'

'He's holding her right now. He can't stop smiling.'

'I can imagine. Luke's cried each time.'

'She looks like him.'

'How did it go?' I ask.

'It bloody hurt,' she says.

'I does, but it's hard to describe it unless you've been through it.'

'Your honesty helped to prepare me.'

'I have your back, you know that. Besides, I told you that you're a strong woman, I had faith in you. OK, now I need details!'

'Willow Catherine Sutton, seven pounds two, born at two twenty this morning.'

'Catherine – after your mum? Oh, Kiki.'

'Dad cried when I told him.'

'He's so proud of you, and your mum would be. She's looking down on you right now.'

'I thought of her when I was in labour – how bloody ridiculous is that?'

'It isn't. Remember what we said?'

'Not to fear her memory.'

'Right – use it for strength,' I say.

I can hear her breathing alter.

'Kate, I have some more news.'

'Me too, but you go first.'

She chuckles. 'You're not pregnant?'

I say nothing.

'Jesus, you are! Oh my God! Declan?' she calls to the love of her life. 'Kate's pregnant.' She begins to laugh.

'I'm pleased to entertain you.'

'I can't help it, babe. But baby number four… Tell me, how many do you intend to have?'

'This is the last and then Luke will visit the doctor…'

I feel an arm around my waist. Of course Luke is awake and listening to my conversation – especially since it concerns him and his most amenable body part.

'It's a girl, Luke.'

'Tell me your news. I need a diversion.'

'Declan has asked me to marry him.'

'That's fantastic.' I hold the phone away from me. 'Declan proposed.'

'About time,' Luke mutters.

'Oh Kiki, I'm so pleased, what did your dad say?'

'He was too emotional holding Willow. I'll need to remind him that I'm going to be a Sutton.'

'Two extra independent women around the Sutton table… How exciting.'

Once again Luke pulls me tight. 'I would say stubborn and argumentative.'

I glance at my husband, who has far too much to say at four o'clock in the morning.

'When did he ask you?'

Kiki begins to laugh. 'Just as Willow's head popped out!'

I can't help laughing. 'Who ever said romance was dead needs to meet Declan Sutton.'

'At least I won't forget it.'

'I guess not.'

'I have to go. Willow needs a feed.'

'OK. I love you so much – well done.'

'Kate, come and see me as soon as you can. I need you.'

'Try and stop me.'

I lie back down, crying happy tears.

'How are they?' Luke rolls to his side.

'Happy. I think that's what hit me – she sounds happy for the first time ever. She just needed someone to love. Willow Catherine Sutton.'

'Willow?' Luke looks at me, slightly confused.

'I love it.'

'I'm not saying a word. I have girls named after herbs.'

'Oi. You said I could choose.'

'And I wouldn't change it.'

'Declan proposed just as Kiki pushed Willow's head out.'

Luke ——— his elbows. 'He's always had a mind of his ow——— one to conform.'

'Run——— y.'

Luke ——— he ribs.

'You ——— he says.

I can——— laughing.

'Yes ——— you know it, that's why I love you.'

He k—ses my lips. 'That's why I need you.'

'Are we made for each other?'

'Yes, baby. Souls together forever.'

'Kiss me, Luke.'

HARPER'S FINALE